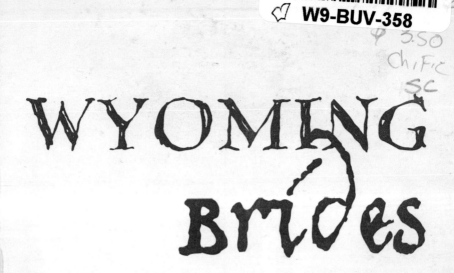

WYOMING Brides

THREE ROMANCES BLOSSOM
ON THE TRAIL OF FAITH

SUSAN PAGE DAVIS

BARBOUR
PUBLISHING

Protecting Amy © 2004 by Susan Page Davis
The Oregon Escort © 2005 by Susan Page Davis
Wyoming Hoofbeats © 2006 by Susan Page Davis

ISBN 978-1-59789-986-4

All scripture quotations are taken from the King James Version of the Bible.

This book is a work of fiction. Names, characters, places, and incidents are either products of the author's imagination or used fictitiously. Any similarity to actual people, organizations, and/or events is purely coincidental.

Cover image © Macduff Everton/Iconica/Getty

Published by Barbour Publishing, Inc., P.O. Box 719, Uhrichsville, Ohio 44683, www.barbourbooks.com

Our mission is to publish and distribute inspirational products offering exceptional value and biblical encouragement to the masses.

Member of the
Evangelical Christian
Publishers Association

Printed in the United States of America.

Dear Readers,

Writing these three books was challenging and exciting. Although I've lived most of my life in Maine, I married a Westerner. During the time we lived in Oregon, I took a special interest in the Oregon Trail. Some of my husband's ancestors moved to Oregon. Others went west with the Mormons and took the trail through Fort Bridger in 1850. This area and period of history are fascinating, and I knew I wanted to place my characters there.

Shortly after we moved back to Maine, I took a class in horseshoeing and became a certified farrier. Although I no longer shoe horses, this experience has been invaluable in my writing. I hope you enjoy reading about Kip, Lady, Wiser, and the other horses in these stories—as well as the human characters!

These stories speak of men and women who underwent the rigors of the frontier. Their determination and faith were key elements for successful pioneers. My main characters grow stronger through their harrowing adventures. Our experiences today are different, but our spiritual and emotional needs are the same.

I've also tried to give as accurate a feel for the period as possible. The research was fun. Nearly all of the characters are fictional, except for Jim Bridger and a few of the officers who served at Fort Laramie. At a museum in Oregon, I learned about the Oregon Escort, a real military unit that was formed in 1861 to escort wagon trains. This duty was later turned over to state units and civilians. Most of the conflicts portrayed in these books are fictional, but in most cases similar incidents took place. The Dakota War of Minnesota (1862), in which Rachel was captured, was a real conflict.

I love to hear from my readers! Come visit me at my Web site: www.susanpagedavis.com.

PROTECTING
AMY

Dedication

To our adventurous daughter, the real Amy,
who went West and found true love with her own "T.R."

Chapter 1

Get my daughter out of here." Major Travis's words came out tight and stark, and T.R. Barkley eyed him silently.

As a civilian scout for the army, Barkley was used to being ordered around, but this time was different. The major was nervous, and with good reason.

"I'll give you two men. I can't honestly spare them, but you've got to get her through to Fort Laramie." Travis swung around and faced him, the cords on his uniform fluttering.

"Sir, I'll get through faster with your message if I go alone."

"You've got to take Amy," Travis insisted, his blue eyes adamant. "Nothing good is going to happen here. You know that."

Barkley lowered his gaze. He had just come in from three weeks of reconnoitering, and he did know. He'd informed the commanding officer himself. The Indians were gathering, making tentative peace among tribes who were traditional enemies. The tribes that had traded freely at the fort had become sullen and hostile, but until Barkley confirmed it, Travis had not believed they would make a concerted attack with the aim of removing the white man's garrison from Fort Bridger. Barkley had made the best count he could, gathered every scrap of information, then hurried back to the fort.

"Might be best to just pull back," he suggested.

"Abandon the fort?" Travis paced angrily to the window that looked out on the parade ground. "I have orders, Barkley. The government just bought this fort from civilians and made it a military installation. It's taken a lot of effort to bring it up to our standards. Washington would not be happy if I gave it up within months of establishing the outpost here. I'm to hold this position no matter what."

The scout ran his hand through his beard. "No offense, Major, but those orders were written a long time ago by men who had no clear view of the situation."

Travis's eyes narrowed. He was near retirement, Barkley guessed. Fifty, at least. The word around the barracks was that if the major could hold Fort Bridger for a year, they'd discharge him honorably with a pension. And he'd done that for eight months, but the way Barkley saw it now, the major had little chance of living out the week.

"Get Amy away from here tonight," Travis demanded. "You know it's her

best chance. If she stays here. . ." He didn't need to say more. His eyes pleaded.

Barkley nodded in resignation. "All right, as soon as it's dark. Give her a good horse, and tell her to pack light."

"Thank you. I won't forget this."

Barkley could only hope the man wouldn't have a tragic reason to remember and regret.

He left the major's office and went out the gate to the bank of the Blacks Fork. There wasn't time to go home. He'd bathe in the river and shave here then sleep for a few hours in the barracks. When dusk fell, he would be in the saddle again.

But this time he wouldn't be creeping alone toward the Indian camps, outfoxing the foxes to learn their ways. He'd be flying toward Fort Laramie with a desperate call for reinforcements and with Travis's precious daughter.

He didn't like it. Travis ought not to have brought her here in the first place. Fort Laramie was one thing, but Fort Bridger was a small post 350 miles to the west and had no amenities. The wives of two other officers had come out in April for two months' visit, but they had left eight weeks ago. Travis, a widower, had brought his youngest daughter out. He'd been away from home nearly a year and craved his family. But he should have sent her back to Laramie when the other women went.

Barkley rarely saw Amy Travis. He only went to the fort when the major needed him. He had a cabin five miles away, where he lived alone. He'd been only a boy when his family came with one of the first wagon trains through the Green River Valley in 1845. His mother became very ill on the trail, and when they arrived at Jim Bridger's trading post, his father decided to stop right there, in Indian territory, and build a homestead within a few miles of the post, or the fort, as Jim Bridger styled it. Bridger himself was still at the fort then, and Barkley's father became friends with the legendary mountain man.

The Indians generally had a good relationship with Bridger and clustered around the fort to trade. For several years, wagon trains heading for California and Oregon stopped there to rest and trade. Now they mostly bypassed Fort Bridger, taking a cutoff farther north, making directly for Fort Hall, but some still came this way, taking the Mormon Trail.

Somehow the Barkleys' homestead, hidden in a peaceful little valley, had been ignored by hostiles. T.R. Barkley thought Jim Bridger's proximity and rapport with the natives had protected his family, and for thirteen years they had lived unmolested. Once or twice his father had had problems with pilfering and had learned to lock up his stock and tools, but for the most part, the Barkleys were left alone. When Bridger sold the fort to the Mormons and moved on to bigger adventures, the climate had changed around the outpost.

Barkley's family had changed, too. His parents were dead now, and his sister,

Rebecca, had married a lieutenant and gone east. His older brother, Richard, was dead; his horse had fallen on him. Young Matt had joined the army and was back at Fort Laramie. If he went to beg Major Lynde for troops to relieve Major Travis, chances were that Matt would be among them.

Returning to the fort after he'd washed himself, Barkley was leading his horse across the parade ground when a flash of color drew his eye. Amy Travis was coming out of the major's quarters, a small house under the wall of the fort. Her deep plum-colored skirt swirled around her as she walked quickly toward her father's office. It was hot, and she wore a white shirtwaist without the formality of a jacket. Her hair was hidden under a lavender bonnet. He'd never been close enough to see her eyes, but he guessed they were blue like her father's.

He'd heard she was a wild thing, always wanting to be out riding the prairie. Her father became exasperated, having to detail men to watch her. She was reputed to be a phenomenal horsewoman and a half-decent shot with a rifle. Barkley didn't know. He usually made a point of staying away from women.

He'd seen her once, across the parade ground, when a chaplain had passed through and held a worship service for the garrison. Amy Travis had sat demurely beside her father that day on one of the benches carried out from the mess hall. She kept her eyes downcast. He'd glimpsed her profile, solemn and earnest beneath the brim of her bonnet. He wasn't sure whether she was beautiful or not, but he liked the way she looked, and he knew she affected him in a way no other woman ever had. That disturbed him. He had stayed away from the fort for weeks afterward.

Which woman was the real Amy Travis? The subdued angel or the rash daredevil?

The sight of her now made him stop in his tracks. Two troopers walked past him, toward the barracks, momentarily blocking his view of her. How could they carry on with their routine while she was in sight? Maybe they feared her father's wrath, or maybe they were just used to her presence.

Miss Travis didn't look toward him, and he let his gaze linger as she walked. If she wasn't beautiful, she was striking at least. That uneasy feeling returned, but it wasn't unpleasant. Barkley felt a pang of regret as she disappeared through the door to her father's office.

"So, T.R., you're back."

He jumped and turned his head. Corporal Jim Markheim was leaning on the doorjamb at the entrance to the barracks.

"Jim," Barkley said in acknowledgment.

"Just admiring the view?" Markheim asked with a chuckle.

Barkley felt his face warm beneath his tan, and he tugged at Buck's reins. He'd have enough time later to decide whether or not Amy Travis was pretty.

He still didn't like taking her with him. She would slow him down and perhaps endanger his mission, but it seemed he had no choice.

"Can I get a shave around here?" he asked, looping Buck's reins around the hitching post and reaching for his saddlebag.

Markheim shrugged. "It's dry, T.R. Don't know as we'd ought to spare the water for a dirt clod like you."

"The well's dry?" Barkley asked. That would be bad news with the attack coming.

"No, I'm pulling your leg. The water level's low, but that well has never gone dry yet, so they say."

Barkley nodded. His older brother had helped dig that well seven years ago. The occupants of Fort Bridger could always get plenty of water from the Blacks Fork, but in the event of a siege, the well would be crucial.

He fingered the damp whiskers on his chin. "Well, I reckon I'll get shaved then."

"Better wash your clothes, too." Markheim held his nose and grimaced as Barkley pushed past him.

⌒

"I won't go," Amy said flatly. She was annoyed to the edge of anger. She'd been separated from her father much of her life as the army sent him from one assignment to another, and she didn't want to leave him now.

He stood up, returning her glare. "Yes, you most certainly will. I was a fool to keep you here this long. It was selfish of me. Now I have to send three good men to make sure you make it safely to civilization."

"You don't need to do any such thing. I want to stay with you, Father."

"I've told you: The situation has deteriorated to the point where that is no longer possible."

"Do you honestly think they're going to attack the fort?"

"Yes, I do. Our civilian scout says they are, and he knows what's what when it comes to Indians."

"But surely you don't think those savages can overpower the fort? You can repulse them."

"It all depends." Her father frowned and studied the map on the wall behind his desk.

"On what?" Amy stepped closer to him. His gravity was beginning to worry her. She'd never before heard him suggest that his outfit might not survive an Indian attack.

"On how many there are of them and how soon we can get reinforcements."

"You're asking Major Lynde for reinforcements from Fort Laramie?" The garrison at Fort Bridger was only fifty men strong at the moment, hardened cavalry troopers. Most had served at Fort Laramie or one of the other western forts before being assigned at Bridger, but still, fifty men seemed inadequate, Amy thought, if an attack was likely.

"Yes. I'm sending Barkley. He'll take you with him and deliver you to Mrs. Lynde. From there, you can go back to your sister in Albany. If things go well here, I'll send you word. If not. . ."

"Daddy." She never called him *Daddy* except when she was frightened. It had slipped out, and she saw when he looked at her that he knew she was afraid now.

"I'm sorry, Amy. The truth is, if we don't get reinforcements fast, things could go badly. I don't like to frighten you, but there are times when you ought to be afraid."

Amy sat down hard on her father's oak chair. She was a tomboy, a daring, fearless girl, or so the boys at home had thought. She would walk a fence rail or ride a bucking mule or jump off the bridge over Walker Stream. In reality, she was scared out of her mind to do any of those things, but she'd felt somehow that she couldn't let anyone see it. So she gritted her teeth and did them. After a while, taking risks had become a series of exciting adventures instead of terrifying ordeals.

Coming west had been the biggest adventure of all. Since her mother had died, she'd lived with her married sister, Elaine, but when their father was selected as the first commanding officer at Fort Bridger, he sent word that she might join him if she wished.

If she wished! It was wonderful! Elaine had fretted about her traveling alone, but Amy had gone off by stagecoach to Cincinnati and from there had joined the wife of a captain stationed at Fort Laramie. After two months of travel, she'd arrived at Fort Bridger exhausted. It had taken her a week to get her energy and high spirits back. Then her father had had his hands full trying to control her.

She knew she'd stretched his patience to the limit, but when the limit was in sight, she eased off and coddled him. He loved that. She mended his uniforms and brought him coffee at his desk in the middle of the morning. She baked the applesauce cake her mother used to make and knit him a pair of soft, black wool socks.

She stood up and put her hands on his shoulders, fussing with the epaulets. "You ought to have told me sooner."

"Maybe. I hoped we could smooth things over."

She straightened her shoulders, knowing there was only one thing she could do to ease his mind. "All right. I'll go, but only so you won't worry."

"Good girl." He leaned over and kissed her forehead. "You'd just be in the way here."

"You've got to be careful, Father."

He laughed ruefully. "I won't give up this fort without a struggle. And if Barkley gets to Laramie in good time, I may have reinforcements before the hostiles make a move."

She nodded, determined not to impede the scout's progress. "There's one thing, though, Father. Please don't make me go back to New York. I'll wait at Fort Laramie, and when it's over, you send for me, and I'll come back."

"Oh, Amy—"

"Please? I've loved being with you. I don't want to give that up."

Her father's eyes were troubled. "I thought it was safe when I brought you here."

"It was. We had a wonderful time together this spring, didn't we, and most of the summer?"

He nodded. "We'll see, my dear."

"Good. I'll wait at Laramie."

"But you must promise to behave, girl. Don't give Major Lynde the headaches you've given me."

She laughed. "I won't. His wife will keep me busy, trying to match me up with the single officers. That's what she did when I came out."

"If only you'd settle down," Travis said in mock exasperation. "I think it will take quite a man to handle you, Amy Margaret."

"Someday, Father."

"Yes. There's plenty of time. Now, you listen to me. Barkley says you must travel light. You're to leave most of your things here. Wear your riding skirt, and take one change of clothing. I'll send the rest of your things when it's safe."

"That old scout said all that? I didn't know he could talk." She laughed, but her father's eyes narrowed.

"You'd be surprised what T.R. Barkley can say when he has a reason to speak. And listen to me, girl. When he tells you something on the trail, you pay attention. He won't waste words, but he knows this territory, and your life is in his hands."

She swallowed and smiled weakly. "Yes, sir. I'll be good."

Travis's eyes softened. "He's a good man, honey. He'll get you through. Now, I've got the supply sergeant packing for you and the escort, other than your personal things. And Amy. . ." He looked keenly at her. "You must promise me you'll take care of Kip."

"Father! You're letting me take Kip?" The joy that spurted up in her was tempered by the realization that he was giving her the swift, valiant horse for a reason. He honestly believed she would be in danger.

"Nothing but the best for you, dear, but don't run him into a chuckhole."

She threw herself into his arms.

"I'll keep him safe for you at Fort Laramie, Father. And I'll be safe, too. When the troops come from Laramie, you'll know I'm all right."

Chapter 2

B arkley stood on the catwalk at the top of the fort's wall, watching the sun go down behind the massive, forbidding mountains to the west. There were wispy clouds, not the serious kind that would bring a soaking rain to the parched land, but enough to splinter the rays of light into glorious color. He watched until the last bits of rose and lavender were swallowed up in the gray of the evening sky and turned toward the ladder. Time to move.

His buckskin gelding was saddled and waiting. Buck wouldn't win any prizes for beauty, but he was sturdy and strong. Half quarter horse and half mustang, Buck was fast, and he didn't know when to quit. Barkley gathered the reins and led him toward the commanding officer's quarters.

Major Travis was saying good-bye to his daughter, and Amy was listening earnestly.

Should have sent her out two months ago, Barkley thought again. Now it was up to him to get her safely to Fort Laramie. Four days' hard ride, if they were lucky. He hoped it wouldn't take longer. Travis would need Major Lynde's troops soon.

She kissed her father one last time, and Jim Markheim led up her horse. Barkley recognized the rangy gray as one of the major's three personal mounts. He was big and fast, and the major thought a lot of him. Good. He recognized the precariousness of the flight and was giving Amy his best horse.

Barkley looked over the two troopers Travis had detailed to go with him. It must have been a difficult decision. Send two sharpshooters to protect his daughter when he'd need every gun he could lay hands on? He'd chosen two privates. Barkley recognized Layton by sight but knew nothing about him. He was short, wiry, and alert. Brown was taller, slouching lazily in the saddle, but Barkley knew he'd be full of action when the need came. He was a decent tracker, a fair shot, and stubborn as all get-out. Barkley was glad Travis had picked him.

Amy Travis put her boot in the stirrup. Her father gave her a little boost as she swung onto the gray's back, then led the horse to where Barkley and the troopers were waiting.

"Amy, you've met our scout, T.R. Barkley."

"Not really," she said, looking him up and down.

Barkley touched the brim of his hat. "Ma'am."

"He'll get you where you're going." Travis said it as if he were taking Amy across the street to visit a neighbor.

She nodded. Her golden hair was up, hidden under a soft brimmed hat, not one of the calico bonnets he'd seen her wear around the fort. In the twilight, he couldn't tell if she'd inherited the blue eyes or not.

"You take care," the major said sternly.

"I will, Daddy."

Travis looked keenly at Barkley, and he nodded. They'd already settled things. Travis had seen that they had food, blankets, water, a little hard money, ammunition. Barkley knew the dire consequences if he failed in his twofold mission. Nothing remained to be said.

The scout mounted and turned Buck toward the trail, not looking back. He heard the other three horses following closely. He wanted to put a lot of miles between them and Fort Bridger before the half-moon rose at midnight.

They rode without speaking, with Barkley ten yards ahead of the others. Amy Travis came next on the long-legged gray, and the two troopers rode behind her.

Barkley knew the gray gelding could outrun Buck, but Amy kept him back, allowing him to concentrate on the trail ahead. They trotted briskly up the valley, paralleling the Blacks Fork, heading for the Green River. As they approached the pass, they rode high above the river on a winding trail that rose between the looming peaks. Barkley kept Buck in the ground-eating trot the horse could sustain for hours, heading east.

To his left, the ground dropped away to the wide, slow-moving stream, which in August was shallow and sluggish. Clumps of trees grew near its banks, and the dark tops of some of those trees were as high as the level they rode on. He knew that when they left the mountains, trees would be scarce for the rest of the journey. When wagon trains reached Bridger, the emigrants always commented on the trees and the acres of green grass in the lush valley. It was a relief to eyes that had seen only the open prairie for weeks, with brown grass, dried and brittle by the time the weary oxen limped into the haven.

After three hours, they left the Blacks Fork and cut across several miles of open ground to the Green River. The bank cut down sharply in front of them. Barkley knew the best place to cross the stream and angled Buck along the edge until he came to the most gradual slope in the bank. He slowed his horse for the descent and heard the others close behind him.

When they reached the bottom, he dismounted and took Buck's bridle off, turning him loose to drink.

Layton and Brown followed Amy down to the edge of the water. Brown snapped a line around his mare's neck before removing her bridle, but Layton let his bay drink with the bit still in his mouth.

Amy rode the big gray close to where Barkley stood. She seemed able to handle the horse, but he didn't want any problems.

"Will that horse come to you?" It was the first time he had spoken to her, really. Her nearness triggered his pulse, and the question came out more gruffly than he'd intended.

She hesitated. "I'm not sure. Kip always comes to Father, but I don't know as I dare turn him loose out here. I have hobbles, though."

She held the reins slack as she hopped lightly down and opened the saddlebag on the near side. Barkley fought the impulse to jump to her side and offer to take care of the task. Better to let her be as independent as possible. He turned to Brown.

"We'll stop twenty minutes and give the horses a breather."

"All right. Seems like a quiet night."

"So far."

The starlight was enough to show where a gravel bar spread halfway across the stream. Barkley walked out on it, then waded the rest of the way over. The water wasn't more than two inches deep. On the other side, he picked up the path and climbed the bank. At the crest, he could look out over the prairie for a mile or more, toward the eastern ranges of the Rockies, where the moon was rising, just pushing above the horizon, big and yellow. The tough grasses waved in a light breeze that at last relieved the heat of the day.

If they could move along undisturbed for another four hours, they would be well on the way to South Pass, although they would still be within hostile territory. He would stop at daybreak to let Miss Travis rest while he scouted the trail ahead as far as the pass. He knew the danger would not be at an end until they were safe inside the walls of Fort Laramie.

He could hear the river, the gurgling swirl of water over the rocks. He could hear the horses, too, pulling grass and snorting below him. He heard her footsteps long before she had toiled up the bank.

He knew it was Amy without turning around. Her skirt made a swishing sound that no man's clothing ever made. He realized she was trying to be quiet, and truthfully, she wasn't all that noisy, but it was a different sound that stood out in the silence of the night as much as the champing of the horses.

When she was nearly beside him, she scuffled a bit, and he thought she might have lost her footing, but he didn't turn and reach out to her. A moment later, she stood next to him, breathing a little fast.

He kept still, looking out at the way they would take. The moon had slowly separated itself from the edge of the earth and sprung above it, smaller and whiter now.

Amy's breathing slowed and grew quieter, and he thought she was purposely bringing it under control. She stood beside him, looking and waiting. He wondered if she expected him to say something, but he couldn't think of anything worth

breaking the silence for.

"Mr. Barkley," she said at last. It was little more than a whisper.

He turned toward her. She had removed the felt hat and held it down at her side. Her hair was burnished gold in the moonlight. In the daytime, she had better keep it well covered, Barkley thought. She wore a dark blouse, not the white one he'd seen her wearing earlier. He was glad; the deep brown cotton wouldn't reflect the moonlight.

"How well do you know my father?" she asked.

He looked off east again, thinking about that. He had met Travis perhaps a dozen times over the last eight months at the fort or out on the plains. They had camped together a couple of times when he rode with one of the major's detachments. They had talked most of those times about the Indians and the land and the life in the West. But they weren't friends exactly.

He respected Benjamin Travis. The major had come into the fort with authority but without arrogance. He was willing to learn from others with more experience in the territory, and he seemed fair where his command was concerned. He'd taken on the difficult tasks of rebuilding the fort and keeping the tension with the Mormon pioneers at a minimum. Barkley found nothing about Major Travis to criticize.

The scout was silent so long that Amy wondered if he had heard her. She felt suddenly very exposed, and she knew she would be frightened out here so far from the fort and her father if this man weren't standing so solid and competent beside her.

"Don't know him real well," Barkley said at last. It was loud enough to carry to her ears but no farther. "I've worked with him some."

Amy looked at the scout's profile. He was handsome, perhaps rendered more so by the moonlight that softened his features. He wasn't scruffy looking; he had shaved that day, she was sure. He wore a dark shirt and pants, not the smelly buckskins she had seen on the shaggy scouts at Fort Laramie. He was young. It had startled her back at Fort Bridger when she'd first seen him up close. He seemed to have years and years of frontier living behind him and intimate knowledge of the Indians' customs and habits, but he was still in his mid-twenties, she was sure now.

He hadn't come to any of the social gatherings at the fort last spring. She'd seen him only occasionally, silently passing in and out of the fort, but she hadn't really noticed him. He was another man among dozens at the fort, a part of the scenery. Until today, she had vaguely supposed he was one of those feral mountain men who couldn't read but knew every beaver lodge between here and Canada.

Now he was very important to her, and she wanted to know why her father had entrusted her to this particular man, the quiet young scout who crept around in the brush for weeks, watching the Indians for him. It occurred to her that the safety she had enjoyed on her rides near the fort might somehow be connected to this man.

"My father seemed a bit fatalistic today." Even her quiet voice was loud in the stillness. He looked quickly at her, and she said more softly, "He's never been that way before."

"Your father's a good man. He knows what he's doing."

"Do you think—is he really in danger?"

"Always in danger out here, ma'am."

She shivered. If her father was in danger inside Fort Bridger, how much danger were they in out here, unprotected? But her father wouldn't have sent her away if he'd thought she would be safer with him.

"We'd best move," Barkley said quietly. He turned and went down the path, waiting for a moment at the stream bank until she had climbed safely down but not holding his hand out to aid her. As soon as her feet were on the level ground at the bottom, he turned and waded into the shallow stream, toward the gravel bar. She followed, trying to keep her leather boots from splashing in the water.

Brown was watching the grazing horses, keeping an eye on the path they had come by. As they walked across the gravel bar, Layton went to the big gray and began bridling him for Amy then stooped to remove the hobbles.

Barkley gave a low whistle, and his buckskin walked eagerly toward him. Amy watched him rub the gelding's forelock then reach for the bridle that he'd looped over the saddle horn. He never wasted a motion, and he slipped the bit easily between the buckskin's teeth.

"All set, ma'am," Layton said.

She walked to Kip's side. The stirrup was high on the tall gelding's side, and Layton's hand came under her elbow, giving her a little leverage as she sprang up onto Kip's back. The private was being attentive, and Amy wondered if she ought to let him know somehow that she wasn't getting personal with any man just now. There was nothing offensive in his manner yet. He might just be more gentlemanly than Brown or Barkley, might have been raised to offer more assistance to ladies. She decided to ignore it for now.

＞

The breeze had found its way into the riverbed, and the treetops ruffled and stirred.

Barkley wanted to get out of the ravine. He couldn't hear all the tiny sounds he wanted to with the trees tossing and the stream trickling. He mounted Buck and pushed him across the water then up the far bank. At the top, he moved out far enough so the others could gain the high ground without running into Buck then halted and listened and looked. Nothing seemed to have changed.

He glanced over his shoulder. Amy had stopped Kip just behind him and was stroking the gray's neck where the black mane fell on the left side. Behind her, Layton and Brown were waiting, their horses sidestepping nervously.

He lifted his reins just a hair, and Buck moved into his trot. Behind him, the other horses picked up the pace and came on steadily.

They rode over the silver-washed hills for hours, dark silhouettes against the ever-swaying grass. Barkley's lips were dry. The wind would be stinging the tender skin of Amy Travis's face, he was sure, but he couldn't help her except to maintain the pace and get her closer to Fort Laramie before the sun rose.

An hour before dawn, he halted Buck suddenly, raising his hand to slow the riders behind him. Before him, the tall grasses lay down in a straight line from the trail they followed toward the river on his left. It was not a worn, well-beaten track, but the trail of several animals that had recently passed that way.

The other horses came up close, and he motioned to Brown. The trooper rode up beside him and silently surveyed the scene, then looked toward the river.

Amy hung back a little, and Layton kept his horse beside hers. Barkley shot a glance at Brown.

"Reckon we ought to check it out?" Brown asked softly.

"You go on," Barkley told him. "Move out away from the river a little. I'll have a look and catch up. Keep Miss Travis between you. If you find some cover, wait for me."

Brown nodded and rode back to where Layton and Amy sat on their mounts. Almost immediately they moved out, away from the flattened grass, continuing east. Barkley moved Buck into the trail and walked him slowly toward the river. Twenty yards from where the land descended sharply, he stopped. There was no cover for the horse; he would have to leave him there. He turned Buck off the trail into the tall grass, dismounted, and tugged down on the reins.

Buck snuffled quietly, then lay down. After petting the horse, Barkley went back to the path. Buck's hiding place would not fool a tracker, but he would not be in plain sight to anyone approaching as the sun rose.

The scout crouched low and crept swiftly toward the river. He could hear it above the wind now. It was wide and low along this stretch, swirling around rocks. He gained the edge of the embankment and stared down into the bottom of the wide draw. The flat, dark water lay before him with the moonlight on it, and willows crowded the brim. And yes, horses grazed down there. He counted seven. Two were pintos, with large splotches of white clearly visible. There was no campfire, no smoke.

At last he made out dark spots under the trees. He thought they must be people stretched out to sleep. He wished he could get nearer, but he didn't dare, not with Amy Travis to protect. He was more than half certain they were

Indians, and even then they might be friendly, but the way things had been going lately, they probably were not.

There might be a guard on duty. Barkley sat for several minutes, watching for any movement, any gleam or any dark spot that was not still. There was so much motion already with the restless horses, the flowing water, and the tossing treetops that it was hard to be sure.

Finally he turned away, satisfied, and went stealthily back to where Buck lay. He threw his leg over the saddle and clucked, and Buck heaved to his feet, his head going up first then his hindquarters. The two of them stood immobile as Barkley looked and Buck sniffed; then they headed for the track Amy and the troopers had followed.

He kept the horse at a quick walk for a quarter mile then urged him into the extended trot. Daylight would be on them soon. He'd have to find a place where they could guard Amy and rest part of the day. They might need to lie low and wait for darkness if hostiles were on the move.

He thought of Major Travis and his urgent situation. It wouldn't be good to wait out the entire day. Travis needed those reinforcements.

Barkley hated being in this position, having to decide what was best or least dangerous for all concerned. Hide the daughter for the daylight hours or move on to get the aid the garrison needed? It would be different if he only had to worry about himself.

He realized suddenly that it wasn't his decision alone. There was always someone who had better foresight than he did. His mother had taught him as a child to take his problems to God. As he rode, Barkley began to pray in earnest for wisdom and for Amy Travis's safety.

Far ahead he saw the dark bulk of a line of trees, and he let Buck quicken his pace. They would be waiting there for him. It might have made a good stopping place for the daylight hours if it weren't so close to the party he'd just seen. They would definitely have to put some more ground between them before they stopped for another rest. If one of the natives rode up out of the river bottom to check on their back trail, the track of the four riders would be obvious.

He slowed Buck as he neared the trees and watched cautiously ahead. He didn't like riding into cover from the open like this.

The trees were between him and the rising sun, but even so, the gray light of early dawn showed him clearly where their horses had passed. He followed the trail of bent grass, watching the verge of the woods. When Barkley drew within ten yards, Brown stepped from between two cottonwoods and stood silently waiting for him. As soon as Barkley was close, the trooper turned and walked into the trees. Barkley followed.

A stream flowed through the copse toward the river, and the three horses were browsing on grass and leaves. Layton and Amy were seated, and Barkley dropped Buck's reins and walked toward them. Brown stood beside him.

"Indians," Barkley reported. "At least seven horses. I couldn't tell much without getting closer than I liked. I think we'd best move on."

"Sun's coming up," Layton said.

"Yes, but our trail's too plain."

"Reckon we ought to stick with the wagon trail?" Brown asked quietly.

Barkley nodded. "Our tracks will be less obvious. Sandy Creek flows into the river up ahead. We'll follow it northeast for thirty miles or so, then we'll have a stretch of twenty-five miles along the Little Sandy to South Pass."

"All right," said Brown.

"We'll stop and rest and water the horses when we get to Little Sandy Creek if we don't run into any problems on the way. I'd like to keep riding until then." Barkley turned his eyes on Amy. "How about it, Miss Travis? Can you ride another thirty miles before we rest again?"

"I'm fine," she said, but he knew she must be tired. She had pluck.

"You hungry?"

"I can wait."

He couldn't help smiling. They'd been riding all night, and she must be starved. His own stomach was crying out for breakfast, even though he was used to going long stretches between meals.

"Layton, get out something we can chew on."

The trooper took biscuit and dried beef from his packs, and they sat eating a cold breakfast while Brown watched the trail behind them, beyond the trees. Barkley wished they had hot coffee, but they couldn't risk a fire.

"You all set, Miss Travis?"

She looked up at him. The sun had risen, and even in the shade of the trees, the blue of her eyes was startling. Odd how his heart hammered when he noticed them. He didn't like it. It made it hard to concentrate on their purpose.

"I'm ready anytime you are, Mr. Barkley."

He was seeing an unexpected side of her—not the unmanageable tomboy, not the submissive daughter. She seemed to be maturing under his eyes.

Barkley cleared his throat. "You must be tired, but I think we'd best not stick around here too long."

A saucy smile crept out as she stood up and brushed off her brown skirt. "If I fall asleep in the saddle, don't let me fall off and be left behind."

He couldn't help returning the smile. "Don't worry, ma'am. I'll tie you in the saddle if need be."

Chapter 3

An hour later, Barkley spotted smoke in the east—just a thin column from a campfire—and he was sure it was at a stopping place in the trail beside the creek.

Amy rode up beside him, letting the gray stretch his legs.

"Someone's up ahead?" she asked tentatively.

He nodded. "Probably an emigrant train camped there last night and hasn't got rolling yet."

They rode side by side, and he found himself snatching glances at her. Her golden hair was up under the hat, and she wore no adornments. She had an interesting face, he thought. Pretty, but more than that, full of curiosity about her surroundings. She could hardly wait to see what they would find at the campsite where the smoke rose and disappeared into the blue August sky.

They came to the place where the approach to the creek had been worn down by many wagon wheels. Barkley took Buck to a vantage point on the bank above for an overview of the low camp.

A train of eleven wagons circled loosely among the trees by the river. He squinted and frowned at the scene. The smoke came from only one campfire and people were moving about it, but they were moving too slowly to be preparing to travel.

"What is it?" Amy asked, watching his face rather than the camp below.

"Unless their cattle are farther downriver, some are missing. They don't have enough oxen there to haul those wagons."

She turned back to the scene laid out below and studied it. He saw her eyes flare as she took in the dozen oxen grazing inside the circle of wagons, a sprinkling of saddle horses among them. The women tending kettles at the fire or washing clothing in the river didn't seem alarmed, however. He could see only two men, and both held rifles. They stood near the wagons, looking back toward the wagon road.

"What does it mean?" Amy asked.

"Come on."

Barkley wheeled his buckskin and rode for the wagon trail. As the four horses approached the camp, heads went up. The two men with guns stiffened and trained their weapons on them, but Barkley raised his hat and waved it, and they slowly lowered the rifles.

He rode in at a trot, and Amy kept pace on Kip, with the two troopers close behind.

"What happened?" Barkley asked shortly.

"Injuns," said a stout, dark-haired man. "They came tearing in here at dawn and drove off most of our stock. Got away with nigh thirty mules, eight oxen, and a few horses. Most of our men have gone after 'em."

"North?" Barkley asked, looking toward the stream.

"No, back south again, into them hills." The man nodded toward the slopes that rose, brown with dry grass.

"Anyone hurt?" Barkley asked.

"One boy took an arrow in the leg," the man said. "It happened so fast, we didn't really have much chance to defend ourselves." He kicked sheepishly at a stone on the ground. "Didn't expect this to happen. Heard the tribes had been quiet lately."

"The boy all right?" Barkley asked.

"He'll mend."

"Show me the arrow."

The man did not question his authority but turned and headed for one of the wagons.

The second man, who was older, stood looking at the riders, and women and youngsters began to gather.

"You with the cavalry?" the old man ventured.

"Sort of. We're on the way to Fort Laramie," Barkley said.

"You been to Fort Bridger?" one of the women asked.

"Yes, ma'am." Barkley looked at the old man. "We saw a small band of Indians twelve or fifteen miles back. They didn't see us. But the tribes have been restless lately." He knew it was too far for these people to go back to Fort Laramie now. "You be alert between here and Bridger."

"How long will it take?" the old man asked. "I mean, if we get our mules back."

"Most a week with wagons, I reckon," Barkley said. Oxen would do well to make ten miles a day, he knew. He didn't like to think of the small band unprotected at this unsettled time.

The dark-haired man came back, holding a twenty-four-inch arrow with the tip cut off. Barkley reached for it and held it up, turning it thoughtfully.

"Lakota Sioux. How many men went after them?"

"Fifteen. Our horses were mostly tied up, so they only got three."

Barkley rubbed his chin. "I'd like to stop and help you, but I can't."

Layton eased his horse up on the other side of Amy's. "We'll tell the authorities at Laramie what happened," he said.

The two men nodded. "Tell them it's the Richardson party," the younger man said.

"How many Sioux?" Barkley asked.

"Seemed like a hundred," a tall, angular woman said.

"No, 'twarn't that many," the old man snorted. "They made an insufferable racket, but there warn't more than twenty of them."

Layton looked at Barkley.

"We can't," Barkley said. "Major Travis was explicit. We can't delay."

Layton crossed his wrists on his saddle horn and looked away.

"You got plenty of ammunition?" Barkley asked.

The young man nodded.

"Well, if you don't get your stock back, you pack everybody up and head for Bridger as quick as you can. Things are looking a mite uncertain just now."

He saw the fear leap into the women's eyes as they looked around quickly for their children. He didn't like to cause that, but neither did he like to think they might sit here for days or weeks in indecision.

He nodded to the emigrants and turned Buck back to the trail. He set a quick pace for the next hour despite the searing heat and was rewarded by the sight of the Little Sandy flowing into the larger stream.

He dismounted and led Buck down to the edge of the water, then unbridled him. While the gelding greedily slurped from the creek, Barkley squatted and removed his hat, dipping one hand in the water. It was very cold, even in mid-August, running down from the high peaks.

He saw Amy turn away Layton's offer of help as she struggled with the hobbles. When her horse was secure, she sat on a large rock and pulled off her tall leather boots.

He walked upstream a little ways, scouting for a likely spot for her to rest. The water was low, and there was a place where the ground beneath tall bushes beside the stream was dry and sandy. He ambled back toward the others.

Brown looked up as he approached, and Barkley beckoned to him. Brown was definitely the one to trust. The trooper came to him, and he said softly, "We'll stop here. You keep watch while I scout ahead a little."

Brown nodded.

"Tell the others to sleep, and keep an eye on the horses. There's a place yonder in the shade where Miss Travis can rest. When I get back, you rest and Layton can keep watch."

Brown gave him a curtailed salute.

Barkley almost told him not to light a fire and to watch the back trail, but he decided it was unnecessary to tell Brown that. It rankled him when people told him to do things he would do anyway, so he didn't say it.

He whistled for Buck, reluctant to take his mount away from the chance to graze, and rode out along the creek, following the deeply rutted trail. After half an hour, he sat and gazed long and hard eastward, toward South Pass then

turned and loped slowly back toward the others.

Brown stood up out of the grass as he approached. Barkley rode up close to him and dismounted.

"Miss Travis?" he said as he slipped the headstall over Buck's ears.

"She's asleep," Brown said with a grin. "Plopped down in the shade with her head on her saddle, and she was out."

Barkley smiled. "Layton?"

"Him, too. You'd best get a few winks yourself, T.R. I can stand another hour."

"All right, but no longer. We all need rest, and we'll need to be awake and alert."

The sun was high overhead when Layton woke him.

"Hate to do it," the private said.

Barkley was on his feet. He didn't feel truly rested, but he knew he could go on for some time now.

"Miss Travis still sleeping?"

"Like a baby." Layton's smile was smug, and Barkley felt annoyance. Had the trooper been watching her as she slept? He had been tempted to take a peek at her himself but had deliberately stayed away. He could see where she was stretched out on her blanket beneath the bushes, but he thought ladies needed their privacy.

"All right, see if you can get a little more rest." Barkley settled his hat comfortably on his head and walked to the stream, where he bent for a drink. At least they would have water most of the way.

He checked on the horses, then ambled up to where he could see behind them, down the almost imperceptible slope. They would be heading upward faster now, climbing to the pass. It was hard work for the horses, but they were all in prime condition.

An hour later, he turned back toward the creek and walked quietly to where Brown lay leaning against a weathered log. He kicked the man's left boot gently.

Brown immediately opened his eyes and looked up at him then stood, reaching for his rifle.

"Let's eat something and move," Barkley said, and Brown nodded.

Layton stirred, and Barkley knew he hadn't gone back to sleep. While Brown rummaged in the packs for food, Layton went to bring the horses closer.

Barkley stared after him thoughtfully. "How do you read Layton?" he asked Brown.

The trooper glanced up at him. "He's all right, I guess. Not my first choice in a pinch, but he's a good shot."

Barkley nodded. He walked slowly toward Amy. Her boots were set neatly beside her, and her stocking feet were drawn up to the hem of the loose divided skirt. She was curled on her right side, her face in the shade. She had folded Kip's woolen saddle blanket over the tooled leather seat of her saddle for a pillow, and her golden hair shone against the dull blue and black stripes of the blanket.

He stood just for the length of two short breaths, his pulse thudding in that disconcerting way. Softly, he said, "Miss Travis."

She didn't respond but breathed on steadily, and he envied her the sound sleep. Her face held a sweetness that caught at him and a vulnerability that brought home to him afresh the magnitude of his mission.

"Miss Travis—Amy," he said gently, leaning down to touch her elbow.

Her eyelids fluttered, and she looked up at him, startled for an instant, then sat up and reached for her boots.

He stood and walked to the log where Brown was rationing out cheese and biscuits. She seemed to know what to do without asking questions, and that pleased him. He was glad she wasn't a chatterbox and could perform simple tasks without detailed instruction. It made his job easier.

"You like working for the army?" Brown asked, handing him his food.

Barkley shrugged. "Travis is fair. Don't think I'd want to enlist, though."

Brown nodded. "I wish now I hadn't."

Barkley raised his eyebrows. "Why did you?"

"Things were really tough at home. We had a fire, lost everything. I took Martha and the boy to my folks', but they didn't really have room for us, and they're struggling, anyway. I figured if I did a year or two with the army, I could at least be sending my pay home. Martha's been putting by every cent she can, and we're hoping when I get home, we'll have enough to start over."

"I hope it works out for you."

Brown grimaced. "I've made up my mind. When I get home, I'm never leaving them again. Just between you and me, I miss them something fierce."

Barkley opened his canteen. "A man's allowed to miss his family."

Layton came to the log, and Brown gave him his ration.

Barkley looked over his shoulder and saw Amy standing up, pulling at the top of one boot, then stamping her foot a little. She stooped for the felt hat and perched it on her head, hiding the gleaming hair, and he took a deep, slow breath.

He turned away and saw that Layton watched her, too. Suddenly he felt foolish. He was an ordinary man, no different from any other. Perhaps she was an ordinary girl, and he only imagined she was special. How could he tell?

He walked toward the trail to eat while he kept watch once more.

Ten minutes later, Brown came up beside him, leading his chestnut mare, and Barkley relinquished his post to go saddle Buck.

The heat of the sun was scorching, and he kept the animals at a slow jog as they climbed the broad pass. The stream grew smaller as they went on, until it was a rivulet tumbling down its rocky course. The trail rose higher, and the air cooled.

Barkley always felt a thrill when he went over the pass. Somewhere ahead was the place he was born, still thousands of miles away. It seemed a foreign land to him: the East. Massachusetts. He could remember the farm there, the farms and shops and the church where the neighbors had gathered each Sunday. His father had kept sheep, and he and Richard had helped wash and shear them in the spring. He wasn't sure how much was really his memory and how much was the stories his parents had told.

He knew there were hundreds of towns close together with thousands of people in them. And they told him he had seen the ocean when he was a tyke, but that memory escaped him. He could remember ponds and a few large lakes but not the Atlantic. Jim Bridger had told his family about a huge salt sea he had seen to the west across the desert, but that, too, was out of Barkley's reckoning. Maybe someday he would go see it. Bridger told a lot of tales of the wonders he had seen, but so far Barkley hadn't caught the wanderlust. He liked the cabin in the mountains by the Blacks Fork.

Amy rode up beside him, the rangy gray stretching his legs, and again he wondered about her. She was reputed to be an adventurous girl, and she did seem to enjoy traveling. She hadn't complained even though the conditions were primitive. Her father had told him he was sending her back to the security of his married daughter's home. Was she ready to go back to Albany and sit in her sister's parlor, spinning yarn and embroidering runners?

She smiled when he looked at her, and his pulse quickened. Yes, she had her father's eyes, but her mother must have been a beauty. Her smile lit her features with an enthusiasm that even the battered hat couldn't repress.

"We've left the creek," she said.

"Yes, this is the Continental Divide. We'll hit the Sweetwater soon—flowing east."

She nodded. "It's beautiful out here. I hope Father permits me to come back soon."

Barkley just hoped her father survived, and uppermost on his list of hopes right now was Amy's safety.

"He's right to send you away," he said.

"Even so, I'll miss it."

"Fort Bridger?"

"Yes. Well, everything." She stroked the horse's neck, leaning forward slightly, and the hat brim hid her features. "I'll miss Father, of course, and the feeling I have out here. There's freedom in the West."

He supposed that was true. A woman could do things here that she wouldn't be allowed to do in Albany or Boston. Wear a split skirt, for instance, and ride hundreds of miles in the company of three men. In Albany, she would probably ride sidesaddle or in a buggy and be closely chaperoned. Amy rode astride here without self-consciousness, and she sat easily in the saddle, even after so many hours. She held the reins lightly with her left hand, barely keeping the contact with Kip's mouth. Even his sister, Rebecca, wasn't the rider Amy Travis was.

"Do you miss anything from the East?" he asked.

"Well, yes," she admitted. "Father's library is quite meager. I suppose books are too heavy to cart all this way, and the traders don't bring any."

Barkley smiled. His own home held a shelf of well-worn books, and he, too, wished for more.

"What does your father have?" he asked.

"You mean besides army regulations and his Bible?"

"Yes. If I'd known, maybe I could have loaned you something."

"You have books?" Her face was animated, and he caught his breath. That look was for him.

"Just a few." He swallowed hard. "Do you have Franklin's autobiography?"

"No. Father has Calvin's *Institutes* and Edmund Burke and William Bradford, and an astronomy book. Oh, and Shakespeare. A volume of Woolman's sermons, too. That's the most of it, I think."

"Don't know Woolman," Barkley said, "but I wouldn't have suspected your father of reading sermons and law books."

Amy shrugged. "Father reads anything. He's wishing he'd brought more books along, too."

"Well, I have John Bunyan and David Brainerd and a volume of Milton's poetry. That was my mother's."

"Men can read poetry," she said with a stubborn note.

Barkley laughed. "Didn't say they couldn't. I've read it three or four times myself." *Milton would have loved her*, he thought. *"So lovely fair, that what seemed fair in all the world seemed now mean, or in her summed up, in her contained."* He looked away quickly, hoping she couldn't guess he was comparing her to Milton's Eve.

"If I do go back East, I'm going to send some more books to Father," she said. "One of the traders can fit a box of books in his wagon."

"It would be the first thing they'd toss out if they had trouble. You see things like that by the trail."

"Yes, I saw a lot of furniture this spring, coming out from Fort Laramie," Amy admitted. "Beautiful, some of it. Such a shame."

He nodded. "Once I saw a whole set of medical books. I'd have packed them home, but it would have been too much for Buck. Folks don't realize what they're facing when they leave Independence."

It struck him suddenly that he was talking more than he had in ages and was certainly having the most detailed conversation he had ever had with a woman.

"How long have you been out here?" she asked.

"Long time." He rode on, thinking about it and wondering if his father had traded away something precious for the open spaces of the West.

"Who taught you to read?" Amy asked.

He smiled. Her blue eyes were wide, and it was obvious she was surprised to find he was educated. "I had some school in Massachusetts, but my mother kept us all at it when we came. I was twelve when we settled out here."

"You were lucky," she said.

He'd never thought of it that way. It was what had happened, that was all. If they'd stayed in New England, perhaps his parents would have lived longer. Perhaps his brother Richard would still be alive. No, he wouldn't say lucky. But he was glad they had come, all the same.

A well-defined track veered off from theirs, almost straight west, while theirs came from the southwest. Barkley nodded toward it. "That's the cutoff. Most folks take that trail to Fort Hall now and don't come down to Bridger."

She nodded. Even for those heading for California, the cutoff was shorter. Fort Bridger was quite isolated as a result, though a few trains went that way, mostly Mormons headed for Utah. Trappers still frequented the outpost, but it hadn't grown into the thriving settlement Jim Bridger had envisioned.

Buck nickered softly, jerking Barkley's thoughts back to the present. "He smells water."

Amy's eyes glittered with subdued excitement, and he was glad she didn't need to chatter on. He was content to ride beside her without speaking for a while. There were things he'd ask her sometime but not now.

They were descending an incline toward the river valley. The sun had dropped behind them, and the air had cooled noticeably.

"You cold?" he asked.

"A little."

"We'll stop soon, when we get to the Sweetwater, and let the horses graze."

She nodded.

Barkley looked behind him. Brown was five yards back, his horse ambling steadily along, while he looked off to the south, then behind them. Barkley was glad the private was alert. It was the first time he had let his mind wander from his purpose and let his vigilance lapse. He hadn't thought a woman's company would do that to him. Layton's bay was picking its path carefully, just behind Brown's horse. Layton was too far back for Barkley to read his expression, but he thought the trooper wasn't happy.

Chapter 4

Amy swung stiffly from the saddle when they reached the bank of the Sweetwater. She tried not to let her fatigue show, but she was glad they were halting. She loved to ride, and having Kip as her mount was a joy, but Barkley's pace was wearing her out.

She unsaddled quickly and let Kip drink then put the hobbles on him. Layton took up the guard's position, and Brown fussed over his mare's feet. She hoped there was no problem. She went to her saddle and untied her pack.

She was wishing she had brought her coat. She'd thought it would be too bulky and heavy for the horse to carry in the searing heat of the day, but the nights were chilly in the mountains. She took out the extra shirt she had packed and pulled it on over her brown blouse. It helped a little. She looked around then scolded herself. She was searching for Barkley.

He came out of the shadows downstream and went to Brown, not looking her way. Amy tied her pack up again on the cantle of the saddle and made herself ignore the two men. Barkley was interesting, she admitted to herself, but she had met other interesting men. She had never lost her head over a man, or her heart. At the fort, she had cautioned herself about forming an attachment for any particular man and had managed to avoid that pitfall. Most of her father's officers were married, and she knew better than to show a preference for one of the enlisted men. She had remained impartial, but it hadn't been difficult, really. None of the men had impressed her as someone with whom she could happily spend the rest of her life.

So why was she being so silly about Barkley? As they rode, she watched his back. He rode straight but not stiff, at ease with Buck's movement. When they stopped, she kept track of him, trying not to let her eyes follow him. She felt safer when he was in sight.

And this afternoon she had risked riding Kip up beside his horse and striking up a conversation about books and freedom and civilization. She had been quite daring, she thought.

The man read Milton. She'd imagined him to be taciturn and illiterate, not an avid reader of poetry and classics. Had he and her father ever discussed books? Their relationship must be limited to business, but she had sensed a deep respect for Barkley when her father spoke of him. And Father had, after all, given her into the man's care. Competence and expertise were not enough. Ben

Travis wouldn't entrust his daughter to any man who wasn't decent.

But Milton! The scout was far more complex than she had supposed.

Brown left his horse at last and came toward her.

"Best eat while we're stopped," he said.

"How long will we be here?"

"Probably an hour or two. T.R. wants to let the horses graze and rest a little, then we'll ride most of the night if you can stand it."

"We need to push on," she agreed. It had almost seemed like a picnic as she rode along with Barkley. Instead of trotting, the horses had walked down the incline, and the conversation had changed her entire view of the journey. For a while, it had become a pleasant outing, very pleasant, indeed. She felt quite the socialite, drawing out the reticent scout. But now reality was intruding again.

If her father and the fifty men at Bridger were to live, they must push onward relentlessly. It was that stark and simple.

"We'll keep an eye on your horse if you want to get a nap," Brown said.

"Thank you." Amy sat down on a rock and chewed her piece of jerky. Brown stood nearby, looking off toward the horses. "Is your mare all right, Private Brown?" she asked when she had swallowed.

"I think so. Thought she was favoring the off front foot for a while."

"Where are you from?" Amy asked. She thought she caught a strange flavor in his speech.

"Tennessee, ma'am."

Ah, he was a Southerner. That was it.

"How long have you been out here?" she asked.

"Came to Fort Bridger when your father came. I was at Fort Kearney for a few months before that." The shadows were deepening, but Amy thought his face had a wistful air.

"Do you miss your home?"

"Oh yes." It was deep and sure. "I hope to be going back East before too many more months."

"Oh? You have family in Tennessee?"

"Yes, ma'am." He hesitated, eyeing her from beneath the brim of his hat. "Got a boy back there, and my wife, and my folks."

"You're married?" It surprised her. She never thought much about the enlisted men's families.

"Oh yes, ma'am," Brown said, and she thought he might have added, "Very married."

"You miss them," she ventured.

"Yes, I surely do. I wasn't thinking to be so far from home for so long."

"You'll leave the army?"

"I believe I will, come January. Not the best time to travel in these parts, though. I've a mind to ask your pa to transfer me after this crisis is past."

"He'll do it."

"Oh, I don't know, Miss Travis. Privates get shuffled around where they're needed most."

"But you need to be with your family."

He was quiet again, and she wondered why he had joined up in the first place.

"How about Layton?" she asked. "Is he married, too?"

"Don't think so."

She didn't ask about Barkley. She was making an assumption that he was single, but it hit her at that moment that he, too, might be as married as Brown. He might even have an Indian woman stashed away in his cabin near the fort.

She glanced surreptitiously at Brown. Maybe she should ask before she let herself think too much about T.R. Barkley. More and more he filled her thoughts. She had never been timid exactly, but this seemed too brazen. She realized she didn't care about Layton but had asked about him with a faint hope that Brown would enlighten her about Barkley's family, too.

She chewed the beef slowly. It made her thirsty, and she reached for the canteen that hung on her saddle. She walked to the edge of the river, stepped carefully out onto a flat rock, and stooped to fill the canteen. She would ask her father at the first opportunity to send Brown east of the Mississippi. He ought to be able to go straight home in January when he mustered out. Of course, there was all this talk about a possible war between the states. If that happened, she supposed Brown's loyalties would lie with the South. Hard to think of the faithful young soldier as a potential enemy. He'd served the United States Army well and would do his utmost to protect her now. She couldn't imagine him lining up opposite her father's troops.

She drank from the canteen and bent to top it off. She heard him come up behind her as she pounded the cork in with the heel of her hand. "Do you think there'll be a war?" she asked without turning around.

"I hope not."

She jumped and whirled around, nearly toppling off the rock into the water. Barkley stood three feet from her in the twilight.

"I'm sorry, I thought you were Private Brown," she gasped.

"Didn't mean to startle you."

She was sure he was smiling.

"Oh, well, we'd been talking about homes and families and such, and he told me he's from Tennessee. I was thinking about what would happen if we went to war."

"Mm." Barkley seemed to ponder that. "Seems kind of far-fetched to me.

We've got enough to worry about with the Indians. But I guess back East, folks are het up about it."

"Slavery, you mean?" she asked uncertainly.

"Oh, that and other things."

She'd heard some talk around the fort but did not consider herself well versed in the topic. It was a world away. Yet her father was a career army officer. If a war broke out before he retired, he would be in the thick of it. She felt suddenly bereft. The peaceful days with her father might be over regardless of the outcome of the situation at Fort Bridger.

She gathered her skirt to make the long step from the rock to the shore, and Barkley reached out to her, ready to steady her if she missed her footing. It surprised her. He'd never helped her with anything before. When she hopped lightly over, his hand settled on her wrist, and he pulled her quickly away from the edge then let go.

"I'm hoping we can make Independence Rock by this time tomorrow. It'll be a hard ride." He looked intently at her, as if trying to gauge her endurance.

"All right." She felt the color rising in her cheeks. She told herself that the feelings of unswerving trust he aroused in her were because of her father's trust in him and because of the steadfastness she saw in him, but his touch had an astonishing effect on her. "That's halfway, isn't it?"

"Better than halfway. You'd best lie down for a while. We'll ride most of the night."

She nodded. "Just tell me when you want to move out."

He watched Amy walk away from him to where she had dropped her saddle. It wasn't the light, narrow, cavalry-issue saddle the men used. It was made from soft reddish leather with intricate tooling. He wondered if she had brought it from Albany or if the major had bought it for her somewhere. She untied her bedroll and spread the dark wool blanket on the ground before she lay down with her head on the saddle and the horse's blanket. It was getting cold. She ought to have something warmer to wear, but the wool blanket beneath her would help.

He went to his gear. Buck's saddle blanket was damp, and he had spread it out to air. He untied the leather thongs that held his own blanket to his saddle and shook it out, then walked over to her, carrying it over his arm.

She was already turned on her side with her eyes closed. He draped the blanket over her gently. Her eyes came open, and she stared up at him.

"Thank you," she whispered.

"It's nothing." He turned away, confused by the feelings that were unbalancing him. He wanted to protect her from more than hostile Indians. He wanted to keep her safe forever.

He went to his saddlebags and took out his second shirt. It was a warm blue flannel, and he put it on over his other shirt, then lay down, pillowing his head on the saddlebags.

He was getting soft. Maybe he would have done the same for his sister. More likely, Rebecca would have taken his blanket without asking. He wondered what Amy Travis would look like with her golden hair uncoiled.

Chapter 5

When Amy woke again, it was dark. Stars glittered overhead, but the moon was nowhere to be seen. Layton had spoken to her and perhaps shaken her a little, but he moved away when she sat up. She looked around, realizing that the three men were all moving, preparing to leave. She rolled Barkley's blanket, and he came and took it wordlessly from her hands. She packed her own gear, then walked quickly downstream, looking for a private spot. Even without a mirror, she could tell her hair was disheveled.

When she came back a few minutes later, Layton was saddling Kip. She braided her long hair as she walked, quickly twisting the braid and fastening it on top of her head with the three hairpins she hadn't lost in the dark.

"Thank you." She reached for Kip's reins.

"You're welcome," Layton murmured. "We'll get down out of these hills; then it's mostly flat prairie from here to Laramie."

She nodded, remembering. "We'll make better time now."

She slid her fingers under the girth. It was a little loose. She didn't want to tighten it with Layton watching, but he didn't move away, so she hooked the stirrup up over the saddle horn and worked at the cinch strap.

"Let me do that." He reached toward her hands.

"It's done." She pulled the knot tight and brought the stirrup down. She didn't want Layton boosting her into the saddle, so she led Kip toward a rock. Holding the reins over his withers, she climbed on the rock and pulled herself into the saddle. She knew Layton was still watching, but she didn't look at him.

Brown was mounting, and Barkley and the buckskin were no longer in sight. She guessed he was above, watching the trail. She walked Kip toward Brown and the chestnut mare, Lady.

"You all set, Miss Travis?" Brown asked.

"Yes."

He turned Lady toward the trail, and she followed. Barkley and Buck were a darker form against the dark grass and rocks. She could hear Layton's horse behind her.

They headed out without speaking, Barkley leading. Brown followed him, and Amy urged Kip into line behind Lady. They were still moving downward, and they went slowly in the darkness. She wondered how long it would be before the moon would rise. There had been quite a large moon last night, but she didn't know if it was waxing or waning. She tried to remember when it had risen. Before midnight, she thought. She ought to have read that astronomy book of her father's. She felt quite ignorant as she rode on in silence.

There was a steep place in the trail where Barkley dismounted and led his horse down, and they all followed suit. On her westward trip, the corporal guiding her had told her the emigrants unloaded their wagons so the oxen could pull the empty wagons up that slope. Then the travelers carried their belongings up the hill on their backs and reloaded the wagons. She imagined her father carrying the handful of precious books up over the rocky path.

Barkley was waiting at the bottom of the steepest part. Brown led Lady down and moved her out of the way as Kip stepped carefully down. A dark bulk loomed beside the trail.

"What is that?" she asked, and Barkley turned his head to take in the shadowy heap.

"Some of that fine furniture we were talking about."

Behind her, Layton's bay slipped and floundered a little. They all turned quickly.

"Y'all right?" Brown called.

"I think so."

Layton bent and felt the bay's legs carefully.

"That's the worst of it," Barkley said. He swung onto Buck's back, and Amy fumbled for Kip's stirrup before Layton could come and try to help her. They rode slowly for another hour without speaking. The muffled ripple of the river and the even *clop-clop* of the horses' hooves reached her ears. They left the rocky slope, and the hoofbeats were softer on the powder-dry trail.

Barkley pushed Buck into a trot, and they all picked up the pace. After an hour or so, Amy let her mind drift. She was weary, but she had expected that. She felt very alive, and she knew that part of it was the danger, being out here so far from anything with three men she didn't know. They were all polite and sworn to protect her, but still, it kept her senses prickling. The possibility that Indians might appear at any moment made it even more stimulating, though how anything could disturb the quiet darkness of the night, she didn't know. The creak of the leather, the thud of hooves hitting the ground, an occasional snort from one of the horses, the softly murmuring water, and the breeze that whistled past her ears continuously—those were the only sounds as they trotted east on the never-ending trail.

Then Barkley stopped. They all stopped, bunching up behind him.

Amy sat still, listening, trying to divine what had caused his caution. Then she smelled smoke, faint, just a trace. It didn't smell like wood smoke, though: more acrid. Buffalo chips, probably.

Barkley looked around at the three of them.

"Stay here," he said quietly, and the buckskin moved out at a walk. Soon the hoofbeats faded, and Amy shivered. She looked quickly toward Brown. His body was rigid as he strained to hear anything besides the river and the light breeze.

Behind her, Layton's horse snuffled and began cropping grass. Amy wondered if she ought to let Kip grab a mouthful but decided against it. She wanted to hear everything.

For fifteen minutes they sat silently. Kip began to paw, and she stroked his neck soothingly. Far ahead a glow silhouetted the horizon. Again the faint whiff of smoke came to her. Yes, the glow definitely had an orange tinge.

She was about to ask Brown if it were a prairie fire and what they ought to do, when she realized it was the moon, slowly creeping into view. She felt foolish and was glad she hadn't said anything.

Hoofbeats came, a swift staccato. Brown tensed and moved Lady between Amy and the sound.

Before she could take a deep breath and brace herself, she knew that it was Barkley. He reined in next to Lady.

"Seven troopers and a couple of trappers," he said. "They're camping by the river on the way to Bridger. No sign of hostiles since they left Fort Laramie."

"Well, that's good news," said Brown.

Relief swept over Amy. The troopers would more than replace those her father had dispatched as her escort.

Layton moved the bay gelding closer. "So are we going down there to get some hot coffee?"

"No, we're going to keep moving," Barkley said a bit shortly. He turned to Amy. "I asked the corporal to tell your father you'd made it safe this far, Miss Travis."

"Thank you."

"They've got dispatches for him; said the command has changed at Fort Laramie again."

"Major Lynde is gone?" Brown asked.

"Yup. The Fourth Artillery moved in August second with a Colonel John Munroe in charge."

"Are they pulling us out of Bridger?" Layton asked.

"Didn't say. I imagine the dispatches have something to say about your outfit, though." Barkley looked at Amy and smiled. "I reckon we're past the worst danger now, Miss Travis, but we still need to hurry and deliver your father's message to Munroe."

"Of course." She noticed Barkley looked less grave than he had before. "Did you tell them about that wagon train?" she asked.

"Yes, ma'am. They'll watch for it."

"I feel easier knowing they're heading for Bridger," Brown said.

"Me, too." Barkley turned Buck. "Let's go."

They rode on and on, up and down hills and across the prairie, with the undulating grass whispering softly around them. Once they stopped in the darkness to water the horses and let them graze for half an hour. Brown stood watch while the rest of them catnapped.

At sunrise, the view was the same: waving dry grass and the low river that seemed to grow more sluggish as it wound its way east over the plain. But far ahead there were hills and eerie rock formations. Amy pulled her hat brim low as they rode toward the rising sun. She was warmer, so she peeled off her outer shirt, stuffing it into her pack. She knew that within an hour or two the sun's rays would be searing through the thin cotton of her blouse.

Suddenly Brown brought his mare up beside her.

"Indians," he said quietly.

She darted a startled glance at him and looked in the direction he nodded, to the south. She saw three horsemen, perhaps a half mile away, riding over a rise in the prairie, from the southwest.

"Do you think they know we're here?"

"Oh, they saw us."

Amy looked at Barkley's back. "Does he know?"

"He saw them before I did."

Amy shook her head. She must be less observant than she'd thought. But it must be all right or Barkley would have said something.

⌁

When the sun was halfway to its apex, Barkley called a halt once more, and they took the horses cautiously down a faint path to the riverbed. The water level was several feet below the prairie, and they were sheltered from the wind, but Amy felt insecure, as if intruders could approach without warning. She felt a little better when Barkley had released his horse and climbed back up to the prairie above, carrying his rifle.

Brown brought her some food in his neckerchief.

"Thank you. Oh, raisins!" She looked up at him in surprise. "You've been holding out on us."

"I was saving them for the halfway point," he said sheepishly. "A little celebration."

"We're halfway?"

"Ought to see Devil's Gate in an hour and be at Independence Rock within two or three. We're making good time."

Amy found a rock where she could sit at the edge of the placid water and pulled off her boots. Layton and Brown were eating together near the grazing horses. Surreptitiously, she peeled her stockings off and stuffed them in her boots, then dangled her feet in the water. The river was warmer than Sandy

Creek had been in the mountains but still refreshingly cool.

She had copied the pioneer women on the trail this summer, for convenience hemming her skirts shorter than was acceptable in the East. Now she arranged her skirt so it was modest without dragging the hem in the water and slowly ate her biscuit and cheese, then chewed the hard, dry raisins one at a time.

Before she had finished, Layton approached.

"You ought to rest while you can, Miss Travis."

She said over her shoulder, "I'm resting. I think this is as good as a nap."

He came closer and squatted at the edge of the water. Amy quickly pulled at her hem, and in the process of trying to cover her ankles, dipped the edge in the water and dropped her last three raisins. Why couldn't the man leave her alone?

"You make a charming picture," he said in a low tone.

She felt her face color. "Please excuse me, Private Layton. I'd like to get up now."

"May I help you?" He held out one hand.

His smile was meant to be engaging, she was sure, but he held no appeal for her. His manner irked her. She didn't want to be flattered.

"No, thank you," she said quickly, perhaps more frostily than was warranted.

"As you wish." He stood and hovered there a moment. "If there's anything I can do, ma'am. . ."

"Thank you. I'm fine."

He went away at last, and she pulled her feet up under her on the rock and stood. The bottom of her riding skirt swished clammily against her legs. She stepped to shore and wiped her feet carefully on the grass, then picked up her boots and stockings and carried them a short way downstream where she could put them on without being stared at. She took out her handkerchief and wet it, wiping a layer of grime from her face.

Brown was lying on a dark brown blanket when she returned, his head on his saddlebags and his hat covering his face. Layton had walked upstream a few paces and chosen a spot where the bank offered a tiny strip of shade. Amy took her blanket and went back to where she had put on her boots. She wanted to take them off again. Her socks were uncomfortably damp, but she didn't want Layton snooping around again when she had bare feet. She lay down on the blanket and shaded her face with her hat.

Its smell reminded her of the day her father had tossed it to her in the sitting room of his quarters. She had been out to ride in the valley with an escort of two privates and come back to the fort flushed and excited. They had seen a bear. Her bonnet was forgotten, hanging down her back by the strings.

"Here," her father had said, flipping the hat into her lap. "If you won't wear a proper bonnet, at least wear this to keep the sun off you. You're turning into a regular hoyden."

But he had smiled, and ever since, when she went out to ride, she had worn it along with her boots, a blouse, and a divided skirt, though in the fort she dressed like a proper lady.

Brown woke her when it was time to move on. The sun hung high in the sky, and the heat was oppressive. Kip was saddled and stood waiting for her. Her braid was coming down, and she coiled it and anchored the hairpins more firmly. Before mounting, she drank deeply and wet her handkerchief once more to wipe her face. They met Barkley up on the trail, and she knew he hadn't slept but had let them all rest while he stood watch. She couldn't remember seeing him sleep since they'd left the fort, but he must have, yesterday, while she had slumbered for hours in the shade.

She rode eagerly forward, looking past him to the east, searching the horizon for Devil's Gate, but she couldn't spot the declivity. She trotted Kip up beside the buckskin, hoping Barkley wouldn't find her a nuisance.

He glanced at her, then looked ahead at the trail.

"Think we'll see any more emigrant trains?" she asked.

"It's late. If they haven't made it past Independence Rock by now, they won't get through the Rockies before snowfall."

She looked over at him, then away. The beard stubble was dark on his chin. None of the men had shaved for two days. She hadn't thought about it with Brown, but it made Layton look predatory. On Barkley it was attractive, very masculine.

"Those Indians this morning were Cheyenne," he said.

She was surprised he had brought it up unasked. "Are they friendly?"

"Mostly. They didn't seem to care about us."

She nodded. "So you think we're out of danger?"

"Not out, but getting there." He smiled at her, and her pulse quickened. "Pretty soon you'll be writing a letter to your daddy, telling him you're at Fort Laramie." He looked ahead again and off to the south.

"When?" she asked and wished she hadn't. It sounded childish. But the end of the journey seemed within reach, and she wasn't sure she was glad. She wanted to know that aid was on its way to her father, but she didn't want Barkley to ride off again, leaving her at the fort. She might never see him again.

"Look yonder," he said softly.

She saw it then, the slot in the hills that rose above the plain. "Devil's Gate."

He nodded. "I reckon we can be at the fort in two days. Two long days. And nights." He looked at her again, swiveling slightly in his saddle. "How you holding up?"

"Well, I think."

He nodded, as if he thought so, too. She felt her blush coming on again, but this time she didn't mind. The camaraderie was back, and it was exhilarating. Their horses ran side by side, Kip matching the buckskin's quick trot and reaching over now and again to snap at Buck's jaw.

The wagon trail veered away from the river, but Barkley led them toward the cleft in the rocks. Granite walls rose on either side of them as they entered the pass, and the river rumbled.

"Can't take wagons through here," Barkley yelled.

Amy looked up and saw a slash of blue sky overhead between the cliffs that towered above them. They moved briskly along in the shade until they came out on the east side, and the prairie opened before them once more.

⌒

They were nearly within the shadow of Independence Rock, the huge humped stone that rose beside the Sweetwater. Emigrant trains usually stopped there for a rest, but there were no wagons at its base today.

Suddenly Layton cried out behind them, and Barkley turned quickly in the saddle.

Far back on the prairie, three horses were coming fast along the trail from Devil's Gate. Barkley turned Buck around and stood up in his stirrups. Brown and Layton came up to them and faced the west, too.

"Is it those Indians?" Amy asked. Barkley could tell she was frightened, and he wished he could instantly allay her fears.

"No, they're white men." He kept his eyes on the riders, straining for clues to their identity and purpose.

"They're in a big hurry," Brown said. He and Barkley simultaneously pulled their rifles from their scabbards.

"What is it?" Amy asked, her voice shaking slightly.

"Not sure," Barkley said. It didn't feel right. The riders made no signals that would communicate friendship or danger. "Could be they've had some trouble. Get behind me." She wheeled Kip and moved him back. The approaching riders were throwing up alkali dust, but Barkley could see them clearly now, three men riding low over the horses' necks, coming down on them quickly.

"I don't like it," said Brown.

Barkley squinted as his apprehension mounted. "Saw a paint horse like that last night at the troopers' camp."

"You think they ran into some hostiles?" Layton asked, pushing the bay gelding forward a couple of steps.

Barkley shrugged. "We'll know in a minute."

Brown looked hard at him. "We can't go back, T.R."

"I know," Barkley said grimly, keeping his rifle at the ready.

Layton's bay walked forward several more steps. "Those aren't uniforms," he called.

Barkley had already noticed the red shirt on the foremost rider and the buckskins on the next.

"Amy, get in those rocks," he said without turning his head. He heard her horse walking toward the large boulders scattered near the trail. "Could be the trappers that were camping with them last night." He wished they had all taken cover.

As the front horse came within fifty yards of them, he saw the rifle come up. "Get back!" he yelled, even as smoke billowed.

Layton, several strides ahead of him, jumped as the report cracked, then slumped in the saddle. Brown spurred Lady forward and grabbed the bay's reins as Barkley returned fire. The horseman swerved to his right just as Barkley pulled the trigger. All three riders rode off to the south and circled, just out of range. Brown led Layton's horse quickly toward the rocks, and Barkley crowded Buck behind them.

Chapter 6

Amy was still astride the big gray, her face chalky. "They shot him," she said incredulously.

Brown dismounted and pulled Layton from the saddle, laying him on the ground in the shelter of the biggest boulder.

"Get down, Amy," Barkley ordered. She was too good a target on the tall gelding. He leaped off Buck's back and found a place where he could watch while reloading, mostly shielded by a boulder. The heat of the rock burned through his shirt as he leaned on it to steady his hands. He poured the powder in from a paper cartridge, followed it with a bullet wrapped in a patch, and rammed it home. He thought he heard a moan from Layton, and he glanced toward Brown as he worked. "How bad, Mike?"

"Real bad. He ain't gonna make it, T.R."

Barkley gritted his teeth, watching the three horses loping toward them again. "They're coming back. Hang on to those horses. We don't want to walk to Fort Laramie."

"I'll hold them." Amy was at his side, pulling Kip along by his bridle.

"You can't hold them all." He relinquished Buck's reins to her and saw that Brown had grabbed Lady's and the bay's.

"Get farther back," he said to Amy. "If they shoot these horses, we won't have much of a chance." Barkley didn't dare watch her as the riders approached again. She came back, panting.

"I hobbled Kip. Let me take the others back there."

Brown let go of the reins, and she ran, pulling Lady and Layton's bay after her.

The three horsemen came relentlessly closer, and Barkley got another round off before they circled away again. Brown fired as well, but the riders seemed unscathed.

"We need to get out of here." Barkley fumbled to reload. He drew his Colt Dragoon revolver and laid it on the rock in case they rode in too close before he was ready. "We'll tie Layton on his horse. Let them come in one more time; then we head out. Stick to the trail. If they get too close, we'll split up."

"I told you, Layton's had it."

Barkley looked down at the wounded trooper and saw the dark blood soaking the front of his uniform blouse on the left side. He glanced toward the marauders again, and they were far out on the prairie. Bending down, he put his fingers to Layton's neck to feel for a pulse.

"Is he breathing?"

"Don't think so."

Brown frowned, ramming the ball down the barrel of his musket.

Barkley looked out at the riders. They had stopped two hundred yards away and were looking toward them, seemingly in conference. "Check him good," he said through his teeth. "I won't leave him if he's alive, but I won't cut Amy's chances for him if he's dead."

Brown crouched beside his comrade and was silent for several seconds.

He stood up, pointing his rifle toward the three horsemen. "He's dead, T.R."

Barkley swallowed.

"Should we leave his horse?" Brown asked.

"Slow us down if we don't. Take his pistol."

Brown nodded.

"Personal effects?" Barkley asked.

Brown stooped again. Barkley didn't look while he searched the dead trooper's pockets. He stood up again, shoving an envelope into his pocket.

"Letter home," Brown said shortly. He held out Layton's gun belt.

"Where's his rifle?"

"He dropped it."

Barkley looked out to where they had waited on their horses, and he thought he could see a gleam off the gun barrel. He measured the distance from the rock to the gun with his eye. "Best leave it. But we'll take the powder and lead from his pack."

"Here's his knife." Brown held out a sheathed, six-inch blade.

"You take it."

"You don't think we can stand them off?" Brown asked.

"They could keep us pinned down here all day. Don't forget, the major's in need of reinforcements. We've got to get through."

Brown nodded. "You take off with Miss Travis first, and I'll stay here for one more round with those three."

"Oh, no. I'm not leaving you."

"I'll catch up."

Barkley looked at him through narrowed eyes. Somehow, over the last two days, his respect for Brown had deepened into friendship.

"It's the best chance," Brown insisted. "She's the major's daughter. You've got to stick with her. If I keep up the fire, they won't realize you've gone."

Barkley knew that wasn't true. "They'll see the dust." He looked out again toward where Layton's weapon had fallen. "Too bad we can't get his rifle."

"Too risky." Brown rested his musket on the rock, watching the riders.

"Take the horses farther back," Barkley told him. "Turn Layton's horse loose, but drop his tack first. No use giving them a remount."

"After this go-round," Brown agreed.

The attackers were riding in again, low over the necks of their mounts. Before they were fully in range, Brown fired, and they veered away.

"Save your lead," Barkley told him.

"Sorry. I knew better." Brown began reloading.

"If they'd come a little closer, I could have got that first one," Barkley complained. "I'm pretty sure they're the ones that were with the troopers last night, but I only saw two then. That one with the red shirt, he's a Frenchman."

"What do you think they want?"

"I dunno. They said last night they were heading up the Sweetwater, scouting for beaver."

"I'm guessing they think we've got something important, like an army payroll or something." Brown poured powder down the barrel of his gun.

"Heading east? That makes no sense."

"Well, the only thing we've got that's worth anything is Miss Travis." Barkley stared at him.

"Did you tell them last night?" Brown asked gently.

"I told the corporal, but I didn't make a general announcement. Someone might have heard, I guess, or he might have told them after I left." He felt sick, realizing he might have caused the attack, Layton's death, and Amy's immediate peril. He reached for Brown's rifle. "Go fix the horses."

Brown slipped between the rocks, and Barkley kept his eyes on the three riders, who stopped once more on the prairie, then faced him again.

"God, help us get her out of here," he whispered fervently, leaning Brown's gun, muzzle up, against the rock and hefting his own rifle to draw a bead on the lead rider's shirt.

He waited until they rode in close. Their bullets ricocheted wildly off the stones, one throwing up chips of granite in his face. He held steady and pulled the trigger.

Brown was back, breathing hard, shoving a bag of ammunition into his hand. "All set. Leave Lady ground tied for me."

"What if she follows us?"

Brown didn't have an answer.

"I'd better bring her up here," Barkley said.

"This is taking too long."

"I know. I think I winged one of them."

He reloaded, seized his six-shooter, and left Brown, dodging through the boulders to where Amy was waiting with Buck and Kip. Layton's horse was free, already moving eastward, snatching grass as he trotted away from the noise. The saddle and bridle lay in a heap, and Lady stood off to one side, content for now to stand patiently, waiting for Brown.

"I'm taking her up there for him." Barkley took hold of Lady's reins.

"Private Brown said we're leaving him behind." Her eyes were huge.

"He'll catch up."

A look of pain crossed her face, and he felt guilty. It had been his own reaction to the plan, but she thought it was his idea.

He took Lady up to a rock just behind the trooper.

"What are they doing?" he called.

"Getting ready for another pass."

"Think they'd talk?"

"What do you think?" Brown replied.

Barkley anchored Lady's reins with a small rock.

"Keep to the south bank, and I'll try to lead them off," Brown yelled.

Barkley hesitated.

"Get going!"

"I'll see you later!" It was a hope rather than a promise.

⇒

Amy struggled to breathe calmly as Barkley ran back toward her. It seemed all wrong to be leaving Private Brown, but she couldn't stop trusting the scout's judgment now.

"Let's go!"

She turned toward Kip and reached for the stirrup, but Barkley came behind her and picked her up bodily, swinging her atop the horse. Startled, she gathered up the reins. He was on Buck, giving a last backward look as shots rang out again.

"Stick with me!" he ordered, and the buckskin pounded down the trail, eastward, away from the shooting.

She let Kip run flat out for the first time. He tore up the ground, and soon his nose was only inches from Buck's flying black tail. They rode on and on, and she looked back once but could not see any movement, could not even see the boulders anymore, just Independence Rock rising calm and solid over the waving grasses.

Barkley slowed his horse. The Sweetwater had tumbled into the Platte, and they had reached one of several points where the wagon trail crossed the river. It was shallow and muddy. In the spring it had been a torrent, and it had been rafted across.

Barkley looked back. "We'll stick to the south bank. Maybe they'll think we followed the trail and went across."

"Can't we wait for Brown?" she asked.

He pressed his lips together and urged Buck into a gallop again.

She thought she heard a shot and looked behind her. Far back, she saw a reddish horse charging up the riverbank.

"It's Brown!" she screamed, and she raised her arm, waving wildly.

Barkley stopped and wheeled Buck around. "Get down!"

"What?"

He rode close to her and pulled her out of the saddle, even as he slid from Buck's back.

"But Brown won't—" She stopped. Brown was splashing into the water at the ford, and now she could see the three horses behind him.

The buckskin was lying down in the tall grass. Amy couldn't believe it. She turned to stare at Barkley and saw that he was pulling Kip's head down until the gray lay down, too. Then she understood.

"They'll kill Private Brown," she choked.

"I hope not."

He grasped her upper arm and pulled her down then crouched beside her, listening. They heard a distant shout, and she could hear the hoofbeats clearly. Her heart pounded. She hoped they wouldn't come to where they hid, but she didn't want them to catch Brown, either.

Barkley half stood, peering intently toward the ford. "Get up. Quick."

He tugged at the reins, and both horses clambered to their feet. Again he picked her up and tossed her into the saddle. She didn't have time to think about how strong he was. She only had time to get her boots into the stirrups and hang on as Kip took off at a dead run after the buckskin. They veered out away from the riverbank and rode for five miles, parallel to the Platte. She looked across the wide riverbed often but couldn't see the mysterious riders or Brown. The ground was rough in places, and they crossed a stream that meandered toward the river. Kip was breathing hard but not gasping. She could see that Buck's sides were heaving.

Barkley led her on at a frantic pace. He regretted pushing Buck so hard, but Amy's peril overshadowed everything else. At last they approached a place where four large cottonwoods grew beside the river, and he headed for them. When they were beneath the trees, he stopped and leaped to the ground.

"Don't unsaddle. We'll let them breathe and cool down a little then give them a drink. Then we go on."

"Are we safe now?" she asked timidly as she dismounted.

"No."

"They followed Brown."

He turned away from her accusing eyes, leading Buck slowly in a circle beneath the trees. "It was the only way. Brown has as good a chance as any man under the circumstances."

"Even you?"

Barkley frowned. He ought to be the one drawing off the outlaws, not Mike Brown. Mike had a family. But he had promised the major he would stay with Amy no matter what. He personally would deliver her to Fort Laramie. He gritted his teeth.

"I've already caused the death of one loyal man," she said. Tears stood in her eyes.

"It's not your fault, Amy."

"You can say that, but if I weren't along, Layton and Brown would be back at Fort Bridger."

"Yes, and fighting Indians hand to hand, no doubt," he flung at her. He stopped and sighed, putting one foot up on a rock, gazing across the river, and praying silently for Brown.

When he turned to look at her, she was holding Kip's reins loosely, letting him crop the dry grass. Her eyes were hard; her face troubled.

"Come on, let's water them," he said. "We need to move."

"Brown is mustering out in January." She blinked hard against the tears.

"I know." He took the reins from her hand and led both horses to the water. He wished they could stop longer and rest them. Buck had heart, but he couldn't run forever.

Amy followed him to the edge of the water. "If Brown escapes—" she began. Then she stopped.

"It's not Brown they're after."

"What, then?"

He said nothing.

"It's me," she said flatly. "You think they want me."

"It's all I can figure," he admitted. "They might be hoping to get a ransom."

"A ransom?" she snorted. "Army majors don't make much."

He was silent. He knew that when they discovered Brown had decoyed them away from her, they would come back.

Buck lifted his head, and Barkley said, "Let's move."

They rode on in bleak silence, cantering the horses. Whenever Barkley looked at Amy, she was looking somewhere else, her face a mask of grief. His heart twisted. Even if he managed to fulfill her father's commission, he had failed her.

Chapter 7

The sun was dropping behind them when Barkley slowed again. Amy thought of how happy she'd felt that morning when he'd told her they would be at Fort Laramie in two days. Now she wondered if they would reach the fort at all. He was calling her *Amy* now. That would have thrilled her a few hours ago, but now it was simply an expedient. He could bark orders at her faster if he didn't say "Miss Travis."

She was so tired, she hardly noticed when Kip stopped. Barkley was standing beside her horse in the dusk, touching her elbow.

"Come on down. We need to rest." She slid off to the side, and he caught her and stood her upright. "You get some sleep. I'll keep a lookout."

They were near the river again, but the bank came right up to the prairie grass. Barkley spread a blanket in the short, curly buffalo grass for her.

"Try to sleep." He pushed her gently toward the blanket.

"It's my fault," she mumbled.

"No. Don't think that." He gripped her arm. "Look at me, Amy."

She turned and looked up into his face, and she couldn't hate him. The sorrow in his eyes was so deep, she knew he was as grieved as she.

"Brown came up with this plan. He wanted to do it this way. He knew I couldn't leave you, and it seemed like the best chance."

Her mind was whirling, and she focused on his brown eyes. He looked wounded.

"Amy, it's not your fault. It's mine. I told that corporal we were taking you to Laramie. I shouldn't have told anyone you were with us. If I'd realized—" He turned away sharply and seized the horses' reins, heading for the river.

"Mr. Barkley," she called.

He dropped the leather straps and walked back to her slowly. Kip and Buck lowered their heads and began grazing. He stood before her, his shoulders slouched, his eyes pleading.

"I'm sorry," he whispered. "It wasn't supposed to be like this."

She nodded and swallowed hard. She felt she knew him very well now, had seen him at his best in the display of staunch courage at Independence Rock. And now she was witness to his worst, the guilt and the agonizing regret.

"Do you have a name besides Barkley?" Her voice was hoarse from the tears she hadn't shed.

His lips twitched. "Folks call me T.R."

"What does it stand for?"

He looked toward the horses then back. "Thomas Randolph."

"Thomas. May I call you that? Mr. Barkley seems a bit formal now."

He licked his chapped lips and looked past her. She wondered if he was uncomfortable with her request and was trying to think of a way to politely say no.

"Tom," he said at last.

She nodded. "All right, Tom. If I'm going to stop blaming myself, you have to, too. We have to concentrate on surviving and getting to Fort Laramie as fast as we can, agreed?"

He reached out tentatively and put his hand on her shoulder for an instant, then backed away. She watched him lead the horses down to the river, then she lay down on the blanket. The evening star shone brightly near the horizon in the west. There was no one to spell Tom Barkley on the lookout. Before she could think about that, her mind shut down and she slept, dreamless.

꙳

He let her sleep for an hour and wished it could be longer. She was bone tired, he knew, but if they lingered here, the riders might catch up. He paced along the riverbank. If he weren't so sleepy, he could think more clearly. His plan had exploded in chaos, and his misery weighed him down. But he knew that somehow this all had to be part of God's plan, whether they survived or not. He couldn't lose sight of that. It was up to him to keep Amy moving toward Fort Laramie. Only that much was in his control.

It was nearly dark. Time to move.

He looked into her innocent face before he woke her, wishing she could awaken to a world where everything was good and true and right. He put two fingers out and touched her smooth cheek.

"Amy." It was barely a whisper. He cleared his throat and tried again. "Amy, wake up."

Her eyelashes fluttered, and she looked up into his face. He caught his breath, and slowly she smiled, just a small smile that might mean recognition or friendship, but it reassured him. She wasn't angry. She was sad, but she didn't despise him for leading the two troopers to death or for revealing her presence to the trappers.

"God knows, Tom," she said softly.

"Yes, I reckon He does. We have to trust Him."

He took her hand and pulled her to her feet then picked up the blanket.

He had brought food from the saddlebag, and she ate her share as they walked to the horses. He hadn't dared to unsaddle in case the riders appeared while she slept.

Amy lifted the stirrup and checked Kip's girth. "What's this?" She was staring at the belt tied to her bedroll.

"It's Layton's pistol. In case we get separated." He heard her take a deep breath. "Can you shoot?"

"A little."

"It's a six-shot, but you have to load each chamber. They're all loaded now."

"I don't think I could reload it." She looked up at him apologetically.

"Well, we'll hope you don't need to."

"Think Buck is rested?"

"Yes, he'll be all right for a while." He'd be glad when they reached the fort and he could turn the faithful buckskin out for a few days.

She was in the saddle before he could offer to help, and he reflected that it was just as well. Feelings for her had taken root in his heart, but his mission was to get her to a place where she could ride out of his life forever.

He mounted, glancing across at her before signaling Buck to move out. Suddenly he stiffened. He heard hoofbeats, distant but coming toward them from the west.

She heard them, too; he could see that. She was afraid, but she sat still, looking to him for direction.

"Ride, Amy. Stick to the riverbank. Keep going no matter what happens! The wagon road crosses the Platte again about ten miles from here, and you can pick it up on this side. Go!"

"I'm not leaving you." It was a sob.

"I'll be right behind you. You go first, and be careful, but don't spare the horse. Now move!" He yanked his rifle from the scabbard.

She headed Kip eastward and tore off, looking back over her shoulder to be sure Tom followed. Buck was running, head down in the twilight.

She turned forward, trying to watch the trail ahead for obstacles. Kip ran so fast that she couldn't focus on objects before they were past. The faint track was barely distinguishable in the growing darkness. She would have to trust Kip, at least until moonrise. She knew now that the moon was waning. It would rise later and be smaller than last night. Clouds had moved in while she slept. Perhaps there would be no moonlight at all.

She looked behind her and saw that Kip was rapidly outdistancing Buck. She knew Tom would have only one shot with his musket. She prayed their pursuers would not come within pistol range.

"Dear God, help us!" Her words were snatched away by the wind. She felt her braid flopping against her shoulders. The last of the hairpins had loosened. She clapped one hand hard on her hat, pulling the band down tight above her ears.

She pulled Kip down to a canter, hating to disobey Tom but unwilling to lose sight of him. Buck was a quarter mile back, and she could barely see him.

She held the gray at the slower pace until half the distance was closed, then she kept him moving steadily on. She wasn't sure how long Buck could keep running, but she knew she wasn't going to desert Tom.

Half an hour later, she couldn't stand it. It was very dark. She stopped Kip and sat listening. The gelding gave a cough and breathed heavily, but she could hear hoofbeats behind her. She couldn't see Buck. What if it wasn't him? What if the strange men swooped down on her out of the darkness? She looked around hopelessly for cover, but there was none.

The buckskin came cantering out of nothing, suddenly appearing a few yards away.

"Tom!"

He checked his horse.

"Amy! I told you to go!"

"I did, but—"

"Keep going!"

She swung Kip into step beside him, and the two horses picked up the long trot they used for travel.

"Are they coming?" she asked.

"Yes, but their horses are tired, too."

"Do you think Brown got away?" she dared to say.

"I don't know. But now they know where we are."

To the north, lightning flashed, and a few seconds later, a deep thunderclap rumbled over the prairie.

"We're in for it," Tom said.

Amy thought the prospect of rain was delicious. She felt so parched. Her lips were dry and scaly, and her hands felt leathery from their constant exposure to wind and sun.

"Ford's up ahead," he said. The wagon road would be plain after that, but its ruts might trip up the horses. "Let's hope these clouds blow over and we get some moonlight."

When they came to the place where the trail came up out of the Platte, he led her to the water. They stayed in the saddle as the horses stretched their necks down to drink greedily. Tom was listening, watching back to the west.

"How far behind are they?" she breathed.

"Not far. Here, fill the canteens, and I'll hold Kip's reins."

She slipped from the saddle, waded a few steps upstream from the animals, and stooped to fill the two canteens. She sloshed back to Kip and handed them to Tom, and he fastened them to the saddles as she mounted.

"Let's go," he said, and she pulled Kip's head up.

Tom kept Buck at a trot, and she and Kip stayed beside them. The two horses kept to the wagon ruts, with a slight ridge of dry grass between them.

The river wound away from them, and they continued more or less straight for a couple of miles. The lightning flashed intermittently.

"This storm could work to our advantage," Tom said.

"Think so?"

"Well, we'll probably get soaked, but it might make them hole up somewhere."

"The horses can't keep on forever." It was really Buck she was worried about. Even Kip was tired; she could tell by his dragging steps and his drooping neck. Buck must be near exhaustion.

Tom was silent a moment, then said, "I don't dare to stop now. They weren't far behind me back there. I can't hear them now, but they know we're here. They might stop to rest for a while and figure they can catch up to us in the morning. We'll just keep going slow for now, all right?"

He was asking her opinion. She wasn't sure she liked that. All her life, she'd depended on strong men to order her life—first her father; her brother-in-law while she lived in his home; then her father again; and now Tom Barkley. She wanted him to give orders again, to be confident, and to know what was best. But then, she wanted Brown and Layton back, too, and she wanted to be safe at Fort Laramie, not out here in the dark wilderness with three evil men pursuing her. She took a deep, shaky breath.

"Whatever you think, Tom."

The rain held off, although the thunder rumbled louder. Tom looked frequently over his shoulder, but the flashes of lightning revealed no one on the back trail. At last they came back to the verge of the Platte, at a place where large cottonwoods clung to the bank. They took the horses down for a drink beneath the trees, and this time they dismounted.

"Let's let them graze for a few minutes," he said. "Keep hold of Kip's bridle, though."

He unstrapped Layton's gun belt and put it in her saddlebag. She wouldn't be able to use it effectively as she rode. Better to keep it dry. They stood next to each other, and the horses began pulling grass, tugging against the taut reins. Tom stretched his arms and legs. He listened as he prayed continuously.

He wondered if Amy was praying. She was his sole reason for living now. She might be his reason for dying. She had mentioned God, and he wanted to know how deep her faith was and where she looked for solace in her worst moment.

"Amy?"

"What?"

"Do you. . .pray?"

"Yes."

"Are you praying now?"

"Yes."

He reached out, and his hand found hers. "Me, too."

She squeezed his fingers, and his heart jumped.

"He won't leave us, Amy. No matter what happens."

She was silent a moment, clinging to his hand. "Thank you."

He listened once more, but the river swirled and the wind moaned. The intermittent thunder blasts dulled his hearing. They couldn't stay here. They wouldn't hear anyone approaching. At least the horses had gotten a drink and a few mouthfuls of grass.

"Let's go."

They fumbled wearily with the reins in the darkness. Amy was in the saddle before Tom could reach her side to help her. The thunder crashed, and Kip squealed and sidestepped.

Tom yelled, "We'd better get away from these trees."

She got the gray under control and followed him away from the water. They picked up the trail at a trot once more.

The horses were fidgety. When Amy stroked Kip's neck, a spark crackled from her hand. The gray snorted and pulled against the bit.

"He wants to run."

"Too dangerous," Tom said.

The wind was suddenly much stronger, and rain began to fall in big, splattering globs. The horses snuffled and twitched, but still they trotted onward. The drops pelted them, soaking their clothing. They puddled on Tom's hat and funneled off the brim, down the back of his shirt.

At first it felt good to be wet and cool all over, but soon his wet clothing started to chafe his skin. The wind stole his body heat, and he began to shiver. It was worse for Amy, he knew. She wasn't used to being out in all kinds of weather the way he was. He had to find shelter.

The lightning struck close, hitting a tree near the river, and Kip reared with a terrified squeal as a deafening crash of thunder broke over them.

"Amy!"

She fought the gelding's panic, speaking quietly and holding his head down firmly. "Ho, Kip, easy."

Tom pushed Buck up beside them, reaching toward Kip's bridle. He seized the reins just below Kip's bit and added his strength to Amy's. "You all right?"

"Yes," she yelled, "but I don't know how long I can hold him."

"Stick close to me!"

⌣

They rode along slowly, so close their stirrups brushed, and Tom kept one hand on Kip's bridle. He watched the trail sharply and looked frequently off to the right. Amy was sure he was searching for something.

She leaned toward him. "What are you looking for?"

"An old man used to have a cabin off here someplace. I haven't been there in three or four years, but I think I can find it."

They kept the horses at a walk. Kip fretted against the bit, trying to get his head down. Amy hated not being able to trust the magnificent horse, but she didn't dare test his loyalty to her. Under ordinary circumstances, she would have been livid if a man implied that she couldn't handle a horse. But Kip was far stronger than she was, and in his present frenzy, she was afraid he would bolt given the smallest opportunity, so she swallowed her pride and allowed Tom to hold on.

Both horses began to slip in the mud that was forming in the wagon ruts. Every time the thunder boomed, Buck shuddered, but he kept on steadily. Kip lunged and pawed at each crash. In a flicker of lightning, Amy saw the gray's head twisted back toward her. The whites of his eyes showed starkly, and foam dripped from his bit as he threw his head from side to side in terror.

Chapter 8

Vainly, Tom looked for a place where they could take shelter. They kept moving in the drenching downpour, and at last he was rewarded by the dark bulk of hills rising on their right. The trail skirted the northern end of the range where it came close to the Platte, and he knew they were near his goal. He thought he saw a faint track leaving the wagon road, and he stopped Buck, calling to Amy to try to hold Kip steady. A bright flicker of lightning came, and Kip jerked against his weight. But in that light, Tom recognized the place.

"This way!" He waited until Kip stopped prancing, then released the reins. He turned Buck in at the overgrown path. Most travelers went right past it, never suspecting there was a dwelling nearby. Trusting the rain to obliterate their tracks, Tom urged Buck up the trail and around a knoll, and there it was: an adobe cabin built twenty years or more ago by old Jim Frye. The codger had been dead several years, and an Irish family had squatted in the cabin one winter, but as far as Tom knew, it was deserted now.

There was no light, no smoke. He rode up and dismounted.

He stood in the doorway until lightning came again, showing him the place was empty. A corner of the roof was missing, and water poured in on that side of the ten-by-fifteen-foot cabin. He led Buck over the threshold and pulled him to one side, then went out again.

"Get down," he shouted up at Amy.

Slowly, she brought her right leg over Kip's back and hung there for a moment, her left foot still in the stirrup. He reached up and put his hands on her waist.

"Jump, Amy."

She kicked the stirrup off and plopped down beside him. He shoved her toward the door and pulled Kip by the reins, one hand on his nose, trying to lower the big animal's head so he could get through the doorway. The horse balked for an instant, sniffing, then plunged through the gap.

Tom shut the door.

"Amy?"

"Here."

He jumped, she was so close in the darkness.

"The roof is leaking over there," he said.

"I h—hear it."

"I think I saw a bunk to the left."

Her hand clutched his wrist. She was shaking.

"You're freezing!" he said. The lightning blazed, and he saw that there was no mattress or bedding, just a plain wooden bunk against the wall.

He led Amy to it. "Sit down," he said in her ear. "I'll get your blanket."

He spoke quietly to the horses, groping in the darkness. They moved restlessly in the small space, snorting and snuffling. Buck stood still for him, and he worked the soggy leather strap until he was able to lift the saddle off, then stripped the bridle off, too, feeling for a place to lay them against the wall. His bedroll felt wet, and he left it on the saddle. Guided by flashes of lightning, he went to Kip and unsaddled him. He fumbled with the rawhide thongs that kept Amy's blanket against the cantle. The smell of wet wool and leather filled his nostrils. At last he got the blanket free and stumbled toward the bunk with it.

"Here, the inside isn't too bad," he said, but he knew the whole thing was too wet to do her much good. They needed a fire.

He had gathered by now that there was a small cast-iron stove in the room, but he couldn't see anything they could burn. He felt the saddle blankets, but they were soaked with rain and sweat.

"You all right?" he asked.

"I think so."

"I wish we could have a fire."

"They'd smell the smoke," she said.

"That's if we had anything to burn."

She chuckled. He was glad she could laugh. It meant the storm hadn't drained as much of her energy as he'd feared. He was freezing but couldn't take off his wet clothes.

"If Buck wasn't sopping wet, we could make him lie down and let him keep us warm," she said in the blackness.

It startled him that she was thinking in the same direction he was.

"There aren't any blankets here?" she asked.

"I haven't seen anything. Just the bunk and the stove. Indians probably pilfered everything else."

Amy tried to concentrate on a different part of the cabin each time the lightning flashed, until she had looked at every inch of it. The horses took up most of the space on the packed earth floor. There were no cupboards or boxes, no pans or clothing. Nothing. At least it had a roof. Sort of.

"Sit down, Tom." She realized he was standing beside the bunk, looking around in the irregular bursts of light the way she was. But the last time, she thought he'd been looking at her.

"I'm dripping wet."

"So am I."

"Hold on."

She heard him working at something and, when the lightning came, saw that he had opened his saddlebag and found his flannel shirt. It was surely the only dry piece of cloth in the cabin except maybe the dirty socks and blouse in her own pack.

Still the rain drummed down in torrents. At least there were no leaks over the bunk. Amy sat upright, shivering on the hard wood, her legs curled under her.

She felt the bunk give a little as he sat down on the edge and thrust the soft shirt into her hands.

"Here, put this on."

"Your extra shirt?"

"Yes."

"You should wear it."

"No, I'm all right. Put it on."

Meekly, she slipped her arms into the sleeves. She felt marginally warmer and raised her wrist to her face, inhaling the comforting fragrance of Tom's shirt.

He got up and went back to the pile of gear, returning with her saddlebags.

"The gun's in this one," he said, guiding her hand to the buckle. "Keep it on the bunk beside you."

He went to the slot that was more of a rifle loop than a window and looked out. She was less uncomfortable but still shivering. Her skirt hung in heavy, wet folds.

"Do you think they're out there?" she called over the noise of the rain.

"I don't know."

"If they know about this place, they may come here."

"I thought of that, but we had to take a chance." He came back to the bunk and sat down beside her.

She had to admit that being inside the cabin was a lot better than being out on the trail. "You're right, Tom. We'll have to pray they don't know about it."

The wind howled around the little house. If it didn't tear off the rest of the roof, they'd be fairly secure.

"Can you sleep?" he asked.

"I don't think so." She wrapped her arms around herself, tucking her hands under her arms. She was so cold! She clamped her teeth together to keep them from chattering.

"Here." He pulled the damp blanket up over her shoulders. She wasn't sure the wet wool army blanket would help, but she accepted it. He shifted beside her, and she leaned back, sitting against the cabin wall.

"What'll we do if they come?" she asked.

"Well, we've got the rifle and two pistols. These walls will stop bullets, I think. But if they start shooting at the door and windows. . ."

She looked toward the two narrow slots of windows. There didn't seem to be any shutters.

"If they come and start shooting in here, get behind the stove," Tom said. "Keep the pistol with you. And if I go down—"

"Don't say that!"

He sighed. "Amy, listen. It could happen. I don't think it will. I think they're huddled under some rock right now, waiting this storm out, but if it does happen, you've got to be ready."

She took a long, ragged breath, pushing down the fear. "All right. What do I do?"

He spoke slowly and deliberately, and his voice was the only reality for her in the darkness. "If I go down, use those six shots well. Don't shoot wildly. Wait until they're close. I think the powder's dry. If the pistol misfires, stay calm and try again."

"All right. But you'll be here."

✑

Tom wasn't sure how to deal with her blind faith in him. Did she think he was invincible? He'd already shown his weakness. He had revealed the existence of his precious cargo to crafty adversaries. He ought to have just told the corporal to tell Major Travis he had met him and that all was well. Once again, he fought guilt and depression. He had to think about this minute and how to keep her safe.

"Funny, we were worrying about Indians all that time." She sounded hoarse, and she had to yell for him to hear over the pounding rain and the wind.

"Those trappers," he said, leaning toward her. "I can't figure it out. I never expected this."

"What are they like?" she asked.

"I only saw two of them by firelight. One's a Frenchman, dark, with a bushy beard. One's a big man that seemed to talk a lot. The third one. . .well, he was wearing buckskins when they attacked us. He might have been in the camp when I was there, but I didn't see him."

She sat thoughtfully for a few minutes, and Tom closed his eyes, trying to picture the men he had glimpsed so briefly.

"The Frenchman," she said, leaning close to his ear. "How did you know he was French?"

"He spoke to me at the troopers' camp. Name's LeBeau or LaBelle or something like that."

She caught her breath. "There was a man named LeBeau at Fort Bridger."

"When?"

"He came in June, I think. Father had him in custody when we left."

"Why?"

"He'd been gambling with the men. There was a fight one night, I think, and they told him to leave and. . . " She hesitated, and Tom wondered how much her protective father had told her. "I think he tried to steal one of the troopers' horses."

"So the major had him locked up?"

"Yes, for several weeks before we left."

"Had he seen you before that?"

"Yes, several times. But it couldn't be the same man."

"I don't see how, either."

"Father was waiting for orders, I think. He had sent word to Fort Laramie about it and was waiting for someone to tell him what to do."

"Maybe they'll hang him," Tom said. "Or if the Indians attack the fort, they might let him go if he promises to fight." He couldn't see what it had to do with the attack at Independence Rock. The men pursuing them had come out of the east with the troopers. He was certain now they had left the troopers and followed them back. There had to be a reason.

"Is your father independently wealthy?" he asked.

In the flickering light, he saw her wide eyes staring toward him. "No, I told you. Are you still thinking they want a ransom?"

"You never know. If the rumor got around that your family was rich. . ."

"Other than his pay, he has nothing."

"Hm."

He settled back against the adobe wall, and Amy leaned back, too. Her shoulder touched his, and he wondered if he should pull away, but she was so warm, he didn't. She pulled the damp blanket around in front of her.

"Here, take part of this, Tom. The bottom end is soaked, but the top part is merely saturated."

He laughed and pulled the scratchy blanket over his legs and up around his chest. "You're exaggerating. This part's hardly dripping."

She chuckled, and he settled back, letting his arm rest against hers. Her heat reached him through their sleeves. The lightning came less often, and he couldn't see her, but he imagined she had her feet curled under her on the bunk again, beneath the blanket.

"Still cold?" he asked.

"Not so bad. What time do you think it is?"

"I don't know. After midnight. Try to sleep if you can." He realized he was talking in a normal voice and she was hearing him. The thunderclaps came less frequently, and the rain had softened from the violent deluge to a steady downpour. "Maybe the storm's blowing over," he hazarded.

"Should we leave?"

"Not yet. But it does seem to be letting up."

She sat motionless. A bolt of lightning flickered, and he saw that she was leaning her head back against the wall, her eyes closed. She looked utterly peaceful, and he wanted to keep her that way. He wished he could block the door somehow in case the marauders came. His fatigue was catching up with him, and he closed his eyes, wondering hazily if he could make Buck lie down in front of the door. There had to be something.

"Maybe we could drag the stove over in front of the door," she said suddenly. "It's not doing us any good where it is."

Tom sat up. "That's uncanny. I was just thinking about it."

She laughed. "If we're both thinking it, we'd best do it."

"Well, it's not big enough to keep them out, but it would slow them down."

"I'll help."

The lightning flashed again. Tom pulled the stovepipe loose, and they hefted the box stove toward the door, crowding the horses aside as they went. It was heavier than he'd expected, and he was glad Amy was bearing a portion of the weight. When it was settled in front of the door, he felt the tiniest bit easier. He looked long out the window loops, but everything appeared the same.

The river will be rising, he thought. There were still a couple of places where the road crossed the Platte. It might be dangerous to ford now. The horses would have to swim.

When he turned back to the bunk, he thought Amy was asleep, her back against the wall. She had removed her boots and pulled her feet up beneath her skirt, but she lifted the edge of the blanket as he sat down, so he settled in next to her. It was hard to get comfortable without feeling too self-conscious, so near to a woman. He sat still and listened to the rain, the heavy breathing of the horses, and Amy's softer breath, close to his ear now.

Why had he stayed out of her path at Fort Bridger? he wondered. She embodied everything in his nebulous idea of the perfect woman. If he'd met her a few months ago. . .but no, he hadn't been ready then, and Benjamin Travis wouldn't have accepted him as a suitor for Amy. Some captain, maybe, or even a first lieutenant, but not a scout. Now if he got her to safety, she was heading into that other world. He doubted their paths would ever cross again. She might insist on waiting at Fort Laramie to hear the outcome of the Indian uprising, but she wouldn't stay there long.

He was nearly asleep when her head settled, very gently, on his shoulder, jolting him awake. His pulse raced. Her breath was even, and he was sure she was sleeping. The major's daughter wouldn't lean on a scout if she were conscious. He didn't move, not wanting to disturb her. She needed to rest, and he didn't want to embarrass her.

All right, he admitted to himself, *I like this.* Maybe it was time to think seriously about finding a wife. Immediately he rejected the idea. He didn't want to go looking. Amy was everything he wanted, but she was far beyond his reach. And any other female he encountered would be measured unfavorably against her.

Chapter 9

When Tom awoke, Buck was nudging his boot as he snuffled around the dirt floor, no doubt looking for something edible. Beyond him, Kip stood, knees locked, sleeping. Dawn was fast approaching.

He turned his head toward the window, realizing all at once that his left arm encircled Amy's shoulders, holding her against his side, and her head was pillowed just below his collarbone. And he was wonderfully warm.

He sat still, breathing carefully, not sure what to do. How had this happened?

The rain seemed to have faded to a light drizzle. He ought to get up and look out the windows and begin to get the horses ready. Carefully, he shifted, easing his arm up a bit. Her head stirred, and she nestled in closer. He held his breath. Her left hand was sliding across the front of his shirt, toward his right shoulder.

This is not good, he told himself. *We'll both be embarrassed when she wakes up. She'll hate me.*

He lowered his head and just for a second let his cheek rest against her hair. Then very carefully, he inched away from her, sliding his arm off her and moving toward the edge of the bunk.

He thought he could settle her on the wooden platform, but as her head gently came down on her arm, her eyelids flew open and she sat up quickly, blinking at him with those huge blue eyes. One hand went to her disheveled braid, where loose hairs danced around her ears and neck. The other pulled the wool blanket around her.

"Is it time?" she asked, her voice husky from sleep.

"I think so. Just stay there, and I'll take a look outside."

꙳

He walked to the nearest window, and Amy sat on the bunk watching him. Her heart was pounding. Tom stood immobile for a full minute, and something made her sit still, watching him. His hair was tousled, and the tails of his soft shirt hung down. He looked like a little boy who needed some mothering. She smiled at that assessment, compared with her first impressions of him at Fort Bridger. He was tough, independent, a loner who would get the job done with no fuss. No one would stand in his way. That was why her father had picked him, wasn't it?

"I'm going to look around outside," he said, putting on his hat. "It's still raining but not hard. If there's no sign of them, I think we ought to go on."

She nodded. "I'll gather things up."

Tom dragged the stove to one side then cautiously opened the door and stood looking down the path that led to the wagon trail and the river. With his rifle in hand, he stepped out and closed the door. A cool draft stole through the room, and Amy realized the heat of the animals had raised the temperature inside the cabin during the night. She didn't relish riding on in the rain and getting soaked again, but there seemed no alternative. They couldn't afford to delay.

She combed out her hair and tied it back with a bit of blue ribbon from her saddlebag. She shook out Kip's saddle blanket and spoke softly to him as she stood on tiptoe to spread it over his back. By the time Tom returned, she had saddled both horses and was fastening her damp bedroll with the leather thongs on Kip's saddle.

"I checked the road. No fresh tracks," Tom said. "We'd better get going."

"The biscuits are getting stale," she said without looking up. "I thought we ought to eat them now."

She nodded toward the bunk, where she had set out four biscuits. Tom walked over and picked one up.

He bit into it and grimaced. "You didn't make these, did you?"

She chuckled and tied the last knot in the rawhide thong. "No, those are army-issue biscuits. I wouldn't claim them."

"That's a relief."

She sneaked a look at him, and his humor changed quickly to dismay. "Your lip is bleeding."

She put one finger to her lower lip, then looked at the trace of blood on it. "Every time you make me laugh, the skin cracks and bleeds."

"Sorry."

"Don't be. Laughing is good." She picked up Kip's bridle. She could see that Tom's lips were chapped, too. "Wish we had some lard."

"Lard? Guess that would help. Wouldn't taste bad on these biscuits, either."

She laughed then winced. "You're doing it again."

"Sorry." He swallowed the last of the biscuit and shook his canteen before opening it for a small sip. "We ought to be at Fort Laramie by tomorrow morning."

"Really?" She felt he was holding it out to her as consolation for all the discomfort she was enduring. She tried not to stare into his intent brown eyes. If she did that, she might give away too much of the confusion that was swirling in her heart. *It's because you have to depend on him right now,* she told herself. *This is not love. It's admiration and respect and tension brought on by danger.*

Tom reached for Buck's bridle. "It's about a hundred miles from here. We can do it in a day if everything goes right. We'll have to rest a few times, but I think we can make it."

His confidence renewed her determination. With that little bit of encouragement from him, she was ready to face another grueling day. They would survive, and her father would be proud of her.

Tom went out first, the musket at the ready. Amy waited, looking over his shoulder, as he stood silent for half a minute, listening. It was nearly full daylight, and the rain pattered down on the trees surrounding the cabin. Faintly, she heard the roar of the river.

He turned and took Buck's reins from Amy's hand. She moved Kip aside, and the buckskin plunged through the doorway into the light with a glad little snuffle.

"They're hungry," Amy said as she led Kip out.

"I know, but we'd better get away from here before we let them graze. We need to get to a place where we can see the trail for a ways."

She mounted quickly, and they walked the horses down the trail, coming out on the wagon road sooner than she had expected.

"What a mess." She looked dolefully at the wet wagon ruts.

"Stay in the middle," Tom said. "You go first. I'll be right behind you. Just keep heading east."

She set out with Kip, and the sun came up, chasing the last of the rain clouds away. It warmed her and dried her wet skirt slowly. She felt grubby and toyed with the idea of taking a swim when they watered the horses. But when the river came in sight again, she gave up that notion in a hurry. The water swirled deep and wide, brown with churning mud.

"The water's so high," she gasped, turning in her saddle to speak to Tom.

"Lotta rain last night."

She trotted Kip onward, not daring to canter on the wet strip between the ruts. As the sun rose higher, she felt the promise of another blistering day. How could it have been so cold last night? Sweat beads formed along the inside of her hatband and trickled down her face.

They rode for nearly an hour before coming to another ford. She looked along the riverbank but could see no ferry or raft.

"Wasn't there a ferry or raft here?" she asked Tom as they dismounted.

"It's probably on the other side. Might have been washed away last night."

The horses snorted and tossed their heads at the muddy water.

"What if they won't drink?" Amy asked.

"We'll find a clearer stream sooner or later."

He didn't seem worried, so she decided she wouldn't worry, either, but she took only a swallow from her half-empty canteen in case it had to last her all day.

"Are we going to cross?" She eyed the swirling water doubtfully.

"We'd have to swim the horses."

"The current looks pretty strong." She was afraid, but if he insisted, she would try it.

"We can stay on this side with horses," Tom said. "It's rougher. We'll have to climb those bluffs and go along the top of them. With wagons, it's a lot easier to cross the river again, but I think we'll be all right."

She nodded, grateful to be spared the plunge into the brown torrent.

"All right, let's go," he said. "We'll get up high where we can see and let the horses graze."

They moved back up the muddy trail from the ford, and Amy realized their tracks would be easy to follow now that the rain had stopped.

They climbed steadily up a grassy slope. At the crest she could look back down at the ford and beyond, down the trail a mile or two.

"You stay with them, and I'll stand watch," Tom said, dismounting. He pulled his rifle from the scabbard and dropped Buck's reins. "We won't unsaddle. If you see anything, yell. I'll watch the back trail and the ford."

She sat down on the grass and adjusted her felt hat to shade her face as much as possible. The horses began eating immediately. When Kip had worked his way several yards from Buck, she got up and brought him closer.

After a while, she lay back on the grass and closed her eyes. *I love him,* she thought then felt guilty and confused. Guilty, because she ought to be thinking about how they could best survive and get help for her father and the garrison at Fort Bridger. Confused, because she still wasn't sure, but it was a captivating thought.

She sent a quick prayer up for her father and his men then allowed the more pleasant thoughts to take over.

Tom seemed to care about her now and with more than just the care that was his duty, the drive to keep her safe, to honor his promise to her father. She tried to analyze the few times he had touched her. He had thrown her into the saddle twice. That didn't count, she decided. But he had held her hand by the river last night, and in the cabin he had sat beside her, their arms touching, and slept that way all night long. At least she thought he had. When she had awakened, it seemed he was trying to get up without disturbing her. But any two people who were in danger of freezing would probably set convention aside and resort to body heat to keep them alive.

If you're honest, you'll admit you weren't at death's door, her heart argued. *You wouldn't have frozen if he'd curled up on the floor with his own wet blanket.*

He had wanted to be close to her. Hadn't he? Or had she pushed him into it?

She squirmed a little, remembering how she had offered him half the soggy blanket. Had she overstepped the bounds of propriety? Was she leading a man on?

The thought shocked and repelled her. She had always been taught to be modest and discreet. Still, the feelings Tom kindled in her were stronger than anything she had ever felt before. She knew love was more than a feeling, yet she was ready to commit herself to him for the rest of her life. But how did he feel? He would do anything, anything at all, to keep her safe—even die for her. But that was his duty. It didn't mean he loved her.

If he wasn't called upon to die for her in the next twenty-four hours, would he want to go on being with her? Would he *live* for her?

She wasn't at all sure. Thoughts like that had probably never entered his head. He was determined to hand her over to this Colonel Munroe like a packet of dispatches, then ride back to the west, back to his isolation on the Blacks Fork.

The more she thought about it, the more she was certain that if he knew she was up here on the bluff daydreaming about marrying him, Tom Barkley would probably make that westward journey as soon as possible and laugh at his escape. Scouts were not family men. They thrived on a solitary life in the wilderness.

Still, Tom wasn't the typical scout. He didn't spit tobacco juice or wear mangy buckskins. He didn't let his hair grow down to his shoulders or hang around with the men who drank and gambled when he visited the fort.

"Amy!"

She sat up quickly, pushing her hat back. Tom was running toward her, over the crest of the hill.

"They're heading for the ford. Come on!"

She jumped up and walked quickly toward Kip. She had almost believed the outlaws had given up, that the remainder of their ride would be peaceful.

"Up you go." Once more he lifted her into the saddle and handed her the reins. He was on Buck and had sheathed the rifle in an instant.

"They'll see our trail," she said.

"Yes, but our horses are fresh now. You go first! If you can't follow the trail, just keep the river in sight. Go as fast as you can."

She wheeled Kip eastward and dug her heels into his sides. He didn't need more encouragement but leaped into a run along the top of the bluff, high above the swollen river. She looked back over her shoulder, wishing they had had a quiet moment together. Wishing she had told Tom she loved him, even if he laughed and told her she was a silly girl. Even if he told her he loved someone else, or that she was not attractive to him, or that she was plumb crazy. She wanted him to know. If she was going to die, she wanted to know she had told him.

Tom was riding hard behind her. There was no sign of the three outlaws yet. Kip and Buck would go fast and might outrun their pursuers. Surely Kip could outrun any other horse. Riding him was sheer pleasure, but that pleasure was displaced now by the fear that gripped her.

She rode on, periodically looking back for Buck. When she couldn't see him, she slowed Kip to a trot until the steady buckskin came into view. After a while, she no longer could discern the track. She wasn't sure if she had lost it from not paying attention or if it had just petered out in the scanty clumps of buffalo grass.

She came to a clear creek that cut between six-foot banks, burbling toward the Platte. Kip high-stepped nervously as she walked him along the edge, looking for a place to cross. Finally she found a spot where the bank was less steep, and she thought that if she rode Kip upstream a few yards, he could climb the opposite side.

He plummeted over the edge, and she nearly lost her balance. When he reached the water, he stopped abruptly, stretching his head down for a drink. Amy was flung forward, almost flying over his neck. Her hands shook as she pulled herself upright in the saddle. She let him drink his fill, but Buck was still not in sight when Kip raised his head.

The streambed was rocky, and she let Kip walk slowly, feeling his way. Her eyes scanned the east bank for the best spot to leave the creek.

Where was Tom?

She was frightened. He ought to have reached the creek by now. She urged Kip forward, then forced him toward the bank. He lunged up and over the top, and she wondered if Buck would be able to do it. She looked back across the stream, and far back she could see the buckskin coming at a dead gallop.

A sudden vision of Buck running unheeding over the creek bank and crashing to the rocky streambed below terrified her, but as the gelding drew closer, he snorted and threw his head.

"Tom! Be careful!" She wasn't sure her voice carried across the gulf between them. The ceaseless prairie wind blew the words back in her face.

"I see it!" His words came faint but distinct as he reined Buck in.

"Follow my trail!"

Buck swerved to the right along the bank toward the place where Kip had leaped down to the water.

Amy caught her breath as Buck scrambled down. He was safe. He stuck his nose down into the stream, but Tom pulled his head up and forced him to trot against the current toward her.

She looked over the creek bed again and saw the reason for his urgency. The three riders were in sight, half a mile back from the creek. Their horses were galloping toward her, and she knew they could see her.

"Tom! Down here!"

Kip pranced along the edge of the embankment. She looked upstream, frantic to find an easier spot for Buck to navigate the bank.

"Ride, Amy!" Tom shouted.

She couldn't make Kip turn and resume his flight until she knew Tom was out of the ravine.

"Don't wait! Ride!" He sounded desperate.

She looked again toward the riders. They were much closer.

Buck lunged at the bank, scrabbling for his footing, and hung momentarily on the edge, fighting for balance. Then he was up and running, past Kip.

Amy turned the gray on his hindquarters and let his reins out. He needed no command but flew into the gallop that made Amy feel she was flying five feet above the earth.

As he surged past Buck, she cried to Tom, "I lost the trail!"

"Doesn't matter! Keep going!"

Kip was soon leading by several lengths, and Tom saw Amy looking over her shoulder again for Buck. The stalwart buckskin went on, and Tom wondered if his horse would run and run until his heart burst.

Tom didn't need to urge Buck to run. The faithful horse would follow Kip anywhere now. And he would follow Amy. He and Buck were her first and last line of defense. He glanced toward the river. He usually took this stretch on the other side, but he judged they still had eighty miles to go, maybe eighty-five. The terrain was hilly, and he knew more streams would cut through it ahead. Kip was so long-legged, he could probably jump right over the smaller ones. Others, like the one they had just forded, were too wide and cut deep channels that were difficult to cross. Buck would lose ground on those.

He looked behind. The riders had gained a little, and he dug his heels into Buck's ribs, hating to ask more of him when he sensed the horse was already giving his best. He'd trained Buck from the time he was a green colt. They'd been inseparable for four years, and now they were having the ride of their lives.

"Just get through today with me, boy, and I promise you'll live high after this." He slapped Buck's withers, and the gelding snorted and dashed on, chasing Kip. The gray was far ahead now, but Tom knew Amy would pull him in if she got too far out in front. She'd been doing that all morning despite his instructions.

He could understand her fear of going on alone, but she would be safer if she would just forget about him and tear for the fort. It would be easier for him to make a stand when the time came if he knew she would go on without stopping.

But he couldn't be sure she would do that. Somehow, she'd gotten her loyalties and her feelings all mixed up. She was forgetting her father's need and the despair that would come over him if his daughter died on the prairie. She was thinking of T.R. Barkley instead, and that wasn't right. He shouldn't have opened up to her so much, let her see inside him. He ought to be expendable in her view, a means to an end. But she wasn't looking at it that way.

She wouldn't have let Brown go if she'd known the plan. When it came down to it, that had been extremely hard for him, too. But he was in charge, and the hard decisions were up to him. His uncertainty of the night before had vanished. It was clear now what he had to do.

He was ready to do it. For honor's sake, for Major Travis, and mostly for Amy. If God gave him the power, he would save her. If the riders came too close, he would stop and steady himself and prepare to take a bullet. But that Frenchman was going down first.

Ahead he saw Kip leap high. There must be a brook there. Buck charged toward it, and Tom concentrated on the terrain.

That girl! She'd stopped again and was looking back at him, making sure he and Buck made it over.

"Go!" he yelled.

She turned the big gray and started off, staring back at him.

The stream was only six feet wide, the banks a couple of feet high. Buck could have jumped it if he weren't tired, but Tom didn't take the chance. The horse leaped down into the streambed and stumbled, splashing cold water up Tom's pant legs and over the tops of his boots.

"No drinks now, fella." Up the other bank Buck charged. As they burst up onto the grass above, a rifle shot rang out behind him.

"Go!" Tom breathed.

Amy was looking back, but Kip was running.

A rifle cracked behind her, and Amy flung another glance over her shoulder. Buck was racing toward her, and Tom was still in the saddle, bent low over the pommel.

The three outlaws reached the bank of the brook. They had never been so close, and she could see their beards and the guns they carried pointed forward. Two of them flew over the brook, the man in the red shirt and the big man on the spotted horse. The other horse reared at the bank then plunged into the water.

Amy turned forward and lay low on Kip's neck. A prayer without words left her heart.

Another shot rang out, and she looked back once more, just in time to see Buck stumble and do a complete somersault, his legs flailing in the air. Tom flew forward and to one side, and she screamed.

Chapter 10

Kip quivered, his ears switching back and forth as Amy pulled hard on the reins and circled him at a canter.

"Tom!" she screamed.

Unbelievably, he was on his feet. She saw him run, stooping for his musket, then head toward Buck.

The horse was struggling to rise, but one hind leg wouldn't hold him.

The three riders were close, the paint horse out in front by several yards, but she was closer. She pushed Kip toward Tom.

Tom stood, his feet apart, using Buck as a shield. She saw the smoke from his rifle before she heard the report, and the big man on the paint jerked and tumbled from his saddle. Tom threw his musket down as she reached him and drew his revolver.

Kip stopped so fast he nearly went over backward. The two remaining riders checked momentarily, just out of pistol range.

Tom turned toward her. "You crazy woman! I told you to go!"

She kicked her foot out of the left stirrup, and he jumped up behind her.

"Go!" he yelled in her ear before he was settled.

Kip bounded away. Amy tried to look back, but all she could see was Tom's shoulder and his grim face.

"Are they coming?" she shouted.

"Not yet."

His left arm encircled her waist, and he held her firmly. She pushed Kip on.

"We need to rest," she said after several miles, turning so he could hear her.

She felt him turn in the saddle.

"Find some cover."

They were coming into an area of rock formations. Amy guided Kip between two tall columns and eased him down to a walk.

"Whoa, Kip."

Tom slid down and reached up to catch her as she jumped from the saddle. "Let him breathe."

"He needs water."

"I know. We'll come back to the river after a while. He'll have to wait until then." He detached the canteen from the saddle and handed it to her.

"I'm sorry about Buck."

Tom shrugged, but she knew he felt the loss deeply. She took a small sip of water and offered him the canteen. He took it and put the stopper in without drinking.

"Too bad I couldn't get that other horse."

"Did they stop chasing us?" she asked.

"No. I think they stopped long enough to reload and see if their friend was dead is all."

"Is he?"

"I hit him point blank."

"So what now?"

"Now I get up on that rock over there and watch behind us while you hang on to Kip. If we lose him, we've had it."

She nodded soberly.

His face was like granite as he stood on the boulder, facing west. He'd lost his hat when Buck fell, so he shaded his eyes with one hand. She held Kip's reins, and the horse stood breathing deeply, not seeming to care about the parched grass anymore.

She wanted to ask Tom what they would do if Kip fell, but she didn't want to think about that.

Tom stood immobile, watching, trying not to let his thoughts stray to Buck. Amy led Kip over to the base of the rock. She started to lean against it but jumped away quickly from its fiery hot surface.

"Maybe Buck's leg will heal, and he'll be all right," she ventured.

Tom said nothing. He knew that if the riders hadn't already shot Buck, the wolves would pull him down that night. He should have put a bullet in the horse's head himself, but the thought that he might lose the battle for Amy for the lack of one bullet had held him back.

His left hip and elbow were throbbing from when he'd hit the ground, but he ignored the pain. He needed to prepare Amy to defend herself and find her way to Fort Laramie alone.

"Get that other gun out," he said.

Amy fumbled with the buckle of the saddlebag and produced Layton's gun belt. She held it up to him, stretching and standing on tiptoe.

He glanced down at her, then returned to watching the trail.

"Put it on," he said. "If we're afoot all of a sudden, I don't want to have to stop for it."

She hesitated, then wrapped the belt around her waist. Although Layton had been a thin man, it was far too large. She took it off and tried slinging it over her shoulder, but it slipped awkwardly down her arm. When they were riding, it would be worse, Tom knew.

"Give it here." He took out his hunting knife and cut six inches from the leather strap then bored a new hole in the belt.

"Try that." He put the belt and holster in her hand then stood up again to watch the trail while she put it on.

"That's better."

"All right. How's Kip doing?"

"He's got his wind back, I think."

Tom hopped down from the rock and prepared to boost her into the saddle again.

"Wait," she said, putting one hand out against his chest. "You take the saddle. I'll ride behind you."

"No."

"Why not?"

He looked down into her vivid blue eyes, wanting to shield her from the stark truth. But she had to know what they were up against. "That saddle was made for you. It won't fit me. Besides, the enemy is behind us, and I'm not going to expose your back as a target."

She swallowed hard, and he thought she would argue. He'd seen that stubborn glint in the major's eyes.

Tom was trying to hold his wits together. The danger to him and Amy had carried him through the fall and the hasty parting with Buck, but that rush of energy had dissipated, and fear was closing in. He had thrown the musket down after he'd fired it, knowing he didn't have time to salvage the lead for it from Buck's saddlebags. Now he couldn't shoot back unless their enemies came close. At least they had Layton's extra powder and ammunition for the revolvers in Kip's saddlebags.

Seconds counted, and he couldn't let his feelings for Amy slow him down. He tried to glare down at her, to stop her from protesting further, but he couldn't.

"We're wasting time, Amy," he said softly.

She was still looking up at him, but she wasn't angry.

"All right." She put her hand up for an instant to his jaw.

He was tempted to scoop her into his arms, but that wouldn't keep them alive. She turned away almost immediately, reaching for the stirrup. Again he picked her up and settled her gently on Kip's back. She pushed her legs forward of the leathers, and he got his left foot in the stirrup and swung up behind her.

He looked off to the west. Was that a puff of alkali dust on the trail? He couldn't be sure. Mirages were common in this territory. The rainwater had kept the dust down all morning, but it had soaked into the ground, and the sun had done its work. If it was their pursuers, he judged them to be a mile away.

He put his arms around Amy's waist, holding her with his left hand and

grasping the saddle horn with his right. Amy squeezed Kip, and the horse took off again at a canter.

Half an hour later, they came to another clear stream, and Tom made Amy stop Kip with the horse's forefeet in the water.

"You stay up there, but let him drink," Tom said, sliding down to give Kip a respite from his weight. "If I tell you to go and I'm still on the ground, you go, you hear me?"

He scowled into her eyes, and her lower lip trembled.

"I hear you," she whispered.

He nodded and went around to the off side and unbuckled the saddlebag.

"Here." He thrust a piece of dried beef into her hand. "Eat."

While she chewed, he took out the bag of lead balls and put half a dozen in the pocket of his trousers, then stuffed as many powder cartridges and caps in his shirt pocket as would fit. He closed the saddlebag and took the canteen, stooping to fill it.

Kip's throat made gulping sounds as he swallowed.

Tom looked up at Amy. She turned away quickly, but he saw tears in her eyes. He handed her the canteen, and she tipped it up for a drink then handed it back.

"Drink more," he commanded.

She did. He took it and filled it then stoppered it and secured it on the back of the saddle.

"Should we drop the blanket and saddlebags?" There was a tremor in her voice.

Tom hesitated. Ounces as well as seconds counted.

"We need the lead and powder. If you want to drop the blanket and your personal things, do it now. I'll take a look behind us."

He scrambled back up the western bank of the rivulet. No riders and no dust clouds were within sight, but because of the undulating prairie, he couldn't be sure they weren't close.

"Take Kip up the far bank and wait for me," he called.

She obeyed, and Tom descended to the stream again, crossing over on foot, hopping from rock to rock, then scrambled up the low bank on the east side to where she waited.

She took her foot from the stirrup, and he swung up into his former position behind her on Kip's back, one arm tight around her waist.

"Let's go," he said quietly in her ear.

It was too hot to be so close to another person, but he didn't care. Little droplets of sweat clung to the back of her neck below the hat brim where her hair was tied. He hoped he would live to be this close to her again, when he didn't have to think about keeping her alive. Whether he died today or fifty years from now, he would always remember how small her waist was and how incongruous the thick leather gun belt felt just below the waistband of her dusty split skirt.

They rode on. Kip seemed to have found new energy and maintained the rocking-chair canter for some time. When he slowed of his own accord, they continued at a trot.

Amy drooped beneath the searing sun. They ought to stop in the shade somewhere. She jerked awake. Tom's arm tightened just a little around her middle.

"It's all right," he whispered, his breath tickling her ear, and she realized she'd nodded off and was leaning back against his chest.

She ought to be embarrassed, but she wasn't. Even though she was in mortal danger, she felt safe. She put her right hand over Tom's on the saddle horn, and he gripped her fingers.

"You ought to have left me back there," he murmured.

"Never." She turned her head against his chest, and her hat shifted. "Take my hat," she said.

"It won't fit me."

She was wide awake now. "Are you all right?"

"Yes. A little stiff. How about you?"

"I'm tired."

"I could tell," he chuckled.

"Do you think they're still after us?"

"Yes. We have to keep moving until we meet someone or reach the fort."

She hadn't thought of meeting a detachment or an emigrant train. They hadn't met anyone going west since the troopers' camp. But it was late in the season, as Tom had pointed out.

"How far now?" she asked.

"I don't know. Sixty or seventy miles, maybe. I don't think they'll chase us right up to the fort. If this horse can keep going, we may outrun them yet."

"I knew he was special," she said dreamily.

"He's incredible," Tom said.

She laid her head back against him, the hat brim coming far down, almost to her eyes. She wished she could stay in his arms always, sweaty and tired as he was. She herself had never felt so filthy. If they made it to Fort Laramie, the second thing she would do was take a bath. The first would be to tell Tom Barkley she loved him.

That would be the appropriate time, she decided, unless it looked like they were going to die short of the fort.

For the moment, she had hope. Kip was still moving, and Tom was holding her in his arms. Not by his own choice, it was true, but she thought his touch was tenderer than was absolutely necessary. And he still held her fingers. He didn't have to.

When this was over and they didn't have to keep close company, she would see if he still wanted to be near her. Maybe he was just trying to keep her from giving up. She hoped it was more than that.

Chapter 11

Another ford. They had worked their way down from the high prairie to the level of the river, and now the wagon road would be on the south bank again.

"I want to swim!" she cried.

Tom laughed, hopping down from Kip's back.

"In that filthy river? It's just thin mud."

"I'm so hot!"

He guessed he was partly to blame for that. He hadn't needed to hold her so tightly—could have let some air get between them.

"Can I at least get down?" she asked.

"All right, but keep your boots on." He lifted her down. Kip was settling for the muddy water this time. When the horse lifted his head, Tom led him away from the river to get a view down the trail.

Amy followed them. She was still beautiful, though her skirt was spattered and stained and the back and sides of her blouse were soaked with perspiration. Her face was streaked with dirt. She took off her hat and mopped her forehead with her sleeve as she walked toward him. He smiled.

"What's funny?" she asked when she was close. "Am I so filthy my own father wouldn't recognize me?"

"Just about," he laughed. The skin of his bottom lip split, and he sucked it. "Can't wait 'til we get some of that lard."

She laughed, too. "We're two of the dirtiest people in the territory, I'm sure. I don't know as they'll let us in the gate at Fort Laramie."

"Up you go." He reached to lift her. He stopped with his hands on her waist. He usually waited until she turned toward the horse to get the stirrup, but this time he'd reached for her while she still faced him.

You're crazy! he told himself. *You can't kiss a woman when the people who want to kill you could pop up any second.* But he wanted to very much.

"Tom."

He swallowed. He really ought to speak to the major before he made advances to his daughter. Besides, his lip was bleeding, and hers were in rough shape, too. Would a kiss like that be pleasant? He'd never kissed a woman, and he didn't want it to be torture when he did.

"We'd better move."

She nodded, still looking up at him, and he wondered what she had been about to say. In her eyes there seemed to be something that answered the deep longing in his heart. Her breath came out in a little puff, and she turned toward Kip. Tom lifted her carefully then climbed up behind her and slid his arms around her. He turned Kip so he could look down the trail then headed east again.

They kept moving for two hours. Tom wouldn't let the hope rise in him that their pursuers had given up. Kip was jogging slowly, his head drooping a little. *As long as he keeps moving,* Tom thought. *Just keep moving.*

The wagon trail was dry, and he doubted the rain had touched this section. Occasional puffs of breeze swirled their own dust around them, making Amy cough and choke. Tom's eyes smarted, and every muscle in his body ached, but he held on to her, and he thought she actually slept for a few minutes, slumped against him, limp and soft.

They came to the bank of a wide stream that had cut a deep gash in the prairie, and he stopped Kip on the edge, looking back for a minute before they descended the slope to the water.

Amy leaned back against him to help the horse balance as he went down the incline. The water was up to Kip's knees, and he stood in it, drinking as though he would empty the stream.

"He's so tired," Amy moaned.

"I know. He's done more than I ever expected he could."

"Should we stop for a while?"

"We should, but. . ." He glanced uneasily over his shoulder. He couldn't see beyond the bank where the wagon road rose several feet.

"How far?" she asked in a small voice.

"Fifty miles. They say this stream is fifty miles out from the fort. I think it's a little less, actually."

"That's good. We're really going to make it, Tom."

"Well. . ." He was noncommittal. Between them and Fort Laramie was a rugged range of stony hills supporting scrub pines and juniper. He knew the rocky country would be hard on a horse already pressed to the limits of endurance.

"What?" Amy asked. "You said they won't chase us right up to the fort."

"Right, so. . ."

"What aren't you telling me?" She swiveled around and stared at him searchingly.

"So they'll want to make their move soon, before we get too close to Fort Laramie."

Her eyes grew large, and he hated frightening her.

"If Kip could rest for an hour or two, he could carry us all that way," she said.

"Maybe. But. . . " He looked west again, and it bothered him that he couldn't see out of the streambed. He ought to have waited up above while she watered the horse. "Let's get up out of here, and I'll walk for a while and give Kip a break."

"I'll walk, too," she said immediately.

"No."

"Why not?"

"You don't weigh much."

"But he needs the rest."

Tom grimaced and took the reins, pulling Kip's head up. "You've got to stay on him," he said as the gray waded across the water. It came up to the stirrups. Amy lifted her feet up along the horse's neck.

Kip heaved up the far bank, and Tom pulled on the reins and jumped down, staggering as he landed. Walking would do his stiff muscles good.

"I want to walk, too," Amy insisted.

"No."

"Why?"

"You know why." He walked alongside the horse. She said nothing, but after a few minutes, he began to worry. She was so headstrong, and she had come charging back for him when Buck fell.

"You listen to me," he said sternly. "If I tell you to go, you go."

"You've said that before."

"And you didn't always do it."

"Tom. . ." She sounded helpless and hurt.

"I'm serious. Kip needs to rest now, and this is the best plan I can think of. If they don't show up, I'll keep walking. If they do, I'll jump on again. But if there's no time and I tell you, girl, you get out of here. You hear me? Ride straight to the fort. Don't stop for anything. Not anything."

She set her chin stubbornly and refused to look at him.

"Promise," he said threateningly.

He thought she sniffed. How could she have enough moisture in her body to cry?

"Amy," he warned.

"I promise," she said bitterly.

"All right." He was not completely mollified. "We've evened the odds somewhat. If they still think they need to do this, I'll do everything I can to make sure they don't get past me. But it's God you should count on, Amy. Not me."

They trudged along in silence for half an hour. Slightly past its apex, the sun beat down cruelly. Every time they topped a rise, Tom turned and looked back, shielding his eyes and squinting. Nothing. He turned and walked on beside the tall gray horse.

If the outlaws never came again, so be it. They would go on slowly. If he walked the last fifty miles, that was all right, too, so long as Amy got there alive. But he really thought they would meet someone soon, now that they were on the last stretch of the wagon trail. The Indians in these parts were generally friendly. They would certainly help them get to the fort. Or a detachment of troopers might be out patrolling. A trader might still be heading for Fort Hall or Fort Bridger with supplies for the winter.

They saw no one, unless three pronghorns and a small colony of prairie dogs counted.

Tom realized he'd been plodding along in the wagon rut for some time without checking behind. They were climbing a long, gradual slope. He glanced uneasily over his left shoulder.

Was it dust, or was it a trick of the sun? Maybe a breeze had stirred and raised a puff of alkali. He stopped, and after a few steps, Kip stopped, too.

"Tom?" Amy called, her voice rising.

He walked slowly to the horse, looking back as he went.

"Do you see dust?" He felt stupid and sluggish.

She looked hard to the west, craning her neck.

"I see it."

"Come on." He started walking again.

"Tom!" She was shouting at him urgently. "Get on the horse, Tom!"

She sidled Kip up next to him, and her leg and the stirrup brushed against his shoulder.

"Get up!" she cried.

That jolted him, and he was able to act. He seized Kip's bridle and jumped up behind Amy. As soon as he landed, she kicked Kip into a trot, and the horse labored to the top of the long hill.

"Turn around," Tom said.

She turned the horse, and they sat staring down the trail.

The dust cloud was nearer, and he thought he could make out a horse.

"It might not be them." There was no hope in her voice.

Tom reached the left rein and pulled Kip's head around. He squeezed him hard, and the gray began to trot.

⌒

Amy's mind was whirling. She had let herself believe they were done with it in spite of Tom's dire predictions.

"Maybe we could hide somewhere until they get close and see if it's really them," she said, turning to speak close to his ear.

"No. I don't have a rifle. The only way I'll do that is if you'll keep going without me."

"No," she said flatly. He was right. The best plan, the only reasonable plan, was to keep going.

They were over the crest of the hill, and Tom was constantly twisting to look back.

"What are you thinking?" she yelled.

"Nothing that would work."

Kip cantered on across the prairie. Tom sat still behind Amy, keeping his weight centered as much as possible, and let her guide the horse. As they climbed another long hill, Kip slowed to a jog. Tom looked back and caught his breath.

"What is it?" Amy asked.

"The paint horse. I shot his rider, but they're bringing the extra horse along."

She put her hand over his where he clutched her waist, and she felt his grip tighten for an instant. She didn't say anything, but she grasped the implication. The riders were close enough that Tom could make out two horsemen and a horse with an empty saddle. They had a remount and could alternate the horses. She and Tom, meanwhile, had one horse to carry them both.

She squeezed Kip a little more, and he halfheartedly broke into a canter again.

"I'm sorry, Kip," she whispered.

"You say something?" Tom's voice was loud in her ear.

She shook her head and blinked at the tears that kept coming. She needed to be able to see. *I'm sorry, Daddy,* she cried inwardly. *Tom's done his best. He really has.*

She knew she was crying out to the wrong person. Her breath was coming in gasps, and she tried to steady it. This was not the time to lose control. She was able at last to form a prayer.

Dear Lord, please help us. I know You're the only One who can. And whatever happens, don't let Father blame Tom. She gulped and fought the urge to turn around again. *Let us live, dear God. But if that's not what You want, let me be strong to the end.*

Tom drew his Colt revolver. "Amy, remember, God is with you." His lips touched her right ear.

She nodded.

"You keep going, no matter what." His arms tightened around her.

Now is the time, she thought. *It's not the appropriate time, but it's the only time.*

She leaned back hard against his chest and turned her face toward his neck. "Tom, I love you."

"Amy!" It was little more than a sob.

A rifle cracked behind them, and Kip leaped forward, faster.

Tom's adrenaline surged. They still had a chance. Their pursuers couldn't reload while riding.

"Keep going," he said relentlessly. "That's one musket discharged. If they keep missing, we'll be down to handguns, and we'll be even again."

Of course, they had three rifles, maybe four if they'd picked up his. More if they'd gotten Layton's and Brown's. He wouldn't think about that.

She loved him. She had dared to say that. Maybe it was just some misplaced surge of emotion for her protector, a panicky declaration she would regret later. He wished there was time to think about it, to savor it, but there was none. He knew vaguely that it was something he couldn't hold her to later, even though his own heart told him he loved her, too.

His legs were very tired from clinging to the horse without stirrups, and he could only hold on with one hand now, since he'd drawn the pistol. It took all his concentration to stay on Kip's back.

He looked back and saw the red-shirted Frenchman dropping back and swinging his leg over the paint horse's saddle without stopping. Meanwhile, the man in buckskins edged forward on a long-legged bay.

Tom felt a wave of despair. They were close, too close. He tried to level the pistol at them, but it would be hopeless to shoot turning backward while Kip was galloping and the targets were moving, too.

"You'll have a better chance without me." He'd been thinking it for some time now, but he'd known she wouldn't like it.

"No, Tom! Don't leave me!"

Her cry was so piteous, it wrenched his heart.

"I can jump and make a stand. You keep going."

"No!"

"We knew it might come to this," he said in her ear.

"No!" she shouted again. "Don't do it!"

Another shot split the air, and even as Amy heard it, she felt Tom's hold loosen. He slipped back over Kip's hindquarters, sliding down the left side.

"Tom!" she screamed. She looked back and was terrified to see him lying on the trail behind her. He didn't jump up and run as he had when Buck went down.

Instead of hesitating, Kip leaped forward with the lessening of weight on his back and charged on up the hillside.

Chapter 12

Tom hit the ground hard and lay staring up at blue sky. The sound of Kip's hoofbeats receded. He had planned to jump off but not quite that soon. Had he lost his balance? He was winded, stunned by the fall. He struggled to breathe deeply. It hurt. When he tried to sit up, fierce pain stabbed through his left shoulder. He knew he was hit and hoped the bullet was high enough to have missed the lung.

With a shock, he realized the two riders were almost on top of him, and he looked around frantically for his pistol. The bay horse charged toward him, and he thought he would be run over, but the man in buckskins pulled the horse up sharply, and the bay stopped, his front hooves landing within inches of Tom's head.

Tom forced himself to a sitting position, but the trapper leaned over from the saddle, pointing his musket at Tom.

"Well, Barkley. Here we are at last."

The Frenchman flew past on the pinto, dropping the reins of the third mount, a brown with white stockings, and Tom looked quickly after him. The pinto was twenty yards behind Kip. Amy must have hesitated again.

God, give her wings.

He knew his prayer was futile.

The trapper leaped down from the bay horse and stood over him, his gun barrel almost touching Tom's chest. His dirty blond hair hung in clumps beneath a battered hat.

"I don't know why you're still alive." The man showed his teeth in a grudging smile. "Say, maybe we'd better fix that."

Tom tried to sit still, staring up at him, not twitching a muscle. His mind was racing. They had fired two muskets. He couldn't see another on the bay's saddle. Surely the outlaw wouldn't hold an empty gun on him? Or would he?

The man's hand moved slightly toward the trigger, just as a scream rent the air from above them on the hillside.

It was enough of a distraction for the man with the rifle. His glance flickered toward the hilltop, and Tom seized the end of the barrel, yanking it hard to one side and forward.

The explosion was deafening next to his ear, and the trapper's eyes were wide with surprise as he tried to maintain his grip on the musket.

Tom pulled and twisted with an effort that wrenched his shoulder violently, but with Amy's life at stake, he ignored the pain. He had the gun now. It was empty, but he swung it by the barrel, aiming for the man's knees.

The trapper hopped back, taking the blow on the shin. He swore and stood sizing Tom up, his eyes glittering.

"Well, now," he said evenly. Slowly he reached for his belt.

I'm dead, Tom thought. *He's got a pistol, and I'm dead. God, help Amy. Don't leave her unprotected.*

Even as his prayer went up, Tom rose carefully to his feet. He dropped the musket and reached for his hunting knife.

He almost laughed when his adversary pulled out his own blade. They were even now, except for Tom's wound and Amy's heart-wrenching screams that made his heart race.

He wanted so badly to look toward her but didn't dare take his gaze off the man whose wolfish eyes glinted at him.

Tom circled slowly until he was facing the hillside. Way at the top, he saw in one quick glance that Kip was riderless, skittering nervously sideways, his reins dangling. The brown horse was cropping grass halfway up the hillside, and the pinto was at the top near Kip. Tom glimpsed the red-shirted man, still in the saddle, against the dark background of the pines, holding Amy half on and half off the horse. He had an impression of flailing limbs and a gleam of light off Amy's golden hair, streaming loose.

He riveted his eyes on his immediate adversary. Amy was putting up a fight. It wasn't over yet. He had a score to settle here before he could finish matters.

"I almost called it quits after you shot Ollie," the man said, his smile a snarl. "That made LeBeau really mad, though. He and Ollie were great pals."

Tom's mind tried to process everything, the man's position, his movements, his words. He said nothing, saving his breath and concentrating, thinking how he could speed things up and come out the victor.

The trapper leaped at him suddenly, and Tom deflected the thrust of the knife with his left arm, tripping the man up and crashing to the ground with him. A jolt of pain ran through his injured shoulder. Somehow they landed beneath the bay horse, and the gelding sidestepped gingerly, whinnying in protest. Tom rolled away, and the other man ducked away from the horse then groped about on the ground. Tom realized he was searching for his knife.

It was the opening Tom needed. He lunged, slicing hard as he brought the man to the ground again. The tough buckskin slowed the blade, and Tom didn't think he'd hurt him much. They struggled, face-to-face on the ground, both determined to control Tom's knife.

Tom's weakened left arm was giving way. The trapper kneed him in the stomach, then rolled away with the knife in his hand.

Tom rose to his knees, fighting nausea. He was in so much pain, he didn't know if he could stand up again. As he tried, he focused, slowly, agonizingly, on a metallic object just inches from his left hand—the pistol he had dropped when he fell from the horse.

He looked away from it quickly. If the other man noticed, Tom would have less of a chance.

The trapper was crouching, weaving slightly, looking for an opening. He was just about to leap when Tom grabbed the revolver and whipped it up, squeezing the trigger.

Click.

The man's eyes widened in surprise; then he smiled.

"Forget to reload, sonny?"

Tom's heart sank. *God, I tried so hard to keep the pistols dry.* In that instant, he knew he must cock the pistol and squeeze the trigger five more times. All six chambers couldn't misfire.

As the man came toward him, Tom aimed at his face, but before he could pull the hammer back again, the hang fire caught, and the powder exploded in the chamber with a roar. The man flew backward, and Tom stood staring, feeling sick.

～

Amy screamed when the man in the red shirt galloped up beside her and tried to pull her from the saddle. She dug into Kip's sides, and he leaped with a squeal, but the man's grip was like iron. She kicked free of the stirrups and tried to leap off the far side, but the man yanked her from Kip's saddle and pulled her to him. Amy shrieked.

She kicked and writhed as he struggled to pull her onto his horse. When he clapped a hand over her mouth, she bit him fiercely.

He swore, and Amy tumbled to the ground. Dazed, she got to her feet and backed away from the pinto then turned and ran toward the tree line. The spotted horse thundered behind her. Suddenly, the ground dropped away, and she found herself sliding down a steep slope into a cleft between the hills. She grabbed at a small pine branch, and the needles sliced her palms, but she held on and stopped her descent.

Above her, the pinto balked, and she heard the man cursing in French. She eased to her feet and tried to move down the slope without sliding again, but her boots slipped, and she sat down hard. Below her, the slope was near vertical with a drop of five feet over the face of a ledge. She looked to the sides but saw no prospect of better footing.

Branches snapped above her, and she looked up. LeBeau had left the horse and was following her down cautiously. A huge lump blocked her throat, and she couldn't scream anymore. There seemed to be no escape.

She reached for the pistol she wore at her side and pulled it clumsily from the holster.

"Go away," she tried to shout, but it came out a whisper.

She raised the gun with shaking hands and struggled to pull the hammer back.

The Frenchman was just above her, holding on to a tree root and reaching out, the sleeve of his red shirt stretching toward her.

Amy pulled the trigger and felt herself falling from the rock as the concussion shook the air in the ravine. She dropped the pistol and tried to extend her arms, but the ground rushed up too fast. Her ankles took the first shock of the landing, but she couldn't gain her balance. She stumbled forward, knowing she was going to hit hard, but she couldn't stop.

Tom realized Amy's screams had stopped, and as the ringing in his ears receded, it was eerily quiet. The brown horse was trotting away to the south, around the side of the hill. He could see Kip and the bay but not the pinto.

He pulled his knife from the trapper's lifeless hand, shoved the revolver in his holster, and ran up the hill. When he came near Kip, he stopped, looking all around and panting. Had they gone over the hill?

A muffled report came from his right, and he ran toward it to where the side of the hill fell away steeply and the trees began. He saw the pinto halfway down the draw, his saddle empty.

"Amy!" he shouted.

There was no answer. He worked his way carefully down the steep hillside, grasping the trunks of the scrub pines to keep from plummeting down the slope. The pain in his shoulder alternately stabbed and ached, and he wondered if he would be able to climb up the hill again. As he came even with the pinto, it eyed him balefully and went on snatching at the meager grass.

"Amy!"

He listened.

A rustling sounded below where the brush was thick. He drew the revolver.

"LeBeau!" he called.

"Halt! Come no closer, Barkley."

Tom stood still, homing in on the voice. "What do you want, LeBeau?"

There was a short laugh. "I have what I want, monsieur, although it has cost me dear."

"Give me the girl. I'll give you whatever you want."

"I do not think that is in your power."

"Do you want money?" Tom asked, taking a cautious step.

"Alas, money will not buy my brother's life."

Tom took another step. "Your brother is the man Major Travis arrested at Fort Bridger."

"*Eh, bien.* You see my difficulty."

"LeBeau, we can work this out." Tom took two steps. He was on top of a granite ledge, and the voice came from the shadows below.

"I told you, stay away. This young lady will ride with me, and I am sure you want her to be in good health when she goes."

Tom thought he saw a tuft of red in the shade of the thick pines, but the sun was setting, and he couldn't be sure. He crouched behind an outcropping of the ledge.

It struck him suddenly that LeBeau might not even have her. Perhaps she had escaped him after all. "Amy?" he called cautiously.

LeBeau laughed derisively. "The young lady does not wish to speak to gentlemen callers just now."

"Where is she, LeBeau?"

"That I cannot tell you."

Fear coursed through him. He looked toward the pinto, where it grazed on the slope. A rifle stuck up from a scabbard on the saddle.

"Can't or won't?"

"She is. . .with me. But you must go away. Take the big gray horse and ride to the fort if you wish. Get reinforcements and chase me across the territory the way I chased you. But I will get to Fort Bridger before you do, and I will do my business with the major."

"What business?"

"It is a tiresome thing. I have what the major wants, you see, and he has what I want."

"Your brother."

"Yes. We can make a trade. The major would not take money to release my brother, I am certain. But he will accept the gift of his daughter's life."

"You were on your way to Fort Bridger when we passed the troopers' camp," Tom said, reaching out with his foot and feeling the edge of the rock.

"I was going to plead with the major to release him. But when I learned the perfect persuasion was within reach. . . Monsieur, let us say I did not expect it to take so long to fetch my trade goods."

As he spoke, Tom leaned forward toward the rim of the ledge, judging the distance to the ground below.

"Get back! I insist, monsieur."

Tom sat still. "It seems to me that if you had a gun, you'd have used it by now."

"Oh, you think I have no weapons?" LeBeau laughed. "Are you forgetting the army pistol the young lady so kindly brought me? Here, I will show you."

The report was loud in the canyon, and chips flew up from the rock that was partly shielding Tom. The pinto snorted and jumped several feet up the steep side of the draw. Tom dove low behind the scant cover and called, "All right! You have a gun. Let's talk."

LeBeau laughed again. "I did not think you were a man who liked to talk. You have killed my friend Oliver, and now I assume that you have also killed Martin. Otherwise, you would not be here. No, Barkley, you are a man who acts, not a man who talks. I am telling you now, leave at once, or I will kill you."

"No. I'm sworn to protect Amy Travis. I'm not leaving here without her."

"I will not hurt the young lady. I will merely return her to her father."

"I don't trust you."

"Ah, that is most unfortunate."

"Let's deal," said Tom.

"What could you have that I could possibly want?" asked the mocking voice.

"You've gotten separated from your horses."

"It is true. This little spitfire led me on a chase and tried to blow my brains out, as you say, but I have her now. I do not see that you have the horses."

"I can keep you from getting to them."

"And I can keep you from Miss Travis. So?"

Tom sat still, thinking. "I'll give you any horse you want and whatever food there is."

"How would this help my brother?"

"It wouldn't, but nothing will help your brother now. Either the major's hanged him or he's let him go."

"I think not," said LeBeau.

"You have communication with Fort Bridger?"

"In a sense. I gave the army corporal a sealed letter for the major before I left his camp. I did not divulge my purpose, but I told him to put this letter in Major Travis's hand, no other. In the letter, I told the major that if he wished to see his daughter alive again, he would release Raymond LeBeau."

"He won't do it."

"You don't think he will? Not immediately, perhaps, but neither will he hang him. When I return to Fort Bridger with proof that his daughter is in my custody, he will reconsider."

"What if Major Travis won't bargain with you?"

"Ah, *elle est belle*. I can find another use for her, I think. I shall not lose on this enterprise."

Tom clenched his fingers around the butt of his pistol, trying to control the rage that filled him. "You're going to need more help than your brother does. You've kidnapped a woman and killed a soldier."

LeBeau said nothing, and the silence lengthened.

"LeBeau?" Tom called. There was no answer. He poised again on the edge of the rock and jumped down, then ran to the thicket, pushing through the branches, stumbling over roots.

In the dusk, he saw the Frenchman moving slowly ahead of him, dragging Amy backward by her upper arms.

"Hold it!" Tom aimed his revolver at LeBeau.

LeBeau pulled Amy up and crouched with her in his arms, producing his own pistol.

"I think it is the standoff, monsieur."

Tom ducked back into the brush. He realized he was shaking. Blood was streaming down LeBeau's right cheek, congealing in his beard, and Amy appeared to be unconscious. "You've hurt her."

"No, no, monsieur. She is a wild little thing. She hurt herself—after she tried to kill me."

Tom swallowed, not sure what to believe, but he knew one thing. "I'm not letting you take her."

"Then we have nothing to say." LeBeau raised his pistol and fired. The ball whizzed past Tom's ear. He jumped back into the thicket and stood still, thinking.

He turned and crept up the slope as quietly as he could. Bit by bit, he worked his way up the side of the canyon toward the horse that was now near the top.

The pinto was wary. He'd worked hard all day and wouldn't like the acrid smell of gunpowder that clung to Tom's clothes. When Tom came close, the horse turned his hindquarters toward him and kept eating. Time after time, Tom tried to approach, but the horse was too crafty. At last Tom managed to chase him up the slope and onto the hillside.

Kip was grazing near where Tom had last seen him. Tom whistled, the way he had for Buck so many times, and Kip raised his head and looked at him, then ambled toward him. Tom was so thankful he could have cried.

When the gray reached him, Tom stroked his nose.

"All right, boy, we've got a little more work to do."

He climbed wearily into the saddle, wincing at the pain in his shoulder. He thought he could see the bay gelding far down the hill beyond where he had fought Martin.

The pinto first. He walked Kip slowly toward the animal, one step at a time. The pinto watched distrustfully. Tom edged the gray in, closer and closer, then made a desperate grab for the trailing reins. The pinto wheeled, kicked at Kip, and galloped down the hill.

Tom grimaced. "If that's the way you want it."

He would shoot the pinto before he would leave him for LeBeau. But first he'd go after the bay.

He trotted Kip down the hill, skirting the body of the man in buckskins. The bay let him approach, and Tom soon grasped his reins. He climbed down and took Kip's hobbles from the saddlebag, glad Amy hadn't discarded them with her blanket and dirty clothes. He fitted the straps around the bay's cannons and removed the bridle then took Amy's decorative saddle off Kip and stood it on its pommel. Throwing the trapper's saddle on Kip, he left the bay grazing contentedly.

The sun had disappeared, and he could not see the brown horse, but he remembered that it had moved away to the south earlier. Time to deal with the pinto.

As Kip jogged toward him, the spotted horse began to trot, too. As the gray gained ground on him, the pinto broke into a run. Tom clucked, and Kip tore after the smaller horse, flying over the prairie. The pinto dodged away, but Kip stuck to his tail and managed to ease up beside him again.

Patience, Tom told himself. He blocked LeBeau and Amy from his mind and concentrated on the crafty horse, trying to predict which way he would veer next.

At last Kip was running next to the animal, inching up until Tom was even with the pinto's head and could seize one rein. Tom slowed Kip gradually. The pinto pulled at the bit, lunging and squealing.

"Calm down," Tom said quietly. "You're making it hard on yourself. Settle down."

At last the pinto stood quivering, and Tom was able to reach over and claim the other rein. After that, the gelding trotted meekly behind Kip. Tom led him back to where the bay was hobbled. He got down and searched the packs from the trappers' two horses, holding the pinto's reins firmly all the time. Coffee, a frying pan, clothing, and lead. He was rewarded at last with a length of cotton rope and a picket pin.

He improvised a rope halter for the fractious pinto then took off the saddle and bridle and picketed the animal. If LeBeau made it up out of the steep ravine with Amy while Tom was looking for the brown horse, the Frenchman would find no bridles for the two grazing horses. Tom put them both in Kip's saddlebags.

The darkness deepened as he rode Kip swiftly around the base of the hill to the south, hoping to find the last of the trappers' three mounts.

Kip whinnied and was answered by a shrill neigh from the darkness ahead.

It was so easy, Tom would have laughed if his thoughts hadn't gravitated back to Amy. She'd been unconscious, he was sure. LeBeau must have struck her. Or perhaps she had fallen, as he'd said.

But Tom had all four horses. Maybe LeBeau would bargain now. If not, Tom would shoot two of the animals. He thought he would keep the bay; it seemed the most tractable. One way or another, he and Amy would be riding into Fort Laramie.

As he rode back to the other horses, he planned his next move. He had to get to Amy as quickly as possible, but he couldn't afford to let LeBeau get past him in the darkness and get to the mounts.

Quickly Tom dropped the brown's saddle with the others and tied the three extra horses together. Riding Kip, he led the animals toward the river and down over the bank. While they all drank, he chewed some jerky he'd found in the pinto's saddlebags.

He trotted the horses upstream half a mile. Around a bend, he found a strip of dry grass ten yards wide between the Platte and the high bank. Tom picketed the pinto there and hobbled the bay and LeBeau's brown gelding. It was the best he could do. Unless the Frenchman was already following him, it would take him awhile to locate the mounts, and their saddles were back near where Martin lay.

Tom was bone weary, and he knew Kip was, too, but the big horse obeyed him eagerly when he turned back toward the long hillside and Amy. She was out there somewhere.

Tom didn't let himself speculate about Amy's condition but prayed earnestly that God would protect her and comfort her and give him the wit and strength he would need to win her back from LeBeau.

Grimly, he headed Kip up the hill. He held a loaded musket in his hand, and a second was ready in the saddle scabbard. He had his revolver at his side and his knife in his boot top. Was it enough?

Chapter 13

Amy awakened in darkness. She hurt. She lay on her side, and as she tried to move, her head throbbed with pain. She couldn't move her hands. It left her feeling very stupid and ill. At last she realized her wrists and ankles were bound, and she trembled with cold and fear. The wind softly stirred the branches above her. Far in the distance, a wolf howled. Closer, she was sure she heard another sound that was not the wind but a regular breathing. When a snore came, she was certain. She began to pray in desperation.

Dear God, let Tom live! No matter what happens to me, let Tom survive!

She had fallen. She had fired the pistol, lost her balance, and tumbled from the ledge. That was all she could remember.

She wiggled her fingers, and the cord that held her hands behind her bit into her wrists. Tears came, unstoppable. She tried to cry silently, but a sob escaped her parched throat.

The Frenchman came and stood over her. She knew it was him. She could smell him, and in a rush she remembered his hands on her, dragging her from Kip's saddle.

"Mademoiselle is awake?"

She said nothing, but he reached down and grabbed her arm, pulling her to a sitting position. There was a bit of moonlight, and she could see a glimmer of lust in his eyes.

"You would be beautiful if you were cleaned up." He reached toward her face.

"Don't touch me," she whispered fiercely.

He laughed. "Still kicking? You must learn to be gentle. Ladies are meant to be amiable."

"Never," she hissed.

He shrugged. "Sometimes it is like the training of a horse, yes?" His hand grazed her cheek, and his fingers settled on her neck.

"You are a filthy murderer. I hate you."

His face darkened. He drew back his hand and struck her.

Amy gasped and cowered, trying not to sob aloud.

LeBeau was breathing heavily. "Sometimes it takes awhile," he said after a moment.

"Tom will kill you."

"Monsieur Barkley? I think not. He is dead, you see."

She felt a deep weight settle on her chest, crushing her.

LeBeau shrugged. "You must not blame me. My friend Martin had to defend himself."

"I don't believe you!"

"As you wish. I will take you at first light to see where he lies." He reached for his belt and began to unbuckle it.

Amy's heart pounded. "My father will hang you." It was a faint whisper.

He laughed. "No, no, he will thank me for bringing him his beautiful daughter. But I must be sure you stay with me until you have learned that I am not so bad. Pardon the indelicacy, but I must ask you to sit over here."

He pulled her to a small pine tree.

"There, sit upright, just so."

She wanted to scream as she watched him remove the belt. He knelt behind her and slid it around her waist. She felt him tug at the strap, and her spine jammed against the tree trunk.

"There, I think that is sufficient for now. Now that I have rested, I must leave you for a short while. I regret that I must close your mouth. You understand?"

She nodded slowly.

He pulled a sweaty rag that might have been a handkerchief from around his neck and rolled it into a strip. "Pardon. It is necessary while I go to fetch our transportation. You will be able to breathe, I promise."

She choked as he tied the cloth around her face.

"Sleep, *ma belle*. When I return, we shall have a long ride before us."

He walked away.

Amy sat still, her heart thumping. He had left her alone, after all. *Thank You, God! Thank You.*

She wriggled against the tree. The belt cut into her abdomen, but she thought she could stand it. She worked her wrists, trying to get hold of the cord that held them. If only she could reach the end, but the thong was tight. Her head throbbed on the left side, and her cheek stung where he had hit her. She leaned back against the tree trunk.

She could hear LeBeau's footsteps, cautious in the brush. He was going after horses, he'd said. Where was his friend?

Her head hurt, and she slumped against the tree trunk, her eyes closed. It came over her very slowly that her protector was gone.

Tom!

She cried bitterly but silently. The last thing she wanted was for LeBeau or his friend to hear her. She drew her knees up and muffled her face in the fold of the dirty skirt.

As the moon rose high above, she turned to God in her silent anguish. *You're all I have, Lord. Tom is gone, and I have only You to keep me safe. Please do not fail in Your promise.* Her own thoughts startled her, and her tears flowed freely. *Lord, I've counted on Tom's strength more than on Yours! I've been very foolish. Forgive me. Whatever You have planned for me, I'm ready.*

She sat quietly, recognizing God's peace and feeling calm. Her cheek stung. The foul-tasting cloth chafed and hindered her breathing. She rubbed her face against her shoulder, trying to dislodge it, but it was tied too tightly.

Suddenly she sat very still.

I must close your mouth. It is necessary. Why was it necessary? If Tom were dead, who would hear her scream?

A bounding hope lifted her heart. Exhausted as she was, she renewed her struggles.

Longing for daylight, Tom trotted Kip up the hill. He rode along the edge of the scraggly pines, hoping LeBeau had brought Amy up from the deep ravine, but he found no sign of them. After scouting all along the hillside to the edge of the defile, he dismounted and let the reins fall. He wasn't sure how deep Kip's training went, but he knew the big gelding wouldn't stray far. He hated to think LeBeau might take possession of the noble horse and reluctantly left Kip grazing.

Tom went to the place where he had made the descent earlier. There was no campfire to guide him, no sound but the wind. Slowly, he worked his way down to the ledge he had sat on when parlaying with LeBeau.

She can't be far, he thought. He wanted to call her name but couldn't risk revealing his location to LeBeau. *Lord, let me find her alive!*

He jumped down from the ledge and ran toward the thick brush, pushing the branches aside.

Here was the place he had seen LeBeau dragging her. He listened for any telltale sound, but the wind in the pines mocked him. He crept along silent as a cat, growing more desperate. If LeBeau had taken her away and was tracking the horses, he might be throwing away his only chance to rescue Amy. He went on, lifting low branches and peering into the shadows.

He came to the place where LeBeau had fired from the thicket and went forward one muffled step at a time toward the last place he had seen his adversary. It was too dark to look for footprints.

"Amy!" he called in desperation. He heard no answer.

For an hour, he crept about in the ravine. He thrashed through every thicket and scrambled up and down the slopes until he was sure Amy was no longer in the small canyon.

At last he sat down. Pain seared through his shoulder, and it was hard to think. But he was close to where he'd last seen Amy, and he didn't want to leave the place.

He lowered his head into his hands. *Lord, help me. What do I do? This is beyond me.*

If I were LeBeau, I'd be out there looking for my horse, he decided. No matter what happened tonight, if the Frenchman lived, he would need a mount. But Tom hated to give up his search for Amy.

He decided to go a little farther, toward the gap at the east end of the ravine where he could hear the trickle of a brook. If he didn't find anything there, he would turn back.

The moon was high, what there was of it, but it was very dark in the bottom of the draw. He went slowly, until a faint rustle ahead stopped him.

"Amy?"

A low moan, more desperate than the wind, made him rush forward, still wary.

Suddenly he saw her. She thrashed her feet helplessly. He ran to where she sat against a small tree. Her huge eyes stared at him from above a strip of cloth that was tied around her head, through her mouth.

"Amy, precious Amy!" He fumbled at the strip of cloth that gagged her. Unable to loosen the knot, he pulled his knife from his boot.

"Hold still."

He sliced through the cloth and pulled it from her face. Amy gasped and stared up at him, tears in her eyes.

"Tom!" Her mouth shaped the word soundlessly.

"Where's LeBeau?"

"He went to look for the horses."

Tom could barely hear her. He decided he could risk a light if LeBeau was not close by. He took a match from his pouch and tipped her chin upward before striking the light. A welt swelled below her right eye. Her face was filthy, and a bruise spread along her left cheek from the temple toward the eye and down in front of her ear.

"What hurts?" he asked.

"Everything. I can't. . .breathe."

He looked behind her, then blew out the match. LeBeau had cut Layton's gun belt into strips and tied Amy's ankles with thongs. Her hands were secured behind her, and a stout brown belt tightly circled her waist and the tree trunk. In the darkness, he felt for the end of the belt and pulled it. She gasped as it tightened; then he released her, and she fell forward against him with a groan. He caught her and held her in his arms, shaking, his breath as ragged as hers.

"Amy, hold on. You're going to be all right."

"Tom."

"Yes, sweetheart."

"He told me. . . ." She gulped air and swallowed.

"Let me get you loose."

"My feet are numb."

He sliced the thongs on her wrists, and she brought her hands around to the front with a groan and rubbed her wrists.

"Are you bleeding?"

"I don't think so."

He checked her wrists, feeling the deep creases where the leather had been. She had struggled against them, and that knowledge strengthened the love and sorrow in his heart.

He slid the tip of his knife beneath the leather that bound her ankles.

"Where are your boots?"

She looked to her right. "Over there, I think. He took them away in case I got loose." Her voice was still a croak.

Tom rubbed her ankles without self-consciousness.

"Can you feel that?"

She shook her head. "Oh! Yes! Now I can." She caught her breath. "My feet are prickly."

"I'm sorry. Just relax. The blood's flowing again. It will stop hurting in a minute."

She nodded and bit her bottom lip.

When the agonizing stabs of pain began to fade, Amy reached down and took over the rubbing. *What would Elaine say?* she wondered. *A man rubbing my feet. That could cause a scandal in Albany.*

Tom got up and searched the brush, returning soon with her boots and hat and the buckle and holster from the gun belt.

"I'm so sorry," she whispered. "I ought to have shot him when he first rode up to me, but I panicked. I forgot I even had the pistol until I'd run partway down here."

He dropped beside her on the ground and took her in his arms.

"It doesn't matter. You're all right now." He pulled her head down on his shoulder and stroked her hair.

She clung to him, letting her hands slide up to his shoulders and around his neck. She never wanted to let go of him again.

Suddenly her fingers felt a stiff, ragged place on his shirt behind his left shoulder, and she felt him flinch. She sat back quickly.

"Tom?"

"It's nothing."

"Let me see."

She clambered to her knees, and he turned slightly. His shirt was caked with dried blood on the left side. She probed gently with one finger where the hole was, and he winced.

"They shot you. I thought you jumped off the horse on purpose."

"No. I was thinking about it, but then I got hit. I'm sorry, Amy."

"Sorry? What for?" She burst into tears, wishing she could control it, but she couldn't.

He held her close again, and she felt him kiss the top of her head.

"Tommy," she gasped.

"Shh."

"No, no. He told me—he told me you were dead."

"Oh, honey, I'm so sorry. He's a liar."

Her breath came in short, jagged gulps. "He said Martin shot you and was watching the horses. They were taking me back to Fort Bridger."

"It was the other way around," Tom said. "I killed Martin. I came down here and tried to talk to LeBeau, but he wouldn't let me near you. I got hold of all the horses then came back to look for you."

Amy made herself take deeper breaths and pulled away from him so she could see his face in the moonlight. His eyes were full of sorrow. She put her hand to his cheek. "I tried not to believe him. He told me that in the morning he would take me to see where you were lying dead. He was smiling."

Tom sighed and tightened his embrace. They sat like that for a long moment.

"We need to get up out of this hole," Tom whispered when she stopped sobbing. "Do you think you can put your boots on?"

She pulled them on gingerly over her sore ankles, then stood up with his support.

"Did you have anything to eat last night?" he asked.

"No."

Tom smiled. "You're going to be so happy. We've got coffee now and bacon. I can even make you some pancakes if the coyotes haven't found the stuff yet."

"We need to get to Fort Laramie," she protested.

"Aren't you hungry?"

She considered. "I think I'm starving."

"I think you are, too. As soon as we find out where LeBeau got to, we're having a hot breakfast. Come on."

Slowly, they inched up the steep wall of the ravine. Tom hauled her up by the hand, one step at a time, stopping three times to let her rest.

"I can't make it," she panted at the third stop.

"Yes, you can. I'll carry you if I have to."

She started to protest but checked herself. Maybe he really could do that. He'd already done the impossible.

She lay against the slope, holding his hand and gathering strength. Pain sliced through her temples every time she moved her head, and her ankles throbbed.

"Let's pray," she whispered.

Tom squeezed her hand and bowed his head. "Lord, thank You for preserving us and bringing us back together. We need some energy now. Please help us to complete our task. I believe You want us to get to Fort Laramie. Please help us do that. Amen."

She gathered up the remnants of her determination. "All right. Let's try again."

When they gained the crest at last, she stumbled forward into the light of the open hillside, and Tom held her up.

"There's Kip," she breathed. "Good old Kip."

"Watch this." Tom gave a whistle, and the gray came trotting, swinging his head with a whicker.

"You clever horse!" Amy stroked his soft nose as he sniffed at her.

Tom stroked the gelding's flank. "He's sweaty!"

Amy reached out in surprise and felt Kip's hot, wet side.

"How long has he been here?"

"I left him at least two hours ago."

"Do you think something's been chasing him? I heard wolves earlier."

"I heard them, too, but they weren't close. And Kip seems calm now. I'm thinking LeBeau tried to get him."

Amy ran her hand along Kip's neck, under the black mane. "Then Kip outran him and came back here to wait for us."

Tom took the canteen from the saddle and opened it for her. She tipped it up and took a mouthful of water then stood for a moment tasting it, feeling the cool wetness in her mouth and down her throat. She took another sip.

Tom picked her up and put her gently in the saddle then walked beside the gray, leading him down the hill toward where he had left the gear.

⌒

"LeBeau's been here."

Even in the half-light, a quick survey showed Tom that the saddlebags had been plundered and most of their contents strewn on the ground. He had left no weapons, ammunition, or bridles. He was certain now that LeBeau had tried to catch Kip. If he had succeeded, he would have been well armed and mounted once more. He had Layton's pistol, though. As far as Tom knew, only three of the six chambers had been fired.

He looked up at Amy and weighed their options. It wouldn't be long until sunrise. Her safety was, as always, his first priority.

"I want you to take Kip and head for Fort Laramie."

"No."

"Look, LeBeau is ahead of us. He couldn't catch Kip, but he's probably tracking down the other horses."

"I'm not leaving you, Tom."

He sighed. He recognized that stubborn note and knew he'd be wasting time if he argued with her.

"Stay here with Kip then. And stay mounted. If LeBeau shows up, you skedaddle." She said nothing, and he stared up at her in exasperation. "Amy?"

"All right." Her grudging agreement made him smile.

"Good. LeBeau doesn't have a bridle, and the three saddles are all here, including yours. So if he does manage to come back here with a horse, looking for the tack, you should be able to outrun him." He pulled his pistol from the holster and held it up to her, butt first. "Just in case."

She shook her head. "I let him get the other one from me. You'd better keep it."

"All right, but you've still got the rifle in the scabbard. Now, promise me you'll get out of here if he shows his face."

She hesitated only an instant this time. "I will. Can I switch the saddles?"

"Better wait. I don't want to take a chance on him surprising you while you're on the ground, and if I take time to do it now, I might lose him."

She nodded. "Be careful, Tom."

He holstered the pistol and reached up to squeeze her hand then turned and ran toward the river, carrying the second musket. He stayed away from the bank, running hard upstream. Banking on LeBeau's moving slowly to track the horses in the scant moonlight, he hurried beyond the watering place, running as fast as he could. His pounding footsteps seemed loud as thunder, but he trusted the flowing river to hide the sound from his enemy.

He swerved toward the bank when he judged he was near the place where he had left the three trappers' horses and peered cautiously over the edge. The pinto was picketed almost directly beneath him. The two hobbled horses had worked their way a few yards upstream but were grazing peacefully. There was no sign of LeBeau. Maybe he was wrong. Tom thought quickly over what he had seen at the pile of gear and concluded again that LeBeau was headed here.

He slid down the steep, six-foot slope, holding the musket pointed skyward. The pinto snorted and lurched away from him, to the end of his tether. The other two horses turned to look at him, still chewing.

Tom flattened himself against the bank and waited. A few minutes later, LeBeau rounded a bend and came toward him, the sound of his steps lost in the river's purling. Tom waited until the man was close to the pinto and had drawn his knife to cut the picket line.

"Hold it right there, LeBeau."

The Frenchman stiffened then shrugged.

"You cannot blame me for trying, monsieur."

"Drop the knife."

The blade fell to the turf near the picket pin.

"Put your hands up."

LeBeau obeyed, moving with stiff slowness. "Let us be reasonable, my friend."

"And what would you call reasonable?"

"I will tell you where the young lady is."

Tom bit back his reply. If he let slip that he had found Amy and she was within easy reach, his enemy would surely try to overpower him.

"In exchange for one horse," LeBeau added. "You can go get her while I make my way west."

"You'd call that a fair exchange?"

"A generous one. It is to your advantage to find her quickly, you see. Without immediate care, I cannot guarantee she will survive her wounds."

"Her wounds?"

LeBeau spread his hands. "What can I say? She was not cooperative." He took a step toward Tom.

"Don't come any closer."

"You are her personal guard, is it not so? You have a promise to keep. She needs you." He took another step.

"Hold it, or I'll drop you right there," Tom growled.

"No, you will not."

"I will." Tom swallowed. He was tempted to just shoot the man and be done with it. He didn't relish the thought of escorting LeBeau all the way to Fort Laramie. No one would know if he executed him here and now and saved the army the trouble.

He thrust the thought out of his mind and concentrated on the immediate danger. LeBeau must still have Layton's pistol. Tom had to disarm him. As long as he was free and had a weapon, LeBeau would try to make Amy his prisoner again. Tom was determined not to let Amy spend another minute under LeBeau's control, no matter what the cost.

He brandished the musket. "Lie down, LeBeau."

"Monsieur?" The Frenchman's eyebrows arched in shock. "What is this?"

"Do you think I'm an idiot? Lie down now."

LeBeau stared at him for a moment then slowly lowered his hands, leaning forward. Tom's trigger finger twitched. He expected the man to make a move.

Don't wait, he told himself. *That's what Amy did. She waited too long. He'll shoot you and take her away.*

LeBeau doesn't know Amy has been found, Tom reminded himself. He would play his last card to get the horses then go back for his hostage. He would find her near the saddles, and he would not give her up again. The thought sickened Tom and made his heart race.

LeBeau whistled suddenly, and behind Tom the horses moved restlessly. "Get down!" Tom shouted.

He was startled as the brown gelding inched up even with him, snuffling. The horse was out of his reach, several paces toward the river but only twenty yards from LeBeau. Even though the brown was hobbled, he was slowly moving toward his master.

It's now or never, Tom thought. *If I don't do something, his horse will get to him.* Even as his gaze wavered between the Frenchman and the gelding, LeBeau's hand went behind him.

Chapter 14

Amy waited, shivering, on Kip's back. As the minutes stretched toward daybreak, she struggled to conquer her dread.

Lord, she prayed, *I know You can help us. Forgive me for trusting Tom more than I trusted You. And if there's anything I can do to help him now, please show me.*

Her bruised cheek throbbed as she brushed a tear away.

Kip tugged at the reins, and she thought he wanted to graze, but when she slackened her hold, he began walking toward the river.

"All right, boy," Amy whispered. "I'm with you. You know where they are." She glanced up toward the velvet sky. *Lord, I told him we'd run if LeBeau came, but even Kip doesn't want to stay here alone. Please, help me not to do anything stupid.*

The gray lengthened his stride and ran swiftly up the riverbank, not checking until they were above where the Frenchman stood, facing Tom. LeBeau's back was to Amy, and in the first ray of dawn, she caught the gleam of gunmetal where the pistol was tucked in the back of his waistband. In an instant, she took in Tom's wary stance, his musket pointed at LeBeau's chest, and with horror she saw that the brown horse was working his way toward LeBeau. In another moment, he would shield the trapper from Tom.

◈

As Tom made his choice, he heard drumming hoofbeats above him, and he saw LeBeau whip the pistol from behind his back. The Frenchman leveled the Colt, and in the instant when Tom would have squeezed the trigger of his musket, a huge body flew off the bank above. As Kip slammed into LeBeau, the pistol discharged in the air. The horses squealed and scattered, and LeBeau sprawled on the ground.

Kip landed hard in the soft earth by the water and stumbled into the shallows. Amy looked tiny on the big gray's back, and she fell heavily forward on impact, flying up toward Kip's ears. She clung tenaciously to the gray's neck, struggling to regain her balance and push herself back into the saddle.

Tom forced his attention back to LeBeau. The leaping horse had knocked him down, but he had rolled with the impact and was crouching, breathing hard and cocking the revolver. He was aiming not at Tom but at Amy.

Tom drew a quick bead on LeBeau's chest, steady and accurate, and the musket roared. LeBeau stood stock still for an instant, seeming undecided whether to fall or not. Then he tumbled back and lay still.

Tom put one shaking hand to his face and swallowed hard.

The pinto crow-hopped nervously, but the picket rope held him. Kip floundered out of the water and stood trembling, with Amy, wide-eyed, staring down from his back at Tom. The brown horse edged away from Kip and put his head down to crop the grass. He was calm now, eating without concern for his former owner.

Tom laid down his musket and walked slowly toward LeBeau, pulling his revolver.

The Frenchman's eyes were open, staring sightlessly at the sky. Tom kicked his boot gently. He stooped and retrieved Layton's pistol, tucking it in his belt, then let the hammer of his own gun down carefully and holstered it.

He turned toward Amy. She held her arms out toward him, and he stepped to Kip's side and lifted her from the saddle.

She took a deep breath, her lips quivering. "I'm sorry, Tom. I couldn't stand being alone, not knowing, and Kip wanted to come, too."

He pulled her close and stroked her shimmering hair. She was shivering. He wanted to scold her, to let loose all the things his father would have yelled at him. *You could have broken your neck. You could have been shot. You might have gotten us both killed.*

He couldn't say any of those things. "Shh. It's all right. Things might have gone differently if you hadn't come. I wasn't thinking very clearly."

He felt her small hands slip around him, and he let himself hold her a few more seconds before ruefully pushing her away. "Come on. Let's see if Kip is all right."

Her eyes widened then, vivid blue in the early light. She turned quickly to the horse, anxiously running her hands along his forelegs, her delicate fingers probing gently.

"Poor Kip," she crooned.

Tom took the reins and urged the gray to walk slowly down the grassy strip. "Is he limping?"

"No, he's fine. But, Tom, everything my father ever said about me is true. I'm reckless and foolhardy. I promised him I'd keep Kip safe, but when I thought LeBeau was going to kill you, I forgot all that!"

Tom looked down at his dusty boots. "I made a promise to the major, too."

Pain flooded her face. "What do we do now?"

"Can you tie the horses together? I'll take care of LeBeau."

He carried the body away from the water and forced himself to go through LeBeau's pockets. He found only a few coins and a folding knife. Around the man's neck was a cord that held half a dozen bear claws and a crucifix. He thought fleetingly of salvaging it for LeBeau's brother. But if justice were served,

Raymond LeBeau would be hanged for horse stealing. To whom would the major send his personal effects? Tom left the necklace.

When he straightened, Amy stood a few feet away, holding Kip's reins and the end of the picket rope. Tom took the rope from her. "You take Kip up the bank, and I'll bring the other horses."

A buzzard rose as they approached the pile of saddles and gear. It flapped south toward the hills. Amy gasped.

Tom said grimly, "I'm sorry. I ought to bury Martin and LeBeau before we leave."

She closed her eyes then opened them again. "We don't have a shovel, and we can't afford to stop that long."

Tom mulled over her words for a moment then nodded. "I'm really sorry. I shouldn't have left him here. All I could think about was finding you."

She dismounted and dropped Kip's reins, coming close to touch her fingers to his cheek. "I'm glad you did. For a while I was hopeful, but then I gave up. I thought I heard your voice in the night, and I told myself it was just the wind. When I saw you, I still couldn't believe it was you. I thought I was going crazy."

He swallowed hard. "Sit down over there, Amy. I'll fix you something to eat. No arguments."

He quickly gathered fuel for a fire and picked up a tinderbox from the scattered stuff on the ground. The pain in his shoulder stabbed deep, and he hoped the bleeding wouldn't start again. In a few minutes, he had a small blaze going and had put some bacon in a pan over the flames. Amy watched as he brought the dented little coffeepot over and poured water from one of the outlaws' canteens into it.

"I can make the coffee."

"All right." He looked hard at her and decided she was over the shock. "I've got to do a few things."

She nodded.

He walked slowly toward where Martin lay. He hated to leave the bodies exposed, but Amy was right; they had little choice. Without digging tools, he couldn't bury them deep enough to keep the wolves from unearthing them.

He braced himself and stared down at Martin's ghastly corpse, then turned quickly away. He'd tell the colonel where the bodies were, but he doubted there would be anything left when the colonel's men arrived.

He walked slowly back to where Amy sat. She threw worried glances toward him as he approached.

"I found the flour and baking powder. I'm making griddle cakes."

Tom nodded, not sure he could eat any. He sat down on the grass a few feet from her.

"Tom. . ." She pressed her lips together and poured batter into the frying pan.

He sat without speaking until she brought him two griddle cakes and a slab of bacon on a tin plate, along with a cup of steaming coffee.

"Thanks. I ought to be waiting on you."

"Tom, you did what you had to, and I'm very thankful."

Her eyes were sober. When he looked at her bruised face, he was still angry.

"If I just could have gotten to you sooner," he began.

She shook her head. "I'll be fine, Tom. You had to deal with other things. It's over now."

He set the plate down and held out his arms. She came to him, and he squeezed her, just tight enough to assure himself she was real and she was safe. Tears trickled down his face.

"Amy, I'm sorry I wasn't there when he hurt you."

"You keep saying that, but you've got to stop. We don't need to think about last night."

"I can't help thinking about it. I felt so helpless while you were with him."

She was silent, but her hands softly rubbed his back.

He remembered her hasty declaration of love before he'd fallen from Kip's back the day before. Did she really love him, even now? He had bungled her rescue badly, allowing the loathsome LeBeau to detain her for several hours. He ought to have been able to avoid that somehow. He ought to have immediately faced down the Frenchman, not let him drag her through the woods and inflict untold misery on her.

"He hit you, didn't he?"

She took two deep breaths before she answered. "Let's not tell Father about this, Tom."

He leaned back to look at her. "I have to report to the major, Amy. We can't just pretend none of this happened."

She sighed. "All right, but please, Tom, don't tell him that. . . " She buried her face in his shoulder, and he held her, shuddering. It was worse than he'd thought.

"I knew I shouldn't have waited," he choked.

She touched his cheek and wiped away a tear.

"The filthy swine—"

"Stop it." She was stern, and he held his tongue.

"Eat," he said at last, picking up the plate and holding it out to her.

"That's for you."

"I'm not hungry."

"Yes, you are."

"No." He glanced involuntarily toward the place where he'd left the outlaw's body. "I really don't think I can."

A frown came over Amy's face. "The first chance I get to cook for you, and you won't eat."

He shook his head, unable to keep from smiling. "All right, but you've got to eat, too."

She went back to the fire and dribbled more batter into the frying pan.

Tom picked up a pancake and bit into it, forcing himself not to think about Martin's face. "This is good." He picked up the cooling cup of coffee and took a swallow.

"Which horse do I ride?" Amy asked.

"Kip, of course, unless you want to give him a rest. But he's recovered, I think."

She smiled. "And which one are you taking?"

"The bay. If you want, we can turn the others loose."

"Don't be silly. We need to take them all back to Fort Laramie. You ought to be able to have them. You need to replace Buck and. . ." She faltered. "I mean, you saved my life."

He laughed shortly. "Well, you saved mine, too."

He got up to saddle the horses. Amy brought him the saddlebags, and he tied the rope between the pinto and the brown gelding so he could lead them both.

"All set?"

"I found this," Amy said hesitantly. She held up a dusty hat. "You lost yours, and you really need one."

He stared at it for a moment then reached out and took it. Slowly, he settled it on his head.

"Let's go." He put his foot in the stirrup of the bay's saddle.

Amy felt a little uncertain, let down somehow. Things had changed. Tom's tenderness was gone. It was more like the first night they'd ridden together from Fort Bridger, when he had let her do everything for herself and kept his distance. For an instant, she wished they were both riding Kip again, with Tom sitting behind her with his arms around her.

They picked their way up the long hill and over the crest. The terrain was rugged, and in a narrow spot, he held back and let her go first. Amy couldn't see him then, but she thought he was brooding, dreading the moment when he would tell her father all that had happened. He had held her in his arms that morning, giving her immense comfort, but apparently it wasn't enough for him.

Perhaps he thought the major would be angry because of her close call. He was probably thinking about Layton and Brown as well. He'd lost two men and almost forfeited her life and his own. She knew Tom felt he hadn't come off very well and that he wouldn't try to make himself look good. She wanted to make him see somehow that he had no cause for guilt.

If Tom could understand how lonely and forsaken she had felt in the darkness of the night when LeBeau told her so blithely that he was dead! She wanted him to know the palpable, bubbling joy she'd experienced when he had come to release her. God had answered her prayer in a way she hadn't thought possible. Her bitter grief had been banished in an instant. She could deal with the rest: the pain, the terror, the hopelessness. She would not forget, but she would heal.

She was not so sure about Tom. He was quiet and had distanced himself from her, physically and emotionally. He had said nothing of love, only of guilt and sorrow.

When they got to the fort, he would probably be glad to have his troublesome charge off his hands. It was a bleak prospect for Amy.

Chapter 15

For two hours they rode in silence, letting the horses pick the easiest path over the hills; then they moved back toward the Platte. They came to the last ford, where a ferry was tied. The wagon road came up out of the river and climbed the bluffs on the south bank, running high above the water toward Fort Laramie. Despite the pain in his shoulder, Tom felt a surge of relief. They were really going to make it.

Amy jumped down and let Kip wade into the water, holding his reins as he drank. Tom brought the other three horses to the water's edge and sloshed into the water, trying to hold them all steady. The pinto pulled at the rope, and it sent a sharp pain through his shoulder.

"We're nearly there," said Amy.

"Twenty miles."

"Should we let them rest?"

"For a few minutes."

When the horses finished drinking, he led them away from the river's edge. He dropped the bay's reins and let him graze near Kip, but he didn't trust the other two, particularly the pinto. He held the lead rope and stood near them, taking a step or two when they moved to new grass. Amy stayed near Kip, a few yards away.

Tom's eyes kept straying to where she stood, small and forlorn. He thought about moving nearer to her so they could talk, but it seemed too much trouble. He was tired, very tired, and his shoulder ached. His head ached, too. He sat down and drew his knees up, leaning his head on them. When the rope stretched taut, he yanked it with his right hand, but the pinto kept tugging insistently. He got slowly to his feet and moved a few paces.

Finally he decided they had stopped long enough and pulled the two horses toward Amy.

"Best go on," he said.

She nodded and pulled Kip's head up.

She was crying, the tears flowing unrestrained down her cheeks.

He turned and put his arms over the pinto's saddle and leaned on the horse. He ought to be able to keep her from crying. It cut deep that he had won her back from the Frenchman and she was still weeping. His fists clenched. Why had he hesitated to shoot LeBeau? He ought to have dropped him the second he appeared.

106

"Tom."

He turned to face Amy. She had come softly and stood beside him now.

"Are you all right?" she asked, her brow furrowed.

She had not wiped the tears away. He wondered if she knew she was crying. The feelings inside him roiled. He looked away toward the river and took a deep breath.

"I'll be fine."

"Maybe we should do something to that wound."

He shook his head. "Nothing but dirty water here. Maybe I'll have the surgeon look at it when we get to the fort."

"You'd better."

He took another breath.

"Tom, are you all right?"

"I just told you—"

"It's more than the wound, isn't it?"

He tried to avoid her tender gaze, but his eyes were drawn back to her. "Amy, I never killed a man before. Until yesterday, I mean."

She nodded, her blue eyes solemn.

"That first one," he said, "the big man...Oliver. He was so far away, it didn't seem so bad. But Martin..." He swallowed.

Amy's touch was delicate on his sleeve. "You had to, Tom. It was him or you. I know that. God knows, too."

He turned away. He had seen men shot before, had seen them die. But the horror of seeing the man's face when the bullet struck was still vivid.

"I know I had to, but it was so..." He let his thoughts trail off. "And LeBeau this morning." He shook his head. "He saw I was weak. I almost couldn't pull the trigger. Even though I knew he was a cold-blooded murderer—Amy, he was going to kill me, and I still didn't want to do it."

"You think that's bad? Tom, it's a serious thing to take a life."

"But I knew what he was. I'd seen what he did to you, and I still couldn't shoot him until he went after you again."

"Tom." She pulled him around gently to face her. "You didn't fail. When the moment came, you didn't fail. If he'd drawn on you, you would have fired, just like with the others. Call it duty or self-defense or whatever you like."

He sighed, and she reached tentatively toward his face. He wasn't sure he wanted her to touch him. He felt unworthy. He might have kept her alive, but he had still failed the test. He hadn't kept her safe. That was part of the major's commission. Alive and safe were two different things.

"Tom, you're burning up!"

His eyes were dull, and he seemed to have trouble focusing on her. Amy pressed her hand to his forehead, below the hat brim.

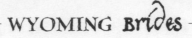
"You have a fever."

"I'm all right."

"No, you're not."

She opened a saddlebag and came up with a dirty piece of cloth. She walked rapidly to the brink of the stream and dipped the cloth in it.

"Here, take your hat off."

He looked at her apathetically. She pulled the hat from his head and sponged his brow with the rag.

"Come on. We need to get you to the fort."

She almost pushed him up onto the bay's back, and she took the lead rope herself.

"Can you sit a trot?"

"Of course I can."

She smiled grimly. He was well enough to let his pride flare up.

"Hang on. If you fall off that horse, I won't be able to get you back on him."

"I told you, I'm all right."

She was torn between making the horses walk gently to spare him pain and getting him to the fort as fast as possible.

They trotted on at a good pace for half an hour. The pinto repeatedly sidled up to Kip and nipped at his flanks. When he nuzzled at Amy's leg and bared his teeth, she slapped him hard on the nose.

"Get out of here, you mangy crow bait!" She wished Tom had tied him on the other side of the brown.

Up ahead, she saw a small tuft of dust. She pulled Kip to a halt, and Tom's horse stopped beside them.

"What is it?" he asked.

"Someone's ahead of us."

Tom stood in his stirrups, staring down the trail. "Going toward the fort."

"Yes."

"Come on." He urged the bay forward, and she followed, pulling the stubborn pinto and the brown horse along.

Tom's bay began to canter, and Amy struggled to keep the three horses under control.

She heard a whoop from Tom, but the dust was flying. She couldn't see the cause of his animation until Kip was nearly on the bay's tail.

Tom leaped to the ground beside a chestnut horse.

"Well, T.R., what do you know!" the man leading the horse cried.

"Private Brown!" Amy wrapped the lead rope around the saddle horn and slid to the ground.

"Well, Miss Travis! You look a bit worse for wear. What happened?"

She laughed. "Private Brown, you're a sight for sore eyes. Tom's been shot, and I've been doing my best to get him to the post surgeon at Laramie."

"Shot?" Brown turned to Tom in surprise. "Can't be too bad."

"Got a piece of lead in my shoulder." Tom shrugged.

"You make it sound like nothing," Amy scolded.

Brown looked at her keenly. "What happened to the riders?"

"Dead," said Tom.

Brown nodded. "Good for you. I thought sure they had you two."

"Your horse is lame," Amy observed. Lady was holding one hind foot off the ground.

"Yes, she threw a shoe on the other side of the Platte. I've been walking all morning."

Tom laughed. "Pick a horse from Amy's string."

Brown grinned. "Sounds good to me." He turned and surveyed the horses, then looked quickly at Tom. "Where's old Buck?"

"Shot out from under me," Tom said glumly.

"Too bad." Brown eyed the pinto speculatively. "How does that spotted horse handle?"

Tom grimaced. "He's pretty and he's fast, but he's got no manners."

"I knew a girl like that once," Brown said thoughtfully.

Tom chuckled, and Amy blushed.

"Guess I'll give him a tryout." The trooper untied the lead rope.

Amy watched Tom anxiously as he put his foot in the stirrup. He started to mount, then settled back on the ground. She took a step toward him, but he was trying again, and this time he heaved himself into the saddle.

She said nothing and mounted Kip. Brown insisted on leading Lady and the dark brown gelding, and they proceeded at a walk to accommodate the mare.

"How did you get away from the riders?" Amy asked. "We saw them chase you across the ford there by Independence Rock."

"Yes, it went just the way I planned it, except they were closer than I liked. I think it wasn't long before they realized you weren't ahead of me. Maybe it was the tracks or just the fact that there wasn't enough dust flying; I don't know. Anyway, Lady gave it her best, and we started to lengthen our lead. After ten miles or so, she was about winded, and I realized all of a sudden that they weren't back there anymore."

"What did you do?" Amy glanced at Tom. He was slouched in the saddle, and she wondered how alert he was.

"Well, I had to let Lady rest awhile. I thought about backtracking and following them, but I figured at the next ford I'd cross the river again, and we could meet up. Except when I crossed, I couldn't tell if you'd passed already; then it commenced to rain. Say, did you two get wet that night?"

"Did we ever!" Amy cried. "The lightning drove Kip wild."

"We holed up in old Jim Frye's cabin," Tom said. "You know the place?"

"I heard there was a house along there someplace, but I never saw it. Too bad I couldn't have found you."

Amy laughed. "I don't think another horse could have fit in that cabin."

"You took the horses inside?" Brown laughed.

"Made it nice and cozy," said Tom.

Brown sighed with envy. "That was the most miserable night I've ever spent. Lady and I snuggled down in a dip and liked to have froze."

As they went on, Amy kept an anxious eye on Tom.

"So, Miss Travis, you took a tumble?" Brown was looking at her face, and Amy realized she must be quite a sight.

"Yes, I—I fell from a rock, then. . ." She stopped and glanced toward Tom, but he was silent, his eyes nearly closed.

Brown said quietly, "I hope you weren't too badly hurt."

"No, it's nothing, really."

Brown nodded.

They went on in silence until Tom slumped low in his saddle.

Amy pushed Kip up beside the bay. "Tom, are you all right? Hold on!"

"Here, Miss Travis, take this."

Brown was beside her, handing her the lead rope. He maneuvered the pinto to Tom's other side and grasped his arm.

"You're going to make it, T.R. Just look up ahead, fella. I can see the top of the west watchtower."

Tom stirred. "Hurts bad, Mike."

"I know. Come on, now, nice and easy." Brown leaned over and took the reins gently from Tom's hand.

Amy dropped back a bit and followed with the lead line, renewing her prayers. Brown kept one hand on Tom's shoulder. They passed the large Sioux village outside the fort complex and approached the gate. Brown hailed the first soldier he saw.

"Tell Colonel Munroe we have urgent news from Fort Bridger, and ask for the surgeon!"

They went on, past the trading post, blacksmith shop, and barracks, toward the commander's quarters.

"T.R.?" A young trooper detached himself from a cluster of men and came quickly toward them.

"You're Matthew," Brown said.

"Yes, I'm his brother. What happened?" The young man looked from Brown to Amy and back to the inert Tom.

"He got shot yesterday. Help me get him to the surgeon." Brown leaned toward Tom. "Come on, fella. We're here."

Tom opened one eye.

"Just lean on me, and we'll help you down. Got to get you to the doc."

"You're not going to carry me in," Tom protested weakly, then slid over the side to the ground in a heap.

Brown looked at Matt Barkley.

"Sorry, son. At least we got him here." He dismounted, handing his reins to one of the troopers who had gathered.

A corporal bustling with importance approached him. "Private, you're in from Fort Bridger?"

"Yes, I'm Michael Brown. This man is T.R. Barkley, and we have dispatches for Colonel Munroe." He gestured toward Amy. "The young lady is Major Travis's daughter. Could someone offer her hospitality?"

"Of course."

Amy sat on Kip's back with the activity swirling around her. Matt called to two of his friends, and they carried Tom toward the surgeon's office. Brown gave instructions for Lady to be taken to the blacksmith and for the other horses to be fed and turned out.

"I'll take you to Colonel Munroe now," the corporal told him.

"May I take your horse, ma'am?" a freckle-faced young private asked.

"Thank you." Amy climbed down wearily, staggering as she hit the ground.

The corporal said uncertainly, "If you'd like to wait, miss, I can send someone to take you to one of the officers' wives."

Brown roared, "This young lady has come from Fort Bridger in four days and is exhausted. What's more, she needs medical attention. You will not leave her standing on the parade ground."

The corporal trembled, and Amy thought he almost croaked, "Yes, sir!" before he remembered Brown was only a private. He looked sheepishly at Amy. "Would you come this way, miss?"

She followed him and Brown wearily, wishing she had followed Tom instead. Within minutes, Brown was explaining their mission to the colonel and delivering Major Travis's dispatches.

"The scout Barkley believes the situation is urgent, sir."

"Hm, yes." Munroe scanned the papers Brown had handed him. "We sent a small detachment out a few days ago."

"We met them on the Sweetwater Tuesday evening," Brown said quickly. "Seven troopers and a few civilians. We believe three trappers learned Miss Travis was with us and left their camp to follow us. They killed Private Layton at Independence Rock and wounded the scout. Miss Travis has had a very strenuous journey, sir."

The colonel looked sympathetically toward Amy. "I'm distressed that you suffered such an ordeal. My wife will be delighted to have you as a visitor until

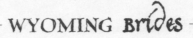

you have news from your father."

"Thank you," Amy murmured, wondering if the colonel's wife would let her have a bath immediately.

"You say three men followed you back along the Sweetwater to Independence Rock?" Colonel Munroe surveyed the map on the office wall.

"Yes, sir. This is where we met them." Brown stepped forward and pinpointed the location. "It wasn't until the next day that we were aware of the pursuit. Apparently the ringleader, LeBeau, had designs on Miss Travis."

"LeBeau?" Munroe asked. "He left here with the detachment. Major Lynde had received word from Fort Bridger that the man's brother was being detained for horse stealing. I was sending back permission for Major Travis to handle the case as he saw fit, but LeBeau asked if he could go along and perhaps speak up for his brother or at least see him again. I let him go. You say there were others?"

"Yes, a big, bearded man named Oliver, with a flashy paint horse, and a fair, snake-eyed man in buckskins."

"Don't know them," said Munroe, "but I haven't been here long. So they saw Miss Travis and—"

"No, sir, they most certainly did not see her that night," Brown interrupted. "Barkley made sure of that. But he did tell the corporal he was bringing her to Fort Laramie. I suspect that after we left, the corporal let it slip."

Munroe frowned. "Miss Travis, my deepest apologies. I'll look into this matter."

Amy took a deep breath. "LeBeau told me he hoped to trade me for his brother's life at Fort Bridger."

"You spoke to him?" Munroe asked.

"Y–yes. He. . ." She looked at the two men. Brown's face was full of compassion, and Munroe's gaze was riveted on her. "Mr. Barkley and I became separated from Private Brown in an attempt to outwit them. Mr. Barkley shot the man Oliver, but the other two came after us. They wounded Barkley, and. . ." She gulped. "LeBeau kidnapped me, sir. He held me for several hours and tried to get the horses back from Barkley."

Brown reached over and patted her hand.

There was a knock at the door, and a woman of forty entered the room, her pleasant face drawn into a worried frown.

"Miss Travis?"

"Yes." Amy stood shakily, and the colonel and Brown leaped to their feet.

"My dear, this is Major Travis's daughter. Miss Travis, my wife, Elizabeth."

It was so proper that Amy thought she might laugh, but instead she found to her dismay that she was crying.

Mrs. Munroe stepped quickly toward her, putting an arm around her shoulders.

"Come, dear. You need a rest and a bath and a good meal."

"I should like to write a note to my father," Amy said.

"Of course," the colonel agreed. "My wife will see to it, and I'll send it out."

The last thing Amy heard was Brown saying, "Please have the surgeon look at her, too, ma'am."

Then she collapsed gently against Mrs. Munroe. Brown reached out hastily and caught her before she could sink to the floor.

Chapter 16

They kept Amy in bed for a day. She protested, but Dr. Johns insisted, and Mrs. Munroe proved to be a fierce watchdog. The first time Amy awakened, her hostess spooned broth into her mouth and urged her to go back to sleep.

"I need to write to Father," Amy said with determination but little stamina.

When Amy had scrawled the note, Mrs. Munroe took it away, leaving her guest to sink back on the soft feather pillow and surrender to fatigue.

It was dark when Amy woke again, and a small lamp flickered at the bedside. A strange woman leaned toward her, saying, "Well, now." She disappeared for a few minutes and came back with a cup of tea well laced with sugar. Amy swallowed most of it, then drifted back into her dreams.

They were not all pleasant dreams. In most of them, she was riding Kip, sometimes pounding across the prairie in an impromptu race with Trooper Brown. At other times, she was frightened, looking constantly over her shoulder as Kip galloped away from some sinister presence. At last she dreamed she was riding along slowly, and Tom was on the horse with her. His arms encircled her, and she leaned her head back against his shoulder. It was so soothing, she wished she could stay in that dream, but then LeBeau came trotting along beside them on the pinto, smiling and calling, *"Réveillez, mademoiselle!"* He pointed a revolver at Tom. *"Pardonez moi,"* he said graciously, "it is the necessity."

She awoke with a start, trembling.

"Good morning," said Mrs. Munroe, laying aside her embroidery hoop. "Do you feel up to having some breakfast, my dear?"

"Tom—" Amy said weakly.

"I beg your pardon?"

"Tom—Mr. Barkley. Is he all right? Where is he?"

"Oh, the scout." Mrs. Munroe smiled. "He's still in the infirmary. The report this morning was that he needs rest. His wound was infected, I believe."

Amy struggled to sit up. She was wearing a soft pink nightgown she had never seen before.

"Do you feel well enough to get up, dear? Because I can bring you a tray. Dr. Johns said that you might get up if your head isn't aching too badly."

"I—I want to get up."

"Perhaps you'd like a bath. I washed you up a bit, but travel is so. . . uncomfortable."

Amy grimaced, remembering her state when she had arrived at the fort. "I'd love a bath."

It was not until late in the afternoon that she was able to convince her hostess that she was up to visiting the infirmary. Private Brown, who had stopped to inquire about Amy, offered to escort her, so Mrs. Munroe let her go.

"Don't worry, ma'am, I'll bring her back shortly," Brown said.

"Thank you," Amy breathed when Mrs. Munroe closed her door. "I was feeling a bit smothered."

"You look charming."

She looked down at her borrowed dress. "Every stitch I have on except my boots belongs to someone else."

"It suits you."

"Thank you. Has the colonel sent relief to my father?"

"Yes, forty men. They left at dawn."

"You didn't go with them?"

"Colonel Munroe asked me to stay to help with some details since T.R. hasn't been able to brief him yet."

"Tom is very ill?" she asked anxiously.

Brown shrugged. "He's tough. They removed the bullet first thing."

He opened the door to the surgery, and she stepped in out of the baking sun.

Tom lay very still on a cot. His shoulder was bandaged, and a blanket covered him to his chest, despite the warmth of the day. His breathing seemed rapid and shallow to Amy, and when she touched his hand, its heat shocked her.

"Has he been awake?" Brown asked.

The infirmary aide shook his head. "Not while I've been here." He wrung out a wet cloth and folded it on Tom's forehead. "We're just trying to keep the fever down."

Brown touched Amy's arm. "Best to let him rest, Miss Travis."

"I want to stay."

"You're hardly well yourself."

She knew it was true. Her head still ached, and her cheek smarted. She had seen her reflection in Mrs. Munroe's mirror after her bath that morning, and the purple bruises frightened her. Her hostess had been generous with gentle soaps and emollients and had offered to help her cover the worst of the bruises with powder.

She touched Tom's cheek with her fingertips. The dark whiskers on his jaw were almost long enough to make a beard now.

"I'll bring you back tomorrow," Brown promised. "I don't think you're ready to sit with him."

Reluctantly, she let the private lead her outside.

Tom opened his eyes and lay still, trying to orient himself. He was indoors but not at his house. Not Jim Frye's cabin. He turned his head and saw a shelf of bottles and instruments.

A man in uniform came to the bedside.

"Well, Barkley, how do you feel?"

He swallowed. "Dry."

The man brought him a glass of water. "Easy now. I'll help you sit up a bit."

The effort sent pain ripping through his left shoulder, and sweat broke out on his brow.

"Where am I?" Tom asked as he sank back onto the pillow.

"Fort Laramie. I'm Dr. Johns."

"We made it."

"You certainly did. I've heard part of the story, and I'd say you are a lucky man."

"Is Miss Travis all right?"

"I think so. Concussed and some bruises on her face and arms, one laceration. But I'd say there's nothing serious. She's been in to see you."

The door opened and another man looked in. "Private Brown is here again," he announced.

"He can come in," said the surgeon.

"Mike!"

"Hey, T.R. You look better!" Brown grasped his hand, and Tom winced. "Sorry."

"I'll send some breakfast in for you, Mr. Barkley," the doctor said. "Some oatmeal, I think, and tea."

"Make it coffee," said Tom.

"You *are* feeling better." Johns went out the door.

"Sit down," Tom told Brown eagerly.

"Fever gone?"

"Don't ask me. How long have I been here?"

"Three days."

"Three—are you serious?" Tom asked.

"Yup. The doc operated on you first thing Friday. Today's Monday."

"The dispatches—"

"All taken care of. Munroe sent forty men out Saturday morning. Your brother went with them."

"Matthew!" Tom was startled. His little brother was off to fight Indians, and Tom hadn't even seen him.

"He wanted to go," Brown said.

"He would."

"Well, that's a kid for you."

Tom nodded. He felt old. He had killed three men. Matt had no idea what he was asking for. To him, war was an adventure. Tom thought he had had enough adventure to last a lifetime.

"How's Amy?" He said it offhandedly, without looking at Brown.

"She's fine. Pesters me all the time to bring her over here."

"She came, the doc said."

"Five times so far."

Tom wasn't sure he liked that. "They carried me in here, didn't they?"

"Had to, T.R. I'm sorry."

He nodded grimly. "Well, she's seen me at my worst."

"She sets a lot of store by you."

Tom only grunted.

"What?"

"What am I going to tell Major Travis?"

Brown shrugged. "Colonel Munroe was sympathetic, seemed to think we acted properly, did all we could to complete the mission."

Tom looked up at the ceiling. "He's not her father."

"Still, he outranks Travis, and he sent him word we got through and his daughter was safe. He questioned me pretty hard about Independence Rock and Layton, but overall, I'd say we came off pretty good, T.R."

Tom frowned. "They're not going to give you any grief about Layton, are they? Because if it's anyone's fault, it's mine. I shouldn't have let him go out in front like that and sit there like a stupid target."

"Take it easy. It's nobody's fault he got himself killed. You see three whites riding up on you—you don't expect them to open fire. Don't blame yourself, T.R. We made it. Layton didn't. That's all."

Tom stared toward the window. He couldn't see much from where he lay, only a patch of sky and the corner of the barracks roof.

"You did the job," Brown insisted.

"I didn't keep her safe."

Brown stirred. "She seems all right now. I heard what she told the colonel."

"What was that?"

"LeBeau got hold of her and held her a few hours. That's about it. She didn't go into detail."

"Then she just smiled and walked away?"

"No," Brown said uneasily. "Then she. . .well, she was very tired, T.R. But she's fine now. At least, I think she is. She's worried about you, but—"

Tom pounded the mattress with his right fist and turned his head away.

"What really happened?" Brown asked.

"I wish I knew."

Brown said slowly, "Maybe it's better this way."

"Her father's going to kill me."

"Whatever for? You brought her back."

Tom faced him angrily. "I should have walked right up to that. . .that. . ." He laid back in exasperation. There was no word bad enough for LeBeau. "I was afraid I'd hit Amy if I shot at him. He had her down in a little canyon. I was within ten yards of him, but he had Amy. I'm glad she was unconscious. She didn't see me walk away."

"Sounds to me like you didn't have much choice."

"Of course I did. I should have just marched up to him anyway and shot him right between those beady little eyes."

"He'd have killed you before you ever got near him."

"So what? Would that be worse than leaving her with him? Six hours, I make it, Mike! I went and rounded up all the horses. It was the only way I could think of to make sure he couldn't leave with her."

"Seems like a reasonable plan to me, and it worked."

Tom shook his head. "It's what did or did not happen between sunset and moonrise that's bothering me, Mike. I should have faced him down right there in the canyon. Killed him or made him kill me. Hauled her out of there or died trying."

"Listen to you." Brown's eyes were troubled. "You really think it would be better for him to kill you and make off with her than what you did?"

Tom sighed. "If you had been there, you wouldn't have waited."

Brown considered. "I can't say what I would have done. I probably never would have thought to get a corner on the horses. Maybe I would have gone down that canyon blazing. I don't know. Wasted all my ammunition, probably. Then what? I'd be dead, and LeBeau would be dragging Miss Travis off to Bridger."

Tom put his fist to his forehead.

"You don't really think—" Brown looked at him closely, then asked softly, "Was she crying when you found her?"

"Yes. She cried a lot that morning. But once we got on the trail, she seemed better. I don't know. We stopped for water, and she was crying again."

Brown sat back. "Well, T.R., I don't know what to tell you. Just be up front with the major. If there's anything more to reveal, she'll tell him."

Tom bit his lip. "What would you do if it was your wife?"

"Well, I guess. . .I'd ask her. But that's not something you can just ask a single gal. Dr. Johns saw her, though."

Tom nodded. "Bruises, he told me. Cracked her head and had bruises."

"The major's not going to hold you accountable for her injuries."

"Why shouldn't he? Mike, when I saw her at dusk, she didn't have that cut on her right cheek. LeBeau did that to her."

They sat in silence.

The surgeon's aide came in with a tray. "Breakfast, Mr. Barkley."

Tom stared glumly at the tray.

"She'll be wanting to come see you." Brown stood up.

"I don't know, Mike."

"You can't refuse to see her. She's been after me constantly to tell her when you woke up."

"Dr. Johns would like him to rest after he eats," the aide said.

"This afternoon," Brown said, backing toward the door.

⌒

Amy stepped cautiously into the infirmary.

"Tom?"

He sat reclining on pillows, a clean shirt pulled over the white bandages on his shoulder, and he had been shaved. He looked younger, she thought at first, but she changed her mind when his dark, brooding eyes met her look.

He didn't speak as she walked to the bedside.

"How do you feel?" she asked to break the silence.

"Awful. But I'll probably be out of here tomorrow."

"Your brother went to Fort Bridger."

"Mike told me."

"I'm sorry you didn't get to see him first. He was very concerned about you." Tom nodded.

Amy pulled the one straight chair in the room over and perched on the edge of it. "I've been praying so hard that you'd recover. You gave us all a scare."

He said nothing.

"Tom, I want to thank you for—"

"No need," he said curtly.

She paused, a little hurt. He wouldn't look at her.

"Colonel Munroe says we ought to have some news by the end of the week. Captain Hollis is under orders to send word as soon as possible about conditions at Fort Bridger."

Tom nodded again.

"Will you stay until we hear something, Tom?"

"I ought to get back." He turned slowly to look at her. She knew the bruises had faded and the red welt on her cheek was nearly gone, but Tom did not seem pleased with what he saw.

He frowned. "You all right?"

"Yes. I'm fine."

He nodded.

"Tom, you won't. . .just leave. . .without telling me?"

"I'll let you know."

"Thank you. I'm at Colonel Munroe's."

Amy stood up. She smiled tremulously. "I'm glad you're better."

He gave a brief nod, and she slipped out of the room, defeated and heartsick. She stood still outside the door for a moment then turned to Brown.

"How's the patient?" Brown asked heartily.

She hesitated. "I'm not sure."

"I'll walk you back to the colonel's."

Tom had had enough. He'd moved into the enlisted men's barracks on Tuesday and stayed at the fort marking time because of Amy's request. For three long days, he hung around the barracks, checked over the horses, went through the equipment, and paid a brief daily call on Amy at the colonel's house.

Their visits were perfunctory. On Friday, he decided it was time to end the waiting. The sooner he stood face-to-face with Benjamin Travis, the better.

"I've decided to head out tomorrow morning," he said as soon as Mrs. Munroe had left him and Amy in the sitting room.

"But. . ." Her blue eyes showed plainly that she was disappointed.

"I might as well go. I'm not doing anyone any good here. If things have cleared up, I'll report to your father then go home. If they still need help, well, I'll be where I'm needed."

"Are you able to travel so far?"

He moved his injured shoulder self-consciously. "I'm fine. A little stiff, but the doctor says I ought to use it."

"I'm glad."

"I've decided to keep the bay horse. He's the only one that didn't try to run off on me."

"He seems like a good horse. Have you named him?"

Tom shook his head. Horses' names were the last thing occupying him at the moment.

"You ought to name him Milton," Amy said with a smile. " 'They also serve who only stand and wait.'"

Tom tried to smile, but it was more of a grimace. He couldn't feel light-hearted. "I came to see if you want anything from the gear."

Amy shook her head.

"All right. I gave one of the muskets to Mike. I'll sell the pinto and the brown horse and give you half the money."

Her eyebrows shot up. "Don't give me anything."

"It will help toward your trip."

"My trip?"

"Back to Albany."

She caught her breath. "That's all right. Father will take care of me."

Like I failed to do, Tom thought. He stood up and walked to the window.

"Tom, take me with you."

He stood motionless, looking out at the parade ground, his heart racing. No, he certainly could not take her with him. One wild ride across hostile territory with Amy Travis was enough for the toughest man. He knew he couldn't survive it again. His heart would give out on him before he reached the Sweetwater. And he had yet to report to her father.

"The major wants you here," he said.

He heard her step toward him. "I want to go back, and Father said I might if it's safe."

Safe. There it was again.

He turned slowly. "Amy, I think I've already proven I'm not able to keep you safe. Major Travis told me to bring you here. I don't think he'd appreciate it if I took you back into danger."

She frowned and opened her mouth as if to argue, but at that moment Mrs. Munroe stepped into the doorway.

"Excuse me, Amy, but my husband just sent a man to tell us that your father is on his way here."

"He's coming here?" Amy faced her, astonished.

"Yes, they say he'll be here tomorrow. He sent a man ahead to tell the colonel. The Indian threat is over, and he wants to meet my husband and discuss some military matters with him then take you back to Fort Bridger himself."

Tom watched Amy. She was excited, happy. Her eyes sparkled the way they had before Independence Rock.

Mrs. Munroe left them, and Amy smiled at him.

"Tom, he's coming here! Isn't that wonderful? And I can go back!"

He picked his hat up from the sofa. "Maybe I'll head out today."

"Today?" she cried in dismay. "But he'll be here tomorrow."

He turned the hat slowly. "If he's that close, I can ride out to his camp tonight, see him there, and then go home."

"But—"

"I ought to get back to my place." It was an excuse, but he couldn't confess to the major, then travel all the way back with them. Travis wouldn't want him along, and Tom would be nervous, not to mention having to look at Amy. He'd lectured himself sternly several times, reminding himself that he was not and never would be on an equal plane with Amy. But his heart seemed to forget that when he saw her. It thumped disconcertingly, and he ached to hold her in his arms again.

Her father would take applications for suitors from stronger men than T.R. Barkley. Someone who could *really* take care of his daughter. Tom thought it might take a general with a brigade at his command to protect Amy Travis.

In the stress of their flight from the outlaws, he had allowed himself to love her, but even then he had known there was no future for them.

"Maybe I'll see you at Bridger sometime," he muttered. She said nothing, and he pushed past her, clapping the hat on, trying to avoid her eyes. If she was going to cry again, he didn't want to know it.

Chapter 17

The major and his men were bivouacked near the ferry on the Platte. With every step the bay horse took away from Fort Laramie, Tom's heart sank lower. He knew he would avoid seeing Amy when she returned to Bridger.

He came to the camp after dark, and Major Travis came toward him from the tents.

"Barkley!" He grasped his hand. "Didn't expect you."

"Well, sir, I heard you were on the way, and I was anxious to get back to my place—"

Travis nodded. "Come, give me the full story. I've only heard bits and pieces."

Tom dropped the bay's reins and walked beside Travis away from the camp.

"Things are settled at Bridger?" he asked.

"Yes. It was a near thing. They gathered two thousand strong after you left, and I was a bit worried."

"Did they attack?"

"Yes, but we did pretty well. I had two men wounded, but we hit at least a dozen of them. They backed off. Wouldn't parlay. I was afraid they'd come back again, and I didn't know as we could hold out. Our defenses are really pretty flimsy."

Tom nodded.

"Then—what do you think?"

"I have no idea, sir."

"Old Jim Bridger himself came riding in on a mule. Once the Indians heard he was there, they agreed to talk. The entire matter was settled within hours, and they dispersed. Bridger said he'd stick around for a few weeks, and I thought it was safe to come retrieve my daughter."

"She's very anxious to see you, sir."

"Your brother, Private Barkley, said he'd seen her. I was a bit anxious about her. I got a note that worried me from that ruffian LeBeau, but I'm told you and Amy got through all right."

Tom cleared his throat. Travis was eyeing him keenly. "She did have some injuries, sir. I'm sorry. I'd like to give you my report if I may."

"Of course. Tell me everything."

They walked along the bluff for half an hour, and Tom held nothing back.

When Tom finished, Travis stood with his hands behind his back, looking down on the river.

"I owe you and Brown a great debt."

"No, sir. It was a matter of duty."

"Perhaps, but—"

"I want to apologize, sir, for not keeping her safe."

Travis looked at him curiously. "But she's with Colonel Munroe. You said so yourself."

"Yes, sir, but I mean. . ." Tom turned his hat in his hands nervously. "That night, on the hill—I ought to have done something different, sir. Got her back quicker. I—I don't really know how much she suffered that night. I'm sorry." He stared down at the ground.

Travis watched the river and said slowly, "You can't go on fretting about the past, Barkley. Every time I give an order, I wonder if I've made the right decision. But you can only do your best at the time and keep going. I don't fault you for the way you handled things."

"Yes, sir." Tom stood, feeling miserable.

"That's leadership. You act, and you take the consequences. I picked you because I figured you could do that and because you know this stretch of trail better than just about anyone. Was I wrong?"

"No, sir." Tom knew he could bear the weight of responsibility for the mission, but he still felt a bittersweet regret when he remembered the time he had spent with Amy.

Travis looked up at the star-filled sky. "You came here to report to me sooner than you had to tonight. I'm wondering if this whole thing hasn't been weighing on you disproportionately."

"Sir?"

"Forget about me for a minute, son. Ultimately, we all stand before God. Can you say in your heart that you did your best? That you took what God gave you to work with and used it to the best of your ability to accomplish His purpose as far as you understood it?"

Tom went over the pursuit again in his mind and took a deep breath.

"Don't answer me," said the major. "Tell your heavenly Father. If you honestly believe you acted the way He wanted you to, then you have nothing to be ashamed of and nothing to fear from me or from God."

Tom stood silent. He wished he could have done better, yet. . .

Lord, I did what I could that night. Thank You for bringing us out of it. Without You, I couldn't have done it. Thank You.

Travis turned and surveyed Tom thoughtfully. "Do you have feelings for my daughter, Barkley?"

Tom was startled. "I. . .well. . ." He cleared his throat. "Yes, sir, I admit I do, but I want you to know I tried to treat her with utmost respect, and I know you would never approve—" He stopped helplessly. "You don't have to worry, sir," he finished, meeting the major's eyes.

Travis held the gaze for several seconds, and Tom breathed deeply, forcing himself to stand still and take it.

"I would never approve?"

Tom opened his mouth then closed it.

"Come back to the campfire with me, Barkley. You can spend a little time with your brother tonight, and there's something I think you ought to see."

Tom's heart began to pound. Had they found some trace of the battle or Layton's body?

As they walked, Major Travis said affably, "My daughter has a stubborn streak. Don't know as you noticed that."

Tom grunted. "Yes, sir. She saved my neck when I'd told her not to."

Travis laughed. "Yes, well, I want you to look at this. Captain Hollis brought it to me at Fort Bridger."

Beside the fire, the major pulled a sheet of paper from his uniform pocket and handed it over. Tom opened it curiously and held it down where he could read it by the light of the flames.

Dearest Father,

I write this hastily to tell you that I am safe at Fort Laramie, thanks to Mr. T.R. Barkley and Pvt. Michael Brown. Although we had a difficult journey and Pvt. Layton was killed on the way, we have arrived, and it is to these two brave men that I owe my life. I hope you can do something for Pvt. Brown, as he hopes to go back to his family soon.

Father, I was badly frightened, and I spent a rather woeful night in the company of the vilest sort of man, but I stress to you that, other than a few bruises, I was not harmed, and you must not let this affect your treatment of his brother, Raymond LeBeau.

It is with deepest sincerity that I beg you not to send me back to Albany. I have come to care deeply for Mr. Barkley, and I cannot leave the Wyoming Territory unless I know for certain that he will never reciprocate. He is very ill now because of the wound he received for my sake, and I am afraid for him. My heart tells me I can never love another man the way I do Tom Barkley. Please do not send me away.

Your loving daughter,
Amy

Tom looked up slowly.

"Well?" Travis asked. "I told you, she's stubborn."

Tom swallowed. "I don't know what to say, sir. It's a relief—I mean, the first part. But I wasn't trying to put notions in her head. I'm sorry."

She still loved him, and she had told her father! His heart raced. If the major sent him angrily away, he would still have that.

Travis said gently, "You go on back to the Blacks Fork if you want, Barkley, but I'm hoping you'll see fit to turn around and ride back to Fort Laramie with me in the morning."

"Are you saying you wouldn't object if I. . ." Tom swallowed hard. "If I courted your daughter?"

"I'd be most disappointed if you didn't."

Amy was waiting anxiously with Colonel and Mrs. Munroe when her father's party rode into Fort Laramie at midmorning. They halted on the parade ground, and her father dismounted and dismissed the troops, handing the reins of his horse to his aide.

He walked toward her, smiling, and she ran to him, throwing her arms around his neck.

"Father! I'm so glad to see you!"

He kissed her cheek and held her at arm's length. "I heard the story from Barkley last night. Are you all right?"

"Yes. Oh, Father, did he apologize and tell you he didn't do his job?"

Travis laughed. "You seem to know Barkley pretty well. The way he tells it, he owes his life to you and that gray horse of mine."

"But Tom was wonderful. He outsmarted that awful man, and—"

Her father held up his hands in protest. "Let's discuss it inside, Amy."

She glanced around and blushed, realizing that the colonel, his wife, and several other spectators were listening eagerly.

Tom watched from a distance. He caught his breath when he saw Amy fly into her father's arms. She was lovely, her golden hair braided and wound on top of her head. She wore an impractical white dress that skimmed her ankles above the leather boots. He watched her go inside with the major; then he turned his horse out with Kip and headed for the barracks, meeting Brown outside the door.

"T.R.! You came back with the major?"

"He asked me to."

Brown was wary. "We're not in trouble, are we?"

"No. He's going to give you a commendation. And Mike, he gave me his blessing."

"You mean—Amy?"

"Yes." Tom gulped. "What do I say to her?"

Brown laughed. "You'll think of something."

"Well, if she'll have me—"

"I don't think there's much doubt of that. But last night I thought you'd ruined everything."

"Really?"

"Yes. I went by to see her, and she was taking it hard that you left."

"I felt like I had to, Mike. If I'd stayed. . . Well, I figured it was better to be a hundred miles or so away when the major told her I wasn't eligible."

Brown shook his head. "Don't know how you could walk out on those blue eyes. She cried buckets on my uniform."

"What did you tell her?"

"That you weren't uncaring, just knot-headed."

"Oh, I care, Mike."

"I know. But she was finding that hard to believe."

Colonel Munroe's aide approached them. "Private Brown? Mr. Barkley? You're wanted in headquarters."

"Time to make my report, I guess," said Brown.

Tom walked with him to the colonel's office. When they entered, Munroe and Travis were deep in discussion.

"Come in, Brown," said the colonel, glancing up. "I'd like you to give the major your version of the engagement at Independence Rock."

Travis looked at Tom. "Barkley, my daughter would like to see you. I believe she's with Mrs. Munroe."

Tom backed out the door and slowly went the few steps to the commander's quarters and knocked. The colonel's wife opened the door.

"Mr. Barkley! Welcome! Won't you come in? Miss Travis is—"

"Thank you," Tom murmured, walking past her into the sitting room. Amy jumped up from a chair and stood facing him, her hands twisting the ends of a blue sash the same color as her eyes.

"Tom!" There was a hesitance in her manner as she greeted him. "Father told me he brought you back, and I ought to talk to you."

He advanced slowly toward her, his hat in his hands. She reached out toward him, then drew her hands back uncertainly.

He walked closer and stood just inches from her, unsure how to begin.

"Tom, if I offended you somehow on the trail. . . I mean, it seems looking back that I may have been indiscreet, and. . .I'm sorry!" Her eyes pleaded for understanding.

He put his left hand up and rested his index finger lightly on her lips. "Shh. Do you still want to go with me?"

The gladness that filled her face was intoxicating. "Of course!"

"I love you, Amy. Didn't get a chance to tell you before I fell off the horse."

She caught her breath, and he was afraid she was going to cry. He let his fingers stroke her cheek. He smiled faintly. "Guess you found some of that lard."

Her eyes flared; then she laughed. He let his hat fall to the floor and drew her into his arms slowly but purposefully. He brought his lips down tenderly on hers, and she melted against him, her hands creeping up onto his shoulders.

"I plan to leave in the morning," he whispered in her ear, holding her close against his thudding heart.

"But Father said he'll be here three days."

"I know. Thought we'd go alone. It ought to be safe with troopers back and forth so much right now."

She drew back quickly and stared at him. "Just you and me?"

He nodded. "We can get married tonight. What do you say? There's a chaplain here, and you could wear that dress. You look beautiful, Amy."

She gasped. "But, Tom, you'll have to ask Father. I mean, he told me he respects you, but—"

"I had that talk with him last night. He'll give us his approval, Amy. Please, will you be my wife?"

Her smile started deep in her eyes and spread to her lips.

"Can we stop at Jim Frye's cabin?"

Tom laughed. "All right, but this time the horses stay outside."

"Yes, and we'll take extra clothes and blankets and some decent food. I'd better tell Mrs. Munroe. Maybe she and I can bake this afternoon. And we ought to have a tent in case we get caught in the rain again."

"Sounds like I'd better line up a packhorse." Tom laughed at her enthusiasm and the joy that was shooting through him.

She caught her breath. "Oh, and can we take a few books? The trader has some."

"You start baking and packing. I'll go see to our gear." He looked down into her eyes, smiling, not loosening his hold on her. "Still love me?"

Amy sighed contentedly. "Always."

THE OREGON
ESCORT

Dedication

To my dear husband, Jim, the perfect husband for me;
the patient and loving father of my children;
my first editor and best friend.

Chapter 1

No, sir, I can't take you." The corporal's slight Southern accent made his words soft and apologetic, but Lydia Jackson could tell from the steel in the set of his jaw that he would not change his mind.

She stood in the shadow of the Gordon family's covered wagon, where it sat outside Fort Laramie in the hot July sun. She had spent the first half of 1860 getting this far, and the cavalryman examining the Gordons' team of mules seemed determined to delay their progress.

"But, Corporal, we have to go," Mr. Gordon protested.

The trooper bent to lift one of the nearest mule's hooves and looked at it, then put it down gently and stood. "Sorry. These animals won't make it to Independence Rock."

Mrs. Gordon stepped forward, her eyes blazing. "Who gives you the right to make that decision? We've come all the way from Pennsylvania with these mules."

Corporal Brown frowned and shook his head. "They're on their last legs, ma'am. Maybe you can trade them for another team or stay here at Fort Laramie for a month or so and rest them."

When the corporal left the Gordons and headed toward the next wagon, Lydia hurried after him.

"Corporal."

He swung around and met her gaze, and she halted in her tracks. His worn uniform suited him perfectly, with the high-topped black boots, blue jacket with brass buttons, and lighter blue trousers with gold stripes down the sides. Like many troopers, he had abandoned the army-issue forage cap in favor of a wide-brimmed, soft felt hat, and the cavalry's crossed saber insignia was pinned to the crown. He pulled it off, revealing thick, brown hair tumbling across his brow.

"Yes, miss?"

Regardless of his dashing uniform, the corporal's most striking feature was his rich brown eyes. They took in her every move as she stepped closer. Lydia made herself break the stare first. There was something about the way he watched her that made her heart race.

"Pardon me," she began, feeling a flush creep up from the high neck of her dress. "I've been traveling with the Gordons since Missouri. Did I understand correctly that you're refusing to let them continue with the wagon train?"

"Yes, miss. I have strict orders from Sergeant Reese. No wagons without fit teams will proceed."

Lydia inhaled deeply. The Gordons' team was lean and footsore, but they'd held out this long. That meant they were tough, didn't it?

"I must get to Oregon City by fall." She lowered her gaze, embarrassed that she had voiced her thought. It was none of his concern.

But the corporal's sudden, empathetic smile sent a thrill through her. "Best be making other arrangements, then, miss. There's a family yonder with two wagons and a passel of children. I expect they could use a hand."

Lydia knew he was referring to the Sawyers, and she refused to consider them. Mr. Sawyer whipped his mules and yelled at his children. But there were other, more peaceful families she could ask.

"You're certain about the Gordons?"

"Yes, miss, they'd be risking their lives to go on with those mules. But they can wait here a few weeks for another train."

Lydia nodded. She hated to see the Gordons turned out of the wagon train, but the officers leading the cavalry unit that would accompany them from Fort Laramie to Oregon had the final say.

"I hope you find a place in the train, miss," he said softly, and Lydia gulped. It would be brassy to reply to such a forward remark. Wouldn't it? She felt her face go scarlet.

"Thank you," she managed to get out, and he smiled again. It wasn't a leering, offensive smile. It was more of an encouraging, friendly smile, she decided as she hurried across the trampled grass toward the Gordons' wagon.

Mike Brown stood watching the young woman as she glided away into the dusk. Seldom did one encounter such a pretty sight on the plains of Wyoming. He wondered what she was doing out here, traveling alone. Her refined speech and high-quality clothing told him she was accustomed to an easier life than he'd known. New England, he guessed from her inflection. Her hair, pinned up on her head, caught the last rays of sunlight and gleamed auburn. She had been months on the trail, yet she walked erect and with grace. And those blue eyes. . .

He took a slow, careful breath and turned away. He had no business looking over the women of the wagon train. Sergeant Reese had reminded him just this morning that they would have to keep an eye on the thirty troopers in their escort detail.

"Can't let the men form attachments with the civilian girls," Reese had said. "It makes for trouble later on."

Mike had agreed with him at the time. But that was before a young woman with the bearing and complexion of a princess had come to talk with him. He realized he hadn't thought about a woman this way in a long, long time. He wasn't sure he liked it.

Lydia went to the back of the wagon and climbed over the tailboard. She'd been with the Gordons for nearly two months. She'd offered her services of cooking, doing laundry, and watching the children in exchange for a niche in the wagon for her belongings and the protection of the family. Mr. and Mrs. Gordon were not warm or sentimental, but they had befriended her in their aloof way, and she had come to care about twelve-year-old John Paul and the three little girls. However, she would not stop a month at Fort Laramie while their overworked mules recovered.

She rooted her belongings from the tightly packed wagon. The three Gordon girls watched her, their faces sad and their eyes wide.

"I've got to leave you," Lydia told them. "Be good, now. I'll miss you." The youngest, Clara, began to cry, and Lydia gathered them to her in a brief embrace. Then she heaved her carpetbag down and climbed out to lift down her small, leather-bound trunk of books. Mrs. Gordon walked toward her, shoulders sagging.

"What are you doing, Lydia?"

"I need to find a berth in the train, Mrs. Gordon. I'm sorry, but if you're staying here, I'll have to part from you."

"No, please. You can stay with us. You've no one to go to."

Lydia shrugged. "You've been very kind, but I need to go on."

"I don't know if I can get along without you. You've been so good with the children!"

"And I'll miss them, but you'll be fine. A few weeks' rest here will do you good."

Mrs. Gordon sighed. "You helped buy supplies for the next part of the journey."

Lydia swallowed. She couldn't afford to lose that.

"Let me speak to my husband," Mrs. Gordon said wearily.

"Thank you." Lydia set her bags to one side. "I should try to make arrangements immediately. The wagons will pull out at first light."

Mrs. Gordon nodded. "You go see about transportation, and I'll pack you up some flour, beans, and bacon."

Lydia headed toward the Paines' wagon. They were one of a dozen families that had come out together from Independence. The rest had been waiting at the fort until the army decreed the party large enough to warrant an escort. Lydia didn't know them well, but she perceived Mr. Paine as a quiet man who cared well for his oxen. His wife, Dorcas, had a good heart and a sweet, cheerful face. Their two children were lively but clean and obedient. Yes, the Paines were Lydia's first choice.

The sun was down, and she felt insecure and alone. The wagon camp sprawled

across the meadow near the fort, and an Indian encampment lay nearby.

"Can we help you, ma'am?" Two troopers appeared out of the dusk, and Lydia shrank from them with distrust. The addition of the troopers to the party aroused mixed feelings in her heart. She ought to feel more secure with an official escort, but the men seemed altogether too eager to socialize.

"No, thank you." She hurried on.

Mrs. Paine was drying the supper dishes, and her husband sat silently beside the fire with a drowsy little girl on his knee. The eight-year-old boy was sprawled on a blanket near the back wagon wheel, staring up at the sky.

"Excuse me." Lydia entered the circle of flickering light.

Mr. Paine stirred as if he would rise but sank back with two-year-old Jenny in his arms, giving Lydia a nod. His wife's greeting was more effusive.

"Well, good evening, Miss Jackson! My dear, isn't this exciting? We shall be off at dawn with a large company, and thirty strapping soldiers to protect us."

Lydia smiled. "Yes, ma'am. I was—"

"They're even sending a doctor along." Mrs. Paine smiled as she lifted the basin of dirty dishwater. "We have it so much better than those who traveled this road in the past."

"Yes, ma'am. I—"

"Although Mr. Miller has done a fine job as wagon master. I'm certain we could have made it on our own, but it's comforting to know we won't have to."

"Indeed," Lydia said with a gulp. Would she ever get to make her request? The stolid man by the fire came to her rescue.

"Mrs. Paine," he said quietly, "I believe Miss Jackson came on an errand."

"Oh." His wife stopped with the tin basin swung back, ready to toss out the tepid water, and stared at Lydia in the dimness. "Forgive me, my dear. What is it?"

Lydia smiled. Dorcas Paine was perhaps ten years her senior, and she was quite pretty, with her blond hair bound in a crocheted snood. She had been a bit on the plump side when they left Independence, but Lydia could see she had lost some weight and was looking healthy and still a bit rounded. Her enthusiastic kindness appealed to everyone, and she enjoyed conversing with nearly anyone, at any time.

"I find myself in somewhat of a bind," Lydia began, glancing from Dorcas to her husband. Mr. Paine appeared to be nodding off, his hair dark against little Jenny's blond curls.

"In what way?" Dorcas asked.

"I need to change my travel arrangements."

Dorcas swung the basin, and the water shot out with a neat *plop* onto the scrubby grass. "You're leaving the Gordons."

Lydia nodded. "The troopers told them they must rest their team if they can't replace them. I felt it best to find another situation."

"Quite right." Dorcas hung the basin on a nail in the side of the wagon box. "I've seen you with the children. You've been a good helper to Mrs. Gordon."

"Thank you." Lydia waited, anxiety creeping over her. It was getting late. She wanted the matter settled.

"I'm sure any family in this train would be pleased to accommodate you," Dorcas said.

"I have a few supplies," Lydia murmured, trying not to let her desperation show.

Dorcas nodded. "I shall speak to Mr. Paine."

Lydia swallowed hard, wondering when that would be. Mr. Paine appeared to be asleep, slouching lower by the minute. But he raised his head at that moment and said clearly, "As you wish, Mrs. Paine." He stood slowly, his little daughter in his arms, and headed for the back of the wagon.

Before Lydia could speak, Dorcas clapped her hands. "There! You see? It's settled."

"Are you certain?"

"Of course, my dear. What Mr. Paine says is so, is so. He's very pleased you're joining us."

Lydia returned Dorcas's smile, wondering how one determined that Mr. Paine was pleased.

"Thank you. I can't tell you how relieved I am. I'll help you in any way I can."

"It will be delightful. Why don't you fetch your things now? It will be simpler in the morning if you're right here. You must be used to sleeping on the ground?"

"Oh yes," Lydia assured her.

"Well, then, I shan't worry about your discomfort, since there's no changing that. We shall have a splendid time together."

Mr. Paine had laid Jenny down to sleep and was stooping over the boy as Lydia walked past.

"Come, Nathan," he said softly. "Let's get your shoes off."

Lydia compared his quiet, solid presence and his gentle way with his children to Mr. Gordon's brusque manner. When Mr. Gordon was around, his whole family was on edge, knowing a reprimand was only a breath away.

She hurried toward the Gordons' wagon, striding more confidently. Things would be better from here on. Dorcas Paine seemed delighted at the change, making the remainder of the harsh trip sound like the most pleasant outing imaginable. Lydia was determined to do her part, helping with the chores and watching the children.

The Gordons' wagon was not where she left it, but John Paul was stretched out on the turf beside Lydia's luggage.

"Where did your parents go?" She tried to keep the anxiety from her voice as she reached for her carpetbag.

John Paul sat up and yawned. "Pa took the wagon closer to the fort so the army will think he's staying."

Lydia stopped with her hand in midair. "What do you mean?"

The boy smirked. "We'll wait an hour or so after the wagons leave; then we'll follow them."

Lydia stared at him in disbelief. "But Corporal Brown says he won't take you unless you have a different team."

"Pa says if we catch up the next day, they can't send us back."

Lydia picked up her large bag. If the Gordons wanted to strike out on their own after the wagons left and hoped to catch up with the train, no one could stop them. But what if the corporal was right? What if they got a score of miles from the fort and the mules went lame? She shuddered to think of the family's fate alone in the wilderness.

She reached for her small workbag. A gunnysack lay on the grass. "What's that?"

"That's your food. Ma says if you want to stay with us, you're welcome. If not, that goes with you."

Lydia hoisted the sack to test its weight. It couldn't hold nearly enough food for an adult for the arduous trip ahead. She had given Mr. Gordon the money for her share of the food back in Independence. She considered marching up to him and demanding a larger share of provisions. John Paul was watching her, and she took a deep breath.

"I'm going with the Paines. Can you carry that little trunk to their wagon for me?"

"You're taking all your books," he said wistfully.

"Well, of course."

John Paul lifted the trunk to his shoulder and nodded toward the burlap sack. "Hope you didn't want any coffee."

Chapter 2

Lydia trudged along beside the wagon. They were only two days out of Fort Laramie, but already she had abandoned all hope of returning to the civilized world. A shack of a house stood near the ferry this morning, but they hadn't met a soul or passed a dwelling since.

Twenty dusty, sun-baked miles from the fort, her lips were cracked, her skin was dry, and her eyes smarted from the alkali dust that swirled in the constant wind. Her purpose had shriveled and shrunk to the basic need of putting this mile behind her.

The wind whipped her skirt around her legs, tripping her up repeatedly. She stumbled and pulled the layers of cloth free then went on. She could ride in the wagon if she wanted, but she wouldn't do that until she was exhausted.

Back in Nebraska, she had tried riding in the wagon, but she hated sitting there while the animals strained to pull her weight across the interminable prairie. She trudged on, telling herself that she was moving herself closer to her goal and not causing more work for the Paines' oxen.

"I've walked over a thousand miles." Unthinkable a year ago, but now it was just a fact, like the layer of chalky dust that dulled her auburn hair and her grimy cotton dress. Already the two-week stop at Fort Laramie, while the smaller wagon trains re-formed into this large one, seemed a hazy dream.

The wind gusted again and caught her skirt, billowing it out in front of her. Lydia gasped and turned into the blast in hopes that would help, but the voluminous skirt and threadbare petticoat beneath it fought her for every inch of modesty.

Just when she was able to smooth the skirt down over her knees, another blast buffeted her, and she struggled once more with the flapping fabric.

A hearty laugh rang out, and she spun around, bending over to hold her skirt against her shins.

"You'd best hang on to something, miss, or you'll be scudding off like a schooner under full sail." The lanky young man was Trooper Barkley, a friendly fellow who was always ready to lend the pioneers a hand. He and another soldier were riding their horses alongside the wagons, and Lydia saw to her chagrin that his companion was the handsome Southerner, Corporal Brown.

"No," said Brown, "she'll just roll off like a tumbleweed in the breeze, until she fetches up in some ravine."

Barkley guffawed. "No offense, miss. Can we help you into your wagon?"

"No, thank you," Lydia said between clenched teeth, walking backward to keep up with the Paines' wagon and trying unsuccessfully to tame the full skirt. She avoided looking at the men but couldn't help snatching glances at Brown. His eyes glittered, and he didn't seem the least bit fatigued.

He was used to this life, she guessed, and he was riding a beautiful bay mare. Anyone would feel more alive riding a horse like that. She'd seen her earlier when her glossy hide gleamed in the morning sun. But now, like everything else, she was coated with dust. Her face had an appealing sweetness, but Lydia had seen the mare sidestep and throw her head, crow-hopping obstinately. She suspected Brown had his hands full for the first hour on the bay's back that morning. Now, after half a day under saddle, the mare walked docilely beside Barkley's dun gelding.

But it was the rider who drew her attention. Lydia found herself looking up at Brown again, and he smiled down at her. Those eyes! She had to quit staring, even if he didn't seem to mind.

"Here you go." Brown fished in his saddlebag and produced a small leather pouch. He stopped the mare and leaned down from the saddle, holding it out to her.

"What's this?"

"Lead shot. Stitch a row in the hem of your skirt."

"The idea!" Lydia shrank away from him, shocked that he would speak to her with such familiarity. Had she somehow betrayed in her glance the way her heart beat faster when he was around? The amusement in his eyes and Barkley's turned her embarrassment into anger. "Keep it! Put it to good use when we're attacked by savages."

"Better'n showing off your laces and linens," Brown replied with a shrug.

"Prettiest view I've seen in a long while," Barkley agreed.

She felt her face go scarlet as she pushed Brown's gloved hand away, but letting go of her uncooperative skirt proved near disastrous. It billowed up, again exposing her pantalets and petticoat.

"Easy, now, Matthew," Brown said to his companion with a touch of annoyance. "That's no way to address a lady."

"Sorry, miss." Barkley had the grace to look chastised.

She turned her back to them and the wind, pressing her skirt down against her thighs as she strode to catch up with the Paines' plodding wagon. She heard Barkley chuckle, and it infuriated her that the men found her situation diverting. She had considered Brown a gentleman, though now it appeared he was only one notch above the other men when it came to courtesy. They trotted past on their horses, and Brown tipped his hat.

"No offense intended, miss."

~

"Brown, two wagons are lagging behind. You and Gleason ride back and hurry them up. Don't want to get too big a gap between them and the rest of the train."

Brown threw his sergeant, Dan Reese, a curt salute and wheeled the mare. How could anything be lagging behind? That meant they were going slower than these overgrown tortoises!

In the two days they'd come from Fort Laramie, the emigrants had settled into the routine. Most were already seasoned travelers, having come from Missouri early in the summer as soon as the grass was high enough to sustain the cattle. They had walked clear across Nebraska beside their lumbering wagons. Brown was thankful that his job entailed riding a horse or a mule. At the moment, it was a horse, and a good one at that. The showy bay mare fidgeted too much, wasting a lot of energy fighting the bit, but once she settled down, she was a good mount. Not one he would choose for a combat detail, but for this duty she was fine, with a more comfortable stride than one of the steadier mules would have.

Gleason joined him, and they trotted along the line of sixty creaking wagons.

"Not bad for summer duty, hey?" Gleason asked with a grin.

Brown nodded. "It beats hanging around the fort pulling fatigue details and drilling in the sun."

In some ways, escort duty was even better than chasing hostile Indians, although 99 percent of the time, that wasn't bad either. It was the 1 percent, when you found yourself a hapless target, that got uncomfortable. The escort service operated from early summer, when the first wagon trains reached Fort Laramie, to late fall, when the last train had been safely delivered to Oregon. For an enlisted man, this was perhaps the best job in the West.

It wasn't like staying at the fort as the emigrant trains passed through. The men traveled along with the same folks for several weeks, helping them and training them to survive the rigorous journey. One could get to know them, even make friends. For most of the men, it was a rare opportunity to socialize with decent women.

Like the girl who had joined the Paines at Fort Laramie. Feisty. A little standoffish. Brown wasn't sure why such a straitlaced girl would want to go west alone. Maybe she had a husband waiting out there. But she had nice clothes. They were becoming shabby, like those of all emigrants who had come this far, but he could see that her dusty dresses were made of good cloth and well cut, not to mention the deep lace flounces on her underthings. He smiled as he remembered her outrage when Matt Barkley intimated that he'd seen them. It wasn't polite to suggest that a lady had anything under her skirt. Pretty girl, though. Very pretty. And she had some backbone.

He noticed that he was nearly back to the Paines' place in line, but when he came even with their wagon, Lydia Jackson was nowhere in sight. Just as well. He and Gleason had a task before them. He urged the mare into a canter.

After the wagons circled that evening, Lydia helped Dorcas prepare the meal and care for the children. Her spirits were still low, and every time she glimpsed a uniform, she turned her back hastily. She tried to pay attention to Mrs. Paine's incessant chatter, but her mind kept straying back to Corporal Brown's practical offer of his shot pouch.

Perhaps she should have taken it. But she was determined not to give any of the thirty troopers reason to think they could take liberties during the trip. Still, the winds were worse than ever, and she couldn't walk all day showing off her ankles and more. Brown was right about that.

She looked down at the ground, wondering if small pebbles might serve the same purpose as the lead.

"Evening, ma'am."

Lydia whirled to see Brown and Barkley approaching the fireside.

"Good evening, gentlemen," Dorcas cooed with a bright smile. The small, vivacious woman had room in her heart for all things motherless, and she looked on the troopers as boys who had been too long away from their families.

"We'd be happy to escort you to get water, ma'am," Barkley said, his glance sweeping over Lydia and back to Mrs. Paine. They had stopped for the night near a stream that was fairly clear before it flowed into the muddy Platte.

"That's very kind." Dorcas brushed her hands together. "We do need water. Lydia, dear, would you mind. . ."

Lydia fixed her gaze on Brown, who was watching her with an enigmatic smile. She flushed, recalling his earlier impertinence. "Yes, I would mind, Mrs. Paine. I shan't go out of sight of the train with these men."

Dorcas blinked at her. "Really, dear, these are gentlemen." She threw a flustered glance toward Brown. "Take Nathan with you, then." The boy was setting out the tin plates and cups but looked up when he heard his name.

"Several other ladies will be along," Brown said. "We're passing the word."

He seemed amused. Lydia refused to be embarrassed. She nodded curtly and walked toward the wagon, where two pails hung from the sideboard.

A few minutes later, she, a dozen other women, and a few children walked to the stream behind Corporal Brown, carrying their buckets. Lydia hung back to avoid him and consequently found herself nearest Barkley, who was bringing up the rear and attempting to look very alert and efficient for the benefit of the three single women in the group.

"Wind's died down," he offered, and Lydia wondered if he was referring to the earlier incident. She decided he was merely making small talk.

"Does it ever quit altogether?" she asked.

"Not out here." He shifted his rifle into the crook of his arm and held a branch back for her. They had come down a steep bank into the flats beside the water, and a few willow trees grew there, with brambles scattered among them. Nathan ran ahead of her with the other children.

"Mike's right about the lead shot."

Lydia stopped short and stared at Barkley. "How dare you!"

Surprise heightened the private's eyebrows. "I beg your pardon, miss. We didn't mean to insult you. All the ladies who come out here learn to weight their skirts down, or else they take to wearing bloomers."

"Bloomers?" Lydia's outrage was mounting. "That's disgraceful!"

Barkley shook his head with such innocence that she wondered if she had misjudged him. "No offense intended, miss. I grew up near Fort Bridger, and we seen a lot of Mormon ladies come through. They all wear 'em."

Lydia eyed him doubtfully. "You don't say."

"I do say. Their church told 'em to. You can see why."

She stared at him. No, Barkley was not toying with her. Still, she had heard all sorts of outlandish tales about the Mormons.

"Is it true they walked all the way across these plains, pulling their things in carts?"

"Some of 'em. A lot of suffering before they got where they was gittin'."

"So your family lives out there?"

"My brother and his wife still do. My folks passed on."

She decided, to her chagrin, that Barkley knew what he was talking about. Perhaps she ought to listen to him and Brown, as much as it galled her.

"So. . .lead shot?"

Barkley grinned. "Yes, miss. Open a little gap in the hem and run a row of pellets in, then stitch it tight. My mother used to do it."

Lydia frowned at the thought of carrying a couple extra pounds around all the time, but that would be better than adopting a masculine costume like bloomers. Aunt Moriah would have been mortified to think her niece would wear the scandalous fashion.

"I don't suppose rocks would do?" she ventured.

"I'll get you some lead when we get back to the train." There was sympathy in Barkley's voice now. "Lead's heavier than most rocks, and it hangs better when they're all the same size."

She nodded meekly.

"And I won't tell Mike I gave it to you."

Her rage surfaced once more at his implication that she cared what Corporal Brown thought. She pulled in a sharp breath. Her instinct was to set Barkley in his place with no question as to her feelings about him, Michael Brown, and the entire U.S. Army. But at that moment she wasn't sure what those feelings were.

"Thank you." She turned and strode quickly toward the stream bank.

Corporal Brown was standing at ease, looking back over the trail, his eyes scanning the landscape. Lydia tried not to look at him, but she couldn't resist one quick glance. He did make a dashing figure in his uniform, tall and clear-eyed. It was comforting to have a man as stalwart and alert as Brown keeping watch while they filled their buckets, she told herself, although his stubborn jaw was a bit annoying.

He glanced toward her then and smiled, and Lydia looked quickly away. Part of her wanted to smile back, but the other part didn't want to give him the satisfaction. Was he presumptuous, or was he simply a friendly person? It didn't matter. She had a purpose in life, and starting a flirtation with a cavalry trooper was not part of it. She called to Nathan and made sure she didn't come close enough for Brown to speak to her.

Chapter 3

It was twilight when they got back to the camp. Brown and Barkley delivered each of the ladies to her campfire with a cheery good night, but when they came to the Paines' wagon, Lydia left their group without a word.

Mrs. Paine, however, was more gracious. "Thank you, gentlemen. It's a comfort to have you along."

Brown nodded and smiled at her. "Have a good evening, ma'am." He moved on with the others, wondering how long Lydia would be able to ignore him. She was a pleasure to look at, with her lovely face, thick, reddish-brown hair, and keen blue eyes, but it would be a long summer if she kept up her stiff refinement.

He reached for Mrs. Adams's bucket, now that they were within the safety of the camp and he didn't need to keep his gun at the ready. He was scheduled to stand watch for a couple of hours after midnight, but he always checked the detachment's livestock himself in the evening. The Sioux would love to pick up some extra animals if they had the chance.

As they left Mrs. Williams off, a stir sounded at the opening on the east side of the wagon corral, and Brown turned toward the noise.

"What is it?" Barkley asked, peering through the dimness. Several men were gathered near the gap they used as a gate each evening, between the lead wagon and the last.

Brown thrust the pail of water at him. "See Mrs. Adams to her wagon." He went quickly to the gathering, arriving on the heels of Sergeant Reese.

"What's going on?" Reese barked, pushing his way to the center of the knot of men.

A tall man straightened, and Brown recognized Thomas Miller, the man elected wagon master by the emigrants.

"The Gordon boy just came walking in," Miller said. "He says his mule dropped of exhaustion half a mile back."

"Gordon?" the sergeant asked.

Brown stepped forward. "It's the family I told to stay at Fort Laramie. Their team was worn-out, and they didn't have replacements."

Reese turned to the boy, who was slumped on the tongue of the lead wagon. "You alone, sonny?"

The boy was shivering, and a worn bridle dangled from his hand. He looked up at Reese and gulped. "Yes, sir."

"Says his folks struck out after us yesterday, but the team gave out," Miller told the sergeant. "They're at least ten miles back, to hear him tell it. They put him on the best animal two or three hours ago and told him to come for help."

Mrs. Miller hovered at her husband's elbow, clucking in disapproval. "How could Mr. Gordon endanger the boy like that?"

Miller shrugged. "Probably figured John Paul was lighter than he was and had a better chance of making it on the last mule."

The travelers had left their campfires and thronged to see what the commotion was. Miller turned to face them.

"We can't take these people with us, folks. They were told to wait at Fort Laramie, but they refused to listen."

"But we can't leave them stranded," Mrs. Carver said uncertainly.

Sergeant Reese faced the crowd. "Do you have an extra team to send back? Do you want to just give them your spare animals? Because Miller's right. Either you give them a team or room in your own wagons. That's the only way. And you all know that cuts your own chances of reaching Oregon. If any of you wants to give up a team of mules or oxen for this family, fine."

An uneasy silence fell upon the group until Miller spoke again. "Folks, I feel bad for the Gordons, but the corporal told them what was what before we left the fort. They chose to ignore his advice."

Brown glimpsed Lydia Jackson at the edge of the crowd. Her gaze never left the Gordon boy's face.

She's feeling guilty because she left them, he thought. So his first favorable impression was not amiss. The haughty Miss Jackson had a heart. The boy had come to these people for solace, and he was hearing them denounce his parents as foolish and negligent. Brown could see that it disturbed Lydia.

Mr. Paine stepped toward Miller. "Still, you can't just leave them there exposed like that."

Sergeant Reese agreed. "I'll send some men with a team of army mules to take the Gordons back to Fort Laramie. It's the best we can do."

There was a murmur of assent, and the crowd began to disperse. Brown watched Lydia, and as the men turned away, she rushed toward the boy.

"John Paul! Are you all right?"

"Miss Lydia." For the first time, John Paul Gordon looked hopeful.

"Corporal Brown," Reese called, and Mike turned away. Of course he was the logical choice for the sergeant to send on this mission. He was glad he hadn't set up his tent yet. He'd be spending the night in the saddle for sure.

⌒

"Come over to the Paines' wagon. We'll feed you." Lydia led the boy along.

"Pa's gonna be madder'n spit if they send him back to the fort." John Paul hung his head as he walked with her to Dorcas's cooking fire.

"Well, we can't help that." Lydia saw that two tears had run down his cheeks, leaving paths that glittered in the firelight. "It's going to be all right." She touched his shoulder lightly, but he sniffed and pulled away.

Dorcas handed Jenny over to Lydia. "Hold the baby, dear, and I'll take care of him. Sonny, you sit down on that box and have a bite." She scurried to fill a plate for him.

Mr. Paine poked the fire restlessly with a stick.

"This boy is asleep on his feet," Dorcas said with a frown. "Do you think Sergeant Reese really intends to take him back tonight?"

Mr. Paine shrugged. "I can ask him." He laid his stick down and ambled off across the camp.

John Paul was wolfing leftover biscuits and lukewarm stew when Paine returned with Corporal Brown beside him.

"Come on, son," Brown said. "We're heading back to your folks."

John Paul stood up, cramming half a biscuit into his mouth.

"This boy's all wrung out," Dorcas said. "Can't you let him sleep tonight and take him in the morning?"

"Well, ma'am," Brown said, "that might be good for the boy but not so good for his folks. The sergeant says we head out immediately, and I think that's wise."

"The corporal is in charge of the expedition," Mr. Paine said to Dorcas.

"That's right." Brown clapped John Paul on the shoulder. "You ready, son?"

"Let me go with him," Lydia said.

Brown turned to stare at her. "Beg pardon, miss?"

"Let me go."

"I can't do that."

"But John Paul knows me. He won't be so frightened if I'm along."

"Ma'am, we're escorting the Gordons back to Fort Laramie. Did you want to go back and stay at the fort with them?"

"Well, no, I simply thought—"

"If you come with my detail, you'll have to ride all night with four men you don't know. Aren't you the gal who didn't want to walk to the river with me?"

She felt her anger rising. The man infuriated her every time she crossed his path lately, try as she would to suppress it. "I was thinking of the boy, Corporal."

Brown looked at John Paul critically. "He doesn't look scared to me. You think he needs a nursemaid?"

"That's uncalled for. He may not be frightened now, but—" She lowered her voice and stepped nearer. "His father's a hard man, sir."

Brown stood silent for a moment, then said, "Assuming his folks are all right when we find them, we'll see them back to Fort Laramie. That should give his father time to cool off."

"And supposing Mr. Gordon refuses to go back?"

Brown set his jaw in that implacable manner that irked her to no end. "I'll make him understand he has no choice this time."

Corporal Brown was giving notice that he could be every bit as obstinate as Mr. Gordon, and Lydia envisioned a heated melee on the plains. Her presence might shame the men into keeping their tempers, at least. "I think I should go."

"You're staying right here." He smiled, but she sensed granite behind the words.

"You can't order me around."

"Can't I?"

"No."

"You got a horse?"

Lydia swallowed. "No. I assumed—"

He laughed. "I'm sure you did. You figured I'd let you borrow a horse. Well, we don't have any sidesaddles, ma'am. We're going to ride hard, do what we have to, and come back."

He gestured for the boy to follow him and walked away, and John Paul trailed after him, his chin low on his chest. Lydia looked to Mr. Paine for support.

"Sir, you have a horse. I'm a good rider."

Mr. Paine wouldn't meet her eyes. "Best listen to the corporal."

Brown and John Paul were heading across the center of the compound, weaving between the loose cattle. Lydia took a half dozen quick strides. "Corporal Brown!"

He turned and looked at her. "This isn't a pleasure ride, Miss Jackson."

She realized several of the other travelers were watching them with avid interest. She felt her flush deepen as her ire increased. "I beg your pardon, sir. You have no call to be rude." She held his gaze, daring him to look away.

Brown took a deep breath. "I didn't intend to insult you. It's just that I have a job to do."

"And I'm keeping you from it."

He shrugged. "I'm taking three other men and six of our extra mules back to Laramie. This train's defenses will be depleted by that much until we catch up with you again. It's my responsibility to carry out my duty as quickly as possible. I'm sorry if that upsets you, but I will not change my mind."

Lydia tried to pull out a withering response, but none came to mind. In exasperation, she whirled back toward the Paines' wagon. Dorcas was feeding the cook fire, with little Jenny hanging on to her skirt.

"There you are, Lydia. Can you take Jenny for a few minutes? I don't know where Nathan's got to."

"I'm sorry. I'll look for him." Lydia scooped up the baby and walked slowly around the perimeter of the camp, crooning to Jenny and watching for Nathan.

I must remember my duty, she thought as she walked. *My loyalties are to the*

Paines now, not the Gordons, and I need to help Mrs. Paine. But she couldn't forget the severe whipping Mr. Gordon had given John Paul when he'd lost his father's hatchet. Somehow she was sure the father would find a way to blame the boy if he was forced to go back to the fort. He couldn't take his frustration out on Corporal Brown. Instead, he would take it out on his family.

But Brown was right. Even if she went back and stayed with the family, she couldn't stave off Mr. Gordon's rage. And she didn't want to go back. She was suddenly overcome with thankfulness for Dorcas Paine and her taciturn husband. Already she was beginning to feel at home with them, although she had yet to learn Mr. Paine's first name. It was obvious that he adored Dorcas. Lydia knew he would always put his family first, and he treated her as he would a respected member of the family. Even in refusing her the loan of his saddle horse, he was acting in her best interest.

Thank You, Lord, she breathed. *As usual, I've been headstrong.* Shame washed over her. *Forgive me for being so impulsive and so rude to Corporal Brown.* As she walked along carrying Jenny, she felt a new serenity.

She caressed Jenny's back tenderly, and the little girl snuggled against her shoulder. She found Nathan near the troopers' tents, where Brown was snapping orders for men to harness the mules that would pull the Gordons' wagon and to saddle enough mounts for John Paul and the four men who were going.

"Nathan, your mother's looking for you."

He looked up at her with huge, wistful eyes. "Wish I could go. John Paul's lucky."

She shook her head, unable to explain to him how John Paul had suffered to catch up with them and how he would no doubt suffer under his father's restless fury while waiting for another train at the fort. That was, if his family was still safe. The thought of Mrs. Gordon and the younger children huddled in the wagon while wolves howled or Indians sneaked around made her shiver.

"Go on. Eat your supper."

The boy trotted off, and she lingered a moment longer. Brown was sliding his saddle onto a fidgety chestnut gelding's back. The horse snorted and stepped away.

"There, now," Brown said softly. "Time for you and me to take a little ride, mister."

She wished she had Brown's freedom and could walk over to the army picket lines and choose whichever horse caught her fancy. The chestnut had long legs and a deep chest, and he looked like he could run for miles without being winded. How long since she'd ridden a horse like that?

She should have told Brown that she could ride as well as any man in his unit, that she wouldn't slow them down or get in the way. Not that he would have listened.

She caught herself up with surprise. Her urge to ride back to the Gordons' wagon was gone, wasn't it? How much of her desire to go with the troopers had been a longing to ride horseback again? To be free and active as she had been in childhood, to escape for a few hours the dreary existence to which she had committed herself?

She would stay with the Paines and seek every opportunity to help them. She would not fret and chafe at the agreement she had with them. And she would find time to read the small Bible she had brought along. She hadn't always made the effort to read the scripture after an exhausting day on the trail, and she regretted that. She glanced up at the star-filled sky. *Lord, help me to be a good traveler, and help me make this trip easier for the Paines, not harder.*

She realized suddenly that Brown was staring at her, and she caught her breath. He walked toward her, leading the chestnut.

"Miss Jackson, I told you I can't take you along. The subject is closed."

She lowered her gaze in embarrassment. "I'm sorry, Corporal. I can see that you're right on this matter. I was extremely rude. I hope you'll forgive me for that and for delaying you."

His tense body relaxed, and she knew he had expected another sparring round with her. "We all have strong feelings about some things. Wanting to help someone isn't a bad thing."

"Yes, well, at times I can't see the best way to do that."

"So you're content to stay here tonight?"

"Yes. God speed you on your errand."

His smile was brighter than the glowing stars above.

Chapter 4

Lydia rode on the wagon seat with Dorcas the next afternoon, carefully feeding lead pellets into the hem of her extra dress, then stitching all around the hem to secure them. She had walked all morning, picking up fuel for their evening fire and watching Nathan chase butterflies with the Paines' long-eared, reddish dog, Harpy. All day she had tried not to think about Corporal Brown, but he kept coming to mind whenever she let down her guard. She liked him. She couldn't help it.

The wagon lurched as they hit a deeply rutted section of trail.

"Ouch!" Lydia sucked at her finger where the needle had stabbed it.

"Up!" Mr. Paine called, prodding the near lead ox.

"Are you all right?" Dorcas was all concern.

Lydia grimaced. "I guess I'll live." She marveled at Mr. Paine's consistency. He plodded beside his oxen all day, matching his stride to theirs and keeping the team going steadily but speaking only when necessary. Maybe that was the best kind of husband. Dependable but not very exciting. Certainly better than the choleric Mr. Sawyer, who whipped his mules on the slightest pretext. Maybe there was a medium. She wondered what a man with Mr. Paine's equanimity would be like if he had an adventurous streak.

Then again, would she ever be married? Perhaps after a teaching career, she would have that adventure. If she did have a husband, she hoped he would not be cruel and unfeeling. She couldn't bear the thought of marrying a man who was mean and autocratic. She could live with a quiet man so long as he wasn't stupid, or with a scholar if he wasn't too dull. She hoped the man she married would have a dash of chivalry. Was that too much to ask?

The thought of Corporal Brown flashed once more through her consciousness. *I mustn't allow myself to be too attracted to him,* she warned her uncooperative heart. *I have commitments, and so does he. He's a personable man with pleasing looks, spirited horses, and an air of authority. What of it? I am not here to find a husband.* Of course, a man like that would be an ironclad insurance against a dull marriage.

She knew all the young women had looked over the men of the escort, picking out the ones they believed were most eligible. Margaret Sawyer and Ellen Hadley had talked of nothing else as they walked along the dusty trail together that morning. Michael Brown and John Gleason, who was rumored to play the fiddle, seemed to be high on the list. So were young Matt Barkley and Trooper

Everett Wilson. Sergeant Reese, they'd learned to their bitter disappointment, was married. His wife was awaiting his return at Fort Laramie.

"Well, I think your idea is very sound," Dorcas said, and Lydia catapulted back to the present, realizing she had stitched nearly halfway around the hem of her dress. "When you've finished, you can hold the baby, and I'll get some of Mr. Paine's lead and stitch my claret skirt."

"Hello, ladies." Both women looked up at the greeting. Brown was riding up alongside them from behind. The fractious bay mare tossed her head with a snort, sending her coal black mane rippling. Brown put his gloved hand to the brim of his hat, smiling broadly.

"You're back already!" Dorcas's eyes were wide in disbelief.

"Yes, ma'am. The Gordons were closer to the fort than they were to us. It was almost midnight when we found them. They hadn't seen anyone since Fort Laramie except the mail rider who passed us yesterday. We hitched our mules up to their wagon right away and took them in."

"Driving all night in the dark?" Dorcas shook her head.

"Yes, ma'am. We rode into the fort at first light, got a hot breakfast, and turned around to come back."

Lydia's heart pounded, and she told herself it was due to the closeness of his beautiful mare. She wished that just once she could ride the bay. Brown must have switched mounts when he caught up with the herd of livestock that followed the train. Her gaze drifted from the horse's sleek head and delicately pricked ears and rested on Brown's face.

"The Gordons must be thankful you came," she said, eager for news and determined not to start another argument with him.

Brown winced. "Well, Mr. Gordon's not too happy with me, sad to say. I had my men put his last mule down. It was in terrible distress."

"You must be tired," Dorcas said.

Lydia glanced at him furtively. Whiskers darkened his firm jaw, giving him a dangerous air, and there were deep shadows beneath his eyes.

Brown shrugged. "Part of the job, ma'am." He nodded with approval toward Lydia's sewing project. "Glad to see you've taken my suggestion."

Dorcas's eyes widened. "*Your* suggestion? Why, Lydia, you didn't tell me this clever gentleman invented the idea."

Brown laughed. "Hardly my invention, ma'am. Ladies out here have been doing it for some time."

Lydia lowered her head and concentrated on her stitching.

"You're an asset to the company, Corporal Brown." Dorcas smiled up at him sweetly.

"Thank you, ma'am. Oh, by the way, Miss Jackson—" He held out a two-pound sack, and Lydia reached for it in wonder. "Mrs. Gordon was extremely glad to see John Paul come back safe, and she asked me to give you this. She said you would understand."

Lydia held the bag to her nose and breathed in the rich aroma. "Coffee." She handed it to Dorcas. "Would you put that with the family supplies, please?"

"With pleasure. Mr. Paine will be delighted."

Brown leaned toward them from the saddle as the mare kept pace. "The boy was fine when I left them. I told his pa he ought to be proud of him."

Lydia nodded. Looking into his deep brown eyes made her pulse accelerate and her cheeks flush. She looked straight ahead. "Thank you."

"Well, it was about all we could do." He grinned. "Don't put too much lead in there, now. The troopers will be disappointed." He tipped his hat and spurred his horse forward until he was hidden from their view by the next wagon.

Dorcas was smiling, her face pink with pleasure. "That is a very nice young man, Lydia."

"I'm not so sure."

"Why, my dear, you don't think he's nice?"

"He has an impudent side."

"Oh, he's friendly, and he likes a joke, but he seems sincere."

"Can two people make each other angry and still like each other?" Lydia asked, and Dorcas looked at her with injured surprise.

"Corporal Brown was perfectly civil just now."

"I suppose he was, but we've had a few moments when he made my blood boil. Perhaps I was unjust."

Lydia frowned, jabbing her needle through the fabric. It was true he was handsome and clever, and he seemed to have a compassionate vein, as well. Was she taking offense too easily? When she considered his motives each time they had crossed swords verbally, she had to admit he hadn't been insufferable. He had a heightened sense of duty, and that had caused their biggest flare-up. She feared it would be easy to let herself be drawn to the corporal, and she mustn't do that. She needed to keep her emotions in check. After all, she had a job ahead of her. Perhaps that was why her mind told her she had taken a dislike to him.

"Mr. Paine and the sergeant were having a cup of coffee last evening, and Mr. Paine asked about Corporal Brown's horses," Dorcas said.

"His horses?" Against her will, Lydia gave her attention to Dorcas.

"Surely you've noticed that Brown's horses are better than all the others. Why, most of the troopers are riding mules, which is all well and good. They're hardy and they're easy keepers, but—" Lydia waved one hand, and Dorcas trailed to a stop. "Don't you care about the horses? I thought you loved them. You said your father bred fine carriage horses."

"Corporal Brown is in charge of their remounts." Lydia hoped to steer her smoothly back to the topic.

"That's right. When a man needs a new horse, he has to go to Corporal Brown for it."

"And that's why he has the best horse. That seems a bit self-serving, doesn't it?"

"Well, the sergeant told Mr. Paine that Brown keeps the horses in good shape for the officers. He rides the most obstreperous animals in the herd."

"Also the most beautiful," Lydia said thoughtfully.

"Can he help it if that gorgeous bay is ornerier than the stubbornest mule? He's training it to be a good, steady mount. Sergeant Reese said that when they get new animals, it's Brown's job to try them out and assign them to the men according to their ability and the animals' temperaments."

Lydia smiled. "Exactly as you say, Dorcas. *He* rides the ornery ones." Even as she reached for the baby, she knew it was a cutting and undeserved assessment of the corporal. "Here, let me hold Jenny. Your arms must be tired."

As the wagon creaked along, Lydia hummed softly to lull Jenny to sleep. Dorcas fetched her workbag, but she decided she couldn't sew after all, with the wagon lurching so, and took out her crocheting instead. As she worked, she prattled on about the disappointing array of supplies at Fort Laramie and the scandalously meager wardrobe of Mrs. Carver and her daughters in the wagon ahead of them.

Lydia found her thoughts straying again to the handsome corporal. It was the mare that drew her attention, she told herself. The rider held less than no interest for her. She would rather drink water from the Platte River than engage Corporal Brown in conversation.

But that wasn't true—far from it.

Lord, help me! she prayed in silent exasperation. *I'm a grown woman, on my way to fill a demanding position, and here I am getting starry-eyed over a dashing man. Help me to focus on what's ahead and to put aside thoughts of Michael Brown. I don't see that he fits into Your plan for me.*

⌒

The first ford over the Platte was a time of testing. The travelers had crossed the river many times in Nebraska Territory, but it was more treacherous here. Since leaving Fort Laramie they had resorted to ferries when a crossing was necessary. But now they were beyond the ferries, and the emigrants were on their own.

The troopers had been through the harrowing experience before and showed the families how to waterproof their loads. Early in the morning, Brown and Barkley tested the ford. Halfway across, the water rose to their mounts' bellies, but Brown was confident the oxen could make the ford without losing their footing. Oxen couldn't swim and pull wagons the way horses could. If the water was too deep, they would have to unload all the wagons and float the goods across in a few watertight wagon boxes, dismantle the other ox-drawn wagons, float the parts across, swim the animals over, and reassemble the train.

But it was mid-July, and the river was fairly low. Most of the men in the company seemed competent with their teams, and there should be no serious problems. Brown sent Barkley back to report to Sergeant Reese that the crossing was not too risky. The settlers would need to keep their teams moving; that was the main thing.

Mike rode on to scout the trail ahead for two or three miles. He spotted a small band of Sioux camped beside the river, but he had no fear of them. The wagon train had four times as many men and ought to pass the Indian camp without incident, unless the Sioux swarmed out to beg the travelers to trade. The wagon train would be well advised to chain their stock up tonight and post a heavy guard, however.

He rode to the top of the next knoll and stopped, looking out over the endless prairie. Bushy yellow and purple flowers grew all across the plain. From a distance, the colored patches were resplendent, waving in the wind. They didn't have masses of flowers like this where he grew up in Tennessee. Martha would have loved to see them.

He took a deep, careful breath. It didn't hurt so much to think about her now. Out here, under the limitless sky, he was able to talk to God about it and to forgive himself for leaving her and Billy behind.

The mare tossed her head and pawed the ground. Mike turned her around and loosened the reins just a hair, and she took off at a canter toward the ford.

Chapter 5

Lydia avoided Brown for the next week, but that wasn't difficult. He seemed to draw a lot of scouting details, riding forward of the train for long periods. Occasionally she saw him across the compound early in the morning, drinking coffee with the other troopers, but then he rode out and was gone all day.

One evening he dropped by to speak to Mr. Paine but declined Dorcas's offer of supper. More often, Mr. Paine would go join the men at the escort's fire in the evening.

The days settled into the routine of the trail. Lydia found her life with the Paines pleasant compared to her stay with the Gordons, but monotony was inevitable. She walked sometimes with the other women or gathered fuel with Nathan. She carried Jenny for short periods or sat on the wagon box holding her to give Dorcas a respite. She was becoming fond of the two children.

When the train halted for nooning and when they circled for the night, each family member began his or her chores. Mr. Paine lit the fire and tended the oxen and his horse, Beauty. Lydia took care of Jenny and brought water, while Nathan gathered fuel. Dorcas immediately began preparing the meal. Most days Trooper Gleason found one excuse or another to stop by their camp spot, and Lydia was afraid he harbored hopes that he might win her heart.

In the long, mindless hours of trudging along the trail, Lydia thought about what lay ahead. Oregon seemed farther away than ever. Sometimes it seemed they would never get out of this vast, dusty plain. Other times she summoned a bright vision of herself teaching eager children. It would be a worthwhile, satisfying life.

She walked along one torrid afternoon with three of the young women close to her age. Frances Bailey's family had joined the train at Fort Laramie, and Lydia felt an affinity for her. The Baileys seemed a bit more refined than some of the others in the company and had been faithful in attending chapel services at Fort Laramie. This morning Lydia had gone early to the Baileys' wagon to invite Frances to fetch water with her and had found the girl reading from a battered volume of William Blake's poetry. At that moment, Lydia knew she and Frances had much in common, and she was eager to learn more about her new friend.

Margaret Sawyer was the oldest girl in her large family, and she escaped the range of her mother's voice whenever possible. Margaret was often required to look after a brood of younger siblings but occasionally was able to slip off and socialize with other young people, especially Ellen Hadley.

Ellen was promised to marry Margaret's eldest brother, Charlie Sawyer. She was seventeen, and according to Margaret, Ellen's parents weren't crazy about seeing their daughter married so young. In Lydia's opinion, it was the intended groom who raised the Hadleys' objections. Charlie was an immature nineteen, given to practical jokes and horseplay. Lydia had trouble seeing him as husband material. The Sawyers and the Hadleys had been neighbors in Ohio and traveled west together. Ellen said her parents had agreed to allow the wedding once they reached Oregon.

"I'll be eighteen, anyway," she'd said airily.

Jenny was napping in the wagon when Frances, Margaret, and Ellen came to coax Lydia to walk with them.

"Jenny will sleep for a couple of hours, and Nathan will stay with his father," Dorcas told her. "Go and enjoy yourself."

Lydia wasn't sure she wanted to get too close to Margaret and Ellen. She had experienced their idle chatter before, with the result that she now knew more about the inner workings of their families than she wanted to know. But Frances's look held such a wistful appeal that she decided to go.

"Just let me get my chip basket."

Margaret laughed. "I've got mine. Ma says I can't go off and leave her with the little ones without bringing home fuel for the cook fire."

They walked along slowly so as not to outdistance the wagons, stooping frequently for dried buffalo chips.

Ellen ran a finger around the collar of her cotton dress. "If it weren't for this breeze, we'd all bake to a crisp."

"We should have brought a water skin," Margaret agreed. "I feel like I'm going to shrivel up and mummify."

Lydia glanced at Frances and returned the shy smile Frances gave her. She was about to ask her how she liked Blake's poetry when Margaret said, "Don't look. Troopers coming up behind us."

Ellen giggled.

"I just pretend I don't notice them," Frances said softly.

"Ladies!"

It was amiable Trooper John Gleason and another man whose acquaintance Lydia had so far avoided. He and Gleason reined their mules to a pace that matched that of the young women.

"Miss Sawyer, Miss Hadley," said Gleason. "And Miss Jackson."

"Good day, Private Gleason," Lydia said. She was not surprised that Gleason had made it his business to know the names of all the single young women.

"Haven't met this young lady," said Gleason.

Frances stared at the ground, blushing.

"Oh, that's Frances Bailey," Margaret said with a saucy smile. "She's quiet as a church mouse."

"Yes," said Ellen. "She generally hides in her pa's wagon, but we dragged her out for a constitutional."

Gleason laughed. "Have you ladies all met Trooper Stedman?"

"Why, no," Ellen said. She and Margaret called a merry greeting to the second man.

"Ladies." The trooper tipped his hat and smiled at them boldly.

"Trooper Gleason, is it true you have a fiddle?" Margaret asked.

"Yes, miss. One of these nights we'll have us some dancin'."

"Oh, how about tonight?" Margaret squealed, and Lydia wished the dusty soil would part and swallow her whole.

Gleason shrugged. "Folks'll be tired tonight. Sometime when we're going to stop a bit, maybe."

"I hope it's soon," Ellen said, her eyes shining.

"You just want to dance with Charlie," Margaret said.

"I'd dance with most anybody about now," Ellen retorted. "I hardly ever see Charlie. He's always off minding the stock."

"What, you gals not getting enough exercise during the day?" Stedman asked, and Margaret and Ellen giggled.

Frances was lagging behind, and Lydia slowed her steps, as well. She didn't want the men to consider her a part of the flirtation, harmless though it may be.

Gleason's voice carried easily. "Well, Pete, when we get an evening for dancin', you'll have to make sure these ladies don't lack for partners."

"It will be a pleasure," Stedman said. "Why, I expect so many gents will stand in line that you ladies will dance until dawn."

The men touched their hats and urged their mules into a trot. Sergeant Reese was coming down the line of wagons toward them, and Lydia guessed the two troopers didn't want him to see them loitering.

"He is just too handsome," Margaret said dreamily.

"Which one?" Ellen asked.

"Either."

Frances winced at Lydia, and Lydia smiled. "Long weeks on the trail can enhance a man's looks," she whispered, and Frances convulsed in silent laughter.

"I wouldn't mind dancing with Trooper Stedman," Ellen said.

"Too bad Gleason can't fiddle and dance at the same time," Margaret added, and Lydia couldn't hold back her laugh.

"Well, there!" Ellen cried. "You can take a joke, after all. You're usually as sober as a judge who lost his gavel."

Lydia smiled ruefully, wondering if perhaps she was too somber. Sergeant

Reese had passed the other two troopers and was cantering his gray horse toward them. He passed a few yards from the girls, and Lydia turned to watch the gelding's springy gait.

"The sergeant's married," Margaret said with evident disappointment.

Lydia jerked her head around to face westward again. "I wasn't ogling the sergeant. I was looking at his horse."

"His horse!" Ellen giggled. "That's likely!"

"I'd love to have a chance to ride some of the horses these cavalrymen have," Lydia said.

"Can you ride?" Frances asked. "I've never learned."

"Oh yes," Lydia said. "I used to ride a lot when my father was alive."

"I'd be afraid," Frances declared. The other girls laughed.

"It's not so hard," said Margaret. "I used to ride our plow horse out to the pasture and back. Now all we've got are those nasty oxen."

"What sort of horse did your father have?" Frances asked, looking at Lydia with huge, admiring eyes.

"He had lots of horses." Lydia saw glances pass between the other girls, and she wished she hadn't said it. She could see that they were wondering whether to believe her or not. "My father raised horses. He trained them for saddle and for carriage teams. His clients came from all over Connecticut, and some even came up from New York to buy at our farm."

"Sounds as if you had it pretty soft," Margaret said.

Ellen clucked her tongue and frowned at Margaret.

Lydia shrugged. "That was a long time ago."

"What happened?" Frances asked.

Lydia hesitated, but Frances at least seemed sympathetic. "Father died. We had a fire, and he was trying to get the horses out of the barn. They were his fortune, you see. The stallion especially. Father was determined to save him." She felt the tears pricking at her eyelids, though it had been more than five years. "He told me to wait while he went in for Jubel."

They walked in silence for several paces, then Margaret prodded, "And?"

"The roof of the barn collapsed. He didn't get out."

Frances's hot fingers clasped Lydia's for a moment. "I'm sorry," she whispered.

"Did the horse survive?" Margaret asked.

"Margaret! That's insensitive of you!" Ellen cried.

Lydia swallowed hard. "No. No, Jubel didn't make it, either."

"What about your mother?" Frances's eyes were also glistening with tears, and Lydia managed a weak smile, wondering how she had allowed herself to be persuaded to tell this tale.

"My mother died when I was quite young. So after the fire I was an orphan."

The other three girls sighed, and Frances slipped her arm around Lydia.

"You poor thing. Is that why you came west?"

Lydia smiled. "No. I went to live with my aunt after that. I was fifteen years old, and she thought I ought to finish my education."

"Really?" Ellen's eyebrows arched in surprise. "Mine was finished long before I reached fifteen."

"Well, it was a bit different there, I expect," Lydia said. Although she now shared these young women's state of abject poverty, it hadn't always been so. Her memories of the comfortable old home at the horse farm and of her aunt's mansion in Hartford were painful now.

"Anyway," she said briskly, "my aunt picked out the school she thought was most suitable and sent me there. I attended for three years, but I didn't have many chances to ride anymore."

"No horsemanship classes?" Ellen asked with a chuckle.

"Wouldn't that be grand?" Margaret's giggle rose once more to an annoying tone. "Do they teach fine ladies to ride in Connecticut?"

"I expect they do," Lydia said, "but not at my school. In the city park, we used to see ladies out riding. They had fine velvet habits and sidesaddles, of course."

"Of course," Ellen said, her eyes twinkling. "And no doubt were escorted by gentlemen in caped coats and top hats."

"Certainly."

"Wouldn't that be lovely to see?" Frances sighed.

"Too bad your school wasn't fine enough to teach you that," said Margaret.

Lydia knew how dearly Miss Clarkson would have liked to add equestrian classes to her curriculum, but alas, the school would have needed a wealthy benefactor for that. As it was, they'd had other innovative courses.

"My teacher was quite progressive," she said. "She was a great proponent of decorative arts and physical education."

"What's that?" asked Margaret.

Frances's eyes were wide. "Is that where you learn all the insides of the body?"

"No," Lydia laughed. "It's where you exercise for your health and learn agility and coordination."

Margaret blinked at her as if she couldn't imagine what Lydia meant.

"Sounds high-falutin'," Ellen said. "We got the three Rs through sixth grade, and that was it."

"I learned to embroider and play the organ," Frances said. Her timid glance told Lydia she considered making this information public a risk.

Lydia smiled at her. "I'd love to hear you play sometime."

"We had to leave the instrument behind."

"Ah. Well, perhaps there will be one in Oregon."

"Perhaps," Frances agreed. "They say some folks send fine furniture around Cape Horn to Oregon by ship."

Lydia squeezed Frances's hand and let it go. "I've enjoyed the company, ladies, but I must see if Mrs. Paine needs me. Jenny has probably finished her nap by now."

As she hastened her steps toward the Paines' wagon, she heard Margaret say, "Ain't we grand?"

Frances's troubled reply came soft but firm. "I think she's wonderful."

"Do you believe that about the fire and all?" Margaret asked.

Lydia hurried on, biting her lip. It would have been much better to have kept her thoughts to herself. Now those who believed her would pity her, and those who didn't would think she'd invented a story to draw sympathy.

Chapter 6

Mike knew they were close to Independence Rock, the halfway point for most of the emigrants. They would leave the muddy Platte and follow the Sweetwater upstream toward the mountains. It was a point of change, and the settlers were filled with excitement. But first they had to negotiate the Platte one last time.

The troopers rode alongside the teams, shouting encouragement to the drivers. It was their third river crossing in five days, and each ford had its treacheries. Now the Platte was swollen from rain in the mountains.

One moment the Anderson family's team strode confidently in two inches of murky water; the next they were breast-deep and floundering, with the wagon careening crazily behind them.

Mike sat on his mount—a big, powerful mule—watching in exasperation.

"Get them over!" he yelled to Trooper Wilson, who was trying to grab the bridle of one of the wheelers. "Three feet to your right, and you'll be fine!"

To Mike's relief, the off mules gained solid footing. The team soon lumbered up the far bank with the wagon intact.

Mike sighed. He had spent most of the day in and out of the water, soaked to his knees. The mule he called Buster was steadier than most of the horses and reliable for this work.

The pioneers were grim-faced, and many had lightened their wagons. Some of the furniture they were trying to tote to Oregon amazed him.

"You'll never get that article over the Rockies, ma'am, let alone the Cascades," he told Mrs. Hunter, as two of his men helped her husband unload an oak credenza. "Trust me. Save your energy for the things you need."

"We should have sold it in New Jersey," her husband said bitterly. "Travel light. That's what they told us."

Mike left them and headed for where the Paines waited. Their wagon was one that had been taken apart and waterproofed with hides and grease and used in the ferrying. Josiah Paine had gone back and forth all day with the troopers, helping others, and Mike felt he deserved extra help now to ensure that his goods and his family passed safely over the Platte.

He and Paine began to load crates, bedding, and pans into the wagon box. Nathan, Lydia, and Dorcas brought them bundles to stow.

A flash of color caught Mike's eye, and he looked up to see Gleason riding his mule up from the ford, carrying an armful of pink and lavender flowers.

"Well, John," he said and laughed. "What are you up to?"

Gleason smiled. "Thought I'd cheer up the ladies. Mrs. Paine, Miss Jackson, this is but a preview of the lovely country across the river."

Lydia laughed, reaching out to take the flowers from him. "Lovely country exactly like the country we left when we crossed six miles downstream, I take it."

Dorcas frowned. "Now, Lydia, be gracious. This gentleman took time to pick us a nosegay, and isn't it fine? Thank you, Trooper Gleason."

Mike chuckled. "Miss Jackson would have liked it better if you'd brought her some of those burdocks we saw growing over the hill yonder for the stew pot."

"Burdocks?" Lydia asked eagerly.

Her face told him she was ravenous. The few root vegetables they'd brought had probably been eaten weeks ago, and there had been nothing fresh available at Fort Laramie.

"Take it easy, Miss Jackson," Gleason said with a smile. "Don't get all het up about burdocks. They're several miles ahead, and by the time we get you folks over the river, it'll be almost dark. No root digging tonight."

Dorcas had perked up, too. "I'd love to get hold of some of those roots. It would make a nice change."

The Paines and the Hunters were the only two families left to cross. This ford was taking longer than most, and unpacking and transferring the loads was disheartening. Miller and Reese had agreed to camp just over the river for the night to allow the people to put their things back in order.

"Time for you ladies to cross," Mike said.

"I'll take Nathan with me," said Mr. Paine. "Mrs. Paine can ride Beauty over and carry Jenny."

"I'll take the little one for you," Mike offered. He caught a shocked glance from Lydia as he reached for the baby. She probably thought he'd never held a baby before and would drop Jenny into the swirling water. As Dorcas lifted Jenny, the little girl looked up at Mike and reached a chubby hand toward his face. Mike smiled. The little girl's clothing was clean and her hair combed. He pulled her to his chest as he would a precious treasure. "Say, John, Miss Jackson needs a ride over."

"Well, I—" Lydia looked around quickly, as if searching for an alternative. The only other trooper still on this side of the Platte was Barkley, and he was speaking with Mr. Paine about guiding the oxen across.

"Why, miss, I'd be honored," Gleason said, flushing beneath his tan.

Lydia hesitated then nodded. "Thank you, I appreciate that."

Gleason slipped his boot from his near stirrup, and she raised her foot to the iron then reached up and grasped Gleason's wrist, swinging herself up in a graceful arc and landing gently behind the saddle.

She's done that before. A stab of envy quickly replaced Mike's surprise as he saw her hands creep reluctantly onto Gleason's shoulders. Just for a moment, he wished he had offered to take Lydia himself and left Jenny to her mother.

Against his better sense, he urged Buster close to Gleason's mule for a moment and whispered, "Don't y'all be afraid to hang on, now. We'd hate to have to pull you out of the Platte."

Lydia scowled at him, and he winked then headed Buster for the water, holding little Jenny cuddled tight against his shoulder. Buster stepped awkwardly into the murky water, and Mike let the mule find his balance. Dorcas's horse stepped in without balking. Mike looked back. As Gleason's mule plunged in, Lydia suddenly grabbed the trooper around the waist and clung to him. Gleason's grin told Mike that John's strategy had worked, and he'd managed to scare Lydia into embracing him. Yes, John was happy to have the plum assignment.

That's all right, Mike told himself. *It's not every day a man gets to hold a sweet-smelling baby.*

～

Mrs. Paine offered supper to the three troopers who had helped them get their wagon and family across the river. Lydia accepted the men's eager response with resignation.

Most of the other women had been on the north bank for hours, and Mrs. Carver invited Dorcas to cook at her fire. It had burned down to a fine bed of coals, and Dorcas gratefully rummaged for her pans in the wagon box and began to fix supper. Lydia helped, wishing they had some of those elusive burdocks. Somehow she would get some tomorrow, no matter what.

Barkley, Gleason, and Brown sat on crates, talking lazily with Mr. Paine.

"We'll feed them first," Dorcas told Lydia in a low voice. "I don't have enough plates for us all to eat at once." She gave Jenny a dry biscuit to gnaw on while they hurriedly prepared the meal.

Frances appeared in the twilight with a pan of fresh-baked corn bread. "Mama sent this over. She made extra for you and the Hunters."

"Bless you, child!" Dorcas cried. "Give your mother a kiss for me, and tell her I'll return the pan in the morning."

Frances smiled. "Is there anything I can do? You seem to have some extra mouths to feed this evening."

"My dear, if you could find an extra coffee mug for us to borrow, it would put us in good order."

Frances hastened to fetch a mug and then offered to watch Jenny. Lydia and Mrs. Paine soon had the meal ready. Lydia filled tin plates with stew for the men and Nathan and carried them to the circle before the Paines' wagon while Dorcas poured coffee.

"Thank you," Gleason said, grinning up at Lydia. He obviously thought she was mad about him, after the way she had shamelessly held on to him during the river crossing. How could she tell him it was only because the horse had lunged so violently that she feared for her life?

"So you fellows have been out here quite a spell," Mr. Paine said as Lydia handed him his supper.

"Oh, I've only been with the Seventh about a year," Gleason said, "but Matt and the corporal have been here a lot longer."

"It's been about five years for me now." Brown accepted his plate with a cheerful nod. "Matt's the one who's practically a native."

Barkley grinned. "Yeah, my folks left Massachusetts when I was just a kid. I grew up in the Green River Valley, about five miles from Fort Bridger."

"Did you ever meet Jim Bridger?" Dorcas asked as she made the rounds with hot coffee.

"Several times," Barkley said. "He's quite the character."

"And how did you get your education in the wilderness?" Dorcas asked. Lydia knew she was concerned about schooling for Nathan and Jenny once they settled on their claim in Oregon.

"Well, I'd had some back East, and my mother kept us kids at it out here. We didn't have many books, but we got along. She had us scratch our sums in the dirt sometimes, because we didn't have paper to waste. Anytime my father had a chance to trade for a book, he did."

Dorcas nodded. "Your mother must have been a courageous and resourceful woman."

"Yes, ma'am, she was."

"We had a dame school when I was a lad," Mr. Paine revealed, and Lydia looked at him in surprise. He rarely said more than five words in an evening, but when he did speak, it was with flawless grammar. She hovered, wanting to hear more.

"I only went through four grades, but it's served me well. How about you, Corporal?" he asked.

"I had a little schooling back home," Brown said. "Not as much as some."

"Probably more than me," Gleason said. "There wasn't any school where my pappy settled in Arkansas. He turned and looked at Lydia. "How about yourself, Miss Jackson? Did you have any teaching?"

She hesitated. "I was tutored at home, and then—"

"And then I suppose they sent you to a finishing school," Gleason said with a laugh.

"Well. . .yes. Miss Clarkson's Seminary for Young Ladies, in Hartford, Connecticut."

"There, now," said Mr. Paine.

Brown was smiling. "For young ladies, yet."

Barkley nodded. "No hoydens allowed."

"In Hartford, Connecticut," Gleason said.

"Yes." Lydia wasn't sure she liked the way the conversation was going. The troopers seemed ready to make fun of her.

"Let me guess," Brown said. "You learned to play the dulcimer and stitch petit point."

She eyed the corporal suspiciously, expecting his sarcasm to blossom. "We did study music and embroidery. Also archery. Developing manual dexterity is important."

"Oh, of course." He smiled and sipped his coffee.

"They do that where I come from, too," Gleason said.

"Really?" Lydia asked with misgiving.

"Yeah, but instead of archery, the ladies chop wood and hoe the corn patch."

"Good for manual dexterity, I expect," Barkley said with a laugh.

Gleason laughed, too, and Mr. Paine smiled good-naturedly, but Lydia didn't find it humorous.

"Take it easy on Miss Jackson, boys," Brown said. "She had a chance to learn something, and she took it."

"There's nothing to belittle in that," Mr. Paine agreed.

Barkley smiled ruefully. "Sorry, Miss Jackson."

Frances had been sitting all the while on a quilt with Jenny, and she asked dreamily, "Did you learn to speak French at Miss Clarkson's?"

"Latin," Lydia said.

"Oh, of course, Latin." Gleason's affable smile made her want to scream.

"That will do you so much good out here," said Barkley. "Especially if we run into some ancient Italians."

"Well, Matt, you know, them Arapaho are always roamin'." Gleason hooted at his own pun.

Lydia felt her upper lip quiver and bit it.

Brown was watching her, and he rose, passing his mug to Lydia. "If it's not too much trouble, Miss Jackson, might I have a drop more coffee?"

"Of course." She went to retrieve the coffeepot, and Brown followed her.

"Don't let the fellows bother you," he said softly. "They're just having fun. They don't get a chance very often. It's true they don't have the best parlor manners, but sitting down with a nice family like this will do them a world of good."

"You're the one who should teach them manners, Corporal Brown." A lump was forming in Lydia's throat, and she tried to swallow it down. She ought to be able to laugh along with them, but the memories of the past hurt too much. She glared at him, hoping she could escape his presence before her tears spilled over. "Your men are churlish, and there have been moments when I thought you were the same."

Brown's merry laugh exploded. "I've never met that word outside a book. Perhaps you'd better introduce us properly." He turned to Paine. "I do beg your pardon if we've spoken out of turn, sir. Miss Jackson thinks we're churlish."

"Not you, Corporal," Mr. Paine said with a frown.

"Yes, me, too."

"Oh, no, miss," said Gleason. "He's from Tennessee."

Lydia sent Gleason a glare that she hoped would give him frostbite. She gathered her skirts and turned toward the wagon, ignoring the men's riotous laughter.

Chapter 7

Trooper Gleason appeared in the center of the camp after supper with his fiddle, and Mr. Adams soon joined him with a mouth organ. The girls were giddy when the dancing began, and even the grown-ups joined in. Mr. Paine took a turn with Dorcas, while Lydia hung back in the shadows, holding Jenny. Finally Dorcas came and coaxed her to join the fun.

"Come on, dear. I'll put Jenny to bed and stay near the wagon in case she cries."

Lydia hesitated then moved toward the center of the corral. One of the troopers immediately claimed her hand, and she danced for an hour, changing partners with each new tune. She was surprised to find that she was enjoying herself with the other young people. But Corporal Brown was nowhere to be seen.

She told herself she wasn't disappointed and resolved not to ask about him, but it didn't matter. Margaret Sawyer pulled her aside, her eyes glowing. "Too bad the corporal has sentry duty tonight. I'd give anything to dance with him! Oh well, Private Wilson is a passable dancer."

"Isn't that Trooper Stedman dancing with Ellen?" Lydia asked. "Where's Charlie?"

Margaret snorted. "Yonder with Tim Anderson. He's madder'n a hornet. Ellen's danced with Pete Stedman three times tonight!"

Lydia decided the less said the better on that topic. "Oh, look, Minnie Carver's dancing with Dr. Nichols!"

Margaret laughed. "Her sister Jean got the first hour, and Minnie's got this hour."

"Are they watching the children turnabout?" Lydia asked, puzzled.

"No, they've only got one decent dress between them, and they had to switch off." Margaret turned a bright smile on the cavalryman approaching them.

"Miss Jackson, isn't it?" the trooper asked, looking past Margaret at Lydia.

"I. . .yes."

"I'm David Farley. Would you do me the honor?"

"Well, I—" Lydia glanced apologetically toward Margaret, but the girl had already turned away and was accepting the attentions of another trooper, so Lydia smiled and took Farley's hand.

It was not an unpleasant evening, she thought, though none of the troopers overly impressed her. Most were homesick young fellows who had been away from their families for months or even years and longed to have someone to talk to. Lydia prided herself on being a good listener. She said very little about herself but drew the men out about their families and the rough life they led in the cavalry.

When the party broke up and Gleason stopped playing, Lydia saw him looking around, and she feared he was searching for her. She slipped away and went back to the wagon. Dorcas was dozing on her pallet with Jenny curled beside her, and Nathan snored gently. Mr. Paine was tending the fire. He nodded to her and stepped over the wagon tongue with Harpy on his heels. Lydia knew they would make their nightly inspection of the family's livestock.

She pulled her blankets and carpetbag out of the wagon and made her bed with the bag as her pillow. Before she settled down, she reached deep inside it. Under her extra clothing was her Bible. She felt around a bit more until paper crackled between her fingers, and she drew out a creased and worn envelope.

It was too dark to read, but she held it close to her heart. Dancing had been fun, but she wasn't out to find a husband. It was because of this letter that she had set out on this arduous journey. She knew it almost by heart. It was the agreement that pulled her to Oregon.

The loss of her parents and later her aunt had set her adrift, alone in the world. Then came the discovery that Aunt Moriah had spent all her resources on Lydia's education. Lydia remembered the weeks of terrifying hopelessness when she had asked one family friend after another for advice on finding a position, but none could help her.

At last she had turned to her beloved former teacher. Miss Clarkson had allowed her to stay at the seminary for three months without paying board. In return, Lydia assisted with some of the lower classes and cleaned the classrooms. At last Miss Clarkson had presented an offer. A town in Oregon wanted a schoolteacher, one who could set up an academy that taught a classical curriculum. It would be an arduous trip, and the pay was low for a demanding job.

"The teacher must agree to one year's service and must not marry during the term of her contract," read the paper the school board had sent. At the time, that restriction had seemed irrelevant. Lydia had no prospects for marriage, and the security of a teaching contract seemed the best possible solution to her problems.

Dear God, Lydia prayed haltingly, as she clutched the envelope containing her copy of the contract, *You have given me this opportunity. Please help me to live up to the terms I agreed to. Help me to be a good teacher and to help many children learn. And help me not to wish for a different life.*

⌒

Mike ambled slowly around the rope corral the troopers had erected to pen in their mounts for the night. Private Haines was making the circuit of the corral in the other direction. Usually the stock was confined within the circle of the wagons for safety at night, but tonight that space had been appropriated for dancing. The strains of Gleason's fiddle had faded, and it was quiet now. The mules stamped and snorted as they vied for the dry grass. Mike watched outward as he walked, searching for sounds and movements that didn't belong in the dark, peaceful scene.

As he came around the side nearest the wagons, he saw a form coming toward him.

"Who's there?" Mike called softly.

"It's me—Paine."

"Evenin'." Mike waited for him.

"Thought I might find you out here," Paine said.

"Walk with me, sir," Mike replied, and they fell into step around the circle. The horses and mules cropped the grass without taking notice of them.

"I've got a riding mare," Paine said after a moment.

"I noticed her. Good, stout horse."

"Yes, well, she picked up some nettles today. I plucked them out of her leg, and I don't think it's serious, but she worries at the spot. Don't want her to rub the skin off."

"I've got something," Mike said. "It's in one of our supply wagons. Better than lard. I'll get it for you when someone relieves me."

"I'm obliged."

They strolled on in a new sense of companionship. A horse nickered and stepped toward the rope barrier. In the faint light, Mike could make out the markings of the bay mare he liked to ride. She thrust her nose over the rope and snuffled.

"Big baby." Mike stroked her muzzle. He and Paine kept walking, and the mare lowered her head to graze. "There's still a lot of rough country between here and Oregon," Mike said. "Be hard for the missus and the young ones."

"Mrs. Paine isn't one to complain when things get difficult."

"That's true," Mike said. "She's held up better than a lot of folks. Are you figuring to farm in Oregon?"

Paine was silent for a moment before he answered. "I want a place of my own. A place where Dorcas and the young'uns can live peaceful."

Mike sighed. "Well, if you're not too picky, you might find it. Most of the best land is taken, but there are still homesteads available."

"I'd never be able to own a farm of any size back East. But out here, they say any hardworking man can make a go of it."

They paced on in silence, and Mike stayed alert to the night sounds.

"What about you, Corporal? What do you want out here?" Paine asked.

"Well now, that's a question. Everything I wanted is gone now."

"How's that?"

Mike took a long, deep breath. "My family. Lost them near two years ago. I was at Fort Bridger and didn't know about it for months. My wife and little boy, that is."

"I'm sorry."

"To tell you the truth, I'd like to have a home again. Don't expect to see it happen, though."

"You never know what God will do."

Mike nodded. "That's so. Thank you for reminding me."

They walked on in silence. Two troopers approached from the camp, and Mike greeted them. The two new guards started out in opposite directions around the corral. Mike and Mr. Paine walked back toward the wagons together. Mike struck a match and lit a lantern at the back of one of the wagons. He rummaged in his chest of remedies for the livestock and came out with a tin of salve.

"Put some of that on your mare's leg. I don't know if it helps the healing, but it tastes bad enough to keep her from licking it."

Paine nodded. "I thank you."

Mike smiled then. "There's one other thing I'd really like to see out here."

"What's that?"

"That gal traveling with you—"

"Miss Jackson?"

"That's the one," Mike said. "She takes herself far too seriously. I'd like to see her laugh."

The next morning Mike rode ahead of the train to evaluate the conditions between their overnight stop and Independence Rock. They could be there by midafternoon, he judged, if nothing unforeseen delayed them.

He reined the bay mare to a halt beneath the huge rock, staring westward toward Devil's Gate. It was here that he and three others had made a stand against a trio of renegades two years back, and one of his fellow troopers had been killed. That was a black moment, and he'd wondered if he would survive his tour of duty in Wyoming Territory. He was a happily married man then and eager to rejoin his family in Tennessee. He had lived through the harrowing ordeal but a short time later had learned that his family was gone.

Funny how a man's values could be turned upside down in an instant. One minute he'd been desperate to stay alive, the next he'd wondered if living was worthwhile.

On the other hand, look how that adventure had turned out for T.R. Barkley, Matt's older brother. He'd made it through the ordeal, along with the daughter of Mike's commanding officer. Now the two were married and settled in the Green River Valley. And if a half wild scout like T.R. could find a new life in this wilderness, maybe he could, too.

The mare nickered and pulled against the reins. Mike turned eastward and cantered back toward the wagons. Yes, life was worth living, he'd concluded after months of agonized study in the scriptures. As long as God wanted him on this earth, he'd do his best to stay healthy. Right now he had sixty families to worry about.

When he arrived at the wagon train, they were stopped for the nooning hour. Mike headed for the escort's camp for dinner but had to pass a dozen emigrants' wagons to reach it. He came even with the Paines' wagon and started to pass it, then reconsidered. Dorcas was pouring water into the dishpan while Mr. Paine and the children finished their meal. Mike dismounted, tying the mare's reins to the wagon wheel.

"Good day, Mrs. Paine. I thank you for your hospitality last night. That was the best meal I've had for months."

"Oh, go on, Corporal. It was nothing special, and you know it."

He smiled. "You have a touch with venison stew, if I do say so."

"We missed you at the dancing."

"Ah, well, duty." He looked around the camp, mentally ticking off the family members.

As if reading his mind, Dorcas said, "Lydia should have been back by now."

"Oh? And where is she?" It was tantamount to admitting he couldn't make it through a day without a glimpse of Lydia, but suddenly Mike didn't care, and his heart was light.

"She went looking for those mouthwatering burdocks you and Gleason were talking about yesterday."

Mike stood still, a sudden fear striking him. "She went by herself?"

"Yes, we were near the place, Gleason told us an hour or more ago, and she had her teeth set for some. Said she'd catch up by noontime, but. . ."

"But, ma'am, we passed a Sioux camp this morning."

Mr. Paine came and stood beside him. "You think she could have run into trouble?"

"That was hours ago, the Indian camp," Dorcas said, taking away Nathan's empty plate.

"It was three miles back, ma'am. These oxen move slowly." Mike hurried toward his horse.

"I'll go with you," said Paine.

"No need. Most likely she's fine, but if I'm not back in thirty minutes, tell the sergeant."

"Take Beauty," said Paine. "Miss Jackson will need a mount."

Chapter 8

Mike waited while Paine threw the saddle on his roan. He would have preferred to bring Lydia back riding with him, the way Gleason had taken her through the river, but he knew the feisty mare wouldn't put up with the weight of them both. If he tied so much as a bedroll behind the saddle, the bay bucked and plunged in fury.

He led Beauty along and trotted both horses through the area where the extra livestock grazed, then cantered a mile along the back trail until he could see the knoll. The burdocks grew on the other side.

Lord, let her be there safe and sound, he prayed as he topped the rise. It was very important to him that Lydia was safe, and he knew it was more than his duty to protect the emigrants that spurred him on. His initial attraction to her had grown into admiration over the weeks since they'd left Fort Laramie. From everything he saw and heard, she was a spirited, hardworking, not to mention lovely, young woman, and whether she wanted to or not, she had stolen his heart. He would hate to see anything happen to her, even though she seemed to have an aversion to him.

Lydia was kneeling on the turf, digging with a large knife. Beside her lay a lumpy burlap sack. Her bonnet hung down her back by its strings, and her mulberry-colored dress was blotched with dirt. Her determined concentration made him smile. She was beautiful even with her nose smudged with grime and the wind tugging strands of hair loose from their pins.

"You'll ruin that blade, using it for a shovel."

She jumped and stared up at him. He dismounted and let both horses' reins trail on the short buffalo grass.

"You!" She stood up, pushing a tendril of hair back with her filthy hand.

"Yes, it's me, herder of stragglers."

"I'm not a straggler. I'm a forager."

"Did you know it's past noon, and the wagons are a mile west of here?"

She swallowed. "Really?"

"Really. The Paines are worried about you."

She flushed slightly and reached for the sack. "I'm sorry. It took longer than I thought to find these. But I don't need you to bring me back like a naughty child."

"Mrs. Paine was afraid those Sioux would be after you."

171

She waved that aside. "Dorcas worries too much. I'm armed, as you see."

He took a step nearer, perturbed because his heart was leaping. He found her more appealing than ever. It was silly, losing his head over a girl like this, especially one who disliked him. But for all her standoffishness, he knew she had a compassionate heart. He'd seen that when she wanted to protect the Gordon boy. She was clever and diligent and a big help to Dorcas. The Paine children loved her. Mr. and Mrs. Paine respected her. . .and she was beautiful.

"All right, I admit I was worried, too. Those Sioux were cordial this morning when we rode by with thirty armed troopers. They might not be so friendly if they happened on a young woman foolish enough to go wandering around by herself." *Especially one with hair that glints fiery in the sun,* he thought.

She drew herself up, ready to do battle. "I am perfectly capable of taking care of myself."

"That may be, in most situations, but—"

"But what? I'm not smart enough to find my way back to the train?"

A taunt leaped to his lips, but he bit it back. "You're not safe out here alone, and you're causing those kind people some distress. Now, get on the horse." Her face contorted in resentment, and he added belatedly, "Please."

"I can walk, thank you."

Mike knew she was just trying to make him angry because of their past encounters, and maybe he deserved that, although it seemed his men caused an awful lot of bad blood between him and Lydia with their thoughtless remarks. But it was partly his own fault.

"Lydia, a lot of people care about you." That wasn't a brilliant opening, but he was rusty when it came to courtship.

"Oh, really?" She glared at him.

"Yes. You've got them worried sick." He closed the distance between them and stood staring into her glittering blue eyes. She was so lovely! Did he really think she would give him a chance? Probably not. She had already made up her mind about him.

The knowledge that he'd been looking at her as an irresistibly attractive woman for weeks aggravated him. He had tried to resist the feelings that lay dormant so long. But not anymore. He was ready to admit the way she affected him, ready to move on beyond his grief, and ready to pursue a future with her. He swallowed hard. "You could at least have brought Paine's dog with you."

"I don't need a watchdog, four-legged or otherwise."

Her defiance made his adrenaline surge, but Mike buried his impulse to seize her by the shoulders and shake her. No, he realized, he didn't want to shake her. More than anything he wanted to kiss her.

She stood her ground, her blue eyes shining. *I ought to step back,* he thought, though he wanted to get closer. In fact, the urge to sweep her into his arms was almost overwhelming. But no, that type of behavior would confirm all her ideas about him, not to mention the trouble he would be in when Reese got wind of it. He took a slow, careful breath, trying to frame a courteous request for her to mount Paine's horse and ride back to the camp with him.

"You're so beautiful," he whispered, and was appalled that he'd let the thought leave his lips.

Her eyes flared. She clenched her fist on the hilt of the knife. Regret flooded Mike's mind as he realized he'd stepped over an invisible line and frightened her with his intensity.

Before he could launch an apology, she glared at him in contempt. "Is this the way you treat all the ladies in your care?"

"No, miss." Mike cleared his throat, anxious to make amends. "To be truthful, I haven't said such a thing to a woman since—well, since I left my wife in Tennessee."

"Your wife?" Her eyes blazed, and quicker than the mare could shy she slapped him.

Mike watched her ruefully as she strode to the roan, gathered up the reins and mounted, the butcher knife still in her hand. She didn't look at him again but turned the horse toward the wagon train and galloped off, riding low over the saddle.

He sighed, watching her go. A fine hash he'd made of this situation. Before she had merely disliked him. Now she had good reason to hate him. His nebulous hopes of courting her were ruined.

He settled his hat firmly on his head and rubbed his scratchy jaw as he walked toward his mare, carrying the sack of burdock roots. "Well, now, that gal packs a wallop, wouldn't you say, Lady? Perhaps I should have said, my *late* wife."

The bay mare nickered and sidestepped as he pulled the stirrup toward him.

Mr. Paine took Beauty's bridle as Lydia dismounted, looking up at her in anxious silence.

"I'm sorry I was late getting back."

Dorcas stood by the wagon, knotting her apron in her hands. One glance at her sweet, troubled face put Lydia in acute repentance. She walked over to Dorcas and held out the knife. "I didn't intend to cause you any worry, but I can see I stayed away too long, and I wasn't here to help you get dinner."

"Don't worry about that." Dorcas handed her the plate she had reserved for her. "I'm just glad you're in one piece."

"Did you get any burdocks?" Nathan asked.

Lydia clapped her hand to her mouth. "I forgot the sack!" She looked from Mr. Paine to Dorcas. "I could ride back and get it."

Mr. Paine shook his head. "Let's forget about it."

Lydia hesitated, and in that instant Harpy began a joyful barking.

"There's Corporal Brown!" Nathan raced across the grass toward the approaching horse.

Lydia turned her back to the horseman, her color rising. "Dorcas, I apologize for my behavior, but I don't wish to speak to Brown again." She took her plate and ducked behind the wagon.

A moment later she heard Mr. Paine call a hearty greeting to Brown as the hoofbeats came closer and stopped.

"There you go, ma'am," she heard Brown say.

"Bless you! Lydia said she forgot to fetch it." Dorcas sounded her usual cheerful self.

Brown said something else, but Lydia was prevented from understanding it by the noise her teeth made as she ground them. Why couldn't he stay out of her life? He thought it was his duty to provoke her on a regular basis. It was time someone disabused him of that notion.

She set her tin plate on the wagon's lazy board, where tired pedestrians could catch a ride, and took one angry step toward the end of the wagon. Then she stopped. Vivid in her mind was the memory of that exquisite moment when Corporal Michael Brown had looked deep into her eyes and said, *"You're so beautiful."* Only for an instant had she let herself revel in that, imagining what it would be like to be his sweetheart, to let him pull her gently into his embrace and kiss her.

Then she had done what any decent girl would do. But how could she dress him down, remembering how she had hesitated, how she had hated to end that blissful moment?

Her cheeks flamed at the memory, and her heart raced. The corporal was married, and she had enjoyed seeing the light of admiration in his brown eyes. It hit her with terrible force that she had wished for just such a moment. All these weeks, she had insisted to herself that she didn't like him, but that wasn't true. He aggravated her, but part of the aggravation was the knowledge that she could never respond to his advances.

What if she had? What if she had simply lowered her lashes and said, "Thank you"? What would have happened next?

She wished she were free to answer the longing she had witnessed in his eyes and voice. The idea shocked Lydia. Was she wicked to feel this way?

No other man was like Michael Brown, she was sure, although she had never been courted, and no one else had ever held this fascination for her. As much as she told herself she disliked the man, she found herself drawn to him. He was so much more alive and energetic than any other man she had ever known. And even though he professed to be uneducated, there was a depth to his conversation that told her he was well-read and contemplative.

And what did this mean, as far as her future was concerned? She had promised to teach school for a year and could not attach herself to a man, any man, but especially not a married man. Shame washed over her. She had fallen for a married man! It was unthinkable.

"Dear God, forgive me," she whispered. "I didn't know!"

But that was no excuse. Her future was settled. She had promised the school board that she would arrive, single, by October 1 and carry out her duty as teacher at their new academy—an unmarried teacher. That fleeting moment between her and Michael Brown must never be repeated.

No, she couldn't march out there now and berate him. It was as much her fault as his. She sank down on the lazy board in despair.

When she heard Dorcas calling, "Good-bye, Corporal. Thank you!" she walked slowly out from behind the wagon.

"There you are, dear. We've got to put the dinner things away." Dorcas clucked her tongue as she noticed Lydia's plate. "You're not done eating? Hurry up. They'll be pulling out any minute."

"How did you learn to ride so well, Miss Lydia?" Nathan asked as she sank wearily onto the dish crate.

"Now, Nathan, let her be," said Dorcas.

"It's all right," Lydia told her. She didn't feel like eating, but she put a forkful of cold beans into her mouth, and as soon as Dorcas turned away to put the skillet in the wagon, she held her plate out to Harpy. The dog made short work of her meal. Nathan watched with wide blue eyes.

"Shh!" Lydia warned him, and he nodded with a conspiratorial smile, glancing around to be certain his mother didn't see. "My father taught me to ride," Lydia whispered.

"Pa lets me ride Beauty sometimes."

"She's a good horse."

"I'll bet you can ride better 'n my pa."

Lydia smiled. "I don't know about that." It wouldn't do any good to make the boy think less of his father. Mr. Paine might be slow moving, but he was a kind, thoughtful man. Now, if Nathan had said she rode better than Corporal Brown... but that probably wasn't true. She had observed Brown enough to know he was an excellent horseman.

"I rode Bright today," Nathan said, referring to the docile lead ox.

Lydia smiled and stood up. "Before you know it, you'll be driving a team." She hastened to help load up the dishes, determined to forget about the mortifying incident with Corporal Brown.

That afternoon she walked alone. She was too embarrassed to face the Paines again so soon and too introspective to enjoy the company of the other young women. She was afraid if she spoke to anyone, they would read in her expression her confusion and know somehow that she had feelings for Michael Brown.

Gleason found her where she trudged along against the wind. He pulled his mule up beside her.

"Miss Jackson, how are you today?"

She barely glanced at him. "I'm fine."

"Some of the folks are asking if I'll play again this evening so they can dance."

Lydia shrugged.

"Would you come if I played the fiddle?"

"I don't know. Maybe."

The mule walked beside her, and after a few seconds, Gleason said bleakly, "Well, so long. Maybe I'll see you tonight."

An hour later Dorcas came toward her carrying little Jenny.

"Lydia, come ride for a while, dear. Please." Her face was creased with anxiety, and Lydia gave in, following her back to the wagon.

When they were settled on the seat, Dorcas laid Jenny on the pile of bedding just inside the wagon cover.

"Trooper Gleason stopped by earlier. He asked me if you were all right."

Lydia nodded wearily. "I saw him."

"He's quite taken with you," Dorcas said.

Lydia shrugged. "I'm not interested."

Dorcas smiled. "I knew it! Corporal Brown is perfect for you. You needn't have been so coy when you came back this noon."

"Coy?" Lydia said dully.

"Well, yes. I mean, if you love him—"

"*Love him?*" Lydia stared at her hostess. "Love Michael Brown? That's impossible."

Dorcas smiled. "And why would you say that? He thinks highly of you."

"Well, I cannot stand the sight of him."

Dorcas's eyebrows arched in surprise. "It didn't seem that way when you came tearing in on Beauty with your cheeks flushed and your eyes all dreamy."

"Please, Dorcas! He's married!" The words nearly choked her, and she was surprised that Dorcas didn't react with shock.

Instead, Dorcas touched her sleeve and said tenderly, "Don't you know?"

"Know what?"

"Oh, my. No wonder you think so badly of him. Lydia, dear, the man's a widower."

Lydia stared at her companion. "Are you sure?"

"Absolutely. He's been out here with the army away from his family for years. He was all set to go back East when word came last year—or was it the year before?—that his wife had died. Poor man. He was distraught. They say he rode out on the prairie alone for two days then went back to Fort Bridger and reenlisted. Couldn't stand to go back to Virginia—"

"Tennessee," Lydia murmured.

"Yes, Tennessee." Dorcas nodded. "You're always correct, dear. Anyway, he decided he'd rather stay out here and keep soldiering than go back and face the emptiness of his old home without his dear wife and little son."

"There was a child, too? How very sad!" Lydia tried to fit the tragic tale with what she already knew, or thought she knew, about Michael Brown. It changed everything, and she wasn't sure she could adjust her image of him so quickly. She cleared her throat. "And how did you learn all this?"

"I wouldn't gossip, of course," Dorcas assured her, "but Mrs. Miller's husband told her, and he had it from one of the troopers." She looked primly at Lydia from the corner of her eye.

Lydia cringed inwardly. Dorcas definitely ran her tongue too much, if in a genteel way. She straightened and gathered her skirts. "I think I'll hop down and walk some more."

Dorcas grasped her arm. "I'm certain he cares about you. Don't you care?"

She sighed. "All that about Corporal Brown is very sad, but if it's true, he would probably prefer not to become an object of pity in the train."

"Pity?" Dorcas stared at her in alarm. "Michael Brown is not a man to pity! He's a fine fellow, and he's a born leader. The troopers all love him. I expect he's one of those rare men who will work his way up through the ranks and come out a general."

Lydia smiled at the thought. "General Brown. Perhaps he will. Dorcas, would you mind if I stretch out inside with Jenny for a while? I find I'm very tired, after all."

"Of course you can! A little rest will do you good."

Lydia crawled into the shadowy interior of the wagon. It was piled high with the family's belongings, and she settled herself carefully on top of the luggage and quilts. If anything, it was hotter in the wagon than out in the full sun, and she couldn't get comfortable on her makeshift bed. She lay on her side, watching Jenny sleep.

Her guilt grew as she went over what Dorcas had told her. If it was true, if Michael Brown was really a widower, then it was no sin for him to pursue a young woman like herself. Was he trying to court her? Or was it just a lark for him? She hadn't supposed he took anything too seriously except the danger brought on by nature and the travelers' carelessness. But if he was free, and if he was indeed attempting to court her, that changed everything. Corporal Brown had done nothing wrong.

She, on the other hand, had allowed herself to develop an admiration for him while she was pledged to fulfill a year's contract. Tears rolled down her face. She wriggled to the back of the wagon and opened her carpetbag. From deep in the bottom, she pulled out the contract and unfolded it.

Her signature and that of the school board chairman stared up at her. There was no changing it. The document had meant so much to her when she received it. It was the beginning of a new life, and it renewed her optimism. It was more than the answer to her sudden poverty and homelessness after her aunt died. It was a chance to launch an innovative school and touch many lives. She had been sure it was God's purpose for her. Had anything changed? Surely God would not want her to go back on her word just because a man was interested in her. That was one thing her father had taught her—never break your word.

She held the paper to her heart, the tears flowing freely now. *Lord, forgive me. I've made a promise, and I intend to keep it. I don't mean to feel these things for Michael Brown. I don't want to feel them. I want to fulfill my contract. Help me, Father.* She collapsed with her arms on Mr. Paine's toolbox and wept.

At last she straightened and wiped her eyes, tucking the envelope into the pocket of her dress. If she carried it around with her, it would be a constant reminder of her duty and her promise. She mustn't let her obstinate heart run away with her again. Even if Michael was eligible, she could not, would not, even for a moment think of the possibility. And she must never allow herself to be alone with him again.

Dorcas's words came back to her. *"If you love him—"*

"I don't, Lord," she whispered brokenly. "I can't love him. I won't." She hopped down over the tailboard and walked out onto the prairie, then kept pace with the ox team as the words cycled over and over in her mind. "I don't love him."

Chapter 9

It was early when they stopped that evening close to Independence Rock. A holiday atmosphere ran through the camp. Women hastened to do a quick wash and a large baking. Young people scrambled up the rock to view the plain from above.

Lydia helped Dorcas wash the children's clothing. The hard work took her mind off her inner struggles, and she plunged into it gladly. She was spreading the wet, clean clothes to dry when Frances Bailey arrived, breathless.

"Lydia! Mr. Miller says we'll stay over for a day of rest. We're making good time, and there's enough grass for the cattle here."

"Joy!" Dorcas cried. "I want to repack the supplies tomorrow. We've got the children's clothes washed, Lydia. Perhaps tomorrow we can do a load for us old folks."

"Wonderful," Lydia agreed. They seldom had time to do a complete laundry job along the way.

"Some are talking about walking over to Devil's Gate tomorrow morning," Frances said.

Lydia shaded her eyes against the sun and squinted westward. The tall cliffs that squeezed the river between them stood a couple of miles away. The cleft in the hills was like a jagged knife cut in a loaf of bread. The wagons wouldn't go through Devil's Gate, as there wasn't enough space between the cliffs and the river for a road, but some folks were eager to get a closer look at the landmark.

"I'll go," Lydia said. "After I help Mrs. Paine with the washing."

"That's capital. I'll tell my mother you're going. Then she'll know I'll be safe." Frances was quite pretty when she smiled, Lydia realized. If she weren't so shy, the men would flock around her.

"Did you dance last evening?" she asked. "I didn't see you."

Frances flushed slightly. "I did. It was early on."

"Be we allowed to ask with whom?" Dorcas asked, her eyes twinkling.

"Well, I took a turn with Charlie Sawyer, but that was no fun. He was fuming because Ellen was carrying on so with that soldier."

"And then?" Dorcas prodded.

Frances didn't seem to mind Dorcas's questioning. "Well, Charlie's friend Tim Anderson asked me next."

Her color deepened, and Lydia wondered if Frances wasn't enamored of

Tim Anderson. She knew the boy by sight. He was good-looking but quiet, and he had lost three fingers from his left hand in an accident when he was little. Dorcas had detailed the story to her shortly after they'd left Fort Laramie. Lydia had thought Tim and Charlie were an odd pair. Charlie was constantly calling attention to himself, while Tim was content to remain in the background. The girls seemed to skip right over Tim when cataloging the eligible young men in the company.

"That must have been a highlight of the evening's program," Dorcas said, and Frances's blush went crimson.

"It was. . .very nice." She didn't look at either of them.

"But I looked for you after Mrs. Paine took Jenny," Lydia protested. "I saw Tim and Charlie but not you."

Frances sighed. "By the time my dance with Tim was finished, Charlie was upset. He started saying vile things about Trooper Stedman. It was very embarrassing. I could see Tim was angry with Charlie for talking that way in front of me, and so I excused myself."

"I'm sure there were plenty of other fellows who would have been happy to dance with you," Dorcas said.

Frances smiled. "I didn't mind."

No, Lydia thought, *you didn't mind a bit. You'd had one magical moment with Tim, and you didn't want to spoil it by dancing with some oaf of a trooper afterward.*

She smiled at Frances. "I'm glad you had a nice time."

Frances had a look of utter contentment, and Lydia felt a stab of envy. Would she have felt that way if Corporal Brown had come along and asked her to dance? She knew she wouldn't. Instead, she'd have been in worse turmoil than she was now.

"I'll come by for you in the morning, after I've helped Mother with the chores," Frances said.

"You girls can take a lunch and have a picnic party," Dorcas said.

Lydia laughed. "That's very sweet. Thank you."

She thought of staying away from the dancing that evening, but she couldn't see much point in that. There were so many soldiers along, it seemed almost a patriotic obligation to give an hour or two to dancing with them. Besides, if she hid out during the festivities, the other women would think it strange. Margaret Sawyer certainly would make cutting remarks about her absence the next day.

After supper Lydia tried to coax the wrinkles from her blue dress with a damp cloth. She'd been keeping the dress in reserve for when the others became too shabby, and it was full of wrinkles from resting in the bottom of her carpetbag.

A sudden thought struck her, and she called, "Dorcas, do you think it would be all right for me to lend one of my dresses to Minnie Carver?"

Dorcas looked up from her mending. "That would be most thoughtful of you. Then she and her sister could both enjoy the dancing. Of course, you'd have to be careful how you phrased your offer."

Lydia nodded. "Yes, I wouldn't want to offend her."

Dorcas bent over the button she was reattaching to her best dress. "I thought of it last night, but those girls are far and away slimmer than I am. They could never fit into one of my dresses."

Lydia frowned. "Don't belittle yourself, Dorcas. I think you are the perfect size, and Mr. Paine does, too."

"Mr. Paine does what?" her host boomed, and Lydia jumped.

"There now, you shouldn't startle her so," Dorcas chided.

Lydia laughed. "I didn't know you were there, sir. Your wife and I were just discussing a matter that is better left unspoken in mixed company."

He chuckled. "Well then, I shan't ask again. Trooper Gleason is tuning his fiddle. Will you be dancing with me tonight, Mrs. Paine?"

"With none other," Dorcas replied. She stuck her needle into her pincushion and stood. "Lydia, if you're going to perform that errand of mercy we spoke of, you'd best be quick."

"I'll be back in time to watch the children while you and Mr. Paine have the first dance." Lydia grabbed the blue dress and hurried toward the Carvers' wagon.

Once again, Michael Brown was absent from the clearing while the music filled the air. After Mr. and Mrs. Paine relieved her from baby tending, Lydia danced and smiled and laughed at several dozen jokes. She gave out minimal information about herself and urged the troopers and farmers to tell her about themselves, and all seemed eager to comply.

She glimpsed Frances once, dancing starry-eyed with Tim Anderson. Margaret Sawyer was rarely without a partner. Lydia saw Charlie Sawyer dancing with anyone but Ellen Hadley, and once she saw Ellen with Trooper Stedman. John Gleason tried to catch Lydia's eye. She gave him what she hoped was an impartial smile and began to wish she were elsewhere. The trooper she was dancing with now, Wilson, was excessively attentive, and as soon as the melody came to an end, she thanked him briefly and slipped away toward the Paines' wagon.

She almost collided with Pete Stedman and Ellen Hadley in the shadows between the wagons.

"Oh, I'm sorry."

"It's all right," Stedman said.

"Oh, Lydia," Ellen stammered.

Lydia swallowed hard, wondering if she'd interrupted an intimate moment.

"Lovely night," Stedman said in the awkward silence.

"Yes."

"Did you see Minnie Carver?" Ellen asked. "She found a new dress somewhere."

"Yes, I saw her. She looks lovely in it," Lydia said with a secret smile.

"It's her color," Ellen agreed. "But if she had it all this time, why didn't she wear it last night? Well, good evening, Lydia." She grasped the trooper's hand and tugged him toward the circle of dancers.

Mr. and Mrs. Paine were sitting together on a quilt beside their wagon, holding hands.

Lydia smiled at them. "Thank you for letting me go. It's not too late for you folks to have another dance together."

"What, you're all done?" Mr. Paine said.

Dorcas chuckled. "Perhaps the right partner wasn't there this evening."

"Some men just don't like to dance." Mr. Paine scratched his head. "Of course, some of the troopers nearly came to blows earlier, fighting over who was *not* going to have sentry duty."

"The married men should stand guard and let the bachelors have a chance to socialize," Dorcas said. "It only makes sense."

"Well, I don't know. Sergeant Reese told me he doesn't like to see the men get attached to our young ladies. It can cause trouble later on, you know."

"How is that?" Dorcas asked.

Mr. Paine hesitated and looked at Lydia, then murmured, "Mixed company, m' dear."

"Not for long," Lydia assured him. "My feet are tired, and I'm retiring. Do go and have another round."

"It's more peaceful here," Dorcas said a bit wistfully.

Lydia supposed the phlegmatic couple had had enough excitement for one evening, but as she climbed into the back of the wagon to grope for her carpetbag, she heard Mr. Paine say softly, "Perhaps a walk in the moonlight."

"Lovely," Dorcas said, "but not too far from the wagons. The sergeant is adamant about folks wandering off at night."

When Lydia descended with her bedroll, the Paines were gone. She settled down next to Jenny and Nathan. The music had mellowed from the rollicking square dances to a dreamy waltz, a sign that Gleason would stop playing soon.

She sent up an abbreviated prayer of thanks, knowing she couldn't stay awake much longer. The exertion of the day coupled with her emotional upheaval over Corporal Brown left her exhausted.

The stars glittered above her in the purple-black sky. She'd never learned much about the stars. Science seemed to be one area Miss Clarkson had neglected. They shone brightly, tantalizingly close. She wondered if Michael could see the same stars. Could he hear the music? And was he thinking about her? She couldn't make herself wish that he wasn't.

Chapter 10

It was nearly a week before Lydia worked up her courage to set things right with Michael. They toiled along the Sweetwater, climbing slowly toward South Pass, and every mile was a struggle. The road going down the other side was even worse. There was less time for socializing, and everyone was too tired to do more than attend to the basic needs of food, fuel, and water.

Lydia watched Michael guardedly, all the while feeling guilty, but she saw no private opportunity to speak with the busy corporal. Her mortification increased as she pondered all that had passed between them. She came to the conclusion that she had been wrong to strike him and that she must express her regret to him, but she was afraid. Of what? Afraid of his disdain? She had scorned him. Afraid of his rejection? She had rebuffed him. She knew she needed to seek his forgiveness regardless of his reaction. Over and over she poured out her heart to God, pleading for the strength to do what was right.

The young women on the train were swooning over Corporal Brown. His tragic tale had leaked out, and the ladies romanticized his plight.

The mothers of marriageable daughters envisioned snagging a handsome, hardworking noncommissioned officer as a son-in-law, and Brown was rumored to have a supper invitation at a different campfire each evening, but Lydia saw him ride in after dusk more often than not and shuffle slowly to the army cook wagon after putting up his horse.

The girls looked for excuses to speak to him and shamelessly sought for him on the one evening since Independence Rock when there was dancing, but somehow Michael seemed to have been assigned picket duty again that evening.

But one night he approached their campfire with Mr. Paine, and Lydia fought the impulse to pay a hasty call on the Baileys. She knew it was past time she faced him. The opportunity came when Dorcas asked her to fetch a skillet Mrs. Williams had borrowed at the noon stop.

"I'd be happy to escort you, Miss Jackson," Michael said. It was what she wanted—a chance to speak to him.

She walked woodenly beside him, wondering how to broach the subject. The Williamses' wagon was only four spots away from the Paines', and the walk was a short one. They were halfway before she slowed and faced him with determination.

"Corporal Brown, please forgive me for my behavior last week. It was uncalled for, and I wish you would excuse it."

He stopped walking. A smile played at his lips.

"And what behavior is that, Miss Jackson?"

She felt irritation rising. "You know very well what I'm talking about. I mean, when you—you rode out after me." She knew her face was scarlet, and she turned hastily away, heading for the Williamses' camp.

"Oh, you mean when you went off alone in Indian territory and I came to fetch you back, and I told you how beautiful you looked, and you—"

"Hush!" She rounded on him furiously, looking around to be sure no one had overheard.

He laughed. "As far as I'm concerned, Miss Jackson, there's nothing to forgive on that score. If anything, I should be the one seeking absolution."

"I. . .disagree."

"Seems we do a lot of that."

She gritted her teeth. "Fine. I've apologized for my behavior. If you won't accept that, I can't do anything more."

His smile was dazzling in the dusk. "I understand. 'She hath done what she could.'"

Lydia's ire rose once more. Why must he tease her? Why couldn't he just be nice for once? "You needn't rebuke me in that supercilious manner, as if I were an uppity prig." She turned again in a whirl of skirts, but he seized her wrist and held her immobile.

"Whoa there, Miss—what did you call yourself? An uppish twig? If you can quote the dictionary at me, why can't I refute you with scripture?"

He was still laughing, she could see, and suddenly she felt very small and vain. "That was scripture?"

"Yes, but I shouldn't have tossed it out so lightly. Scripture's not meant to be trifled with."

Lydia gulped. "I–I'm sorry, Corporal. Truly."

"It's Mike."

"No, it's not. It can't be."

"Why not?" His voice was almost tender now, and when she glanced up, his melting brown eyes seared her conscience.

"I—I can't be more than friends with you."

He was quiet for an instant and then said softly, "Are we friends now? I couldn't tell."

She sobbed, and he released her wrist, bending to look closely at her, full of concern. "Miss—Lydia, I'm sorry. I shouldn't bait you, but you must know you're lovely when you're angry."

"No," she choked. "Don't say things like that. You make me—"

"What?"

She shrugged helplessly. He looked around and then pulled her quickly between two wagons, over the tongue of the Carvers' wagon, and a few steps out onto the darkening prairie.

"What is it, Lydia? Something's got you all worked up."

She stood trembling, trying to keep back the tears. She would not cry in front of him. It would give him too much satisfaction to know she had shed tears over him.

"It's just that the way you talk to me—"

"I admire you, Lydia. I don't mean to upset you."

"But you do. If you're attempting to make advances toward me, you have to stop," she choked.

"My intentions are honorable. Isn't it obvious that I'm wildly attracted to you?"

She looked away helplessly. "And you expect me to believe that? At first I thought you despised me."

"No, never that."

"And now. . .well, now I suppose you find pursuing me a diversion."

"Lydia, I've admired you from the first day I met you. But you seemed remote, beyond my grasp. I've teased you because I didn't think you'd look twice at me. If you'll let me, I'd like to court you in earnest." She felt his fingers rest lightly on her sleeve, and she stepped back.

"Don't, please."

He nodded. "You can't be more than friends."

"That's right."

Mike frowned. "You must know by now that my wife is. . . deceased."

"Yes, I heard, and I'm sorry I thought so badly of you. I should have known you wouldn't do such a thing."

"How could you know it? I'm the churlish type."

She hid her face with one hand, wishing she had never begun the conversation. After a moment, she cleared her throat and looked up at him. He was watching her intently. "Mr. Paine thinks highly of you. He says that you're loyal. That tells me, by implication, that you wouldn't desert your wife or seek other female company if she were living. Mr. Paine wouldn't like you if you were that type of man."

He nodded slowly. "Mr. Paine is wiser than most give him credit for."

"Yes."

"For instance, he wouldn't lend you his horse the time you—"

"Let's not get into that," she said hastily. "I think we've established the fact that I misjudged you. I'm very sorry I. . . struck you. And I would like to be your friend, as the Paines are your friends, but that must be the sum of it, Corporal."

"Michael," he said softly.

"Michael." He held her gaze, and she felt an overwhelming desire once more to be in his arms, to have a man like that care for her so fiercely that it wouldn't bother her in the least when he laughed at some little absurdity, because she was secure in knowing he would love her always.

"Mr. Paine is right, Lydia. I'm not the type to toy with a woman's affections. I'm sorry that I made you uncomfortable. What I really wanted was to win your heart, but I could see that I hadn't much chance. Tell me I was wrong."

She made herself look away from his eyes. "Michael, I have a contract. I cannot break it."

There. It was out. She glanced up at him, and a deep sadness had settled over his features.

"I see."

She pulled in a shaky breath. "I have to get the skillet back to Dorcas."

"Of course." He touched her elbow and led her back to the slight gap between the wagons. Mr. Carver was about to close it by piling sacks of feed and household goods about the wagon tongue.

"Oh, Corporal Brown. Didn't see you there."

Michael stepped into the enclosure and held out his hand to help Lydia over the barrier. Carver raised his eyebrows. "Miss Jackson."

"Mr. Carver."

Minnie Carver's curious face appeared in the opening behind the wagon seat.

Michael touched his hat brim and walked on toward the Williamses' wagon, still holding Lydia's hand. *Oh, dear. There'll be gossip in camp tonight,* she thought, but she savored the brief moment, only pulling her hand away when they came to the Williamses' campfire. *I'll never touch him again,* she thought sadly.

On the way back, he carried the cast-iron skillet, and Lydia marched along with him, hastening because she knew Dorcas was waiting.

"It's ironic," she said when they were nearly there. "All the girls in the company will be heartbroken when they hear that you were out walking with me, but there's nothing to it."

He smiled. "I'm sure they'll figure that out in a few days, when they see how you avoid me."

"I shan't try to avoid you anymore, so long as you understand my position."

"I don't fully understand it, but I respect your wishes."

"Thank you."

She went to help Dorcas with supper, leaving him to resume his conversation with Mr. Paine, who was cleaning his rifle.

Lydia picked up the water bucket and looked around for Nathan. They were camped close to the river tonight, and there was no need for a guard when she went for water.

"Let me get that," Michael said, reaching for the bucket.

Lydia eyed him in surprise. "I can get it."

"The corporal and I will give you a recess this evening," Mr. Paine said, rising and setting his rifle aside.

Michael grinned. "That's right. Give us all your buckets while you have the chance, ladies."

Dorcas quickly gave them the three pails she could lay hands on, and the men struck out for the water with Nathan tagging along.

"You know my opinion," said Dorcas, looking pointedly at Lydia.

"Yes, ma'am, I do." Lydia smiled. She knew Dorcas couldn't refrain from voicing it again, anyway.

"That," said Dorcas, "is a very nice young man."

Chapter 11

Mike took Pete Stedman with him on scout duty. The corporal had been over this trail many times. He didn't expect any problems in this area, though the trail was steep in places. They'd make it past the mail relay station today and within days would reach the cutoff that would take them north into the Oregon Territory.

"You keep clear of Charlie Sawyer," Mike told him as they rode along.

Stedman nodded. "The sergeant read me those lines a week ago."

"Yes, well, he's serious. The wagon master told him yesterday that one of the boys heard Charlie threatening to kill you if you didn't stop seeing the Hadley girl. It doesn't take much for a lovesick young man to lose it out here."

Stedman grimaced. "It wasn't my intention to stir up trouble, Corporal."

Mike shook his head. "Then what was your intention? I can't see any good way for this to end."

"I care about Ellen."

"She's too young to be an army wife. What could you offer her? Best end it and let her go on with her family."

Stedman was silent, and Mike left him to his thoughts.

A Pony Express rider galloped past them when the two scouts were only a couple of miles out from the relay station. He waved, but as Mike expected, he didn't stop to talk.

"Let's go as far as the Pony station and see if we can pick up any news," Mike suggested.

"Sure," said Pete.

They went at a much more leisurely pace than the mail carrier, and by the time they reached the small outpost, the rider had passed his mail pouch to the young man heading out for Fort Bridger and was eating his dinner.

"You got Sergeant Reese with you on that emigrant train?" he asked, eyeing the yellow chevrons on Mike's sleeves.

"Yes, we do," Mike said.

The boy grinned. "Tell him Mrs. Sergeant Reese says, 'It's a boy.' She didn't have enough money for a letter, but the fellows told her we'd pass the word along until we either caught up with his wagon train or hit Bridger. I'd have stopped to tell him, but we're not supposed to, and I knew it would take too long to locate him. Folks always want you to stop and gab. Can't do that in this business."

Mike was glad he had some good news to share for a change. It would lift the spirits of everyone on the wagon train.

Dan Reese whooped when he heard the news. "Get your fiddle out tonight, Jack!" The troopers poked fun at him good-naturedly all evening and took to calling him "Pappy."

Mike spent an hour at the Paines' fireside before he took the evening watch. It was the nearest thing to a home he had visited in months, and he would gladly have spent more time with the family.

"They had a newspaper at the relay station. Congress has approved funding for the transcontinental telegraph line they've been talking about," Mike said.

Mr. Paine shook his head. "Won't be long before folks can go clear to Oregon by stagecoach."

"Railroad," Mike corrected him. "I don't see many more years for this type of wagon train."

"What will the escort do?" Nathan asked.

"You'll be out of work," Mr. Paine said with a smile.

"I expect they'll find us another detail."

"Fighting Injuns?" Nathan asked.

"Could be," Mike said. "There's a lot of war rhetoric back East right now, though. Might be other worries than Indians, as far as the government's concerned."

"You wouldn't fight against Southerners, would you?" Mr. Paine asked, frowning.

Mike inhaled slowly. "I don't know."

"You're a United States Army man," Dorcas said indignantly. "Don't tell me you'd fight against your own country."

Mike stared at the fire, thinking about that.

"Let's hope it doesn't come to that," Mr. Paine said.

Dorcas shook her head. "I'm glad we're out here. If there's going to be fighting in Massachusetts, I don't want to hear about it."

Mike sneaked a look toward where Lydia sat by the rear wheel of the wagon. She was busy with some needlework, taking advantage of the fading light. He hadn't spoken to her once, but he knew she was listening to every word he said to the Paines. She seemed to be making intricate lace out of common cotton string, yards and yards of it.

Music came to them across the camp, and Lydia smiled as she bent over her tatting shuttle. Mike smiled, too, as he recognized the tune. John Gleason was playing "Rock-a-Bye, Baby."

He stood up. "I'd best get to my duty."

"You were in the saddle all day," Mr. Paine said. "Can't you have a whirl with the ladies?"

"Oh, I'm not much of a dancer," Mike replied. "They won't dance long tonight, anyway. Folks are all wrung out from the heat and the terrain we've been wrestling."

"Come by again, now," Dorcas said.

"Thank you, ma'am. Mr. Paine." He glanced toward Lydia. She looked up for a moment and met his gaze for the first time that evening. "Miss Jackson," he said softly with a nod then turned and walked away.

Mike rode leisurely back toward the wagon train, his chestnut gelding trotting placidly beside Josiah Paine's roan. They'd had a successful day of hunting in the foothills, and a pronghorn was draped over the rump of Mike's horse. Four grouse dangled from Paine's saddle. Mike was feeling content.

"I'll give Dorcas a couple of these birds, and you take the rest to your cook," Paine said.

Mike shook his head. "No, you'll have some venison, too, Josiah. You earned it."

"We're close to the cutoff, aren't we?"

Mike nodded. "Tomorrow or the next day we'll head off north."

"Toward Fort Hall?"

"Well, yes, but they don't use Fort Hall anymore. There's talk of building a new camp, but the army doesn't have an official presence there."

"What are the natives like?"

"The Snake Indians are generally all right. We could run into some hostile Blackfoot, but I doubt it. It's a lot better than this area, with the Sioux. Still, I'll probably be out scouting most of the time once we get through the worst of the mountains."

Paine accepted that without comment. The more time he spent with him, the more Mike liked him. Josiah Paine was a deliberate man, but he was staunch. Mike decided to take a chance. "You've had Miss Jackson with you more than a month now. What do you think of her?"

Josiah looked off toward the river for several seconds, and Mike almost wished he hadn't spoken. But Paine didn't laugh the way Dan Reese would, and he didn't smirk the way Wilson did when women were the topic of conversation. And John Gleason would surely get angry if he hinted that he was interested in Lydia, Mike knew.

Paine scanned the horizon. "She's one of the family now."

Mike nodded, waiting for more.

At last Paine rewarded him. "She's a mite high-strung, but she's good for Dorcas."

"She says she doesn't hate me anymore, but I don't know. She's mighty cool. Is it an act?"

"Hard to say."

Mike swallowed. "She told me the other night she wouldn't avoid me anymore and we'd be friends, but she still doesn't seem to relish my company." The chestnut reached out to nip Beauty's neck, and Mike slapped him on the withers. "Quit that, mister!"

"She's got something pulling her up ahead in Oregon." Paine's frank, gray eyes invited Mike to give his opinion.

"She said she's party to a contract," Mike said slowly.

"I don't know anything about that."

"I make that out to mean. . .well, do you think it's a marriage contract?"

Paine sniffed and looked at him. "Seems like she'd tell Dorcas that."

Mike nodded, feeling only marginally better. "Could be a business contract, I guess."

"She aims to be a schoolteacher, you know. Bide your time, Mike. That's my advice."

"Guess I don't have much choice. Still, I wonder if there's a gent waiting for her out there."

"Could be, I suppose."

Mike smiled. "You know, I seem to recollect that courtship was a whole lot easier in Tennessee."

"No," Paine replied, "it's not where you are, Mike. They say the older you get, the harder it is."

The wagons were in sight now, and dusk was falling fast. They rode up to the camp and around to the gap that was the gate, then went straight to the Paines' wagon. Dorcas was working over her fire, and Jenny was playing nearby with a rag doll.

"Ah, you brought some meat in." Dorcas's face lit up as her husband dismounted. Paine nodded and began unfastening the thongs that held the birds to the saddle.

"I'll take this antelope to our cook and have him send you a haunch, ma'am," Mike said.

"Thank you. That will be wonderful, Corporal Brown."

Paine handed him two of the grouse. "Come back for supper, now."

Mike darted a glance toward Dorcas, and she smiled at him.

"Of course you will," she said.

"Where's Nathan?" Paine asked, looking around the encampment.

"He and Lydia went for blackberries. They're ripe down in the river bottom, and she begged to go for some."

Paine frowned. "It's nearly dark, Mrs. Paine."

Mike stiffened. Hadn't they learned anything from the burdock incident?

"They took the dog with them," Dorcas said plaintively, but her lower lip trembled.

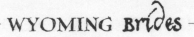

"Well, that's something," Paine said. "All the same, I think I'll go fetch them. Where did you say?"

"Just downstream a bit from the watering place."

"I'll go with you." Mike quickly dismounted and untied the rawhide strips holding the pronghorn against the cantle of the saddle. "Mind if I leave this meat here for a few minutes, ma'am?"

"N–no," Dorcas said. She picked Jenny up, holding her close to her chest. "I thought they'd be all right, Mr. Paine."

Paine had one foot in the stirrup, but he put it down again and turned toward her. Mike turned away and mounted the gelding he called Sam, but he heard Paine say softly, "Don't worry, missus. I'll bring them back."

They trotted toward the river. The twilight was deep as they rode down toward the willows by the water. Heading eastward, they soon saw the dark bulk of bushes ahead.

"Nathan!" Paine called, and they listened.

"Miss Jackson!" Mike yelled louder. Only the breeze stirring the branches answered.

Paine put his fingers to his lips and let out an ear-piercing whistle that Mike had heard him use before to call his dog, but there was no response.

"I don't like this." Paine looked at him, and Mike nodded.

"Come on." Mike pushed Sam forward toward the berry patch and squinted in the failing light for footprints, broken twigs, bushes that had been stripped of their fruit—any sign that Nathan and Lydia had passed that way.

A faint but definite track ran among the laden bushes, and he forced the horse through the brambles, then pulled up short. Paine's red-brown dog lay still on the ground, a dark stain spreading from his neck. Mike caught his breath and sent up a quick silent prayer. He'd need all the guidance, wit, and courage he could get.

Paine came up beside him and reined in Beauty. He grimaced.

"Come on."

Mike fell in behind him. Paine had the right to lead now, and Mike admired him for his coolness. He didn't waste time swearing or climbing down to examine the dog. They went a few paces; then the roan stopped abruptly.

"There," said Paine.

This time Mike dismounted. A small pail lay on the turf, a quart of blackberries spilling from it. He bent to see the ground better, discerning shoe prints and gouges in the soft earth. "They had a bit of a scuffle." He pushed onward and soon found the hoofprints of several unshod horses behind a thicket.

"They waited here. Figured they might get something. Or maybe they were just waiting for dark when they could slip in and try for a few horses." Mike straightened. "Best get more men."

"No, it's late," Paine said. "They might be just minutes ahead of us. Mike, they've got my boy. They say they don't like to trade children back. They'll raise him wild like one of their own. And who knows what they'll do to Lydia. Every minute counts."

Mike looked back uneasily. If they didn't go back to the wagons soon, Dorcas would raise an alarm. Dan Reese would eventually follow.

"Leave a sign for the sergeant," Paine said.

"All right. Let's go." Mike pulled a handkerchief from the pocket of his blue uniform trousers and dropped it a few paces along to mark the faint trail. "They're heading northeast. Probably for that big village Wilson saw yesterday on his scouting duty."

It was difficult to follow the signs in the growing darkness, and he considered ignoring the faint trail and heading Sam at a gallop in a straight line toward the Sioux encampment Wilson had described. He was about to suggest as much when he spotted an item in the short grass. He swung down to retrieve it.

"It's Nathan's shoe," Paine said. He turned it over and looked at the worn sole, shaking his head. "The boy needs new shoes."

Mike decided not to discount the tracks, and they rode without speaking for half an hour.

"How long you figure before we get there?" Paine asked at last.

"Well, their camp was at least twenty miles from our camp, maybe more. That's assuming this party is heading there. I don't know. It seems like we're going more north than we ought if they're headed for the village."

"What does that mean?"

Mike shrugged. "Could mean Wilson was off on his calculations, or it could mean they're not heading there."

"Where, then?"

"Who knows? There are hills up ahead. Could be a band is camped up there. Or they could be from farther away, just out on a raiding spree. They could have a war lodge in the hills."

They rode on under the white slice of moon. Mike wondered what to do if they found that the raiding party had reached the village. The two of them couldn't just storm in there and demand the return of the captives.

The broken terrain slowed them, and Mike let Sam pick his pace as the footing allowed. They approached a stream, and while Paine let Beauty drink, Mike scouted along the bank eastward. When he saw what he was looking for, sixty yards downstream, he gave a low whistle. Paine led his gelding toward him.

"They crossed here," Mike said. The hoofprints close to the stream looked fresh, with water seeping into them.

They forded the stream, and Mike picked out a trail of bent grass in the moonlight. He was so intent on following it that he didn't notice anything else until Paine rode up close to him and hissed. He immediately pulled Sam in and listened. There were definitely soft hoofbeats ahead.

He looked out over the prairie northward and saw irregular rock formations in the distance.

"They're not going to the village," Mike said. "They're heading for those rocks and hills."

"Do you think they know we're here?" Josiah asked.

"Maybe."

"What do you suggest?"

Mike frowned. His impulse was to spur the chestnut and race to catch up with the band of Sioux, but Paine's steadiness in itself was a moderating force. "I don't think there's all that many of them," he said at last. "I've tried to work it out. There's four ponies, at least, but I doubt there's more than six of them."

Paine said nothing, and Mike knew he was waiting for his decision and would follow him without question.

"You primed and loaded?"

Paine drew his rifle from the scabbard. "You said it."

Mike nodded. "Let's catch up but keep quiet if we can. Could be they haven't caught on to us following yet. The closer we can get before they know, the better."

"Right." Paine's eyes gleamed in the faint light. "If I don't make it, you tell Dorcas I did everything I could to get the boy back."

The thought appalled Mike. When the troopers went into combat, it was normal for them to give final instructions to their closest buddies. But Paine. He couldn't imagine going back to the wagon train without him and breaking the news to Dorcas.

"I will." A thought flitted through his mind to give Paine a final message for Lydia, but he couldn't think what to say. *Tell her I'm sorry.* For what? *Tell her I loved her.* That would only distress her. Maybe they should wait for Sergeant Reese to bring the company of troopers up. But no, the Sioux would get away if they didn't strike soon. He lifted the reins and urged Sam forward.

Chapter 12

L ydia clung to the sturdy mustang's saddle. They had ridden for nearly an hour, and she couldn't sustain terror that long. A slow, hot fury rose from deep in her heart. The horses pounded over the turf, through tall grass and wiry brush, up and down over the knolls and swells in the land.

She was used to the faint light of the moon now and could see the other horses running, one ahead of her and one on either side. She knew there was one more behind. The rider to her left held Nathan in front of him.

It was an uncomfortable position. Her captor had somewhere obtained a light cavalry saddle—probably stolen. She would have been much more at ease riding behind the Indian, but she supposed he didn't trust her and assumed she would try to escape. Which she would.

If it weren't for Nathan, that is. She couldn't leave the boy alone on this horrifying journey.

She doubted they would hurt Nathan, but she couldn't be sure. Wild stories had flown from time to time through the wagon train. Michael hadn't seemed unduly worried about the natives, but he'd also been cautious and insisted the women and children not wander off alone, as she had that fateful day when she'd hunted burdocks.

It was tiresome, being tied always to the wagon train and the same people day after day, much as she liked the Paines. When they'd gone for water that afternoon and Nathan had spotted the tempting blackberries, she had immediately begun trying to convince Dorcas that she and the boy would be safe if they took the dog with them. Dorcas had suggested adding a few more young people to their party, but Lydia had declined. Frances's mother insisted that she stay close to their wagon that evening, and Lydia couldn't bear to hear the other girls chatter on about how dreamy Private Gleason or Private Wilson or, worst of all, Corporal Brown was. Surely she and Nathan would be safe with Harpy along.

She sobbed, and the warrior tightened his grasp on her. He was not gentle, and the stench of his unwashed body and buckskin leggings was nauseating. Mentally Lydia christened him "Skunk."

To her left, Nathan yelped, and she saw that he was slipping down the side of the pinto mustang his captor rode. His horse had no saddle, and she was amazed the boy hadn't rolled off sooner.

"Nathan!" she cried, and Skunk squeezed her roughly. Their horse moved ahead of the other as Nathan tumbled to the ground, and she tried to look around and see what happened to him, but her kidnapper went on relentlessly, ignoring his companion's trouble.

Run, Nathan, she thought, but no, he could never outrun the horse, and they were too far from the wagon train now for him to make it back on his own. Little cover was available for him to hide in, although they seemed to be approaching a line of jagged hills.

Several minutes passed before she heard steady hoofbeats, coming fast from behind. She turned her head and caught a glimpse of Nathan, small and meek in front of the garishly painted warrior who brought him. She hoped he hadn't been injured or punished for falling off the mustang. Skunk jerked her arm sharply. She gasped and turned forward, concentrating on not sliding up too far on the horse's neck.

The warrior on the horse in front stopped, and they all came to a halt and clustered around him, the horses breathing deeply. The man who led them grunted, and the others stilled themselves and their mounts, listening. Lydia was suddenly afraid but at the same time hopeful. For the last hour she had prayed silently to God for a rescue but had doubted it would come soon. Dorcas probably hadn't started worrying until after full dark.

I don't ask for an earthquake or a legion of angels, Lord, she prayed. *Just let us live.*

Then she heard it—faint and rhythmic, the hoofbeats coming over the dry prairie behind them. Quick words were exchanged among the Sioux. While they were occupied, she stared at Nathan, trying to communicate silently to him her growing anticipation. She could make out his wide, frightened eyes and pale face. She wished she could speak to him, but she was afraid to. If she spoke, she would draw the wrathful attention of their abductors.

The leader wheeled his horse and headed off again, and the others followed. They went faster this time. The rugged mustang lunged into a rough canter, lowering his head, and Lydia was terrified. If the horse stumbled, she would fly forward headfirst. She laced her fingers tightly in his coarse mane. The warrior's arm was like a bar of iron around her waist, holding her firmly against him, and she could feel his breath on the back of her neck. Hard objects that formed his large necklace pressed into her back, and she wriggled. It only made the poking worse, and she wondered if the thing digging into her shoulder blade was a bear claw. *God, help us,* she pleaded.

They tore on over increasingly broken ground, dodging rocks and hollows. They came to the shadow of the hills and began climbing, and she felt a bit more secure as the horse met the incline, head still lowered.

She could hear the pursuers clearly now. The Sioux obviously did not relish an encounter with them. There was always the off chance they were Indians, too, perhaps from a rival tribe, but Lydia would not think of that. Surely God had answered her prayers, and the soldiers from the wagon train were in pursuit.

The warrior with Nathan came alongside them, and she saw the boy sliding once more toward the off side, clutching wildly at the pony's mane and the woven hair reins.

Skunk allowed his mustang to slow to a punishing trot, and she felt herself tossed about as badly as Nathan. The Indian transporting him was less skillful than Skunk at keeping an active hostage subdued. It seemed inevitable that Nathan would fall again. He was almost close enough for her to reach over and touch him if she had dared to let go her hold, and his mouth and eyes were wide in horror.

"Nathan! Jump!" she cried, confident that the pursuers were now close behind them. Skunk shoved his arm into her stomach so violently she felt faint. She gulped air and watched as Nathan began to struggle against his captor. The horse gave a squeal and hopped to the side, and Nathan catapulted to the ground.

They were close, very close. Mike knew they would have only a brief moment of opportunity. As soon as the Sioux realized only two men pursued them, they would probably turn on them. It was darker now, and scrub brush grew more thickly in the hills. The ground was rockier, and he knew their quarry could hear the hoofbeats of their shod horses. If the Indians stopped to listen well, they would know how few pursued them. He had to keep them on the run as he closed the distance so they wouldn't stop and know what they were facing.

Lydia was the one he was most worried about. Nathan could survive for days or weeks if it took them that long to retrieve him. He was young enough to see it later as a grand adventure, to brag about it to his friends by the fireside.

But Lydia. That was another story.

The Sioux were supposed to be friendly now. There had been some trouble last summer, but the situation had cooled off, and there hadn't been any Indian incidents along the escort's section of the trail other than horse stealing and pilfering. Some mules and trade goods had been stolen from a band of merchants on their way from Fort Laramie to Fort Bridger a month ago, but they were thankful to have gotten through uninjured and considered it a business loss. Still, that was why the Oregon Escort operated. There was no guarantee. The problem remained heated enough for the government to consider building another fort between Fort Laramie and Independence Rock, a new outpost to provide added security for travelers.

The riders in front of them were climbing a rocky hillside. Although they didn't seem to be following a trail, the Sioux knew where they were going. Maybe they had reinforcements up ahead. Mike decided to press them hard, to force a confrontation as soon as possible.

Paine's roan came along beside him, breathing heavily. Mike was surprised Beauty hadn't fallen back yet, exhausted and heaving, after their long day of hunting. Life on the trail had toughened the horse. Still, he regretted not taking a few minutes to ride back and tell Reese about the kidnapping and choose a fresh mount. If he'd known how far ahead the Sioux were, he'd have counted the time well spent. He'd been foolish and listened to Paine, the distraught father. The lives of the captives might depend on their strength, and the odds were against him and Paine.

He spurred Sam, exulting as the gelding edged up little by little, chasing the white rump of a mustang that trailed the other ponies.

There was a sudden shuffle up ahead, and the last mustang shied and leaped over something. Mike realized that one of the Indians' horses had stopped, and he was swiftly riding up on a mounted Sioux warrior.

He reined Sam in and raised his rifle, squinting to determine whether the Indian had either Lydia or Nathan with him. Then he realized that the shadow on the ground was moving. One of them had fallen, and the warrior had stopped to retrieve the captive.

Before Mike's brain told his finger to pull the trigger, Paine's rifle cracked close beside him, and Sam squealed and hopped away from Beauty. The Sioux sat still for an instant, staring at them. The ringing in Mike's ears receded.

"Couldn't have missed him clean," Paine said in disgust.

Mike hesitated no longer, but even as he fired, the warrior sagged and toppled from his mustang, and he knew Paine's shot had been true.

The others were far ahead, not stopping to make a stand with their companion. Mike urged Sam forward and stopped beside a dark heap on the ground.

"It's Nathan!"

Paine was already dismounting, and Mike jumped down beside him.

"Nathan, it's your papa!" Paine cradled the boy in his arms.

Mike's heart was racing. The boy could have broken his neck in the fall. He squatted beside his friend and said gently, "Let me check his pulse."

The boy moaned, and Paine laughed in relief. "Thank You, Lord!"

Nathan opened his eyes. "Papa?"

"Yes, yes, son. Are you all right?"

"My leg hurts something fierce."

Mike quickly reached to feel the boy's legs, tenderly running his hand from Nathan's right ankle up to his knee and beyond. When he touched the left ankle, Nathan gasped and shuddered.

"You'll be all right," his father assured him.

"Harpy?" Nathan gasped.

"He's dead, son."

"I thought so. That Injun that's got Miss Lydia hurt him when he started barking at them. Papa, I was scared."

"We've got to get Miss Jackson," Paine said.

Mike looked toward the dark hills. "The boy's hurt. We can't go chasing after them with Nathan, but we can't leave him here alone."

"We'll lose those savages in this terrain. We've got to get her back, Mike."

"I know." His mind whirled, but he could see only one way. "If I wait for Reese's detachment, we could lose her forever. Or we might not find her again until—well, we need to find her soon. Now that they've lost the boy and one of their clan, they'll be angry. They might take it out on her."

Paine nodded somberly. "I'll head back with Nathan. No other choice. You take care, Mike."

"I think Nathan's leg is broken. You should wait here for the others and make a travois to haul him back on."

Paine shook his head. "Can't, Mike. You need help. What if Reese decided to wait until daylight? We can't take that chance." He looked down anxiously at his son. "You're tough, boy. Can you make it back with me on Beauty?"

"I'll try, Papa."

"We'll go," Paine said to Mike, "even if I have to lead the horse and walk every step, but we'll keep moving."

"That mustang's foraging yonder," Mike said, nodding toward where he could discern the bulk of the Sioux pony. "Maybe you can get him for Nathan. Can you splint his leg?"

"No wood around here." Paine stood up. "Don't worry about us, Mike. And don't give up on us. We'll be back in force. If those Sioux reach a village, you'd better just sit back and wait for help."

"We'll see. I just know I've got to stick with them now, and I may have already waited too long. God be with you, Josiah."

Mike swept Sam's reins up and leaped into the saddle, heading off to where the four warriors had disappeared with Lydia. He wanted to reload his rifle, but it was dark, and every second counted. He decided to wait until he could hear the horses up ahead of him again, until he knew where they were. If need be, he would rely on his pistol and knife.

Lydia writhed and wriggled, but Skunk was not about to let her escape. The other three warriors surged ahead of them on their horses, easily outrunning them with their lighter loads. She'd heard shots fired, and she tried to twist around and see if Nathan's captor was following them, but Skunk punched her in the side, knocking the air out of her. She sat as still as she could, sucking in ragged breaths, her knees gripping the horse's withers and her hands tangled in his mane.

The horse slowed, laboring up the rocky slope. Lydia strained for sounds of pursuit but heard nothing save the hoofbeats and the heaving and snorting of the Indians' mounts.

"God, keep Nathan safe," she breathed. Things were changing too quickly for her to form a coherent prayer. Either Nathan had been recaptured, or she was alone in the nightmare now.

The horses' hooves struck stone with each step. The troopers wouldn't be able to track them. Lydia considered her options and hung on.

They rounded the side of the hill and wound along a ledge until she could see a great distance in the moonlight and realized they were high above the plain. Was there a Sioux village up here? Or were they counting on eluding the troopers in the craggy hills?

A long time had passed since they had left Nathan and his captor behind, and Lydia began to lose heart. Skunk was last in line, and she had heard nothing from behind them for some time. If Sergeant Reese and the men of the escort had been coming, they must have lost the trail of the Sioux party.

Suddenly Skunk reined in the mustang, and Lydia listened as the warrior did. He sat still and stiff, inclining his head toward the back trail. There! Surely she had heard metal on stone.

Skunk urged the mustang forward toward the others, and she saw the three horses ahead jostle each other, heading swiftly toward a declivity in the rocks. The leader halted and turned to face them. He had chosen the ground for a standoff. Lydia took a deep breath. Skunk's horse was still twenty yards behind the others. *It's now or never,* she thought.

She strained forward against his grip, then jerked back, smashing his nose with her skull. His grip loosened, and she jammed both elbows back hard into the warrior's ribs, kicked hard with the solid wooden heels of her shoes, and dove forward over the left side of the mustang's neck.

Chapter 13

They struggled for a moment, Skunk grappling and Lydia squirming and kicking on the trotting horse. She fell with a *thud*, landing hard on her shoulder and hip. Ignoring the pain, she rolled away from the mustang, down the incline. She slammed against a boulder and lay stunned for an instant, then scrambled into its shadow.

Hoofbeats sounded quite close to her, but she didn't dare raise her head. Crouching behind the rock, she renewed her fractured prayers.

Several shots were fired in rapid succession, and she cowered lower, hoping she was invisible in the darkness behind the rock. She had seen a rifle in a scabbard on the leader's pony when they were captured, but she was certain that Skunk's only weapons were arrows and a gruesome knife.

The squeal of an injured horse tore the silence, and Lydia waited, breathless. She heard a thrashing and thumping then dead quiet. She fought the impulse to sit up and look, and instead squeezed lower, tinier.

"Easy, Sam, easy."

Her chin jerked up before she considered her peril, and Lydia stared with uncontainable joy into the darkness. There were more thrashing sounds and loud panting and groaning. She was certain the horse was in dire straits, and she was also certain it was Mike Brown's calm voice she had heard.

"Michael?" she called cautiously.

There was an instant's silence; then his voice came, soft and incredulous. "Lydia?"

"Over here." She moved to the side of the rock.

"Keep down," he hissed, and she flattened herself.

After a long moment she rose a few inches on her elbows and peered toward the voice. She could see the dark mass that was the gelding. He didn't seem to be moving now. Brown was crouched beside him, working with frenzy at the saddle and gear.

Lydia inched toward him on all fours, her weighted skirt hindering her. She tugged it impatiently from beneath her knees and scrambled toward him.

"Have you got Nathan?" she breathed.

"His father took him and headed back to camp for reinforcements. Nathan broke his leg when he fell, or Paine would have stuck with me."

"You mean, there were just the two of you?"

"Unfortunately, yes."

Lydia swallowed hard. "I was hoping for the entire escort."

"Yes, well, I should have brought them. I'll regret that decision for the rest of my life."

"Under the circumstances, I'll settle for you."

He laughed shortly. "You may change your mind if those savages attack us now."

"Where are they?" She stared into the gloom.

He nodded toward the heights. "Yonder. Are you hurt?"

"Not badly. A few bruises."

"Thank God." He bent to his task again.

"What are you doing?" The blade of his knife gleamed as he sliced the leather strap that suspended the saddlebags from the cantle of the saddle.

"The other saddlebag is trapped under the horse, but this one has the cartridges and caps for my revolver." He pulled the leather bag free of the saddle and grabbed her arm. "Get down. I'm not sure how close they are."

"Is Sam dead?"

"As good as. Shot him right out from under me. I didn't know they had rifles."

"Only one, I think. The one who grabbed me didn't have a gun; I know that."

"How many are there?"

"There were five at first, but Nathan fell off his horse, and the one who was bringing him stopped."

"You don't have to worry about that one."

She caught her breath. "Good. Four, then."

"Come on, we'd better get away from Sam. They may be analyzing the situation. If they know I'm the only one out here with you, they'll move in for sure." He grasped her hand and pulled her down the slope toward a large cluster of rocks. Lydia sank to the ground and sat with her back to a boulder, rubbing her sore shoulder.

"All right," Mike said. "Let's get our breath."

"Then we head back to the wagon train?"

"No. We hide until daylight or until some help comes. But we'll have to find a better place to hole up. We don't stand a chance in the open on foot against those Sioux. Besides, my ankle took a beating when Sam went down."

"Is it broken?"

"I don't think so, or I wouldn't have been able to get this far. But we need a hideaway with a small opening or a high spot with a good view of all approaches. Someplace where I can defend our position."

They sat without speaking for several minutes. In the faint light, Lydia watched him reload the empty chambers of his Colt Dragoon revolver.

"Do you have a rifle?" She almost hated to ask.

"It's back there. I'd fired it earlier, and the ammunition was in the other saddlebag. You hungry?"

"I—well, yes."

He thrust something into her hand. "Eat."

"Jerky?"

"Yes. Josiah and I took some with us hunting."

"Who?"

"Mr. Paine."

"It's Josiah? Really?"

"Really." He carefully stowed his equipment back in the leather pouch. "I've got my pistol, Lydia. That and my knife. Our best defense is to stay hidden. You understand?"

"Yes."

"All right. I'd like to get farther from the horse, to a more secure spot, but in this darkness we might stumble around and make enough noise to draw their attention. If they're scouting for us, we might even run into them."

"You're sure they'll come back?"

"Pretty sure. The Sioux like to recover their dead. They may have circled back to pick up their friend's body, but then they'll want revenge."

"How will we know if our friends come?"

"Don't worry. You'll know when the cavalry arrives."

They sat silent for a long time. Lydia was very tired and sore, but her nerves kept her wide awake. Over and over, her mind reviewed the scene by the river when she and Nathan had gloated over the plump, fragrant blackberries.

Suddenly, Harpy had stiffened and growled at a thicket.

"Come here, Harpy!" Nathan had called, but the dog had taken a step toward the thicket, still growling. Lydia felt fear then. A bear could be behind those bushes. They were entering the mountains, and she'd heard enormous bears lived out there.

Harpy barked and leaped toward the bushes. He was in midair when the brambles parted and a copper-skinned man met his lunge. Before Lydia could register what was happening, the dog lay bleeding on the turf, and strong hands seized her from behind.

"Nathan could have got away," she whispered to Mike. "They caught me first, and he grabbed a stick and ran at Skunk."

"Skunk?"

She smothered a laugh. "That's what I called the one who caught me. Oh, not to his face, of course."

"Of course. You're too well-bred for that."

"Well, if you could have smelled him—"

"I'm gratified that wasn't necessary."

A giggle burbled up in her throat. "Stop it. You're making me laugh."

"Laughter does good like a medicine."

"Not when your life depends on silence," she said ruefully.

"That's true. But I'm glad you can see the humor of it." His warm hand found hers, and he squeezed her fingers. Lydia's heart began to pound. "So Nathan tried to defend you," he said.

"Yes. He should have run away."

"They would have caught him, maybe killed him."

She thought about that. "I'm glad you're here, Michael."

He sighed. "Can't help it, I guess. I'm glad, too. I mean, since you're here. If you weren't, well, there's lots of places I'd rather be." He shifted and stretched his left leg out gingerly.

"Should you take your boot off?" Lydia asked.

"I don't think that would be wise right now."

Mike thought once that he heard faint hoofbeats, but he wasn't certain. Lydia was drowsing, slumped against the rock, breathing softly. His ankle throbbed, and now and then a stab of pain shot through it. He watched the quarter moon move slowly across the sky. It would set soon. He gritted his teeth and moved forward to where he could see a larger area of the night-shrouded hill, surveying the terrain while he still had the moon's light.

He picked out a likely spot they could move to, a tumble of large rocks at the bottom of a cliff west of the path the Sioux had taken. He judged the distance and wiggled his toes. His painful ankle might give out on him if he tried to run on it. But with Lydia's help, he could make it to the sanctuary below the cliff. He frowned, eyeing that cliff. It would be much better if they could gain the top, but he doubted his injury would allow that.

The stealthiest *swish* reached his ears, and he froze against the rock. He looked all around, slowly, deliberately, his revolver poised, trying to shelter behind the rock as much as possible. He couldn't see anything unusual, and he sat still, waiting and listening. He had just begun to relax when he glimpsed an unnatural movement between a large rock and a bush. Something had made a move, using the terrain for cover, and it was coming closer.

"Michael?"

He'd thought she was sound asleep.

"Stay back," he whispered, not taking his eyes from the brush.

"What is it?"

"They're getting ready."

She was quiet, but he could feel her nervous energy. She was dying to ask more questions, to wriggle her way up beside him and look out over the landscape. But she stayed put.

Lord, I've been a foolish man this day, and now I've wound up in a bad spot. Out here in the middle of nowhere with a helpless woman, and I've got four savages trying to kill me. That wouldn't be so bad if it weren't for her. If they get through me, she's a goner, Lord, and I just can't let that happen. You can't. Please.

The prayer was only in his mind, but he had no doubt that it was heard. He thought of David hiding out in the hills of Palestine and his pleas to God. *"Lo, the wicked bend their bow, they make ready their arrow upon the string, that they may privily shoot at the upright in heart."* He sat waiting, watching, listening, and struggling to put together the fragments of information his senses brought him.

He heard another tiny sound. They were out there, all right. The moon was setting, and they would soon have nothing but starlight. He had hoped they would wait until dawn, but these were crafty enemies. They probably knew he was alone by now. They'd found Sam, and the single set of shod hoofprints wherever there was dirt would tell the story. They knew he was at a disadvantage. They would also realize that if they waited, a larger force would come after the girl.

A dark wraith tore from the bush to a hollow in the ground, and he almost fired the pistol but steadied himself. *Wait until you can't miss,* he counseled himself.

He heard Lydia stir behind him. *Don't talk now,* he pleaded inwardly. He hugged the rock, hoping the moonlight wasn't glinting off his gun barrel.

A rush of movement came from behind him, and Lydia screamed. He turned and found a warrior had jumped to the top of the rock she was leaning on, knife ready to strike.

Mike fired, then whipped around. As he had feared, another Sioux was only yards away, with his bow drawn. Mike fired his pistol again and dove behind the rock. An arrow zipped past him and plunked when it struck behind him.

Lydia!

He peeked out, but the archer was no more to be seen. With dread, he turned and took a deep breath. Lydia was lying prone, staring at him with wide, luminous eyes.

"Where's the Sioux I shot?"

She looked toward the top of the rocks. "He fell backward over the rock. I think it was Skunk. I smelled him."

Mike exhaled shakily. "We need to move."

"They'll see us."

"The moon's almost down. It will be darker. We can't stay here." He heard a faint scrabbling sound and reached quickly for Lydia's wrist. "Shh. He's out there."

"Behind the rock," she agreed, worming closer to him. "He's alive."

Mike looked out toward where the bowman had been. "Come here."

She crept up beside him and stared out at the night.

"I've got four shots left before I have to reload. You see those rocks over there?"

"Yes. It's too far, Mike."

"No. See, there's some jack pine between here and there, and some more rocks. We can make it. Head for that rock first, and I'll be right behind you."

"What if there's an Indian behind that rock?"

"They don't want to hurt you. And I won't let them take you again, Lydia."

She hesitated.

"On three." He put steel in his voice so she wouldn't argue. "One, two—"

She broke from the cover of the rock and bolted to the next refuge. Mike followed, darting glances toward the most likely hiding places for the Sioux. Lydia flung herself behind the rock, and he looked back at their old hiding place. A shadow grew tall by the rocks, and he fired his revolver in its direction, knowing it went wild, but it was enough to make the Indian take cover where they had been seconds ago.

"You all right?" Lydia said in his ear. Her hands grasped his shoulder and his arm. Something hard poked him in the side.

"I'm fine. What's this?"

"The arrow they shot at us back there. It stuck in the ground right beside me."

He blinked. A souvenir? At a time like this, she was picking up mementos? "Let's keep moving. That was way too close."

"That brush over there?"

"Yes, and keep going right through it until you hit those scrub trees. Wait for me there."

"You should reload."

"No time. Go."

Chapter 14

Ten minutes later, Lydia lay panting in a hollow between several large rocks. She'd feared they would be exposed from above once more, but Mike had found a place where she could ease back into a crevice with the rocks meeting over her. They were both gasping for breath while he fumbled with his cartridges in the dark.

"How's your ankle?" she asked, setting the arrow carefully beside her.

"Bad. I forgot about it while we were running, but I'm paying for that now."

"I wish I could do something."

"Is this where you rip up your petticoats to make me a bandage?"

She laughed. "Wouldn't you just love that?"

"No. It would be a waste of good cloth and expensive lace."

"That's all you know. This one has a simple tatted edging."

"Made it yourself?"

"Of course. It was part of our training. It took three yards to trim the flounce."

"Well, I'm glad I didn't get shot. You'd have to take all that lace off before I'd let you rip your linen into bandages. There." He sat back, and she knew he was finished reloading.

"How can you do that in the dark? I can't see a thing."

"There's a little light here. Not much. Take this."

"What?" She reached toward him, and her hand bumped something hard. She felt it and realized it was his bone-handled knife.

"But I—"

"Take it." He wasn't looking at her but instead out between the rocks toward the small pines.

Lydia grasped the hilt of the knife.

"Squeeze back between the rocks. Make yourself small."

"Michael—"

"Now, Lydia. Please."

She obeyed, sitting down in the snug niche and pulling her knees up before her. She tucked her skirt around her. When she sat back, she could barely see Mike's silhouette against the opening. The silence was frightening. He sat motionless, and if she hadn't known of his injury, she'd have thought him ready to spring, catlike, at whatever showed itself at the edge of the rocks.

"Michael," she whispered.

She thought his mouth curved upward for an instant as he turned his profile to her in the starlight. "What is it?"

"I think I misjudged you."

"Oh, you changed your mind, and you think I'm a gentleman now?" He was definitely smiling.

"I wouldn't go that far, but I was wrong about you."

"You thought I was an indolent churl."

"I never said indolent. You're a hardworking man."

"Oh, excuse me, I meant insolent."

She couldn't help chuckling but sobered as she noted his wary posture and the way his keen glance roved over the area and avoided resting on her.

"I wanted to say. . .well, if things go badly—"

He waited a moment. "Well, if what?"

"Thank you."

"Forget it. Just concentrate on living."

"Yes, but—"

She broke off as he raised his left hand suddenly. It hung motionless for an instant; then he brought it together with his right, on the butt of the pistol, steadying it.

Lydia held her breath and stared out between the rocks where Brown stared. What did he see?

They came in a rush, all four of the warriors, and Mike fired rapidly. Lydia pressed her hands over her ears, but the noise was painful in the tiny cavern. Each shock reverberated, numbing her.

He used four shots in quick succession, but even so, one warrior made it to the entrance of their haven. Terror welled up in her as she watched him come closer and closer. Mike's gun must be empty. She clutched the knife.

At the last possible second, Mike pulled the trigger, and the Sioux fell within a yard of the gap in the rocks. She listened, but her ears still rang.

"Are they gone?" She could barely hear her own words.

Mike shook his head.

She rubbed her ears. After a long moment, the ringing lessened. She touched the back of his gray cotton shirt, and Mike reached back and found her hand while still watching the opening.

"How are we doing?" she asked.

"This nearest one's dead for sure. I think I hit one of the others, but he didn't fall."

"Get me the bow."

He turned and stared at her then. "What?"

"The bow! You can reach it."

"Are you crazy?"

"I told you I learned archery."

"Oh, right, Miss Cluckson's."

"Clarkson's."

"You can't mean to use that thing."

"I won the medal three years running."

"What did you shoot at?"

"Paper targets set up against a straw stack."

"Well, if I see any paper targets for you to shoot at, I'll let you know."

"Let me get it," she insisted, trying to shove past him.

He pushed her back, a bit roughly, Lydia thought.

"You stay put," he hissed. He looked out again, cautiously, then took his hat off and held it outside the shelter of the rocks. All was quiet. He bent swiftly forward and grabbed the fallen warrior's bow. As he ducked back inside the hideaway, a gunshot cracked, and chips splintered from the stone by his head.

"Get back!" He pushed her to the rear of the cavern again, tossing the bow after her, and sat motionless and wary, listening.

After half a minute had passed, he said softly, "I'm sorry. Are you all right?"

"Yes, but. . ."

"But what?"

"You didn't get me any extra arrows."

⬯

Lydia was quiet for a long time, and Mike's admiration for her grew. He heard her fingering the bow. Well, let her. It gave her something to think about. Still, he shouldn't have risked his neck for it.

"Think they're gone?" she whispered at last.

"No. They'll make one more attack."

"How do you know?"

"They went for me and got my horse. That wasn't according to plan, I'm sure. They'd have liked to keep Sam. They always want more horses. Then they attacked us at our first hideout and followed us here for another go-round. One more time before they decide whether or not to call if off. Four times."

"Four times? Is that lucky for them or something?"

"It's a sacred number. They're funny. Sometimes they quit when the first man falls. But if they decide they want revenge, then look out!"

"There's three of them left, you think?"

"Maybe. Did you get a look at this one? Is it Skunk?"

Lydia sidled up to him, and he felt the warmth radiating from her and realized he was cold. He'd left his wool uniform jacket in camp that morning when he and Paine set out for a day of hunting in the late July sun.

"I can't tell," she whispered.

The warrior was lying face down. "You said he had a knife. What about his clothes? His hair?"

"No," she said quickly. "Skunk had a big necklace with lots of beads and things hanging from it. Bones, too." She grimaced, and he imagined she'd been all too close to the Indian's jewelry.

"Well, I'm pretty sure Old Skunk is hurting, and one of his buddies, too. Maybe they'll call it quits."

"You don't believe that, though."

Mike looked up at the stars. "It's still a long time 'til dawn."

"How can you tell?"

"By the phase of the moon. It's down now, but it'll be awhile before you see the sun."

"Huh. It seems like we've been out here for hours."

"Not so very long. Did Miss Parkman teach you any astronomy?"

"Clarkson."

"Right."

"No, she didn't."

He shifted and reached for her hand. "Well, now, that school needs some improvement in its curriculum. Bend over here. Can you see those stars that form sort of a square? Over the trees there."

She peered upward in the direction he indicated. "I'm not sure."

"See the tallest pine? Let your eyes travel straight up from it. There are four stars in a box and three that form the handle of the dipper."

"You mean that's the Big Dipper?"

"Yes."

"My father used to try to show it to me, and I could never see it."

"But you see it now?"

"I think so."

"Well, then, let's see if you can see the Little Dipper. Look at the two stars that make the front edge of the Big Dipper. They're the pointers. Follow a straight line up from them until you see a bright star."

"Way up there?"

"Yes. That's the North Star. It's the tail end of the Little Dipper."

"You're joking."

"No, I'm not. The little one's tipped opposite the big one, like it's pouring syrup into it. That's what my daddy taught me."

"I see it! And to think I had to almost lose my scalp to learn to find the North Star." Lydia sighed and crumpled into a little heap.

"What's the matter, darlin'?" He pulled out his most Southern drawl to distract her, but for once she didn't scold him for his flippancy.

"It seems like years since Nathan and I went to pick blackberries."

"Sleep if you can."

"No. If they're coming back, I need to be alert. You'd better reload."

"If I start, that's when they'll come."

"They can't know. I'll watch while you do it."

"All right. I'm down to one shot, and I guess that wouldn't do us much good. But don't stick your head out there." He worked quickly, but even so, it took him a couple of minutes to fish the components from the saddlebag and reload the pistol in the gloom. When he was done, he looked at Lydia. She was sitting back from the opening but was watching intently, scanning the rough hillside. The bow she held across her lap looked almost like a toy. Her mouth was set in a grim line as she searched for the smallest movement.

Lord, keep her safe. I surely can't do this on my own. I'll take whatever You hand me, but we can't hold out forever, and this gal. . . He remembered her woeful demeanor during their conversation the night he'd gone with her to fetch Dorcas's skillet. *Lord, give her peace.*

He slid toward her, feeling a renewed resolution. "All set."

She didn't move back. "Michael, I could get his quiver."

He smiled. She was scrappy, all right.

"Better not chance it, darlin'."

She looked at him sharply, then crawled back into the depths of the crevice.

◦

Lydia ran her hands over the strung bow again. It was much shorter than the ones they had used in Hartford. The springy wood was smooth on the belly of the bow, but it was backed with something hard as a fingernail that seemed to be elastic. Maybe animal sinew. The string was a tough, twisted cord. She tested the pull. It was much harder than what she was used to, but she thought she could draw it back far enough to make her arrow deadly. There was barely room in the tiny cave, but if an enemy filled the doorway, she could hardly miss.

She picked up her one arrow. The point was bound into a slit on the end of the slender shaft. It felt like metal, but it might be stone. She thought of the blunt brass tips they had used at Miss Clarkson's and gritted her teeth. Mike was right about one thing—this wasn't target practice. Those were real, living men out there. Could she use the lethal force of the short bow against them?

It took only the memory of Harpy to tell her she could. How swiftly and unfeelingly they had killed the dog. They would have killed Mike, too, with as little concern.

Mike tensed, and she sat up straighter. "Stay back there. Get over to the side so you're not in the line of fire."

She obeyed him but slipped the nock of her arrow onto the string and held the bow at rest in front of her. She was more comfortable with it in her hands than with his razor-sharp knife. She slipped that into her high shoe top, just in case.

A rifle shot sounded, and Mike ducked back behind the rock. "Just stay under cover and let him use up his ammunition."

Her heart raced, and she was trembling. She hated that. If she had to fight tonight, she wanted her hands to be steady.

Chapter 15

Mike edged toward the gap to look out again, then moved rapidly to fire his pistol. Lydia covered her ears, slipping one hand through the bowstring and clinging to the arrow so she wouldn't lose it. The opening in the rocks was gray before her, and Mike crouched low, almost lying down.

She lowered her hands, but all she could hear was that awful ringing. Gradually she became aware of her own loud breathing.

"Michael!"

He didn't answer, at least not that she could hear, but he sat a little taller, looking outside.

She waited, trying to calm her breath, and without warning a volley of several arrows hit the rocks near her and shattered.

"Get down!" Mike shouted.

Another cascade of arrows whistled into the cavern, and Mike knew he had to stop them. He had pinpointed the location of the warrior with the rifle behind a gnarled clump of brush. He wasn't so sure about the other two. He'd hoped at least one was out of the action, but from the intense fire, there had to be three of them left.

Doggedly, he watched the spot from which the gunfire had come, praying for a clear shot. It was close enough, but he couldn't just blaze away at them. His supply of lead and powder cartridges was nearly gone, and he wasn't known as a sharpshooter. Every bullet had to count.

He saw movement to his left and turned, knowing it was too late if the aim was true. An arrow hit the rock near him, shattering into pieces, and he fired at the archer. Finally, he found his mark. The jolt of exultation was short-lived. As he swiveled to deal with his other foes, the rifleman rose behind the bushes, and Mike steeled himself to get off two good shots, no matter what. Something hit him just below his collarbone. He aimed the revolver again, but it was very heavy. Pain shot through his arm and shoulder and chest. Using both hands, he leveled it as the Sioux lowered his own weapon. Mike pulled the trigger once more.

It was satisfying to see the warrior fall like a stone, his rifle barrel catching the starlight. Mike sank back against the rock, breathing in deep gasps, trying to realize what had happened. His shoulder was on fire, and his arm was going numb. The pistol fell from his hand with a *thunk*.

I can't quit now, Lord. There's one more out there. If he saw me go down, he'll close in for the kill and take Lydia. Please don't let it end like this.

"Michael!" Lydia was pulling him away from the opening. "Mike! Get back!"

"My gun's empty, darlin'." His tongue didn't want to form the words, and she knelt close beside him, staring at him. He caught the glitter of fear in her eyes.

"Are you hit?"

"Afraid so."

"Michael! You can't—"

She tugged at his boots, pulling him clumsily to the side. He moaned at the pain that shot through his ankle and his shoulder. A tearing sound jerked him to full consciousness.

"What are you doing?" She didn't answer, but he knew. "Don't do that!"

"This is the time, Michael. No jokes now. You're bleeding."

"Three yards of lace. . ." He hated the way his voice trailed off.

"Is it bad?"

"No."

"You're lying, aren't you?"

"Yes." He took a deep breath and focused on the stars above, then pushed himself up on his good elbow. "Lydia, forget about me. He thinks you're alone now. He thinks you're defenseless."

Lydia stopped her frantic preparations. "Aren't I?"

"Only if you think you are. I'm not dead yet, sweetheart, but I can't be much help to you. You've got several things going for you, though, the biggest one being God's power."

She exhaled slowly. "I've never felt very powerful, Mike."

"You don't have to. It's not a feeling. It's knowing that if God doesn't want that savage to haul you out of here, it won't happen."

"I've been praying," she said hesitantly.

"That's fine, but God's also given you some resources."

She caught a sharp breath. "You mean the bow?"

It sounded ludicrous, even to him, but he knew he couldn't fight the last Sioux off with only a knife in his present condition.

"He may be coming, even now. Get over there and watch."

Still she hesitated.

"Lydia! I don't want to have to tell Dan Reese I got them all but one, and then lost you again. I'd never live it down."

She scurried to the opening, and he leaned back with a sigh. It wasn't his reputation he was worried about, but that seemed to have jolted her into action. He closed his eyes. *Lord, it's up to You now. Don't let me lose her again. Please!*

Lydia sat panting in the doorway, shivering and staring out into the night. Her faith had always been an important part of her life, but right now it seemed tiny and fragile. Would God really give her the strength to fight for her life? *Lord, I can't do this,* she cried silently. *Mike says You'll give me power, but I'm so frightened! I don't know if I can hold the bow steady!*

She fingered it tentatively.

"Don't let him get close to you," Mike's weary voice came from behind her. "Don't let him get within arm's length, because once he gets hold of you, it's all over. You understand?"

"Yes." She crouched between the rocks, sending up broken prayers. Had the Sioux given up? Was their fourth attack ended? And would she sit here all keyed up until dawn wondering while Mike's life drained from him?

She thought she heard a sound. Maybe it was a breeze in the stunted pines. There had been no wind all night, though. She eased the bow into position and nocked the arrow.

Lord, help me now. If Michael dies, I'm not sure I want to live, either.

She thought of just standing up in the open, inviting the warrior to put an end to this miserable contest.

"Sweetheart, be careful."

She turned toward his voice.

"Don't look at me. Look for him."

Quickly she faced the opening again. "There's only one?"

"I'm pretty sure. If he's shooting, get down. If he's running toward you, wait until he's three strides away."

She willed her heart to ease its thumping. "I don't know if I can do it, Mike."

He laughed, and she caught her breath.

"You? You took the medal three years running."

Yes, she thought. *Yes, I did. Lord, Your will be done.*

He stirred behind her, and she asked shakily, "Are you going to make it, Mike? Tell me the truth."

"Well, it didn't hit my lung. Where's my knife?"

"In my shoe."

"Left or right?"

"Right."

"Come closer."

She inched back toward him, watching the doorway, and felt his hand grasp her ankle.

"Sorry, darlin'. I'm not much use right now, but I'll be your last line of defense. Just remember, that man doesn't want you dead. He's determined to ride into his village with all his friends' horses and a captive."

"You guarantee that?"

"Nothing's guaranteed with the Lakota. He could be gone now, slinking off toward home, but I don't think so."

She faced the opening again with determination, keeping well to the side behind the rock. Another arrow whizzed into their refuge.

"Easy," Mike said. "If that didn't split, you've got another arrow. And if we keep over to this side, he can't hit us from out there. Just be careful about showing yourself. If he thinks you're me, he won't hesitate to fire."

Lord, only You can help us now, she prayed. *Help me not to be foolish and waste all of Michael's effort. I want us both to live. If we can't be together after today, so be it. Just please, don't let this fine man die in vain.*

Cautiously she leaned to her right, almost expecting a hail of bullets in response. All was quiet. She held her breath and peered out into the night. Suddenly she saw him, crouching, as still as she was, in the shadow of a boulder scarcely ten yards away. He was looking at her. She recognized his cruel sneer, and fear surged up inside her. She wanted to duck back into the dark, to get away from his piercing stare, but she sensed that if she wavered now, he would come and drag her from the hiding place.

She moved forward into the gap between the rocks, and he rose on his knees, raising his bow. Lydia held her arrow on the string, knowing that once she drew it back she would not be able to hold it long.

"Skunk!" He might not understand her derisive name for him, but he would recognize her voice. She saw the surprise register on his painted face. The dawn was coming, and with it light enough to let her see her enemy's lips twitch.

He stood and began walking toward her.

"Stop!" she called.

Skunk came on slowly with the placid smile of a cat.

She gulped a breath and raised her bow, drawing back the string with the same motion. He stopped a few paces away, eyeing her with speculation, then said something in his own language. Lydia didn't move an eyelash. He stooped and laid his bow down.

He spoke again, almost gently, extending his hand toward her. Lydia didn't know if she could hold the string back much longer. She clenched her teeth.

Skunk snarled and pulled his knife from its sheath and took a step toward her.

She let the arrow fly and watched in mixed relief and horror as it found its mark. Skunk opened his mouth in utter surprise, and she watched him fall. It was like the game Statues she and the other girls had played at Miss Clarkson's, whirling around with hands clasped, then letting go and freezing in whatever odd posture they found themselves. Skunk sank to the ground, still holding the knife out menacingly.

Chapter 16

Mike battled the sharp pain and inched toward the opening in the rocks where Lydia stood. She had shot her arrow, and now she was exposed to any enemies left outside their haven.

"Get back!" He pulled himself up beside her, leaning against the largest rock. She turned to look at him, tears streaming down her cheeks.

"I—I did it."

He looked past her and squinted, a strange, expectant awe overpowering his pain and hopelessness. The last of the warriors lay still on the hillside, just five yards from their shelter. Mike swallowed hard.

"Well! I can't wait to see your fancy stitchery."

Lydia sobbed, and he immediately regretted his callousness. She was trembling, and he reached to pull her to him.

"Darlin', I'm sorry. Let's take a second to thank God here."

She collapsed against him, weeping uncontrollably, and Mike gasped as the pain shot through him. He despised his weakness and set his back more firmly against the rock, determined not to fall over.

"Lord, we thank You for life," he said, holding her perhaps more tightly than was proper, but it was necessary if he wanted to stay upright. "We thank You for victory. Now let us rejoin our friends if that's part of Your will, Lord."

"Thank you," Lydia whispered raggedly, and he squeezed her. She had stopped crying, and if his shoulder hadn't hurt so badly, he'd have tremendously enjoyed holding her in his arms.

"Sweetheart, if I don't sit down right now, I'll probably fall down."

She jumped back. "Oh, Mike, I'm sorry."

He settled on the ground, keeping his back to the rock, grimacing as he extended his injured ankle.

"Your shirt is all blood! You've got to let me do something." She turned away, and he knew she was about to sacrifice her petticoats for sure, in spite of his earlier pleas.

"I knew you could do it," he said, hoping he could make her smile again.

"You did not. You thought I was bluffing."

"No, but maybe I did think you were a little optimistic."

She laughed without mirth. "He had almost the same stubborn look you get sometimes." She paused with the finely woven white cloth in her hands. "He was so human then. I didn't know if I could—oh, Mike, it was awful."

"I'm sure it was."

"He changed all of a sudden, and I knew that if I didn't go with him, he would kill me." Her eyes were huge. She scrambled to look out between the rocks, then came slowly back to his side, the white petticoat trailing from her hand.

"He–he's still lying there." Her lower lip quivered.

Mike sent up a quick silent prayer.

"Do you know that verse in Psalm 18 that says, 'He teacheth my hands to war'?"

She shook her head, her eyes glistening. "I loved archery. I never thought. . ."

Mike said quickly, "But God knew. He prepared you for this moment. I'm sorry I made fun of your education before. It did seem a bit frivolous at the time, but I was forgetting that with God, nothing is wasted."

She nodded. "Perhaps you're right. Now let me at that wound."

Mike tried to unbutton his shirt, but his right hand wouldn't function that well. He sighed and let her take over. "I've come to a momentous decision, Lydia."

"And what is that?" She bit her lip as she worked the buttons free from the stiffening fabric.

"I'm going to send all my children to Miss Clarkson's. Well, all my daughters, that is."

She looked into his eyes, startled, then laughed. "Hush, you. You're not trying to distract me while you breathe your last, are you?"

"Hardly. I'm tougher than that."

"Tough enough to ride a mustang back to the wagon train?"

"Oh, I don't know."

"There must be some ponies tethered near here," she said, working tenaciously at the buttons.

"Probably at their war lodge. I think we're close to it."

"What's a war lodge?"

"It's a hut they use when they're out raiding. Just a small, hidden place made out of logs or hides or whatever's handy."

"You've seen one?"

"No, a friend told me about it. Trooper Barkley's brother. He's a scout for the army, and he's spent a lot of time with the Indians."

"I could go and look for it."

"No."

She arched her brows. "Why not?"

"Lydia, you must realize what we've just come through. It may not be safe out there, even now. I'm not letting you out of my sight."

"So. . .we wait here for the soldiers? What if Mr. Paine never made it back to the wagons?"

"He did. I won't believe otherwise, so don't say it."

She nodded slowly. "All right. Then they should be here soon."

He avoided looking directly at her. He'd expected Sergeant Reese and his men hours ago. They must not have started out until Paine returned to camp. If he returned. He glanced sharply at Lydia. He'd just told her not to say it, but the thought was still nibbling at the edge of his hope.

As they talked, Lydia tore a long strip of white cotton from the bottom of her petticoat and ripped off the lace edging. She folded the cloth into a thick pad. "Here. You're losing a lot of blood. We need to stop it."

He sprawled against the rock and let her pull the front of his shirt back and press the wad of cotton against the torn flesh. He winced but sat still as she pushed firmly on it. His eyes closed. The pain was intense, but the pressure gave him some relief.

Lydia sat for half an hour, pressing the folded cloth against his wound. Mike appeared to be drowsing, and after a while she was sure he slept. She was glad. It meant his pain was not sharp enough to keep him awake. She watched him as the sun rose and bathed the hillside in light.

Lord, please let him recover, and let us get back to the train.

He jerked awake suddenly and stared at her, then sighed and shifted his position.

"How you doing?" she asked softly.

"Could be better."

"Do you think you're gaining strength? Because if you're getting weaker, there's no sense in waiting. I'll go look for those ponies and ride for help."

"No." She frowned at him, and Mike shrugged then winced at the pain. "I'm not letting you go alone."

"I can find those mounts, Michael."

He shook his head. "Still stubborn."

"Still rude."

He smiled, watching her with half-closed eyes.

"Are you in pain?" she asked.

"Yes."

"Please let me go. I can't stand the thought of you bleeding to death while we sit here."

"I'm not bleeding to death."

"Well, this cloth is saturated, and I need to change it. Can you hold it for a minute?"

He reached over and pushed on the front of his shirt, where it covered the blood-soaked bandage. Lydia took his knife and started a tear at the edge of her petticoat then ripped off another row of fabric.

"I hope you have more underthings in Paine's wagon."

"Insolent man. A true gentleman would never mention the source of these bandages." She folded the strip carefully then faced him. "Ready?"

He opened his eyes. "Do you have to?"

"Your wound is still bleeding, Michael. It's soaked the bandage and your shirt."

He looked down at her blood-stained hands and the fresh wad of fabric. "Lydia, there's a missionary in the territory, west of Fort Hall."

"A missionary?"

"Yes. A preacher. Won't you please consider becoming my wife?"

She stared at him for just a second and wondered if he was delirious. She ignored the question and leaned forward to remove the bloody dressing from his wound.

"That's assuming I don't bleed to death," he amended.

"I told you, I can't." She pulled the old bandage away in one quick motion then applied the fresh one firmly.

Mike groaned.

"Sorry. I'm afraid it's still oozing blood." She kept her gaze on her hands. She didn't think she could bear to look into his eyes just then.

"Why not, Lydia? You know you like me."

"Rubbish. I can't stand you."

"Is that so?"

"Yes, and you're much too ardent for a dying man."

He laughed then sobered, and she couldn't keep from looking at him. His soft expression almost melted her determination to keep him at arm's length.

"What is it, darlin'? This contract you mentioned. It's not. . .a marriage contract, is it?"

"Of course not. Do you think I would actually. . ." She stared at him. The idea that she would put up with his attempts at flirtation while promised to marry another man was appalling. "Really, Michael."

He relaxed visibly, sinking back with a sigh. "I hoped it wasn't that, but I couldn't be sure. For all I knew, you were married already or had signed away your future and were planning to wed some fur trapper."

Lydia laughed. "That's silly."

"Well, there's only one other logical explanation. Mr. Paine said you were going to teach school, so I guess that's it—a business contract."

"Yes. It's very simple, really. I signed a document stating that I will not get married while I am teaching."

He was very still, and she concentrated on the bandage, holding it steadily with both hands and avoiding his gaze. He was just too magnetic. She wasn't sure if it was his personality or his tattered uniform or the possibility that his proposal was not part of the banter.

"They can do that?" he asked at last.

"They can. They have."

He reached up and stroked a loose lock of her hair back where it hung over her cheek. "Someone must have told them how beautiful you are, and they put that clause in the paper to make sure you didn't abandon your purpose when the men started buzzing around you."

She couldn't look at him. His fingers rested lightly on her cheek, just in front of her ear, and she was afraid that if she moved the slightest bit and met his eyes, he would pull her into his arms. But that was silly. He was badly wounded. How could a man in great pain think about courting, especially when the lady had told him she wasn't available?

He raised his chin suddenly and stared at her. "Is that the only reason you told me you couldn't be more than friends?"

"Yes."

"There's nothing else in the way?"

"Isn't that enough?"

She glanced toward him and realized immediately that it was a mistake. His fingers slid back into her hair, and he pulled her closer to him. "Lydia, I love you." His lips were inches from hers.

"You're serious." It came out as a whisper, as she realized he was about to kiss her.

"Dead serious."

She didn't draw back but closed her eyes and lost herself in that moment of delight, all the while trying to remember what it was she was supposed to be doing. She wanted to ease her hands up around his neck and return his embrace, but suddenly she remembered.

"Your wound," she gasped, pushing away from him, trying not to jostle his injured shoulder.

"Can you stand me now?"

"If I can, I shouldn't." Her pulse was thundering from the effect of his sweet kiss.

"What town are you going to be teaching in?"

"Never mind."

"Why?"

She shook her head. "I know you, and I don't want any knights in shining armor stirring up trouble for me with my employers."

"What, you think I'd challenge the school board to a duel?"

"I need this position, Mike." She looked into his eyes and nodded. "I do.

And without even meaning to, you could get me fired. Just by making your presence known, you could cause trouble for me."

He was silent for a moment then said, "If the security of a place to live is what you need. . .or an income. . ."

"Please stop."

"But Lydia, we're talking about the rest of our lives."

"Are we?" It was a timid squeak.

"I won't claim you love me, but you have to admit you at least like me."

She looked off toward the hillside and the plain beyond, breathing slowly and carefully. "Look, the troops may never come. Those Sioux ponies can't be far away."

"Quit changing the subject."

She scowled at him. "I don't want to talk about the school board."

"All right, fine. What do you want to talk about?"

"Why don't you tell me about your family?"

He said nothing for a moment, and Lydia felt her color rising. She didn't think she could stand it if he kept on talking about a future she knew was impossible.

"I really want to know about your family," she said.

"All right, come sit here beside me."

"I need to hold this."

"You can hold it from here."

"No."

"What? You doubt my motives?"

"Yes, actually."

"Oh, Lydia." He tugged gently on her arm, and she gave in, settling beside him on the ground. Somehow, she ended up in the curve of his left arm. He was warm, and it felt wonderful to be so close to him with her left hand reaching across his chest to keep the bandage in place.

"I think the bleeding's stopped. It's less, anyway."

"Good." He squeezed her shoulders lightly, pulling her closer against his side.

"Mike."

"What?"

They looked at each other. She knew she should move away or at least admonish him, but she didn't want to. They sat that way for a long moment, neither one of them moving.

"So," he said at last. "I grew up in Smith Creek, Tennessee. I had two brothers and three sisters."

"And?"

"What else do you want to know?"

"Everything."

"For a woman who intends to walk out of my life soon, you're nosy."

"No, I just thought we should put the enforced waiting period to good use."

"Ah, yes. Idle hands and all that."

"Michael, really!" She shifted so she wasn't so close to him.

"So tell me about yourself," he said.

"All right, that's fair. You know that my parents died some time ago."

"No, I didn't."

She nodded. "They did. And I went to live with my aunt, who saw to my education at Miss Clarkson's, to her ruin."

"How is that?"

"She apparently bankrupted herself to pay for my schooling."

Mike grimaced. "She mustn't have had much to begin with. Either that, or she had some bad financial advice."

"Well, however it happened, she passed away a year after my graduation, and I learned that I was destitute. Miss Clarkson helped me find this job, so here I am, out to conquer the West and civilize the children of the pioneers."

He smiled. "You'll do it, too."

"So...your family?"

He squinted at her in the shadows. "You want to know about Martha."

She swallowed. "Do I?"

"Don't you?"

"Perhaps I do."

He was silent for a moment, then stirred. "She was my first love. My only love. We knew each other all our lives, grew up in the same valley. It just seemed the natural thing to get married. There was no one else I ever felt close to."

"You loved her."

"Of course." He shook his head slightly, as though he didn't enjoy confronting the past. "Well, we were quite young, and I don't really have anything to compare it to, but looking back now, yes, I would say we loved each other very much." He chuckled. "There were times when I thought she hated me. She'd yell at me, and I'd yell back. But that never lasted long."

"Sounds like us." Lydia immediately wished she hadn't said that and asked hastily, "What did she look like?"

He looked toward the rock that formed the back wall of their hiding place, and his brow wrinkled as though he struggled to focus the memory.

"She wasn't at all like you."

"Is that good or bad?"

He smiled. "Her hair was pale gold. When she washed it in rainwater, it looked pretty in the sun."

Lydia kept silent, thinking how dull her own hair was after months on the dusty trail.

"She was shorter than you and thin. They never had enough to eat at their house. Her folks died when she was fifteen, and it seemed logical to get married." He looked at her suddenly, with a crooked smile. "She wasn't the independent type, and her older brothers were already married. Now, you'd do differently in that situation."

"Would I?"

"Certainly. You'd want to prove to the world that you could survive on your own. I expect you'd have stayed on in your pa's cabin alone for a while."

Lydia swallowed hard. It sounded dreadfully bleak compared to the prospect of marriage to Michael Brown. "How long were you married?"

"About five years. Billy came along a year later, and then. . . well, we lost a baby after that."

"I'm sorry."

"It happens. Martha took it hard. Then we had the fire. We had to live with my family, and that was tough, but we had absolutely nothing." His lips skewed into a grim smile. "I figured I'd enlist for a year or two and send my pay home, and then we'd be able to start over. Didn't work out that way."

Lydia pushed down the memory of the fire that had taken her father's life, but Mike's loss was more real to her because of it. "Did you miss her when you came out here?"

"Sure."

Lydia looked into his face. The carefree, teasing expression was gone, replaced by a thoughtful sorrow.

"I'm sorry you lost them, Mike."

He drew a deep breath, and she felt his lungs expand. *What am I doing?* she asked herself. *I mustn't allow myself to become attached to this man.*

But when his scratchy cheek came down gently against her forehead, she didn't resist. She let go of the bandage and hesitantly reached up to stroke his thick hair. It was cool and satiny. She closed her eyes and rested against his shoulder, unwilling to think beyond this moment to the wagon train and the weeks of trail ahead and the school in Oregon.

Suddenly Mike stiffened, and she was alert at once.

"Listen."

Far away, she heard a bugle sound and, a moment later, faint hoofbeats.

"Darlin', you'd best get out there and wave whatever's left of your underskirt so Dan Reese can find us."

Chapter 17

It took Reese's men only a few minutes to locate the Indians' mustangs. He assigned several troopers to carry the dead Sioux down the hillside and bury them where the ground was less rocky.

Lydia stood near where Mike was stretched out on a blanket. Mr. Paine had removed Mike's left boot and was binding his ankle while Dr. Nichols swabbed out the shoulder wound with water from his canteen.

"No way you can sit a horse all the way back to camp, Brown," Reese was saying.

"I'll make it."

"Better make a travois," Dr. Nichols said, and Reese nodded.

"Oh, wonderful." Brown scowled up at the sergeant.

"He's not a very good patient, is he?" Lydia asked.

Mike struggled to sit up, but Dr. Nichols pushed him back down. "Take it easy, would you? I'm trying to see how bad you're hurt."

"It'll mend in time. Let's get going," Mike replied.

Dr. Nichols shook his head. "You've still got the lead in your shoulder. I'm not digging it out until we get back to camp."

"It won't take long to make a travois if we can get some poles long enough," Reese said. He looked doubtfully toward the scrub pines. "Gleason, take some men and hunt up two good, straight poles."

Dr. Nichols had Mike moved into the shade. It was another half hour before the travois was ready, and in the interim Mike instructed Mr. Paine to go to the rocky cavern and gather up any unbroken arrows he could find and the short bow Lydia had left there.

"I wondered about the brave we found with an arrow through his chest," Reese said, eyeing Lydia with awe.

"She saved both our necks by shooting that last one," Mike said.

Lydia sat down beside him. "Hush now. I did what I had to is all."

Mike's face was gray. His smile skewed into a grimace. "If I pass out on the trail, just make sure they get me back to camp, all right, sweetheart?"

"If you weren't hurt, I'd lambaste you."

He lay back on the blanket, smiling.

The men from the burial detail returned carrying various articles they had stripped from the Lakota. Lydia recognized Skunk's necklace and looked away.

225

Mike stirred and eyed their plunder keenly.

"Hey, Shorty," he called.

A large private walked over to where he lay.

"That quiver goes to Miss Jackson."

"What, this?" Shorty held up an elk hide quiver with four arrows in it.

"That's right."

Lydia felt a flush infusing her cheeks. "No, really, I don't want it."

"You earned it, Miss Jackson," said Reese.

"It'll be a good conversation piece for her class in Oregon," Mike said. "She's a good horsewoman, too."

Reese nodded. "Miss Jackson, you and Nathan Paine can each keep one of the ponies. Corporal Brown can add the other three to our string."

Private Barkley escorted her to where the five mustangs were tied. "You want one of these critters, Miss Jackson?"

Lydia looked them over. "That's the one the leader rode." She indicated a stocky brown and white pinto, made garish with black painted stripes on his legs and the imprint of the warrior's hand on his shoulder. "What does all that paint mean?"

"Mostly it's to scare you. The hand means he killed an enemy in battle sometime."

She looked at the other horses. When she saw the one that was Skunk's, she turned away, her stomach suddenly squeamish. She didn't want to ride that pony again.

"I'll take the one with the black hand."

Barkley smiled. "That's fitting, Miss Jackson. You've earned the honor."

Lydia caught her breath in a little sob. "I didn't—"

"I know, miss. You weren't saying you deserve the war paint. I said it, though. You were a real soldier, and God was surely looking down on you and Mike."

⁀

Thomas Miller and three other men from the wagon train rode out and met them five miles from the camp.

"We sure are glad to see you, Miss Jackson," Miller said, sweeping off his hat for a moment. "Mrs. Paine was beside herself worrying about you and the corporal."

"How's Nathan doing?" Lydia asked.

"He's in some pain, but his mother's making him as comfortable as possible."

It was past noon when they reached the wagon train. Lydia was cosseted and fussed over by Dorcas, and most of the other ladies came by as she ravenously ate her dinner.

"My dear, you'll have to give us the whole story tonight when we make camp again," Mrs. Kemp said, looking her over. Lydia flushed, wondering if that fastidious lady could tell she was not wearing a petticoat. Her ride home on the mustang had been less than modest, but all of the men had been courteous and managed not to stare at her exposed ankles. She was reconsidering her opinion of bloomer costumes, especially with the prospect of riding her new mustang.

Jean Carver leaned toward her eagerly. "Is it true that Injun wanted you for his bride?"

"More likely for his slave," Margaret Sawyer said acidly.

"Margaret!" her mother scolded, but she listened avidly for Lydia's reply.

Lydia suspected that Margaret was jealous because she was not the one who had had an adventure and been rescued by the handsome corporal.

"I doubt he had any such designs," Lydia said evenly. "The sergeant says they might have traded me back for some horses."

Margaret smirked as though that idea was clearly a fabrication.

"There now, ladies," Dorcas said. "Mrs. Miller tells me we'll be pulling out any minute. I must pack up my dishes. Off with you."

The next morning, Mike waited impatiently. He had sent Gleason to the Paines' wagon with a plea for Lydia to visit him. He wasn't at all sure she would come, but he thought he would go crazy riding in the escort's supply wagon all day. The swaying, bumping motion of the wagon sent jolts of pain through his body. There was no way he could read or otherwise occupy himself while riding in this torture chamber, except to think about Lydia.

It wasn't until the nooning stop that she climbed up over the seat of the wagon carrying a tin plate and a basket.

"Good day, Michael. I've brought you some dinner—Mrs. Paine's biscuits and some cold prairie chicken. Mr. Paine says he'll come by and see you this evening after we camp."

He struggled to sit up in spite of the searing pain it caused, and Lydia arranged the rolled up blankets he was using for pillows, to help him into a position that was nearly upright.

"There you go. I'm glad to see you looking so well. I'll come back later for the dishes."

"Don't leave," Mike said.

"I must help Dorcas. We'll be moving out soon."

He realized how long the afternoon would be riding alone in the uncomfortable wagon. "Please. I've been starving for company all morning. Tell me what's going on."

"Well, Nathan cried quite a bit this morning. He's terribly jostled. Mr. Paine spent most of the nooning trying to rig up a hammock for him inside the wagon."

"That's a good idea. I wonder if it would work in here." Mike looked around at the crammed interior of the supply wagon.

"All of the other boys were jealous when they heard Nathan and I have Sioux ponies. They think we went off on a lark and came back with fabulous loot." Lydia smiled. "At least it took Nathan's mind off his leg for a while when Chub Hadley and Ralph Miller came by to see him. Then Private Gleason let Chub and Ralph help him take the ponies into the river to wash the war paint off."

"Which one did Nathan pick?"

"The one with the most white."

"Bad choice."

Lydia scowled at him. "He's eight years old. The boy doesn't know anything about horses yet. Just let him enjoy it. Besides, they're all healthy. If he picks the worst one, why should you care? You'll get the better ones for your remounts."

"The boy needs the one that's calmest and best behaved. That dun."

"The small one? What boy would choose the runt?"

Again Mike felt the chafing of his confinement. "When I'm on my feet again, I'll bring the extra mounts by the Paines' wagon and show him their good points. If he wants to choose another one, I'll let him."

"Mr. Paine rode the pinto before he let Nathan choose. He didn't see anything wrong with that horse."

"Fine. Josiah's not a bad judge of horseflesh. And how do you like your pony?"

"We're getting along well."

"Sit, Lydia."

Immediately her eyes darkened. "I mustn't."

"Gossip?" She didn't answer, and he gave a short sigh of disgust. "It's not like I'm in any shape to be accused of molesting you."

"Please don't speak so. I was starting to reclassify you as a gentleman, you know."

"I'm sorry. I just get so tired of these biddies. Mrs. Sawyer is the worst, and her daughters aren't any better, or so I'm told."

"By whom?"

"Ask any trooper."

"Ah, so the men of the escort gossip, as well." The corners of her tempting lips seemed to twitch.

Mike laughed. "You got me. But seriously, can't you spend ten minutes with me, the poor wounded man who rescued you?"

"You're going to use that to your advantage all the way to Oregon, aren't you?"

"I hope I won't turn into a malingering invalid," he said with a smile.

She sat down on the edge of a crate of staples, smoothing her delft blue skirt. Mike didn't think he had seen that dress before. She'd worn a green dress occasionally, but when she was captured she had been wearing her habitual mulberry dress. That one was probably ruined during the ordeal, he realized, from rough treatment and the stains of his own blood.

"I'll stay a few minutes," she said. "After that I must go help Dorcas with the children. But if you behave yourself, I'll come see you again tomorrow with breakfast. Maybe I'll bring Jenny."

"That would be nice. I should be in the saddle again in a couple of days."

"Surely your injuries won't permit that."

"We'll see."

"Yes, we shall."

She smiled, and Mike felt a pang in his heart that wasn't caused by his wound. Why did she have to take this teaching job? He didn't want to think about leaving her in Oregon and riding back over the mountains to the fort.

"Lydia, do you have to take this position?"

She blinked at him. "That's why they asked me to sign a contract, Michael. To be sure I'd honor the commitment."

He looked up at the canvas above him. The sun had beat on it all morning, and the air inside the wagon was nearly stifling. "But couldn't you explain to them. . ."

Lydia rearranged the folds of her skirt unnecessarily and smoothed down a wrinkle. He could tell by the set of her mouth that she wouldn't seriously consider backing out on the arrangement. "They've lost a lot of prospective teachers to marriage out here. The school board thought it best to have me sign a very rigid agreement before they advanced me the money for my train ticket to Independence and my expenses for the trip."

Mike sighed. Money had changed hands, and it was clear Lydia saw this as a matter of honor. "You've prayed about all this, I suppose."

"For many months now. Michael, I must keep my word."

"I can see that. I'm sorry I urged you not to. I didn't realize how binding it was." Mike lay back on the blankets.

"Your bandages should be changed," she said.

He looked down. She was right; blood was oozing through the bandage on his shoulder. He smiled at her. "I hope you won't find it necessary to sacrifice any more of your wardrobe for me."

She darted a cool glance at him, but her reply was indulgent. "The doctor will take care of it, I'm sure."

Pain from the wound still stabbed him with each breath, and his ankle throbbed, but he was able to ignore the discomfort while he considered his future with Lydia, or the impossibility of one. Dr. Nichols had said that morning that he expected the injuries to heal well, so they were the least of Mike's worries.

"He said he'd come by and tend to it after he sees Mrs. Sawyer and Nathan," Mike admitted.

"Did he give you anything for the pain?"

"He offered me laudanum, but I turned him down. I don't want to be rendered senseless for a flesh wound."

She picked up the basket. "Really, Michael, there's nothing more to say about my employment. I'm going to teach this fall. I feel God would have me do this."

"Wait!" He struggled to sit up as she stood. "Lydia, you know I care about you. If it weren't for that contract, I'd be on my knees begging you to marry me."

She pressed her lips firmly together, and her eyes glistened with unshed tears. "Thank you. I shall always remember that. Good day, sir."

"A few moments ago you were calling me Michael."

She avoided his piercing stare once more. "I came here as a friend. We went through a lot together in the last couple of days. But this must be the extent of it. You understand."

He sank back. "I'm sorry. And I'm sorry for all the times I made you angry. Forgive me, Lydia."

She smiled at his contrition. "Of course. That's part of life, Corporal, when two strong-willed people cross paths. But that's what this has been. We met, we travel along together for a few months, and then we part."

~

That night, Lydia lay awake for hours. The knowledge that Mike loved her and would gladly have married her was sweet and painful. But no matter how she turned the issue around in her mind, she knew that she couldn't give up the teaching job and ride back to Fort Laramie with the escort.

She sighed and rolled over. Would the image of handsome, laughing Mike Brown haunt her dreams for the rest of her life? Would this be the one huge regret she fostered? Or would God bring some other man into her life later on when she was free of her obligation to the school board? Lydia rejected that idea immediately. She would never love this deeply again. Surely she couldn't feel the same way when another man kissed her as she had when Mike did. She never should have allowed him to touch her in the rocky cavern, as glorious as that one kiss had been. The memory would spoil any other man's chances of winning her affections.

It was confusing, and she rolled over again, hoping to find a comfortable spot on the ground and drift off to sleep, but slumber eluded her.

She stared up at the brilliant stars. *Lord, I'm sorry. I was foolish to let myself care for Michael. Please forgive me, and help me not to let this affect my ability as a teacher. I truly want to do a good job, to please the parents, and to help the children love learning.*

She took a deep, shuddering breath. *Help me to be true to my promise, Lord. I know it's the right thing, and I must honor my word.*

She sighed and followed the two pointer stars of the Big Dipper up the black velvet sky to the gleaming North Star. It was easy. As usual, Mike was right.

Chapter 18

M ike waited restlessly for Lydia the next morning. He was afraid she wouldn't come, and it nearly drove him to action, but when he tried to stand, he realized he was very weak from loss of blood and sank back, breathing deeply and berating himself.

He could smell food cooking outside, but still she didn't come. Cattle were hustled to their places to be yoked, and mules were harnessed. His stomach rumbled. He was very hungry, but no one brought him anything to eat.

He was thoroughly exasperated by the time the sergeant poked his head in. "How you doing, Mike?"

"I'm starving to death. Thought you forgot about me."

"No, Miss Jackson said she'd bring you something before we head out. She hasn't been here?"

"No, she has not."

"We're nearly ready to move. Need some help this morning?"

"I want to shave."

Reese frowned. "No time, Mike. Maybe Miss Jackson will help you when we stop for nooning."

"I don't want Miss Jackson to help me. I can shave myself. Just fetch me my razor and some soap."

"We're going to start moving. You'd cut your throat. But I'll send Gleason in to help you dress."

The wagon gave a lurch and started rolling ten minutes later, after Gleason had left him reasonably comfortable but still feeling scruffy. Mike was sure Lydia had forgotten him and he would go hungry until noon.

But before they had fallen into the rhythm of movement, she scrambled up over the wagon seat, juggling a coffeepot and a basket.

"I'm sorry. Jenny was fussy this morning, and Mrs. Paine is afraid she has a fever. I had to cook breakfast and pack up everything."

"It's all right." Mike felt hypocritical as he spoke. "You don't have to do this. One of the troopers could have brought me breakfast."

"Well, I said I would do it, and I always try to keep my word. I just didn't realize how hectic things would be at the Paine camp this morning."

She was removing items from the basket, and Mike sat up eagerly as she lifted the inverted tin plate that covered his breakfast. The smell of the golden griddle cakes and bacon was enough to drive a man wild.

"You're feeling better."

"I am. I feel as if I could do some scouting after a good breakfast."

Lydia frowned as she rummaged for a fork. "You take it easy. I'm afraid your food's cooled off. I left the coffee on the hot rocks 'til the last second. It should be piping hot." She poured a tin cup half full and offered it cautiously as the wagon rolled forward.

Mike held it carefully, hoping the mules pulling the wagon wouldn't lurch into a rut while he asked a blessing for his meal. After a few seconds of heartfelt prayer, he opened his eyes to find Lydia watching him unabashed.

"Lydia, I've given your situation a lot of thought, and I can see that you're right. Please forgive me for suggesting that you break your contract. That was wrong."

She shrugged. "Everyone gets a little excitable when discussing a sensitive topic. That's partly why I wanted to see you today. To be sure you know I'm settled in my mind. I think God would have me fulfill my promise."

"Yes, I see that now." He began to eat, and the food was a comfort to his empty stomach, but his spirits had reached a new low. Lydia would not change her mind, which was as it should be, but it did not ease his grief. He drained the tin cup and set it down. "I appreciate you bringing me this delicious breakfast, but don't feel obligated to keep coddling me. If you'd rather not come again. . ."

She shook her head with impatience. "This is not penance, Michael. You're a friend to me and the Paines. And after all, you did save my life."

"You would have survived."

"Perhaps, but the prospect of survival with the Sioux is not one I want to contemplate."

He knew the terror of her capture would be with her a long time and decided that with a spirited girl like Lydia it might be best to make light of it. "They would have treated you like a princess once they were safe in their village. It wouldn't have been long before one of those Lakota braves dropped a deer carcass in front of your teepee."

Her eyes widened. "I assume you're saying one of them would court me."

"That's what they do. It sort of proves he could support you, feed your family."

She shuddered. "I don't think Skunk was worried about courtship rituals."

He pressed his lips together. Wrong tactic. "This was a fine breakfast, Lydia. Thank you."

"Was it enough? I had to douse the fire and—"

"It's plenty." They sat looking at each other in the shade of the wagon cover. A little frown wrinkled Lydia's forehead.

"I'm sorry," he said at last.

"For what?"

"I can't help loving you, but I shouldn't have pressed you on that score. You've made a pledge."

"Yes," she whispered. "It's one thing my father taught me very young. You don't go back on your word." She began packing the dishes in the basket. "Would you like more coffee? There's a little left."

"Thank you."

As she poured it, he regretted not saying no and just letting her go. She was unsettled again. It seemed to happen every time they were together, and he didn't know how to change that.

"You were wonderful through the whole ordeal, you know," he said at last.

"No. I was terrified. If you and Mr. Paine hadn't come. . ." She straightened suddenly and faced him. "Look, Michael, I know we became very close out there in the wilderness. I'm not sorry about that. You were the one man I was longing to see, and since I had to go through all that, I'm glad it was with you. But that doesn't mean. . ."

She stopped, and he thought she was blushing as she reached for the coffeepot and thrust it into the basket.

"I shouldn't have kissed you."

She sat very still. "Perhaps not." Her voice was very small.

He waited, but she didn't acknowledge that she had kissed him back and had made no complaints at the time. The tenderness and desire that filled his heart was overwhelming, and he reached for her hand.

"Lydia, dearest Lydia, I'm not sorry that I love you or that I kissed you, only that it's bothering you now. I never expected this to happen, to fall in love again. And I had no idea you were obligated to a life that can't include me. If it weren't for the promise you made many months ago—"

"But I did!" She jumped up and seized the basket, backing away from him. "I can't break my promise, Michael. I've gone round and round with the Lord about this, and I truly feel He would have me keep my pledge."

Mike sighed. "Of course. You're right, and I won't speak to you of this again."

She stared at him for a long moment then nodded. "Very well. I think that's best. You should rest now."

"Psalm 15, darlin'."

"I beg your pardon?"

Mike reached for his battered Psalter and winced. "Do you have a Bible?"

"Yes."

"Psalm 15. I was looking at it this morning, and it helped me to understand that what you're doing is right. It may help you, too."

⤸

Lydia hurried back to the Paines' wagon, her blue skirt swirling about her ankles. She had worn it this morning to help her decide whether or not to alter it. All of the Sawyer girls, and even Frances, were dividing their long skirts into billowy trousers. Frances wore hers under another skirt. As much as the fashion had shocked her at first, Lydia knew that if she wanted to spend much time riding the Lakota pony, she would have to adopt the frontier mode.

The blue dress was her favorite, and she had been saving it in the bottom of her carpetbag so that she would have one fresh outfit when she reached her destination. She had loaned it to Minnie Carver for a night of dancing but had not worn it herself on the trip until yesterday.

Now, with Oregon City still two months away, that seemed shortsighted. The prospect of riding the sturdy pinto was enticing, and she knew as she climbed up on the wagon seat beside Dorcas, pausing to lift her cumbersome skirt, that she would be wearing bloomers before the week was out. She winced at the pain in her bruised hip. It had plagued her since she fell from the Indian's pony, but it wasn't bad enough to worry about.

"How's Jenny?" she asked.

Dorcas sighed. "Sleeping at last. I laid her down beside Nathan."

Lydia bent to peer into the wagon. Nathan was watching her from his hammock, and she smiled and waved at him.

"Hey! Would you like me to read to you later?"

Nathan nodded. His face was pale, and Lydia was sure he was holding back tears.

"He'd like that," Dorcas said. "This jostling is hard on him."

Lydia turned to assess her friend and saw that the lines around Dorcas's eyes and mouth had deepened since Nathan's adventure. "You're exhausted. You should lie down, too. Mr. Paine will keep the oxen going."

"There's no more room in there," Dorcas said, raising one hand in futility. "I'll be all right."

"Well, if Jenny wakes up fussy, I'll be the one to tend her."

They rode in silence for a few minutes.

"How's Corporal Brown doing?" Dorcas asked.

Lydia bit her lip, considering on what level she would answer that question. "He seems to be doing better. He's dressed, and he sat up to eat. I think he still has a lot of pain, though."

"Mm-hmm."

Lydia eyed her uneasily. Dorcas definitely had something on her mind.

"I'm going to split this skirt," she said, hoping to draw her hostess off into a discussion of fashion. Anything was preferable to discussing her feelings for Mike Brown.

"It's so pretty."

"Thank you, but I've got to do something."

"So you can ride the horse modestly?" Dorcas nodded in approval. "Perhaps you can salvage the maroon one."

"I don't know. The stains will never come out."

"But you might be able to hide them in the folds."

Lydia frowned. "You may be right. Maybe I should practice on that and keep this one for best. Still, I don't know how modest it will be. It's a bit scandalous to think I can ride astride. Back in Hartford, that would be socially reprehensible."

"Really, dear."

"Oh, yes. Ladies might ride sidesaddle for exercise occasionally but never astride. But out here, it seems to be accepted, and—"

"Why did you not tell me your teaching position would prevent you from accepting the marriage proposal of one of the finest men on earth?"

The sudden question threw Lydia off guard, and she checked for an instant, then went on. "No one seems to care if a woman wears bloomers or— Oh, Dorcas, what have I done?"

Her tears came so quickly, it shocked her, and she sobbed, burying her face in her hands. Dorcas's gentle fingers smoothed her hair, and Lydia was drawn into her kind embrace.

"How did you know?" Lydia sobbed.

"Mr. Paine visited the corporal last evening. He thought Brown might have trouble sleeping, and he was right, but it seems it wasn't because of his injuries. He's pining for you, my dear, because you've gone and pledged yourself to a career as a schoolmarm." Dorcas pushed a frayed but dainty handkerchief into her hand, and Lydia mopped her cheeks.

"Oh, Dorcas, please, you mustn't tell anyone I turned Mike down. It's almost a relief that you and Mr. Paine know, but I'd be mortified if the whole wagon train was talking about it."

Dorcas turned to look ahead over the broad backs of the oxen, and Lydia was filled with remorse.

"I'm sorry now I didn't tell you. You and Mr. Paine have been so good to me! And if Mr. Paine and Corporal Brown hadn't come after us right away, Nathan and I might be sitting at a Sioux campfire right now."

"That's neither here nor there," Dorcas said, but her face softened and she sat a little straighter. "Lydia, I've come to love you like a sister."

Lydia nodded. "That's true, and I should have known I could trust you. And Dorcas—"

"What, child?"

"I've never had a sister. It's nice that you feel that way. If I did have a real sister, I'd want her to be just like you."

She saw a tear glitter on Dorcas's lashes. Lydia reached toward her and hugged her tight for a moment.

"Thank you, dear. That's very sweet," Dorcas said softly. "If we're sisters, then perhaps you'd like to know a family secret."

Lydia leaned back and looked at her.

"An auntish sort of secret," Dorcas said.

Lydia gasped. "Do you mean there will be a new baby in the Paine family soon?"

"Not very soon, but next winter if all goes well."

Lydia squeezed her fiercely. "And I won't get to see him!"

"It will be very hard for me to leave you when we get to Oregon. I expect everyone will know by then. I won't be able to hide it."

"Dear Dorcas, you mustn't fret. God will take care of me. And God and Mr. Paine will take care of you! He won't let you do any heavy work. And all the troopers adore you. They'll stand in line to fetch your water. Have you told Mr. Paine?"

"Oh, yes. He's very good about these things." Dorcas flushed a becoming pink. "We've lost two wee ones, you know, between Nathan and Jenny."

Lydia shook her head. "I had no idea. How ever did you stand it?"

"God knows what's best."

Lydia felt naive. She'd been so involved with her own concerns that she hadn't given much thought to uncomplaining Dorcas's situation. "But this trip is so strenuous! The sergeant says we'll have some very difficult slopes to maneuver in the Blue Mountains next month. Will you be all right?"

"I think so. I hope so." Dorcas smiled at her. "I feel well this time. Perhaps the exercise and fresh air have strengthened me. Now you must get your bonnet before the sun gets any stronger. And you mustn't be angry with Corporal Brown for divulging your secret. Mr. Paine said the corporal told him about your rejection of him in confidence."

"I'm not angry with him. Did Mr. Paine say anything else?" Lydia asked carefully, examining the edging on the crumpled handkerchief.

Dorcas squeezed her arm. "Only that his friend is feeling quite dejected just now."

"I told Michael yesterday I would take Jenny around to see him, but if she's ill, we'd better keep her away."

"Yes. You'll have to go alone, I'm afraid."

"No. No, I shan't visit him anymore. There's no point in spending time with him when nothing can come of it."

Dorcas inhaled deeply. "Just so. I expect he'll be up and around soon, anyway."

Chapter 19

Jenny was still fretful that evening, and Lydia and Dorcas took turns holding her, but the little girl seemed to have lost her fever. Nathan begged Lydia for story after story. Lydia attempted to keep him occupied and also do the chores he would have done if he were healthy. At last, when the dishes were done, the fuel and water in place for morning, and both children asleep, she was able to bring out her Bible and sit down with it beside the wagon wheel. It was still too hot to sit near the fire, and they had let it die out after supper.

She leafed to the Psalms, her heart pounding as she recalled Mike's words. What message was he giving her?

The Psalm consisted of only five verses, and in the fading light she read with increasing curiosity the passage that described a righteous man. What did Mike mean? It was the end of verse 4 that stopped her, and warm recognition flooded her. "He honoureth them that fear the Lord. He that sweareth to his own hurt, and changeth not."

She leaned back against the wagon wheel for a long time, letting the twilight settle around her. At first the sky was dark. Then all at once, she could see a handful of stars. The Big Dipper leaped out, and she wondered why she'd never been able to find it before, it was so prominent in the sky to the north.

Lord, is that what I've done, sworn to my own hurt?

It hadn't seemed so. Back in Connecticut, she'd been certain the job offer was God's answer to her many prayers for guidance. The Lord would honor her for keeping the promise. That was Mike's message to her. It wrenched her heart to realize he was suffering as he watched her try to do right.

The Paines came from the river path, and Dorcas picked up the cooling coffeepot.

"Let me do that," Lydia said, rising quickly.

Dorcas glanced toward her Bible. "You're in the middle of a conversation, I'd say."

"I think we've finished for now. I'll fill the coffeepot for breakfast and put these things away. You go ahead and retire, Dorcas. It's been a long day for you, and Jenny's quiet now. Take advantage of that."

"Howdy, folks." They all turned toward the voice. Trooper Gleason sauntered toward them. His gaze settled on Lydia. "Evening, Miss Jackson."

"Hello," Lydia said, and the Paines greeted him.

"I'm on an errand of mercy for Corporal Brown." Gleason smiled amiably. "He's getting a bit fidgety. Nichols just told him he can't get out of bed for at least two more days, and he's fretful, so I'm making the rounds to see if anyone's got some reading material to occupy him tomorrow."

"Haven't got any books," Dorcas said. "Just the Bible."

"Mike's a big reader, is he?" Paine asked.

"Oh, yes, sir. Whenever we get a new book at the fort, he's always eager to get his hands on it."

"I'm sorry we can't help you," Dorcas said. "Books are too heavy to cart up and down these mountains."

"Yes, ma'am, I agree with you there," Gleason said.

"I have a few small volumes," Lydia said.

The trooper's grin was triumphant. "There, now. I told Mike you'd have something for him."

"Of course!" said Dorcas. "Miss Jackson plans to be a schoolteacher, you know."

"Don't surprise me none," Gleason said with a smile. "You speak so proper and all."

Lydia went to the back of the wagon, opened her little trunk, and chose two slim books. Gleason peered at them in the twilight. "Well, I'm sure he'll be grateful, miss. I'll bring them back when he's done."

"I'll do up these few chores," Lydia said to Dorcas.

"Thank you," Dorcas replied. "Good night, Private Gleason."

Mr. Paine nodded at the trooper and ambled off to check his livestock.

"Mind if I set a spell?" Gleason asked.

Lydia tried to think of an excuse to turn him away. "I—"

"You seem to be fully recovered from your misadventure." Gleason grinned as he settled down on the crate Mr. Paine used as his stool for meals.

Lydia considered that. "I suppose I'm none the worse physically. I wish I could take some of the pain for Nathan."

"How's the boy doing?"

"He's miserable. Cries a lot."

"That's sure a shame."

"Yes. He's a brave little boy, but unrelieved torment wears on the best of us."

Gleason nodded. "That's for sure. Mike Brown's grouchy as a grizzly bear."

"He seemed to be doing better this morning."

"Oh, he is. That's half the problem. He wants to get on a horse, and the sergeant won't let him."

"He'll heal quickly." She stowed the last of the supper things in a wooden box and started to pick it up.

Gleason jumped up. "Allow me."

"Thank you. I was just going to set it under the corner of the wagon there."

He deposited the crate where she indicated, then turned to her expectantly. "I'd be honored if you'd stroll with me, Miss Jackson."

"Oh, no, thank you. I'm very tired." She untied her apron and began to fold it.

His disappointment was evident. "Of course. I just wanted a chance to tell you how much we fellows admire you and the way you got out of that scrape with the Sioux."

Lydia tried not to let her confusion show. The last thing she wanted was to be admired for killing a man. "I do hope the troopers aren't making large of the incident. After all, I was foolish enough to get into the predicament in the first place."

He grinned. "Most of us think you'd be just the woman that a man would want to have beside him. Of course, there's a few who pretend they'd be afraid to be alone with you."

"Oh, really?"

"They're just joshing. They don't mean anything by it."

"I wish the men wouldn't talk about me."

His pale eyebrows arched. "Why, that's impossible, Miss Jackson. Your narrow escape is a wonder, and until something more sensational happens, folks are bound to talk about it."

"I suppose so. We're like a small village here."

"Exactly. Sergeant Reese says you're a heroine, and the corporal would have been done for if you hadn't of skewered that Injun."

"Excuse me, please." Lydia turned away, feeling a little queasy. The macabre image of Skunk's body was still vivid in her mind—his sightless eyes staring at nothing in the first rays of dawn, a smear of blood darkening his cheek. She turned toward the wagon.

"Evening, miss," another male voice called, and Lydia turned back to greet the newcomer.

It was Dr. Nichols, carrying a small bag. "Thought I'd check on the boy."

"He's resting," Lydia said.

"Good. The willow bark tea's doing some good, then."

"It soothes him for a while."

Dr. Nichols nodded. "Well, tell his mother I said to give him a little of that laudanum if he needs it in the night. Not too much. I told her the dose."

"Thank you. I will."

Dr. Nichols smiled. "I'll come back in the morning, then. But Mr. Paine can fetch me in the night if he needs to. Don't want the boy thrashing about."

Dr. Nichols left, and Gleason smiled sadly at her.

"Good night, then."

"Good night."

Gleason followed the doctor, carrying the books. Lydia took a deep breath and let it out in a sigh before she took her blanket roll down from the wagon. Nathan's uneven breathing told her that the boy slept fitfully. She hoped the medicine would give him enough relief that he wouldn't wake the family and all their neighbors with his crying, the way he had for the last two nights.

Her troubled thoughts plagued her as she prepared for bed. Maybe it would be better if she let it be known in the camp that she was not open to receiving suitors. Maybe then the troopers would stop talking about her and Gleason would give up trying to woo her.

She shuddered at the thought of keeping company with John Gleason. He was a nice enough fellow, but his indelicacy repelled her. She supposed he wasn't bad-looking, but beside Corporal Brown, he was clumsy and insipid. And even though Brown had been reared in a remote Appalachian valley, his education was broader than that of most of the men. Apparently he was an insatiable reader and had educated himself. That was important to her in a man. One who couldn't think deeply held no attraction for her. And Mike had a way of taking things he had read and fitting them into the world he lived in.

She caught herself up sharply. How had she gone from her dislike of Gleason to admiration for Brown? She wouldn't allow her thoughts to take that direction. No more pining over a man she couldn't have. She would think instead about her students and the lessons she would prepare for them.

She shook out her bedroll with the bleak realization that she could have faced spinsterhood more cheerfully if she had not tasted love.

⌒

Lydia saw Mike again three days later from a distance. He was riding a calm, rather swaybacked mule. The toes of his left boot barely touched the stirrup, but he was in the saddle and apparently attempting to resume his duties.

He didn't come around the Paines' wagon, but a few days later, when they were well on their way northward toward the Snake River, Mr. Paine brought back her Tennyson and slipped it into her hands without comment.

Lydia carried it with her that day as she walked, leafing through it, wondering which of the poems had caught Mike's interest. She had marked "Maud" with a pencil when she first read it because the lyrical cadence had thrilled her. She flushed as she wondered if Mike had noticed the slash beside the title and drawn any inferences from that.

There was a small stain on the page with "Charge of the Light Brigade," and she wondered if Mike had spilled his coffee on it as the wagon lurched.

"While horse and hero fell, they that had fought so well came through the jaws of Death..." Yes, Mike would relate to that poem. She wondered what he would make of her Oliver Wendell Holmes.

Frances came to walk with her. They took Jenny and Frances's younger sister,

Rachel, with them. It wasn't long before Margaret and Eliza Sawyer joined them.

"Charlie's talking of leaving us," Margaret announced.

"Why?" asked Frances.

"Because of Ellen. She won't give him the time of day anymore. Charlie's furious. He says he's going back to Fort Bridger and see if the Pony Express will take him. If not, he might head up north and join the argonauts."

"Gold hunting?" Frances gasped.

Margaret shrugged. "He just wants to get away. That and he wants adventure, I guess."

"Isn't this journey adventure enough?" Lydia asked.

"Well, maybe if he'd gotten to chase the Sioux that captured you he'd be content." Margaret's exasperated tone surprised Lydia. "There's a whole lot of young fellows who wish they were in Corporal Brown's boots, I'll tell you."

"That's crazy," Lydia said. "The man was almost killed, and he's suffering terribly now."

"Tim and Charlie don't see it that way," Frances told her. "Brown lay low for a few days, but he's on scout duty again and looking none the worse for wear."

"He hasn't fully recovered," Lydia insisted.

"Makes no difference to them. It wouldn't surprise me if every young man on this train joined the cavalry because of Corporal Brown and his derring-do."

"Well, that might be better than having them go off up the Snake for gold," Lydia said.

Margaret shook her head. "All the troopers got to gallop off to rescue you, and the boys had to stay here and guard us and the livestock for nothing."

Lydia winced. "So all the men in the wagon train are discontented, and it's my fault."

"I'm sorry." Frances grabbed her hand. "We're making too much of this."

"I don't know," Margaret said sharply. "You've got a perfectly gorgeous man eating out of your hand, and you ignore him."

Lydia stopped walking. "What on earth—"

"Lydia, everyone's talking about how shabbily you've treated the corporal."

"That can't be true."

Margaret raised her eyebrows. "Whether it's true or not, I don't know, but they're saying it."

"You know I didn't mean it that way."

Frances sighed. "Yes, Margaret. You're not being kind."

"But why would folks think there was anything between the corporal and me?" Lydia was fairly certain Dorcas had kept her promise and not discussed her secret with anyone else, but she might have let something slip.

"He used to hang about the Paines' wagon," Margaret said.

"He and Mr. Paine are friends. And anyway, he hasn't come around at all

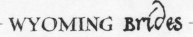

since—since before the incident in question."

Margaret sniffed. "Minnie Carver saw you walking with him before that. She said he was holding your hand."

"That was courtesy," Lydia said weakly.

"Margaret, do be quiet," Frances begged. She turned to Lydia. "It's just. . . well, everyone knows Brown saved your life, and it seems you hardly speak to him. People assume something happened between you."

"Yes," said Margaret. "Did something happen out there? Was he shockingly forward?"

"No, he was very polite."

"Well then, what kind of woman are you?"

It hurt to inhale. Lydia swallowed hard. "Should I throw myself at a man because he helped me? I assure you, I've conveyed my sincere thanks to Corporal Brown."

Frances looked very uncomfortable. "Forgive us. I know you wouldn't snub anyone who made a sacrifice like that for you. Some folks assume Brown is enamored of you, and apparently it's not so."

Margaret's face was more skeptical.

Lydia wanted badly to tell Frances the truth, but with Margaret standing there, she knew she couldn't. Every scrap of conversation Margaret heard would be front-page news throughout the train by suppertime. She would have to keep Dorcas as her only true confidante.

Lydia looked at Margaret. "Next time someone tells you what an inhumane monster I am, please squelch the rumors by telling the truth. Corporal Brown is a true gentleman. We shared a harrowing experience, but that is all. When this train reaches Oregon City, I expect the corporal and I will never see one another again."

Chapter 20

Lydia hoped she would have a chance to speak to Mike, but all week he left camp at dawn and returned at suppertime, never coming near the Paines' wagon.

As the sun lowered in the west on Saturday, she went to gather up the laundry she had spread earlier to dry on the grass. She was startled when Mike rode up to her on the bay mare.

"May I help you?" he asked.

She straightened, unsure what her response should be and conscious of a riotous gladness.

"You must be feeling better."

"Ninety percent, I'd say." He grimaced as he dismounted but faced her with a grin. "Are you in the talking vein, as 'The Autocrat of the Breakfast Table' would say?"

"Oh, you've been reading Holmes." She smiled and folded one of Dorcas's dish towels.

"Never laughed so hard in my life. I'll have it back to you soon, but I'm enjoying it immensely."

Lydia looked toward the wagons, wondering how many people were watching them. "You're putting your reputation at risk by talking to me."

"I'll take the chance."

Lydia sobered. "You really shouldn't."

"Has it been so bad as all that for you? Josiah told me you were upset over the gossip."

"Aren't you?"

"No, I just laugh it off. I told the fellows in my detachment that you're not nearly as haughty as some are making you out to be, that you're actually a pleasant companion and a good scout to have along when things are tough. So if they inundate you with invitations to dance tonight, I suppose it's my fault."

"But Margaret thinks—"

Mike laughed. "Margaret tried to dress me down a few days ago for flirting with you when we were off alone together. I put on a woebegone face and told her quite sadly that I had no idea what she was talking about and that I never learned to flirt. It just isn't done in Tennessee. I think she half believed me."

"That won't last. She'll be after you, trying to get you to flirt outrageously so

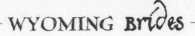

she can prove you lied."

"Ha! That won't go over. I'm leaving soon."

"Scouting?"

"Yes, Barkley and I are going ahead, all the way to Fort Dalles. We'll be gone a couple of weeks, I expect. We heard there was a lot of rain in the Blue Mountains, and Reese wants a full report on the trail between here and the Columbia."

Lydia caught her breath. "Should you be riding so much? It's too soon."

"I thought you were a great proponent of physical exercise."

"Not while you're convalescing."

"I'll be fine."

She thought he looked too thin and his eyes had lost their glint, but she didn't say so. "When are you leaving?"

"First light."

A bleak loneliness settled over her. She would miss him, but she couldn't say that.

Mike smiled. "Don't fret about us. We'll be back in time to help you over the mountains. We'll need every man for that."

"Keep safe, Mike."

He nodded and looked into her eyes for one sober moment. "You, too. And stick to your guns. This is what God wants you to do."

"I will." She felt her face flushing.

Mike handed her the last of the laundry and put his hand to the brim of his hat. "All right, then. I hope I haven't caused you any trouble by speaking to you. I'll see you in two or three weeks."

⁓

The wagons were already climbing the lower slopes of the Blue Mountains when Brown and Barkley returned from their mission. They were out of hostile Indian territory, so there was less tension in the camp.

The trail was rougher than Lydia had anticipated. She'd assumed they had passed the worst of it, but the mountains that stood between them and their goal were fierce guardians. Sergeant Reese assured the travelers that the trail was much improved since the days of the first wagon trains. Even so, as they wound their way up from the plain, the wagons were tested, and several had to stop for repairs. One crashed down a steep incline and had to be abandoned. The owners salvaged their clothing, tools, and what supplies weren't scattered, and used their two surviving mules as pack animals.

Private Wilson and Sergeant Reese helped the Paines get their wagon down safely, and Lydia occasionally glimpsed Mike going from one family to another to aid them. She noticed that Mike limped when on foot. He was working too hard too soon, she had no doubt. She tried not to worry about his health. Instead, she focused on the future, asking God to prepare her for what lay ahead.

Private Barkley came by the Paines' campsite one evening. They were perched on the side of a steep slope. Reese and Miller had hoped to reach the valley floor that day but decided camping on a slant was preferable to navigating at dusk.

"Did you see any Indians on your scouting trip?" Mr. Paine asked Barkley.

Lydia listened while she stirred up bread dough to set for the night. If she rose early, she could bake it before they broke camp.

"Just a few, and that was back near the Snake River. We ran into a band of Nez Perce. They have the most gorgeous horses! Some are spotted all over, and some just on the hindquarters. They're sweet-natured, and they run like the wind!"

"Better than those scrub mustangs the Sioux were using?" Paine asked.

"Sir, you wouldn't believe it! Those horses could sweep any racetrack in the East. And they're pleasing to the eye."

"They certainly made an impression on you." Mr. Paine lifted the coffeepot. "Cup of coffee, Barkley?"

"Thanks! Mike and I are planning to go back there next summer."

"Up the Snake River?"

"That's right. My brother's starting a horse ranch down near Fort Bridger, and he's always looking for good stock. I don't think he'll find any better than those Palouse horses. Mike thought we could convince T.R. to go up there with us after spring planting."

Lydia spread a linen towel over her bread pan and placed it on a warm rock at the edge of the fire pit. So Mike was done grieving over their love. She could almost picture him laughing about it with Barkley as they rode the trail together. "Oh, well, she gave me the mitten. Can't do anything about it." Now he was making plans for the future that didn't include her.

She went to where Dorcas was holding Jenny. "Let me get her ready for bed. She's half asleep already."

Dorcas passed the baby to her and scanned Lydia's face. "Is anything wrong?"

Lydia smiled. "No. Just feeling sorry for myself. The trip is nearly over, and I shall miss you all."

"Perhaps you'll be close enough to visit us now and then."

"Perhaps."

Dorcas patted her arm. "You're young, dear. You'll have a family of your own one day."

Lydia drew a deep breath. "Am I that transparent?"

"You'll make a fine teacher. And someday, I've no doubt you'll make a fine wife and mother."

"Thank you. That is my prayer."

With a nod, Dorcas said, "Mr. Paine and I shall continue to pray to that end."

Mike was relieved when all the wagons were down the western side of the mountains. There was a good enough trail by land to Oregon City now. No more rafting down the Columbia, the way folks had done in the old days. A few families had already left the train to set off on their own, but most were heading for the land office in Oregon City to claim a piece of property.

The escort would sell its mule teams and wagons there and buy supplies for their return trip. They would ride back quickly, getting over the mountains again before the snows set in. Mike couldn't say he looked forward to it. Ordinarily he would have been glad to see the detail ended and head back to the fort and the familiar routine. But that would mean leaving Lydia behind forever.

He tossed the dregs of his coffee onto the ground. Time to check the animals before turning in.

Josiah Paine met him near the picket line, and Mike smiled. He would regret leaving the Paines, too. He'd kept away from their camp for more than a month now to avoid causing Lydia further embarrassment, but he and Josiah often spent an evening together.

"How you holding up, Mike?" Josiah asked.

"A mite stiff but otherwise all right."

As they made the rounds of the animals, Mike checked the cavalry's mules and horses.

"Not long until we part ways," Paine said.

The big mule, Buster, stretched his neck to nuzzle Mike's shirt, and Mike scratched his forehead. "How's Lydia?"

"She's quiet. Spends a lot of time reading to Nathan."

"The boy ought to be up and about soon."

"Doc Nichols says give it another week. Don't want to take a chance on him breaking the bone again now."

"It still pains him?"

"Not so much. He says it itches a lot. Dorcas rubs it with grease every evening."

Mike sighed and looked up at the sky. "I'll miss your family. Makes me want to go civilian again. Start a family all over." He shook his head. "But we both know that's not about to happen."

"You're staying with the army, then?"

Mike shrugged. "I don't know. I got to thinking about mustering out in December, but. . .I just don't know. My first family is gone. I didn't envision starting a new one. Does God give a man a second chance on something like that?"

"Sometimes."

"If I'd met Lydia under different circumstances. . ."

Josiah reached out to pat one of the horses. "You sound like it's now or never, Mike."

"She won't have me."

"That's today. It doesn't necessarily mean forever."

Mike stared at him. He had taken Lydia's declaration as final, and somehow he was unable to let the ashes of hope rekindle.

"She sets a lot of store by you," Josiah said.

They walked on, past the end of the picket line and onto the prairie. Mike had no fear of hostile Indians in this area. It felt good to be out away from the sounds and smells of the camp.

"If only she hadn't signed that paper," Mike murmured.

"I don't see it quite that way."

"No?"

Josiah shook his head. "The way she tells it, she was penniless. She prayed for a solution to her plight, and God gave her this. Mike, if she hadn't gotten the job offer, you never would have met her."

"No, I s'pose not."

"You and Lydia, when you're not scrapping, make quite a team."

"Always pulling in opposite directions." Mike's ankle began to ache, and he favored it slightly. He turned in a wide arc, heading back toward the wagons.

"Be thankful the Lord put her here on this train and you had the chance to see the stuff she's made of."

"You mean. . .when the Sioux took her?"

"Yes. Could you ask for a woman to acquit herself better?"

"No. I love her pluck, even her stubbornness. She never gives up."

"There you go. Be glad she wants to stick to her promise."

"That's an admirable trait, isn't it?" Mike looked at Josiah in the moonlight.

"Well, sure. If she'd made a promise to you, you'd want her to keep it."

"Naturally."

"I've said it before: Bide your time, Mike."

"I expect that's good advice."

⤳

They approached Oregon City three weeks later. Lydia was restless, alternately eager and depressed. They camped three miles from town one clear night in early September, and everyone bustled about, preparing for the big day.

When they sat down for their last supper together beside the wagon, Mr. Paine offered the blessing, then said to Lydia, "We'll take you to meet the school board chairman tomorrow afternoon, once I've filed the paperwork at the land office."

"Oh, you needn't do that," Lydia said as she dished out the stew.

"Nonsense." Dorcas added a biscuit to each tin plate and handed the children their portions. "We wouldn't think of doing otherwise."

Lydia felt tears rising, and she brushed them away with the hem of her apron. "You've been most kind to me. I shall always think of you as my family."

"That suits us just fine," said Dorcas.

Her husband smiled. "So long as we don't cause you any 'Paine.'"

Lydia laughed. "On the contrary, you've chased away many of my aches on this journey."

"Well, Mr. Paine and I have agreed, and we hope you will, too, that if at all possible, you'll come and spend Christmas with us." Dorcas sat down and pulled Jenny onto her lap, balancing the child's plate just within her reach.

"We'll read stories and play games," Nathan said.

"And eat Christmas pudding," added Mr. Paine.

"Now I am going to cry." Lydia favored them all with a watery smile.

Mr. Paine looked beyond her then smiled and started to rise. "Mike! Just in time for supper."

Mike stepped into the family circle. "Thanks, but I had a bite at the escort's fire. I just came to say how much I appreciate you, sir." He and Mr. Paine shook hands, and Mike turned to Dorcas. "You, too, ma'am. It's been a pleasure to know you all."

Dorcas passed Jenny to her husband and stood up. "We shall miss you sorely. Come here." She stood on tiptoe and kissed his cheek.

"Thank you." Mike hesitated and darted a glance at Lydia.

"Have a safe trip back," she said softly.

Mike bit his lip. "I was hoping I could speak with you privately, but I see you haven't eaten yet. . . ."

"It will keep," Dorcas assured him. "Won't it, Lydia?"

It was suddenly hard to breathe. Lydia swallowed. "I guess it will."

"I won't keep her long. I promise," Mike said, smiling at Mr. and Mrs. Paine. "And I'll behave with perfect propriety."

"Of course you will," said Dorcas.

"Go on, git," said Mr. Paine.

Mike extended his hand and looked into Lydia's eyes. She untied her apron and placed her hand in his.

"There's a full moon rising in the east," Mr. Paine noted.

"Then we shall walk eastward and enjoy the view," Mike said, and Lydia was able to laugh.

When they were away from the wagons and the snorting, shuffling livestock, Mike slowed his steps and halted. Lydia stood beside him in silence, waiting to hear what he would say. He stood staring up at the brilliant moon. His face was tense and his expression very sober.

"I don't want to lose you," he said at last. "Does it have to end here?"

Lydia swallowed hard. *Thank You, Lord,* she cried inwardly, a tumult of praise and joy lifting her spirits beyond all expectation. "What do you suggest?" she whispered.

"Well. . ." He turned and looked down at her. "I was wondering how long your contract is for."

"One year."

"Twelve months?" He reached up and touched her cheek lightly with his fingertips, and Lydia's pulse hammered in her temples. "That's not so long."

She cleared her throat. "One school year, sir."

Mike smiled. "It always helps to be precise."

"Yes."

"Because I make a school year out to be. . .what? Nine months? Ten?"

"I believe school will break after the summer term by July 1 next year. I—I may be mistaken."

"And does your contract forbid you to enter a betrothal during that time?"

"Yes."

He grimaced. "How does the contract feel about suitors in general?"

Lydia smiled. "I'm not to entertain gentleman callers."

"Are you allowed to correspond with. . .say, a lonely noncommissioned officer in the Seventh Dragoons?"

"So far as I know, it's not forbidden."

He nodded and drew a deep breath. "Lydia, my enlistment is up at the end of the year. I've been struggling with what to do after that. I'm thinking I'd like to return to civilian life."

"What would you do?"

"T.R. Barkley wants me to go into the horse business with him, raising horses for the army and the settlers. There's always a shortage of remounts out here."

She nodded. "I think you will succeed. My father raised horses, and he did well at it. If not for the fire that destroyed his buildings and killed most of his stock, I would probably be quite well off."

"In Hartford, Connecticut," Mike said, and she laughed.

"Yes. Isn't it amazing how God works?"

"Do you believe He bankrupted you to get you out here, Lydia?"

"Perhaps. I only know that having made your acquaintance has made me grateful for this journey in spite of all the hardships."

Mike cleared his throat. "Could you give me an address so that I can send you letters this winter?"

"I'd like that."

"Of course, once the passes are snowed in, there won't be mail for months."

"Then I'll look for a packet of letters in the spring," she said.

He reached to enfold her in his arms, and she didn't hesitate but went to him willingly. He held her close, and Lydia clung to him, slipping her arms around his waist and basking in his warmth and nearness. She felt that he stood between her and the world. For that moment, she couldn't hear, see, smell, or feel anything that wasn't Michael Brown, and it was wonderful. It was the safest, most secure place she had ever known.

"It had to be this way," he whispered, and she raised her face to look up at him. "I asked God to take the memory out of my mind, but He didn't. I just kept remembering that morning in the rocks, when I kissed you. My shoulder hurt like a hot poker was stabbing me, but I forgot all about that when you let me kiss you. If you'd accepted my proposal that day, I would have healed a lot quicker, I'm sure."

"Quit your silliness, Corporal."

Mike's eyes widened. "Is that an order?"

"Yes, sir, it is."

"Fine, then, how's this for gravity?"

He kissed her with all the fire he'd held back on that other occasion, and Lydia melded into his embrace, reveling in the sweetness of the moment. The months ahead would be difficult, but she would not be lonely with this lingering, captivating kiss to remember.

"I feel as if we ought to pray," he said softly when he released her.

"Yes," she whispered.

He folded his arms snugly about her. "Thank You, Father, for this moment. Now show us where to go from here." He buried his face in the crook of her neck. "I love you, Lydia."

"So you've told me," she said, remembering his declaration after the attack by the Sioux.

"Well, that was nothing compared to what I feel now," he said. "You know that if it weren't for the contract, I'd be asking you a certain question right now. When spring comes, as soon as the passes are clear, I'll be back."

"I thought you were going to trade horses with the Nez Perce," she said with a smile.

"I'm coming here first—that's a promise. T.R. and Matt can meet us at old Fort Boise afterward, and we'll jump off from there. If I know T.R.'s wife, Amy, she'll be along, as well. What do you say?"

She laid a hand on his chest. "Careful now. We mustn't—"

"Right. No betrothals yet. I won't stir up any trouble for you with the school board, but when the time comes, you be ready, sweetheart. I intend to be prompt."

As she looked up into his eyes, a deep joy enveloped her. She felt like laughing and singing and shouting at the top of her lungs. She hoped he could read her eager love in her face as she lightly caressed his cheek. Although her words were within the strictest bounds of propriety, the message she conveyed was one of elation. "Thank you, Michael. I shall look forward to it."

Epilogue

July 1861
Fort Bridger, Wyoming

I should have stayed in the army," Mike groaned, pulling on the coat of his new suit.

"Why?" asked his best friend, T.R. Barkley. "So you could get married in your uniform?"

"This suit feels funny."

T.R. shifted his year-old son, Ben, to his other arm. "Aw, that's just because you've spent so many years in uniform. Anything new takes some getting used to."

Mike sighed. He probably would have had nothing but his threadbare old uniform to wear today if Amy Barkley hadn't badgered him into having some new clothes sent out from St. Louis.

"I think you're a little nervous," T.R. said.

Mike ran a hand through his dark hair. "Can't help it. I should have gone to Oregon and fetched her myself."

T.R. shook his head. "It made more sense this way. That mule train of traders was heading out from Oregon City two days after Lydia's school closed. No sense in you riding all the way out there to get her when she could travel with the traders' families. And it gave you time to finish the house."

"True." Mike shoved his hand in his pants pocket and pulled out the gold wedding band he had purchased for Lydia. "Still, when I saw her yesterday, it was like..."

"Like you hadn't seen her for most of a year."

"Well, yeah."

T.R. smiled. "She was obviously glad to see you again."

Mike bit his lip, then grinned. "How could she not be? Oops!" The ring fell to the floor, and he watched it roll across the bare boards.

"Uh-oh," said little Ben.

T.R. laughed. "Uncle Mike dropped the ring, didn't he?"

Mike bent to retrieve it. "Do you think she'll like the house?"

"Relax, Mike. She'll love the house. She'll love the ranch. She'll love living next door to Amy and me. As long as you're there, she'd love anything."

"Yeah." Mike smiled then thought of another concern. "She's never seen me out of uniform."

His friend shook his head. "It should be a relief to her to see you in civilian clothes, right? No more orders sending you off to who knows where. But, hey, if it will make you feel better, I'll see if Amy can sew a stripe down your pant leg real quick." T.R. watched him expectantly.

Mike laughed.

The door to the barracks opened, and T.R.'s brother Matt stepped inside. "The chaplain's ready."

"Great. I don't think I can hold Mike down much longer. Tell the major." T.R. handed his son over to Matt. "And can you hold him during the ceremony?"

"Sure." Matt turned away, and little Ben waved at his father.

Mike exhaled deeply.

"You all right?" T.R. asked.

"I'm fine."

T.R. nodded. "Good. This is the right thing, Mike."

"I know. I'm so thankful God brought her to me. It's just hard to believe it's finally happening. And that she agreed to love, honor, and obey."

"Guess she got that part out of her system, from what you've told me."

"She's headstrong, but she's a wonderful girl, and I wouldn't want her any other way. When you and Amy get to know her better, you'll love her."

"We already love her. She's making you happy, and it's not difficult to see why. She's beautiful, and she's spirited. She's got a lot of heart, Mike."

"You make it sound like I'm buying a horse."

T.R. shrugged. "You know what I mean. I'm not one to make flowery speeches. You got a good one. Come on; we should be over at the chapel."

They stepped out of barracks and walked across the parade ground to the new structure of rough boards. Entering by the side door, they were met by the chaplain and guided to stand at the front. The room was filled with cavalrymen, with a sprinkling here and there of wives and other civilians. The band, made up of troopers, was playing Beethoven's "Ode to Joy," but when Mike and T.R. took their places, they began a somewhat shaky rendition of Wagner's "Bridal Chorus."

The men filling the benches in the little chapel quieted as lovely Amy Barkley entered the front door and walked slowly down the aisle to stand near Mike, T.R., and the chaplain. There was a hushed moment; then Amy's father, Major Travis, in his full dress uniform, entered with Lydia on his arm.

Mike's pulse pounded as he stared at his bride. She was breathtaking. Her bouquet of wild flax blossoms brought out the blue of her luminous eyes. It registered in his mind that she was wearing the white dress Amy wore when she married T.R. at Fort Laramie three years earlier, although Lydia was taller than

Amy. Mike smiled as he noticed that several inches of delicate lace had been added to the hem of Amy's dress. In her letters during the winter, Lydia had described to him the long evening hours she spent tatting lace. She didn't know what she would use it for, she'd written, but that and correcting her pupils' papers helped keep her mind off how much she missed him.

Their gaze met, and Lydia smiled at him. Mike waited for the moment when Major Travis would hand her over to him, and he could clasp her hand. The future was bright. He had never been so happy—or so certain he was doing the right thing.

"I love you," he whispered as Lydia reached him. Tears glistened in her eyes as she joined him and faced the chaplain.

"Dearly beloved. . ."

"I love you," Lydia whispered, so low he could barely hear it.

WYOMING
HOOFBEATS

Dedication

To my third daughter, Page Miriam Davis,
who loves horses and adventure.
There's never a dull moment when you are home.

Chapter 1

Matt Barkley sat on his fidgety paint gelding, looking down at the Arapaho village below.

"That's Red Wolf's camp," his brother Tom said.

Matt nodded, surveying the valley below them. "Are you sure we're welcome?"

Tom shoved his hat back and smiled at his wife, Amy, who had pulled her big gray horse up on his other side. "Oh yeah, I haven't been up here to visit him for a while, but I'm sure Red Wolf will be glad to see me."

"There hasn't been any trouble with the Arapaho lately, has there?" Amy asked, frowning.

It was the first time she had been on a camping trip with her husband since their second child was born, and Matt could see that she was a little nervous. The intrepid Amy Travis had settled down and become the ultimate housewife Amy Barkley. Still, he knew she loved riding and exploring. She'd probably been chafing to get off on a ramble with Tom for months. Little Molly was two years old, and Ben was four. Amy hadn't left the ranch and the immediate vicinity of Fort Bridger for quite some time.

"Don't worry, sweetheart," Tom said. "We'll be treated like old friends. That's what we are."

"I guess that's good," she said. "It's better than having you be the chief's son-in-law."

Tom gave a good-natured laugh. Matt was surprised his brother had told Amy that story, but apparently it was now a family joke. Tom, or "T.R.," as his male friends and family often called him, had met Red Wolf years ago and had spent so much time hunting with the Arapaho chief that they became fast friends. Red Wolf had informed Tom that his daughter, Elk Calf Woman, was interested in bringing him into the family. Tom, the quiet scout, had gracefully managed to talk his way out of it without alienating the tribe. After that he spent less time in Red Wolf's village, and a year later had told Matt with relief that Elk Calf Woman had taken an Arapaho husband.

Matt had never been chummy with the tribe. His six years in the U.S. Cavalry had given him a different perspective of the Indians than his brother had, but he trusted Tom's judgment. Since Jim Bridger left the area, Tom was the most knowledgeable white man in western Wyoming when it came to Indians. That was why Tom was in demand by the army for scouting purposes, and the commander at the fort consulted him often about tribal movements and attitudes.

Matt spotted a herd of horses grazing near the creek bank on the edge of the village. "Looks like they've got plenty of horses. I just hope they've got the one you need and are willing to trade."

"I'll be happy if we leave here with a good stallion." Tom urged his gelding forward with Amy's gray close behind. Matt looked over his shoulder then followed them down the trail, letting his paint, Wiser, pick his footing.

As they rode down into the village, the Arapaho people watched them. Matt had sensed their scrutiny from far up the trail. They passed two men who served as sentinels for the tribe, but the sentries made no move to stop them.

They reached the valley floor, and the boys of the tribe left playing their hoop and stick game and ran to meet them, trotting along beside the horses and calling to each other. They seemed most interested in Amy and her big gray gelding.

As they came close to the village of tepees, people of all ages gathered to stare at them. Amy was the object of avid curiosity, but she rode without showing any discomfiture. Instead, she nodded and smiled at the Arapaho women as she kept Kip, her gray gelding, in pace with Tom's horse.

In the center of the camp, Tom halted and spoke to a middle-aged man, the eldest among the crowd. A couple of dozen younger men were sprinkled throughout the onlookers, and Matt surmised the rest were out hunting—or raiding, though this tribe was known to be more peaceful than most.

The man spoke to a boy of about twelve, who immediately ran toward a large tepee fashioned of buffalo hides. Wiser tossed his head and pawed the ground restlessly, and Matt stroked his neck. The Arapaho women began surging in to surround Amy's big gray horse.

"Stay close to me," Tom said, and Amy urged Kip nearer to Milton, his bay gelding. Matt lifted his reins slightly, and Wiser closed in on the other side of Amy.

Of course the women were in awe of his gorgeous sister-in-law, with her long, golden braid and azure eyes. Six years ago, Amy Travis had been the most sought-after belle of the Green River Valley. Matt had never quite figured out why the major's daughter had settled on his older brother as her life mate, but it was true love, no question. T.R. had done himself proud.

The women began to chatter. Matt had never learned the lingo, though he had picked up a little of the sign language the Plains Indians used. Even that was rusty now, after three years back East fighting Rebs. He listened but was able to pick out only a word or two.

The boy returned, walking proudly beside two older men, and Matt knew at once that these were the pipe keeper and the chief, the principal men of the tribe. Tom had told him and Amy on the way here that this village was entrusted with the keeping of the Great Pipe, the most sacred ceremonial object of all the Arapaho people.

Matt watched his brother and saw his eyes focus on the younger of the two in pleasure. This was Red Wolf then, T.R.'s old friend.

So the elder of the two men was the pipe keeper. His shoulders were stooped and his thin braids were iron gray. If the village moved, would this old man have the strength to go before them carrying the pipe bundle?

Red Wolf was a bit younger, but his hair was also touched with gray. His limbs were still muscular, and his eyes glittered as he met Tom's gaze. He stopped before the three riders, nodded, and spoke a greeting.

Tom replied then gestured toward Amy and spoke again.

"I remember," Red Wolf said in English, "your woman with hair of gold. Very pretty woman." He smiled up at Amy. "We are honored that you come again."

"Thank you, Chief," Amy said. "I would have come with my husband last summer, but I have two little ones at home now."

Red Wolf nodded with a smile and spoke to Tom in the Arapaho language.

Tom laughed. "He wants to know if the babies have blond hair."

"Tell him yes," Amy replied.

Tom spoke at length, and the Indians gasped and stared at Amy with renewed wonder.

"What did you tell them?" she asked.

"I said that our son's hair is as yellow as the flower of the fever plant, but our daughter's is as white as the breast of the sage grouse. And both have eyes the color of the sky in corn gathering time."

Matt laughed. He'd never guessed his brother could wax poetic in two languages.

Tom glanced at him then turned back to the chief. "Oh, and that's my brother."

The chief looked hard at him, and Matt tried not to squirm as he remembered past battles. Could the chief tell by his army-issue boots or his bearing that he was not long out of the military? Before going back East, Matt had been part of several expeditions meant to intimidate the Plains Indians, but he couldn't recall an engagement in which he actually went up against the Arapaho. They were generally at peace with the whites, although they were friendly with the Cheyenne and sometimes sided with the Sioux in times of contention.

"Welcome, brother of my friend," said Red Wolf.

Matt nodded. "Thank you."

"My brother's name is Matthew Barkley," Tom said.

The chief nodded at Matt then asked, "Do you journey beyond our valley, or do you stop here?"

"I want to discuss trading with you," Tom said. "You know I have a horse ranch now, and I am looking for a stallion for my herd."

The chief spoke to his own people in their language then said to Tom, "You and your brother are welcome to discuss your purpose in my lodge. My daughter will show Yellow Hair Woman a place by the fire."

Matt grinned as he dismounted and gave Wiser into the care of an Arapaho boy. If he knew Amy, the last place she'd want to be in July was near the cooking fire.

Tom told Amy, "Let them put Kip to graze. He'll be safe. And you'll be fine, sweetheart."

Amy gave them a crooked smile and went with the young woman assigned to her, merging into the crowd of dark-skinned women and children.

"Are you sure they won't pull her hair out in clumps?" Matt asked his brother.

"She's an honored guest of the chief. I think they'll treat her with respect." Tom frowned and threw a last glance back toward his wife. "Although Elk Calf Woman. . ."

"That was her?" Matt hissed. "You let Amy go with her?" He stared after Amy and saw her trying to communicate with the chief's daughter. She was touching Elk Calf Woman's arm with one hand and gesturing toward the river-bank with the other.

Tom chuckled. "She'll get a bath out of this stop; wait and see if she doesn't."

Chief Red Wolf was waiting at the entrance to his tepee. The pipe keeper entered before them, and half a dozen mature warriors waited in deference for the guests. Tom, who stood six inches taller than the chief, ducked his head and entered the lodge, and Matt followed him.

Rachel Haynes stood still in the shade of a large pine tree. She wished she had brought her bead pouch with her. She might be exiled until darkness fell. If she'd brought her beads and the leather she was decorating, she could do a good bit of work while she waited.

Yellow Bird Woman had found her by the riverbank and told her outsiders were approaching the village. Rachel knew what that meant without the old woman explaining it to her. She was to stay hidden until either the visitors left or she was told she could return to the camp.

Now she waited in the trees near the edge of the river, peering toward the village. She had seen three riders come into camp, but she was so far away that she couldn't tell much about the visitors surrounded by the people of the village.

If there was no danger to her, Yellow Bird Woman would come and fetch her soon. If she didn't forget. The old woman was apt to set out on an errand and stop halfway there, forgetful of her purpose. Rachel sighed and sat down with her back to the tree trunk. At least she had her knife. She could work on the buffalo carving she had started for West Wind's baby.

Voices reached her from the clearing near the water, and Rachel held her breath. After a moment, she relaxed. It was Elk Calf Woman. Rachel peeked out through the brush that concealed her just inside the tree line and gasped.

Elk Calf Woman stood at the place where the women approached the shallow river to wash and was gesturing down the path toward the pool where they bathed. Beside her stood a white woman. Rachel stared unabashed. The woman's face and hands were deeply tanned, but still much lighter than those of the Arapaho woman beside her. *Like mine*, Rachel thought, looking down at the backs of her own strong hands.

The woman was turned partly away from her, listening intently to what Elk Calf Woman said. The chief's daughter was fairly fluent in English. No doubt she had been detailed to keep an eye on this woman while the men did business.

It had been a long time since Rachel had seen another white woman so close, and she stared from her covert position, fixing the details of the other's clothing in her mind. The stranger wore a long, brown cotton skirt that seemed to be divided into billowy trousers, a light blue blouse, and a man's soft, gray felt hat. The grass hid her feet.

Elk Calf Woman seemed to be arguing a point with her guest, and the white woman shook her head vehemently. Rachel strained her ears and caught the English word "privacy." She knew Elk Calf Woman spoke fluent English, though she might feign otherwise if she thought it prudent. But the two continued to talk, and at last the white woman seemed to win her point, and the chief's daughter left the stranger alone and headed back toward the village.

The white woman removed her dusty hat and unbraided her hair. The sun gleamed on her golden locks, long and shining, like burnished brass.

The woman stood still for a moment staring toward the woods, and Rachel froze. The natural inclination to duck lower behind the brush tugged at her, but she knew it was crucial to stay immobile if she wanted to remain undetected. After a moment, the golden-haired woman sat down and pulled off her boots.

They were leather riding boots, Rachel could see now, such as a man might wear, but daintier for her small feet. Rachel wished she had a pair like them for winter, but her supple moccasins served her well most of the time.

The white woman rose, looked around, then unbuttoned her skirt and took it off. In her lace-trimmed pantalets, as white as new snow, she waded into the water. When she was waist-deep, she began washing the brown skirt. She looked around again, then unbuttoned her blouse and took it off, giving it the same treatment. After rinsing the garments well, she wrung them out and waded up onto the bank. With water dripping from her hair and white arms, and her chemise and pantalets clinging to her, she spread the skirt and blouse out to dry on some low bushes, then plunged back into the water and thoroughly rinsed her hair.

Rachel knew she ought to leave and grant the lady her wish for seclusion, but the desire to speak to the visitor almost overcame her caution. She hadn't spoken to another white woman in more than two years. Would disaster really follow if she showed herself now?

The woman was fit and strong, she realized, as she saw her swim swiftly across the pool and back. Then she emerged from the water and sat down where she had left her boots and hat. She picked something up, and after a moment Rachel saw that she had a comb. Her hair seemed paler and brighter with each stroke, as the sun dried the shimmering golden locks.

At last she stood, and her glorious hair floated about her, hanging down to her hips in a rippling cloud of gold. She went to the bushes and felt her clean clothes. They were still damp, Rachel supposed, but the woman pulled on the blouse, anyway, then the dark skirt. She sat in the grass again and put on her stockings and boots then quickly braided her hair and pinned it up. Rachel smiled to herself as the lovely woman stood and capped her costume with the incongruous hat.

Rachel's mouth went dry. The woman was walking toward her. She stood stock-still and closed her eyes. A few moments later, she couldn't resist opening them just a bit and peeping out. The woman stood only a few yards from her, and she was staring frankly at Rachel.

"Hello."

Rachel swallowed hard. She opened her mouth but nothing came out. The people of the village would be incensed when they learned she had allowed herself to be seen by the outsider. She whipped around and darted behind the large pine tree. There was a bushy spruce close by, and she ran for it, hiding behind its spreading branches, and again stood still.

She could hear the woman's soft footsteps then silence.

"I won't hurt you," came the melodious voice.

Rachel said nothing.

A footstep, and the branches of the spruce stirred. Rachel's heart raced as she hesitated, knowing she could lose the woman in the woods if she ran, but she was unable to turn away again.

Suddenly, she was staring into brilliant, blue eyes.

Chapter 2

Rachel gasped but didn't move.

"I'm Amy Barkley," said the golden-haired woman. "What is your name?"

Rachel pulled in a shaky breath and whispered, "They call me Stands in Timber."

The woman's delighted laugh sent a thrill through Rachel's body. Amy Barkley's teeth gleamed white, and her smile was warmer than the summer sun.

"How appropriate!"

Rachel frowned. The words sounded strange, yet familiar. She took a deep breath and stepped from behind the spruce.

"I was. . .also called. . .Rachel Haynes."

Amy caught her breath and stared at her.

What does she see? Rachel wondered. *My eyes are blue but not like hers. She sees a young Arapaho woman with hair and skin too light, and with eyes the dull gray blue of river ice.*

"My dear child! How long have you been here?"

"I have been here. . .that is, here in this village. . .about one year."

"A year? And before that?"

Rachel reached deep into her memory, searching for the English words she needed. "Before. . .before I came here, I was with the Dakota Sioux."

Amy touched her arm gently, and Rachel looked down at her hand. Although the white woman's fingers were lithe, the softness of Amy's skin amazed Rachel.

"With the Sioux." Amy's brow furrowed as her gaze probed Rachel's. "How did you come to be with them?"

A lump formed in Rachel's throat, and she felt the burning sensation that preceded tears. "I. . .was taken."

Amy stared at her then peered toward the path. "Rachel, are you being held here against your will?"

Rachel swallowed and fought the tightness in her chest. In either language, she couldn't answer that question.

"You needn't be afraid," Amy said, giving her arm a gentle squeeze. "My husband is a friend of Chief Red Wolf. He's in the chief's lodge now, talking to him. If you have been mistreated, he will—"

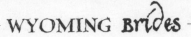

"No," said Rachel.

Amy stopped talking and arched her eyebrows.

"The Arapaho have not mistreated me," Rachel said, wrangling with the long unused words.

"But you were kidnapped."

Rachel shrugged. "It was. . .war."

Amy frowned at her. "I don't understand. There have been a few clashes with the tribes, but nothing like an outright war."

"It was not here." *She doesn't understand,* Rachel thought. *How can I explain my past to her?* "I come from a place far east of here."

"East? How far east?"

"Many days toward the sunrise. It was called. . .Minnesota."

Amy exhaled and stared off toward the river for a long moment. When she turned her attention back to Rachel, she nodded. "My father is a military man. I came with him to Wyoming Territory about six years ago, and I met my husband here. I've not kept up-to-date on all that's gone on east of here. . .the war with the Confederate states and all. . ."

Rachel tried to follow what she was saying and make sense of it. Vague memories stirred. Her father and some neighboring men had talked about the war to the south. Slavery. Secession. At the time, everyone was worked up about it, but it seemed so long ago.

"But I do recall my father saying something about a Sioux uprising in Minnesota a couple of years back," Amy went on. "He told me the leaders of the warriors who raided the white settlements were caught and hung."

Rachel caught her breath. "I. . .don't know. I don't know anything of what happened after I was taken from my home. My. . .parents and my. . .sisters and brothers. . ." She shook her head, not wanting to think about that day.

"Was your family harmed?" Amy asked softly.

Rachel looked up into her startlingly blue eyes. "Yes. I saw my mother and my two little sisters killed. I don't know about the boys, except Ralph. When the Sioux hauled me from the house, I saw my father and Ralph lying in the dooryard."

"I'm sorry." Amy lifted her hands as though she would embrace her, and Rachel pulled back slightly. She was not used to being touched, and the idea repelled her, although Amy Barkley was clean and pleasant to look at.

"How old are you?" Amy asked.

"I. . ." Rachel thought hard. She had tried last spring to determine that very thing. "When I was taken, I was. . .I believe I was sixteen summers. . .sixteen years."

Amy nodded.

"The Dakota Sioux gave me to a band of their relatives. They brought me west. Always west, for a long time. I stayed with them one winter. And then. . ." She remembered the awful cold months and how hungry all the people had been. After that came spring and better hunting, and in early summer the tribes united in a huge gathering of celebration. Rachel shivered, recalling her fear when one of the Sioux women hinted that she might be sold to another band in exchange for horses. "Then I came to the people. . .the Arapaho, you call them."

"Yes. How long—"

"One winter," Rachel said with certainty. "They told me I would have a winter to mourn, and then. . ." She looked into Amy's eyes, suddenly afraid.

"Then what?"

Amy's features were frozen in sympathetic expectation. It hurt to look at her. Deep in Rachel's chest, the lump that hindered her breathing grew larger. She cherished the memory of her mother, whom she considered to be the loveliest woman she had ever known, but Amy Barkley was more beautiful than even Rachel's dear mother.

She blinked, trying to conjure up the memory of her mother's face for comparison, but all she saw was the bloodied horror of those last few moments in their house in Minnesota.

"My father went there to plant," she said. "To farm."

Amy frowned, and Rachel realized she had not answered the woman's question. But Amy's next inquiry showed that she was following Rachel's meandering thought trail. "You were homesteading?"

"Yes."

"As I said, I heard about the Dakota War. My father had a newspaper. By the time we read about it, the hostilities were over."

"I wondered. I didn't know if the Sioux had taken all the land or not."

"No," Amy said.

"They carried me off, and I never knew what happened there."

Amy laid a gentle hand on her shoulder. "Do you have relatives elsewhere? Aunts and uncles, perhaps, in other parts of the country?"

Rachel tried to reach back, beyond the move to the homestead when she was quite young. "Before Minnesota, we lived in New York State."

Amy laughed, and the clear trill of her voice startled Rachel. "I grew up in Albany! What town did you live in?"

Rachel groped for the name, but it was gone. "I. . .can't remember."

"It's all right," Amy said.

"I. . .don't remember any other relatives. I had grandparents, but they died." A sudden wave of bereavement washed over her, and she pulled in a ragged breath. "If there is family left who knew me, I suppose they think I died with the others."

"Rachel, you started to tell me how the Dakota brought you west and traded

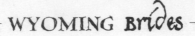
you to the Arapaho."

"Yes, it is true. Those who attacked the farms in Minnesota passed me to another band, and they brought me out here. Then, the next summer, they wanted to be rid of me. I think they feared the white soldiers would see me and be angry with them. So they made a trade. They got three horses for me."

A faint smile flickered across Amy's lips. "Is that good?"

Rachel shrugged.

"And what has happened this last year, since you have been with the Arapaho?"

"They have been kind to me. Mostly. I try to work hard. But I am made to hide whenever outsiders come."

"I'm sorry we caused you distress today."

"I am used to it."

"Come sit down with me." Amy looked toward the sunny riverbank.

"No, I mustn't." Rachel could only imagine the wrath of Elk Calf Woman if she found her talking to this stranger. She remembered an English word that fit the situation. "It is forbidden."

Amy's troubled eyes brought an uneasiness to Rachel's spirit.

"Do you want to leave the Arapaho? Would you like to go back to your own people? Because that is your right. We can help you."

"No! I cannot do that." Rachel raised her hands in supplication. "Please, you must not anger the chief."

"Chief Red Wolf has never been a violent man. My husband finds him quite amicable."

"I. . ." Rachel shook her head. "I don't understand this."

"They are friends."

"Yes, but your husband does not live here."

"He spent many months with Red Wolf when he was younger. The chief honors him when he visits the tribe."

"I. . .do not know about this." Rachel looked deep into Amy's eyes. This white woman was sincere, but she did not understand the convoluted relationships within the tribes; that was certain. "There are others besides Red Wolf who would be angry, and I do not wish to cause strife."

"What do you mean? Rachel, you are an American citizen, and you have been kidnapped. Those Indians cannot make you stay with them. Tom and his brother and I can help you gain Red Wolf's permission to leave if that is what you want."

For an instant, Rachel allowed herself to imagine being back in Minnesota. Her parents were gone, though. There was no one there to welcome her. And if she went all the way back to New York, the place of her childhood, what would she find? No one there would accept her. Her two years among the Plains Indians would make her a pariah among civilized people. Better to remain in the position where God had placed her and accept what her new people planned for her.

"You don't understand. Soon I will become an Arapaho, a full member of this tribe."

"You mean, they are going to adopt you?"

Rachel shook her head. "No, I. . ." She looked toward the path once more in anguish. She must end this conversation now. "The chief has not told me, but his daughter has hinted to me. . .I am to be married soon. I will be one of them, and there are some who would be. . .very angry if I upset those plans. There are warriors who would kill your husband if he interfered."

Amy stared at her. "They will force you to marry one of their men?"

"Please, Mrs.—I'm sorry, I can't remember your name." Rachel put her hand to her forehead and closed her eyes for a moment. *What am I doing, talking to this stranger?*

"It's Barkley. Amy Barkley. My husband is Thomas Barkley. Remember that name, Rachel. Let us help you."

"I can't."

"Do you want to marry this warrior?"

Rachel shook her head, at a loss for the way to explain. "I left the Dakota willingly. Don't you see? I was at the age when I was likely to be married off. I prayed to God that I would not be given in marriage to one of the Sioux men. Out of His grace, He permitted me to come here. These people are much less violent than the Sioux. For the most part, they are peaceful. They do not go about attacking each other the way the Sioux and Cheyenne do. And since I have been here, at least, they have been at peace with the whites."

"That's true," Amy said. "But, still—"

"I thought that if I went with the Arapaho, I would gain time before I was expected to marry. I told God that if He allowed me to go to a peaceful tribe, I would be content there. And when I came to Red Wolf's band, I was told I would have a year to mourn and learn the new ways. But that time is up now."

"So you think they expect you to marry."

Rachel looked down at the ground. She and Amy stood toe-to-toe, only a foot of pine needle-strewn earth between her moccasins and Amy's fine leather boots.

"I know they expect it," she whispered.

"And you wish to marry? Are you. . .in love with one of their warriors?"

Rachel felt her cheeks grow warm. "No, quite the opposite. The man I believe has been chosen for me. . .or rather, who has chosen me for his wife. . .is not one I would choose, but. . . God has honored my prayers, and I cannot dishonor the chief by refusing to marry his son."

Amy straightened her shoulders. "Wait a minute. Chief Red Wolf expects you to marry his son?"

"I fear it is so. And the chief has been kind to me. I cannot refuse, even though Running Elk is the last man of the tribe I would wish to marry."

"He is not kind like his father?"

Rachel swallowed hard, remembering the nights she had cowered in Yellow Bird Woman's tepee after Running Elk and his followers returned from a raid. The noise of their reveling had chilled her, and she had kept herself hidden until the stillness of morning.

Against his father's wishes, the young man promoted aggression against the Sioux. His boasting may be exaggerated, but the warriors who followed him came home just a few nights past with three stolen horses and tales of counting coup on their enemies. From what the women said in her hearing, Rachel was beginning to fear that if Running Elk was not checked, he would bring retaliation on the village. Now he was gone again, with a hunting party, and she dreaded his return.

"He and his father disagree on many things," she admitted.

"Is there another man you would prefer?"

"No, no!" Rachel bit her lip in frustration. "If I object or try to leave the tribe, there will be much distress and anger. Please, Mrs. Barkley—"

"Amy?"

Rachel gasped and stared toward the voice. A tall, handsome white man stood at the edge of the trees, watching them. Amy whirled toward him, and Rachel took advantage of her distraction to duck behind the plump spruce.

"What's going on, Amy?"

"Oh, Matthew, you startled me, and you've frightened Rachel."

Behind the tree, Rachel huddled into a small, still hump. *Now I'm in trouble! If the people learn that the white man saw me, there will be arguing, and perhaps the village will have to move!*

She could hear the intrigue in the man's voice as he joined Amy in the shadows. "Who's Rachel?"

There was no answer, and Rachel sensed Amy's discomfiture.

"Did I interrupt something?" His voice was deep and smooth, and the English words evoked a longing in her that Rachel had tried to suppress for many months. "I'm sorry. Tom's finished trading, and he's getting the horses ready to leave. I told him I'd fetch you."

"Rachel," Amy called softly. "It's all right, Rachel. It's only my husband's brother, and he won't hurt you."

The only sound was the breeze that swayed the upper branches of the trees as Rachel held her breath. In her mind she pleaded, *Go away! Please, Amy Barkley, go away now!*

"Rachel, you mustn't be afraid."

Behind the tree, Rachel closed her eyes and tried to squeeze herself smaller.

The light pressure of a hand on her shoulder jerked her alert.

"I'm sorry we frightened you, but Matthew won't hurt you. We won't tell anyone that we saw you."

Slowly Rachel unkinked her legs and stood. "Please go."

Amy nodded. "All right. But first, I want you to meet my brother-in-law."

Against her better sense, Rachel allowed the beautiful woman to draw her around the spruce tree. She glanced toward the tall white man then turned her face away. The melting look in his eyes was different from the leer she saw when Running Elk stared at her. She saw compassion and empathy in this rugged young man's face. The attraction she felt to him startled her, and it was followed by a heavy trepidation. It could do no good to imagine a future in the world of the whites now. The sooner she parted company with Amy and this man the better.

"This is my husband's brother, Matthew Barkley." Amy smiled, and Rachel forced herself to look at the man again.

Her heart thudded as his gaze met hers. She nodded at him but stood immobile when he extended his hand.

"This is Rachel Haynes, Matt."

"I'm pleased to meet you, Miss Haynes."

Despite Amy's encouraging smile, Rachel did not move to greet him. She tore her gaze away from his face.

"You must go."

Chapter 3

I s there a problem?" Matt looked at Amy, and she frowned.

"Rachel is an unwilling guest of the Arapaho."

"No," Rachel said. "They have treated me well. I wish no bad feeling between Red Wolf's people and the whites. Please go and say nothing to anyone."

Matt's fascination grew with each moment. The girl's features were softened by the twilight of the forest, and her Arapaho dress and braided hair did little to enhance her appearance. Still, her delicate cheekbones and heart-shaped face gave her a classic loveliness that even her rough garb couldn't hide.

He pushed his hat back a little. "We wouldn't want to cause you any distress."

"Thank you. I'll be fine. Truly. If you'll just leave."

Amy hesitated. "Surely it wouldn't hurt to let Chief Red Wolf know we've met you."

"No, don't!" Rachel's eyes leaped in fear.

"But if you don't wish to accept his son's addresses. . ."

"I'm not sure what you mean. But I have been told, and I'm sure it has truth, that a woman who shames a chief's son will regret it."

Amy leaned closer to Matt and whispered, "We can't leave her here! Matt, we have to do something."

He looked from her to Rachel, sending up a swift prayer for wisdom.

"Miss Haynes, I'm sure the tales you've heard were told to scare you into subjection. Surely these people wouldn't harm you for choosing your own mate."

"It is not choosing a mate that would anger them," Rachel replied, staring down at her beaded moccasins. "If I wed the chief's son, all will be well. If I refuse to marry, I will be considered a disobedient. . .shrew." She looked up at him with a question in her eyes, as though not certain she'd spoken the right word.

Matt nodded to tell her that he understood.

"The Arapaho do not treat such women well," Rachel said. "I have heard stories from the other women. In most cases, a woman is allowed to choose her mate, but it is different with the chief's son. No woman would refuse Running Elk. It is. . . not to be considered. And besides, his temper is short. I should not like to be the object of his wrath."

"Come with us!" Amy reached for her hand, but Rachel stepped back.

"You do not understand. Trying to leave with you would be the worst thing I could do. It would cause strife between the chief and his son. Already they disagree

270

on many things. This would make it worse. I cannot do that."

Matt touched Amy's sleeve. "Come on, Amy. We'd better do as she says. T.R.'s bought a fine stallion from Red Wolf, and he's ready to go. If we don't get back to the village soon, someone will come looking for us, and we don't want to cause Miss Haynes further difficulties."

Amy's eyes shone with determination, but Matt stared back with a frown meant to convey his uneasiness. The last thing they wanted to do was cause Red Wolf to resent the intrusion of the whites. As much as he disliked the idea, Rachel's words rang true with what he knew of the local Indians. To refuse the advances of a man who was revered as a great warrior without good reason would lead to ostracizing the woman, or worse. She was already a misfit in the tribe. He supposed it was possible the Arapaho would mistreat her if she didn't conform to their wishes.

"We'll ask T.R. about it," he told Amy. His brother was much more in tune with the Plains Indians' ways than Matt was. "He'll understand the situation. He'll know whether meddling would put Miss Haynes in danger or not. I suggest that for now we get moving and make sure she's not seen talking to us."

"All right," Amy said at last, and Matt exhaled in relief. She turned to Rachel. "In my saddlebag I have a small Bible. I'd like to give it to you."

Rachel recoiled from her. "No, you mustn't."

"How would you get it to her without them knowing?" Matt asked.

"He is right," Rachel said. "You would endanger me and yourselves if you did this. Besides. . .I'm not sure I could read it."

"But. . ." Amy's face crumpled in defeat.

"I learned to read some as a child," Rachel said, "but when we moved to Minnesota, there was no school, and we didn't have time to study. Now. . .I just don't know. I haven't seen English words in a long time."

"Come on, Amy," Matt urged. "We've got to get going. Miss Haynes, we won't forget you. I'll talk to my brother about this. He'll know what's the best course to take."

Amy sighed and reached for Rachel's hand. "You said you trusted God to protect you when you were with the Sioux."

Rachel pressed her lips together for a moment. "Yes. And He brought me here."

"I agree," Amy said. "God delivered you to a better place. But He's not done protecting you. Consider that God brought us here today. Consider that He might use us to deliver you and take you back where you belong."

Rachel stared down at the ground. "I. . .am not sure where I belong."

The forlorn quirk of her mouth tore at Matt's heart. He understood Amy's longing to rescue this poor girl. He felt it himself—the desire to cradle her in his arms and assure her that all would be well. But it wasn't their place to offend the tribe leaders and set them at odds with one another, especially when the woman they wanted to help didn't seem to welcome their interference.

"I remember a saying," Rachel whispered.

Matt strained his ears to hear, not wanting to upset her further by stepping closer.

"Before the Sioux attacked our home, I was learning a. . .a Bible verse. 'I will say of the Lord, He is my refuge and my fortress: my God; in him will I trust.'"

Amy nodded. "That's from Psalm 91, I think."

"I said it many times over when I was afraid."

"It's a good verse to remember," Matt said. "Keep on trusting Him, Miss Haynes. And if you ever need help, send word to Fort Bridger. We live near the fort. You can always locate us by inquiring there for the Barkleys."

Amy reached for the girl, and Rachel did not shrink from her but let her embrace her and kiss her tanned cheek.

"We'll not forget you," Amy said.

Matt nodded. "Now come, Amy. We've overstayed as it is."

He led the way out of the woods, into the dazzling sunlight. Rachel Haynes did not follow them, and when he looked back, there was no trace of her near the spruce tree. Matt almost could believe their encounter wasn't real, but the fear and longing in her gray-blue eyes would stay with him, he knew.

"I hate walking away from her," Amy said through gritted teeth.

"I know, but we have to. Just don't say a word about her until we're well away from the village."

"But Tom can—"

Matt stopped in the path and glared at her. "No, Amy. You could do that girl great harm by spilling the beans before we're clear of Red Wolf's camp."

Amy's eyes flickered. "All right. I'll trust your judgment on that."

"Thank you."

They walked swiftly toward the tepees. A warrior held a long braided leather strap attached to the head of a regal stallion. The horse's head, neck, and hindquarters were coal black, and in between his muscular body was randomly splotched with black and white. He held his flowing black and white tail high as he pranced and tugged at the lead line.

Tom stood talking with the chief and holding the reins of his gelding. Wiser and Kip fidgeted nearby, in the charge of two Arapaho boys.

Amy's excitement when she saw the stallion was contagious, and Matt found himself grinning all the way down to his toes. Tom had finally found the perfect stallion for his horse-breeding operation. His long search was over, and the ranch would thrive. Matt could envision next year's crop of colts, all with straight legs, deep chests, and proud, intelligent faces like the stallion's.

Tom normally hid his emotions, but Matt saw his brother's smile burst out at the exact moment he locked gazes with his wife. Matt hoped he had a marriage like theirs someday: a man with a dream that, fulfilled, would bring security to his wife, and a woman whose hope is a happy and contented husband.

They spoke their polite good-byes to Red Wolf and the pipe keeper, and Amy thanked Elk Calf Woman for her hospitality. They all mounted, and the Arapaho man placed the stallion's leather lead in Tom's hand.

Matt saw Amy look off toward the river and frown.

Don't say a word, he pleaded silently. *This is not the time. Don't betray her.*

To his relief, Amy said nothing about Rachel Haynes, and they turned their mounts toward the trail that would lead them over the mountains and south toward Fort Bridger. Matt led the way, with Amy behind him and Tom coming last, leading the black-and-white stallion.

They topped the pass that led them out of the valley, and Matt sighed. As soon as they stopped to make camp, he would tell his brother about Rachel and ask him what he thought they should do.

Most likely he'll say, "Don't meddle. Let the chief deal with it."

But Matt knew an answer like that wouldn't satisfy him. He'd seen Rachel's fear, and he would never forget the wistfulness on her lovely face.

Apparently Amy's patience had frayed. Matt heard her speak, and he looked over his shoulder. She held Kip in check so that he was walking just in front of Tom's horse, forcing Tom's bay gelding, Milton, to go slowly.

"Tommy, there's a white girl back there," she said.

Tom's attention was on the stallion, which was snapping at his gelding's flanks, causing Milton to fret and prance.

"Cut that out!" Tom growled, cuffing the stallion on the nose. He settled the gelding into a placid walk once more. "What did you say, sweetheart? A girl?"

"That's right. She was captured in a Sioux raid. They dragged her all the way out here from Minnesota."

"That right?"

Matt smiled to himself. Good old T.R. In his laconic way, he would settle Amy down and show her that there was no cause for panic.

Amy's voice grew more strident, though, and Matt had no trouble hearing her say, "We ought not to leave her with them. I wanted to speak to the chief about it, but—"

Matt lost her words as Wiser picked up speed on the down slope. It wasn't too steep, so Matt let him trot until he reached a level stretch that led through a stand of mature fir trees. Entering their shade, he glanced back and saw that Tom and Amy had stopped speaking and were busy guiding their mounts along the trail.

As he swung forward once more, Wiser snorted and stopped so fast he almost sat down on the trail, and Matt lurched forward, his heart hammering.

Shapes sprang from between the trees, blocking his path.

Before him were eight fiercely painted, mounted warriors, each armed with a rifle, a bow, and a glinting knife.

Amy had come up so close behind him on Kip that Matt heard her intake of breath when she saw the war party. A second later he heard Tom's low, "Whoa, Milton," to his horse and a squeal that could only come from the stallion.

Matt kept his eyes on the leader of the band. The other warriors eased into a horseshoe, surrounding them on three sides.

They were Arapaho, of that much Matt was certain, though their clothing and decorations were much like those of the Cheyenne. A beaded turtle amulet hung about the leader's neck. He was perhaps a year or two younger than Matt, but his expression was hard, and the black streaks on his cheeks gave him a ruthless air. The red stallion he rode pawed the ground, and Matt noted the black hands painted on his flanks and feathers plaited into his tail, indicating that he was a trained warhorse.

Matt held his ground, and the warrior looked beyond him. Still Matt didn't turn around, but he could hear the shuffling of the horses behind him, and he knew without seeing that Tom was moving his own mount closer to Amy's.

Soon Milton's dark head edged up beside Wiser.

"Greetings, Running Elk," Tom said.

Matt exhaled. *Of course. The chief's son. He and his party are returning from the hunting expedition Chief Red Wolf told us about.* The elk quarters on a travois behind one of the horses bore out his conclusion.

"Barkley," the leader said.

Tom nodded. "This is my brother."

Running Elk's eyes narrowed as he stared at Matt for a moment, and Matt steeled himself, staring back.

At last the warrior's gaze shifted back to Tom.

"Your woman."

"My wife," Tom confirmed, not looking back toward Amy.

"My horse," said Running Elk.

There was a moment's silence; then Tom said, "You mean the stallion?"

"My horse." The Arapaho men sat like statues, and Matt's mouth went dry. He darted a glance toward Tom and noted that he no longer held the lead line. Amy must be holding the stallion behind them.

"I paid your father for that horse," Tom said.

"You cannot have it."

Tom pushed his hat back and sat in silence for the space of two breaths. "Chief Red Wolf is a man of honor. I traded with him in good faith."

"Chief promised me any horse I choose when I come back. I choose this horse."

Matt's mind raced. If he thought Running Elk was a reasonable man, he might argue that he hadn't technically returned to the village and therefore could not choose yet. When he did reach the village, this horse would not be among those the chief offered him, and so Running Elk would have to choose another. Several other young stallions were available, and Matt might even argue the merits of a likely buckskin colt they had seen. If Running Elk was a reasonable man.

His demeanor and the challenge in his eyes told Matt that attempting to reason with the chief's son would be folly.

Tom said, "Tell you what, Running Elk. You know me. I know you. We've shared the same campfire. You are a great hunter. I see you are returning to your village bringing meat. You've had a good hunting trip."

Running Elk grunted but did not relax his tense posture.

Tom smiled, though how he managed Matt couldn't imagine. His own stomach was churning.

"Let's ride back to the village together and talk this over with your father," Tom said. "I'm sure he can help us work this out."

"No. You give."

The warrior on Matt's flank pushed his horse forward past Wiser, seizing the lead strap from Amy's hand.

Tom wheeled Milton and forced him between the Arapaho's horse and Amy's. All of the warriors but Running Elk brought their rifles up, aiming at Tom and Matt.

"Keep away from my wife." Tom's voice was low and menacing.

"You keep away from village," Running Elk returned.

"I've paid your father well for this horse."

To Matt's surprise, Running Elk dismounted. He pulled his worn cavalry-issue saddle and scabbard from his mount's back and walked with them toward the black-and-white stallion.

"We trade." He tossed his blanket and saddle over the horse's broad back and nodded toward the bright chestnut horse he had been riding. "Is a good horse. He will give you fine colts."

"I paid for this one," Tom said.

The warriors closed about them with their rifles lowered. Tom sat still on Milton beside his wife, one hand lightly touching Amy's sleeve. Matt knew he was ready to make a move if necessary to protect her.

Another warrior dismounted and took the hackamore off the horse Running Elk had been riding and took it to the leader. Matt had the presence of mind to pull his rope from the saddle and slip a loop over the chestnut's head. The Arapaho nearest him watched but did nothing to stop him.

Running Elk leaped onto the black-and-white stallion's back. The horse snorted and pulled at the single rein, throwing his head and causing the horses near him to spring out of the way. Running Elk steadied his mount, using his muscled legs and low, firm voice commands. When the stallion stood still except for his tossing head, the warrior raised his chin and stared once more at Tom.

"My horse. You go. Do not come back. I let you take your woman and other horse. If you wish to fight, you lose both."

Chapter 4

Matt could see the muscle in Tom's cheek twitch. *Don't move, T.R.! You could get us both killed!*

At last Tom broke the stare, and Running Elk turned toward the village. The other warriors sat motionless until their leader had a start of fifty yards then wheeled their mounts and followed him up the trail. The red stallion nickered and tried to push past Wiser to join them. Matt held on to his rope and let the loop tighten around the chestnut's neck.

They all sat immobile, watching the band of Arapaho disappear over the rise; then Amy turned to stare at her husband, her lips parted.

"You did good, sweetheart." Tom sighed and reached for the stallion's lead line. "Thanks, brother."

Matt nodded, understanding the turmoil Tom was stifling.

He was a bit surprised that Amy said nothing. She usually spoke her mind, but a glance at her vivid blue eyes showed Matt her real strength. She knew her husband's sacrifice of his pride and the stallion he'd sought so long was for her sake. She reached out and touched Tom's hand in silence.

Tom managed a wry smile. "This stud's not so bad. He's ten years old, if he's day, but still. . ."

"Tommy!"

Matt turned Wiser homeward, but he heard her quiet "I love you."

If only he could find a wife like that! A woman who would love him no matter what. Who would work beside him and give her strength for their common goals. Who knew when to keep silent and when to speak her encouragement.

Matt had seen Amy in action before. He had no doubt that if there had been three warriors instead of eight, or even four or five, strong-willed Amy would have charged at them in fury. But outnumbered as they were, she'd sat and watched her husband stripped of his dignity to save their lives.

His thoughts flew back to the frightened girl Amy had discovered. Would Rachel Haynes soon be standing by Running Elk as his wife, supporting him in his bullying and raiding? If the young man turned against his father, would she go with him into a life of hate and violence?

He sent up a prayer for Rachel, not certain what he should ask for. *Lord, keep her safe. Give her strength to face whatever You bring into her life now. She's trying to honor You the best she knows how. I ask that You spare her the agony of a bad*

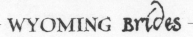

marriage. Bring her closer to You and let her know You're still watching over her. Give her courage.

Rachel walked with Yellow Bird Woman back to the village.

"They did not stay long," the old woman said in the Arapaho tongue.

Rachel nodded. "Long enough to do business with Red Wolf."

"This white man, Comes as a Friend, usually stays with the chief two, three days. This time he says his woman wants to hurry home to her babies."

"How do you know?"

"White Bull told his wife. He heard Comes as a Friend say this to the chief."

Rachel wondered if Thomas Barkley had used his family as an excuse for leaving his friend's village so swiftly.

"White woman bathed herself," Yellow Bird Woman said.

"I. . .saw her," Rachel admitted, not looking at the crone.

"Did you stay hidden?"

"Yes." She gulped, wondering if the old woman could read her thoughts. She had not concealed herself well enough, and sharp-eyed Amy Barkley had found her. Worse yet, she had brought her husband's brother to meet Rachel, too.

At the thought of the tall, handsome young man, Rachel felt her cheeks color. She turned away as they reached the first tepees. "I will help with the hides."

Working hides into soft leather was a grueling job. There were always more cured hides to soften, and the women worked at it whenever other jobs did not claim their attention. Rachel took a stiff deerskin from the waiting pile and positioned herself before a post stuck in the ground. She laid the leather over the post and began to work it back and forth to wear it into suppleness. The wife of one of the tribe's young warriors came to help her.

"The hunters have not returned?" Rachel asked with a smile.

West Wind shook her head. "Soon."

"Your husband is a good hunter. They will bring a lot of meat."

"Perhaps." West Wind grasped the opposite edge of the hide, and they worked together steadily for a few minutes, pulling the hide across the top of the post.

"You saw the whites?"

Rachel's hands stilled, and her heart began to race. *She is only asking out of curiosity,* she told herself. *She does not know, and she won't if you don't tell her.*

"I hid."

"Ah. Then you did not see the golden-haired woman."

Rachel pulled in a slow, painful breath. "Did you think she was. . .pretty?"

"Very pretty, as the white man judges a woman." West Wind repositioned the hide, and Rachel resumed her work.

"She has been here before."

"Oh? When?"

"Maybe three summers ago." West Wind smiled. "Elk Calf Woman was very jealous."

"Why should she be jealous? She has her man."

"Yes, but she wanted Comes as a Friend many winters ago, when he was a young man and she was a girl. The chief asked him to join our people for his daughter's sake, but he refused."

Rachel stared at her. "I have never heard this before."

"It is true. Everyone knows. It is why she is so mean to her husband. She was spurned by the white man, and Broken Wing Hawk is her second choice."

"But the white man. . .he is still a friend of the tribe."

"Oh yes. The chief holds him in great esteem."

"Why?"

"Many years ago this man came to the village in winter. Many were ill, and the people were starving. I was a child, but I remember. Comes as a Friend went away and came back with food for the people. He stayed and helped until enough sick ones recovered to tend those who were still weak."

"That is a noble service for the tribe."

"Yes. The chief loves him. And Elk Calf Woman did, too. She was very young then, and much prettier than she is now."

Elk Calf Woman, with her aristocratic bearing, was a handsome woman. Rachel could only imagine her as a softer, lovesick girl. It was difficult, but imagining an Arapaho girl falling in love with Thomas Barkley was easy. If he was anything like his younger brother was now, all of the girls probably yearned to be his wife.

"But she has outgrown her feelings for Comes as a Friend." Rachel threw West Wind a curious glance.

"Perhaps. He comes less often. At least she has learned to hide her feelings when he is here. And she was kind to his woman."

Rachel nodded. Hospitality was an important characteristic among the people. "So the white men came to trade?"

"He bought a stallion. You know, the spotted one that Running Elk has been gentling?"

"Red Wolf sold that horse?" Rachel asked.

West Wind frowned. "He did. Comes as a Friend would take no other. But he paid much money for it. The chief wanted the white men's rifles, but they would not part with them. Comes as a Friend gave the chief a pouch of money and told him to go and buy what he wanted with it. He said it was a fair price. Red Wolf and the pipe keeper both say he is honest."

Rachel worked in silence. The chief's son would not be happy when he learned that in his absence his father had sold the horse he favored, and to the man who had rejected his sister. Still, it was the chief's right, she supposed. She did not know whether the chief had previously given ownership of the horse to his son, but it seemed that West Wind and the rest of the village knew Running Elk had his eye on the paint stallion.

A cry from the other side of the village alerted them, and Rachel straightened, staring toward the mountain trail.

"Someone is coming." Did she need to run back to the trees? Perhaps the Barkleys were returning. Had Amy told her husband of Rachel's plight and persuaded him to speak to Chief Red Wolf? Fear clutched at her, and Rachel let go of the edge of the hide.

"It is the hunters," West Wind cried with joy. She dropped the deerskin and ran toward the center of the village.

Rachel followed her, straining to count the warriors, to make sure all the men had returned. Suddenly she stopped and stared at the lead rider. Running Elk had gone out on a red horse, she was certain, but he was returning on a paint—the beautiful, high-strung stallion he had recently begun to train.

⁓

On the second day out from the Arapaho village, Tom tried to put Milton's bridle on the chestnut stallion. The horse fought him so savagely that he decided to wait until they were home and he could confine the animal. Matt thought that was wise. No sense risking losing the horse in the open spaces. Tom continued to ride Milton and lead the stallion. Matt could tell from the set of his mouth that Tom was disappointed in the trade he'd been forced to accept.

Although the reddish stallion was healthy and well muscled, he lacked stamina, and his pronounced Roman nose was a deplorable trait that would probably be passed to his offspring. That evening Tom minutely inspected his new acquisition and proclaimed him to be at least twelve years old.

"What do you want to do?" Matt asked. He didn't relish the idea of heading back to Red Wolf's village, but if Tom insisted, he'd go.

However, his brother only glanced toward where Amy prepared their supper of beans, bacon, and coffee and said, "I won't chance doing anything with Running Elk in the mood he's in."

"Whatever you say, T.R. We could take Amy home then go back."

Tom shook his head. "No, I can't see how it would help things to confront the chief and tell him his son is nothing but a thief. That wouldn't endear me to Red Wolf, and his friendship is valuable to me and the other settlers in these parts."

"This horse isn't worth what you gave for the paint, T.R."

"I know. But there's more at stake than embarrassing the chief over his son's behavior. There's that white girl to think about. I wouldn't want to risk causing her any trouble. From what Amy tells me, we could make her life get worse in a hurry if we interfered." Tom smiled and gritted his teeth. "Guess I'll name this horse Sadder, to go along with your Wiser."

Matt chuckled. "Do you really think going back there would endanger Rachel Haynes?"

Tom looked off toward the northwest, where the mountains were backed by a rose and amethyst sky. "It could. And do you really think Amy would let me go back there again to talk horses with Red Wolf and not bring up the subject of Miss Haynes?"

Matt sighed. "I've been thinking a lot about her, too. Rachel seems to respect the chief, and she says they haven't mistreated her, but she's afraid of Running Elk, T.R. She doesn't want to be tied to him, and I can't say as I blame her. But she seems to prefer marrying him and maybe taking abuse from him to causing a rift between him and his father."

"The rift is already there." Tom smiled, and Matt turned to see Amy approaching them.

"Supper's ready," she called.

"Good," Tom said. "The smell of that bacon has been causing my stomach no end of consternation."

They sat down near the campfire, and Tom asked the Lord's blessing on their meal. The four horses grazed peacefully in the mountain meadow as the light faded and darkness settled about them.

"Can we stop at the fort on the way home?" Amy asked.

"I thought you wanted to tear home and cuddle your young'uns," Tom said. "I do, but. . ."

"Want to see if there's a letter from the major?" Matt asked. Amy's father had left Fort Bridger at the start of the Civil War. But instead of his planned retirement in Albany, Major Travis had gone to Washington, D.C., as an aide to the secretary of war.

She shrugged. "That and. . .I was hoping maybe we could send a telegram to Minnesota."

"Minnesota?" Tom stopped with a spoonful of beans halfway to his mouth.

"That's where Rachel Haynes was captured," Matt said. "But she thinks all her kin were killed that day."

"We could find out for sure." Amy's pleading gaze was for Tom only.

Matt rose, stretching. "I'll take first watch, T.R."

He ambled away from the fireside. At least Amy wasn't begging her husband to turn around and go back to Red Wolf's village. Maybe this was the best way. Find out if Rachel had relatives living. If she did, that might make it easier to persuade her to leave the Arapaho.

Why can't she simply refuse to marry Running Elk? Amy would, in her situation.

Elk Calf Woman would. If Rachel could only see beyond her fear and stop viewing herself as a captive, she might dare to assert her independence, even against the chief's son.

As he approached the grazing horses, Wiser raised his head and whickered softly. Matt strode over to him and stroked his forelock. He wanted to go back, he realized. No matter how belligerent Running Elk was, Matt wanted to see Rachel again. See her and take her out of the Indian village.

Rachel, his heart cried, *let us help you!* Her solemn eyes and trembling lips were clear in his memory. She wanted her freedom; he knew she did.

Matt checked the picket line on the stallion and circled the other horses, praying as he walked.

Lord, show us how to help her. You brought us into her life. Surely You have a purpose in that. Is she hoping, even now, that we'll do something in spite of her words?

The thought that Running Elk might have returned to his father's village demanding to choose not only his horse but also his wife turned Matt's blood as cold as the mountain stream they camped beside. He tried to fight the urgency that rose in his breast.

Keep her safe, Lord. Strengthen her. Help her to rely on Your grace. Show her that You haven't forgotten her. And, Lord. . . He paused, looking back toward the campfire where Tom and Amy were spreading their bedrolls. *Lord, if You can use us to help her, I'd be much obliged. And if not. . .if You'd at least allow me to know that she's safe, Lord.*

He tried to imagine her back among the whites, dressed in a calico gown and a broad-brimmed sunbonnet, her hair falling in loose curls about her shoulders, not confined in plaits bound by rawhide thongs. The vision made him draw a sharp breath.

Knowing that Rachel was safe was suddenly more important than any other purpose in Matt's life. She needed a champion. Why not Matthew Barkley?

Lord, I'm finding it real hard to ride away from her, he confessed. *I need a big dose of wisdom and patience right about now.*

He compassed the campsite slowly, focusing on the night sounds, but still in his mind he saw Rachel Haynes's shy glances, tossed toward him almost unwillingly. In spite of her words, had he seen a plea for his help in those glances?

Chapter 5

Matt rode up the winding trail to the Barkley ranch. The barn's roof came into view, then the house, woodshed, and other outbuildings. Every time he approached the ranch these days, Matt marveled at how it had changed. His father had made a good start on the homestead, but under Tom's loving labor, it had become a thriving enterprise.

The barn was three times as large as the one their father had built nearly twenty years earlier. The old barn was now a henhouse and feed storage shed. The house had grown, too. Tom had enlarged it after little Ben was born, adding two more rooms and a wide porch. The result was an airy, comfortable home with room for a few more kids, if Tom and Amy were so blessed.

Meanwhile, the couple made it clear that Matt was welcome to stay in their home as long as he wished. He'd helped Tom enclose the old loft, and that was his room now. He came and went often when he was stationed at Fort Bridger, five miles away, staying with Tom and Amy whenever he had a night's leave. Before his cavalry unit went back East to fight the Confederacy, Tom had signed over half the original sixty-acre homestead to Matt.

Matt had protested, saying Tom was the settled one and the one who had made all the improvements to the property. But Tom insisted. When Matt got out of the army—when, not if—he'd want a place to come back to, a piece of land to call his own.

Their father's homestead on the Blacks Fork of the Green River was small, but over the last decade Tom had gained title to another one hundred twenty acres that included some grazing land. When his best friend, Mike Brown, left the army in 1860, Tom had sold him a forty-acre parcel on the side of his property farthest from the homestead. The two had delved into the horse-breeding business, and from what Matt could see, they were on their way to success.

As Matt rode into the barnyard, Tom raised his hat and waved to him from the fence bordering one of the corrals. He stood outside the fence, holding his young son, Ben, secure on the top rail. Matt could see that Mike was inside the enclosure, riding Sadder. Tom's name for the bright chestnut stallion had stuck.

"Any mail?" Tom called as his brother rode closer.

"A letter from the major, and there's something for Mike from Kentucky." Matt slid off Wiser's back and leaned on the fence on the other side of Ben. The little boy immediately wrapped his arms around Matt's head and squeezed, knocking his hat off.

"Hey, Benjamin!" Matt protested. "You hug rough!"

"Uncle Mike says that horse is gonna earn his keep, or he'll make jerky out of him!"

Matt laughed and retrieved his hat then hoisted Ben onto his shoulders.

Tom shook his head and plucked a piece of grass to chew on. "Worst bargain I ever made. I'm not sure I even want to breed this stud to any of our mares, Matthew. I mean, look at him! That buckskin we saw down Echo Canyon last spring moved better than this plug."

Matt watched the red horse trot around the corral with minced steps, fighting Mike's hands. "What does Mike say?"

"Says he's probably never had steel in his mouth before, and he may be too old to retrain."

"So put a hackamore on him."

"I did."

"And?"

Tom spat in the dry grass. "Tossed me off like a sack of laundry."

Matt tried to hold back his laugh but couldn't suppress a grin. "Wish I'd been here."

"Daddy went flyin'!" Ben chirped.

"Ha! I hope your momma didn't see it."

"No, she didn't," Tom said, "and you don't have to tell her."

"It's our secret," Ben said solemnly.

"Well, sure." Matt held on to Ben's feet to keep the boy from kicking his chest. "Hold still, fella. You're squirmy today."

Mike stopped the stallion in front of them.

"I dunno, T.R., this one's not what we wanted, but we might make something of him."

"But do we want to?"

Tom's morose delivery brought a smile from Mike. "Beats fightin' Indians."

Matt grinned as he fished in his shirt pocket for Mike's letter. His brother couldn't have asked for a better business partner. Mike's sunny temperament countered Tom's pessimism. Tom could pick the best horse out of a herd in seconds, and Mike had a way of making the most ornery equines behave. Between the two of them, they couldn't go wrong in this business.

"Got a letter for you, Mike." He held out the envelope.

Mike stretched forward and took it, squinting as he eyed the address. "Would you mind giving it to Lydia? Looks like it's from my cousin, and I'll read it later."

"Sure." Matt craned his neck and tried to look up at his nephew. "You coming in with me, Ben?"

"Huh-uh. Put me down, Uncle Matt."

"Sure thing." He lifted the boy high and swung him into Tom's arms then accepted the letter from Mike.

"Nothing from Minnesota?" Tom asked.

Matt shook his head.

"Well, it's only been a week or so since you sent the telegram." Tom shrugged. "Might be we won't hear anything back."

"Somebody's got to tell us something, even if it's just that they don't know of any Hayneses." The thought that Rachel Haynes might truly be forgotten by the world at large dismayed Matt. She was a courageous woman, and she deserved to be remembered. Someone should be crossing the plains to claim her and protect her.

"Maybe they're making inquiries," Tom said.

Matt nodded. "I hope we hear something soon. T.R., if we don't—"

"What if we don't?"

That stymied Matt. A thousand times in the last two weeks he'd asked himself that question. Was it his obligation to do something for Rachel if there was no one else to fight for her? Was it his right to claim an interest in her life?

He was interested, there was no denying that. Every time he closed his eyes, he saw her poignant face.

"She needs help."

Tom shook his head. "Not if she doesn't want it. She's strong, Matt. She's survived two years under harsh conditions, and she told you she doesn't want to leave them."

"That's not what she said."

"Isn't it?"

"She said she couldn't leave. It would cause trouble."

"Oh, and us riding back up there wouldn't?"

Mike Brown had followed the exchange in silence, but now he smiled at Matt. "I dunno, I keep hearing about that Haynes girl, and it seems to me you're taking it a mite personal, Matthew. Have you considered that they may have held the ritual and she's now Mrs. Running Elk?"

Tom chuckled at Mike's phraseology, but Matt was angered by the thought.

"T.R., we've got to go back."

The stallion began to throw his head and prance. Mike forced him into a controlled canter, circling the corral.

"Best take Amy her father's letter."

"But—"

"No buts." Tom's eyes were hard for an instant, and Matt's old resentment of his big brother flared on principle, but then Tom's face softened. "Look, you know Lydia's going to have that baby any day, and Mike won't leave her this close to her time. Amy won't, either, and the two of us can't go off on a wild goose chase alone, leaving them here to deliver a baby and take care of Ben and Molly."

"Are you saying you'd go back to Red Wolf's village with me after Lydia has the baby?" Matt searched Tom's face for a sign of encouragement.

"I dunno." Tom frowned and slouched against the fence, holding Ben steady. "Maybe if we found out she has some folks to go to."

"I won't leave her there, T.R."

They locked gazes, and Tom pursed his lips. "Have you thought about what it would do to Red Wolf's village? We could ride up there with a military detachment and demand they release her, and then what? Pray, Matt. It's clear what you want. It's not clear what Rachel Haynes wants, and I'm not sure it's clear what God wants."

Matt stood another long moment, trying to reason his way out of that, but he couldn't find a hole in the fabric of Tom's statement. He turned abruptly and grabbed Wiser's reins. He would put the horse up before taking the letters to the women. That would give him time to soothe his thoughts and banish the image of Rachel's pleading eyes from his mind.

When he entered the house a few minutes later, the smells of roasting meat and baking bread enveloped him. Amy stood over her dishpan scrubbing dishes, and Lydia Brown sat at the kitchen table stitching what appeared to be a tiny undershirt.

Baby clothes, Matt surmised. Lydia and Mike's first child would arrive soon, he hoped. He knew she was uncomfortable in the summer heat, and it was all he could do to keep from staring at her enlarged form. Little Molly, Tom and Amy's youngest, toddled toward him, giving him a welcome distraction. Matt placed the bundle he'd brought on the table and stooped to swing the flaxen-haired tot into his arms.

"Matt!" Molly cried, holding on to him with a fierce hug.

"That's *Uncle* Matt," Amy said, glancing up from her work with a smile.

"I brought you ladies the black thread you wanted." Matt nodded toward the package. "They had some brown, too, so I threw in a spool of that."

"Thank you, Matt," Lydia said.

He smiled at her, thinking how pretty she was, even in the imminent motherhood stage. He knew she had miscarried twice already, and that she and Mike were ecstatic in the knowledge that this time she was able to carry the baby to full term. It was an unspoken matter for the most part, but Tom had clued him in when he first came home from the army.

It took some getting used to—babies underfoot all the time and women in a delicate condition. Matt was with Mike Brown when he met and courted Lydia along the Oregon Trail four summers ago, and he knew that under normal circumstances, Lydia was as robust and active as Amy. Despite her Eastern finishing school education, she'd helped Mike stand off a war party of Sioux before Mike finally persuaded her to marry him.

Looking at her now, that was hard to believe, but Matt had been there. He'd ridden out with the cavalry unit and seen the carnage on the hillside after the battle the two had survived. Lydia still owned the Sioux pony the sergeant gave her after the skirmish.

"There's a letter from Mike's cousin," he said, pulling the wrinkled missive from his pocket once more. "He said to give it to you."

"Well, thanks." Lydia grinned and put aside her sewing.

Matt nodded. "How are you doing?" It was the closest he could bring himself to allude to her condition.

Amy laughed as she dried her hands. "She's about as comfortable as a coyote sitting on a cactus. What do you think?"

Matt felt his cheeks flush. Should he apologize?

Lydia's smile was genuine, though dark smudges beneath her eyes told him she was weary of her pregnancy.

"Actually, I'm doing pretty well today, thank you."

"This is the coolest day we've had all week," Amy agreed. "That's why I'm baking."

"It smells like Mom's apple pie." Matt took a lingering breath, savoring the spicy trace in the air.

"I'm pleased to hear that. I used her recipe." Amy's blue eyes turned sober. "Any mail for us, Matt?"

"Sorry, I almost forgot. There's something from the major." Matt handled the letter reverently as he delivered it to her. He had served under Major Benjamin Travis at Fort Bridger. Only later, when they had both gone east into the fray, had he realized what a fine officer Travis was. On the battlefield and off, Matt had observed officers whose ineptitude made Travis appear to be a genius, and a godly one at that.

"Nothing from Minnesota, then?" Amy took her father's letter without her usual enthusiasm, and Matt knew it was because she'd hoped for word of the Haynes family.

"No, nothing. The telegraph operator says he'll send a rider out here if they hear something."

"That was good of him."

Matt shrugged. No need to tell Amy he'd bribed the operator with two dollars from the hoard of back pay he'd received on mustering out last spring.

"Is your father going to retire?" he asked as Amy eagerly opened the major's letter.

"Not until the war is over, I'm afraid." She scanned the neat lines silently.

The old feelings of guilt nagged at Matt's heart anew. Was he right to leave the army when the conflict wasn't over? After Chickamauga and Knoxville, his zeal for the war had dissipated. He was worn-out and discouraged, and he'd prayed for the chance to return to Wyoming. That opportunity came in the spring of 1864, and he took it, fleeing the bloody East and separating from the army without regret.

But now, hearing reports of his former comrades in arms striving to finish the job, doubts assailed him. Was it right for him to be in a cozy home with his brother's family when others were on the battlefield, desperately fighting to save the Union?

Maybe I ought to reenlist. The thought scared him. He realized he had broken out in a sweat and sent up a fractured prayer. *If You want me here, Lord, give me peace.*

If only he had a purpose, like Tom and Mike did. But Matt felt footloose, not a true part of the ranching operation. He was welcome here; that was not in question. Tom had even asked if he wanted to help with the horse ranch. But that business would probably not support a third household, Matt realized. The thirty acres in his name, half their father's original homestead, might be enough for him to eke out an existence. If he ever married and had a family, he'd have to consider enlarging his holdings.

That line of thinking brought him back to Rachel Haynes once more. But that was a futile thought. Given a choice, she wouldn't have the chief's son for her husband. Why would she have a war-weary ex-soldier like him? Still, Tom and Mike had both found brides on the Wyoming plains. Why couldn't he? Maybe it was time to start building a cabin on his land and trust God to provide him a wife to share it.

"Father wrote this from Baltimore a month ago," Amy said with a frown. "He was on his way north on business for the army and hopes for a chance to visit my sister in Albany before returning to Washington."

"That would be nice," Lydia said.

"Yes, he hasn't seen Elaine in years."

The door swung open, and Tom ducked inside, setting Ben on his feet and reaching over the lintel for his rifle. "Two Indians riding up from the river. Got your gun, Matt?"

"In the barn with my saddle."

Tom glanced at Amy. "Get Lydia and the kids in the back room until we know what's going on."

Matt followed his brother out the door, wondering if he had time to reach the barn and get the Spencer repeating rifle he'd brought home from the war. Mike had dismounted and was taking cover behind the gate, his musket aimed at the trail. Peering toward the river, Matt saw the two horses coming.

Tom hopped off the end of the porch and slipped around the corner of the house, prepared to defend his family and property, but Matt stood on the porch, his gaze riveted on the approaching mounts.

"T.R., that's the paint you wanted."

Tom and Mike both stared at him. Tom lowered his rifle and stepped back up onto the porch.

"There seems to be just the two of them," Mike called. "Are they friends of yours?"

Tom smiled and relaxed. "That's Red Wolf."

"Himself?" Mike straightened and squinted toward the old warrior.

"Sure enough," Tom agreed.

Matt said nothing. He had long since left eyeing the chief and instead was watching the other rider. His chest ached as he inhaled. There was no doubt.

"Rachel."

Tom threw him a swift glance. "You didn't tell me she was pretty." He laid his rifle on the boards at his feet and jumped off the porch, striding out to meet the riders. Matt went more slowly down the steps and followed.

Red Wolf's eyes lit when he recognized his friend, and though he did not smile, Matt could tell he was pleased to have found Tom. The paint stallion he rode still stepped high but was streaked with sweat. Rachel's sorrel mare stumbled as they entered the barnyard but recovered quickly, plodding on with her head drooping in near exhaustion.

Matt couldn't look away from Rachel. After what must have been a grueling journey, she sat on the mare's back with dignity, balancing effortlessly on the flat leather saddle the Indians sometimes used. She wore the short buckskin dress of the native women over soft leather leggings, with beaded moccasins on her feet, and her hair was bound in braids, the way it was the first time they met. Her gaze swept over the ranch house and barn then landed on Tom. She was frightened, Matt guessed, or worried at least.

She looked toward Matt then, and he smiled. Something leaped into her eyes—recognition? No, more than that. Welcome. Pleasure. Satisfaction.

Joy careened through Matt's body. He wanted to laugh and to run to her and help her off the horse, but his brother's measured behavior reminded him of Arapaho etiquette.

"Welcome," Tom said as the horses halted before them. "It is an honor to have you visit my home."

Red Wolf nodded. "It has long been my desire to see your lodge."

"Won't you come inside?"

Matt stepped forward. "Chief Red Wolf, let me take care of your horses while you and Miss Haynes greet Mrs. Barkley."

The chief looked at Rachel then back at the brothers. He focused on Matt with a stern frown, and Matt shivered. His military training warned him to be alert. This was a potential enemy. But his caution was tempered by the knowledge that Red Wolf was known to be a peaceful man, and even more by the fact that Rachel was watching him.

"Brother of Comes as a Friend."

"Yes, sir." Matt raised his chin and returned the chief's gaze. For a long moment he stared into the dark, intelligent eyes. He could see why Tom liked this man and felt he could learn much from him. He hoped the old man could see honesty and goodwill in his face.

At last the chief nodded.

"Stands in Timber asked me to bring her to you."

Chapter 6

Rachel followed the chief as he walked with Thomas Barkley toward the house. Her heart thumped as she approached it. She had not been inside a building since Minnesota, and a knot seemed to tighten in her chest. She looked over her shoulder and saw another man join Matthew Barkley as he led the stallion and the red mare toward a fenced corral.

I thought this was their home. How many people live here? And where is Amy, the golden-haired woman?

Thomas Barkley was holding the door open, waiting for her, and she hastened to climb the porch steps. She gulped and nodded to him, passing quickly into the dim interior.

The chief stood in the middle of the room, and Rachel looked around. What did Red Wolf see? Did he feel as uneasy as she did? Cooking smells assailed her. *Bread!* How long since she had smelled the yeasty fragrance of wheat bread baking? A sweeter odor tickled her nose and made her salivate.

Their kitchen is larger than the chief's tepee! A quick survey showed her both a fireplace and a cookstove, two windows with clear glass panes, shelves holding dishes and containers of all descriptions, two tables and a half dozen chairs, as well as a rough stairway leading to an upper level.

"Amy! Sweetheart, we have guests," Tom called, stepping toward a closed door.

The door opened, and Amy Barkley came into the room. Her gaze lit on Rachel, and she broke into a smile that could not be feigned.

"Rachel! My dear, how wonderful!" Amy hugged her, and Rachel breathed in her spicy scent.

Amy turned toward the chief, her golden braid swinging against the back of her blue cotton shirt. She strode toward him, both hands extended. "Chief Red Wolf, this is indeed an honor. Won't you join us for some refreshment?"

The chief allowed her to grasp his hands and gave her the closest thing to a smile that Rachel had ever observed on his face.

A small boy peeked around the edge of the door to the next room, and then a tiny girl wearing a short yellow dress toddled out and grabbed Amy's skirt.

"Hey now, Molly!" Tom whisked the baby up into his arms.

Chief Red Wolf eyed the child with delight. "Your girl child?"

Tom grinned. "Yes, sir, this is Molly Louise Barkley."

This time there was no doubt the old man was smiling. "Hair like the breast of a sage grouse."

Amy beamed. "You must meet our son. Come, Benjamin."

Little Ben came slowly into the room, staring up at the chief.

Tom knelt beside him and placed one hand on his shoulder, holding Molly in his other arm. "This is Red Wolf, son. He's a great chief of the Arapaho nation. He's a guest of honor in our home."

Ben swallowed hard and stuck out his right hand.

Solemnly the chief clasped the boy's fingers. "You will be tall like your father."

"Yes, sir," Ben whispered.

Red Wolf nodded. "In my village, your father is known as a friend. If you come with him to my village, you will also be welcomed as a friend to the people."

The young boy could only nod.

From some hidden pouch or pocket, Red Wolf brought out a small wooden carving and held it out to Ben. The boy looked up at his father, and Tom nodded at him.

"The turtle is a sign of our people," the chief said.

Ben took it and examined it then smiled up at the old man.

Red Wolf took out another carving and held it before Molly. Her gaze riveted on it, and she reached for it, pulling it toward her mouth.

Red Wolf laughed. "A grouse for the white-haired child."

Tom smiled and looked toward his wife. "Maybe we'd best put that away until she's a little older, Amy." He stood up. "Won't you sit, Chief? My wife will bring us some cider and some..." He glanced toward his wife as he passed Molly to her.

"Apple pie," she said quickly. "And I hope our guests will stay and have supper with us later. Roast beef, biscuits, carrots, and fresh peas."

The chief gave her a slight nod that seemed to Rachel a bit regretful. "I must not stay long. But Stands in Timber will stay."

Rachel's pulse raced as she noted Amy's pleased smile.

Tom placed a chair for Red Wolf and drew another out for himself. "Then sit with me a few minutes, sir, and tell me what has brought you here alone with the young woman."

Amy whisked the two children back into the other room, and Rachel caught another voice—a female voice she was sure—before Amy gently closed the door and went back to her cooking area.

Red Wolf sat gingerly on the edge of the chair, and Rachel knew he would be more comfortable outside, sitting on the ground. But when Thomas Barkley came to visit the Arapaho, he sat on the buffalo robes and smoked the pipe. Red Wolf would return the courtesy by sitting in a chair and eating apple pie.

The door opened, and Matt Barkley and the other man entered. Tom said to the chief, "Sir, you know my brother, Matthew. The man with him is a true friend, Michael Brown."

"Brown."

"Yes, sir."

The chief nodded.

"Mike Brown and I work the ranch together. We are partners in raising horses. He's very good at training them."

Red Wolf eyed Mike with respect. "You have many horses."

"We're building our herd," Mike said.

Tom asked, "Sir, do you mind if these two men sit with us and hear what you have to say?"

The chief glanced at Rachel then at Amy who was taking a pie from the oven.

"If you wish, the women can leave us," Tom said.

"No. They stay. It is the white man's way, and we have come to your lodge."

Tom smiled. "There's truth to that. I never make an important decision without consulting my wife."

Amy set the pie down. "I'll bring you men and Rachel some refreshments, Tom. Go ahead and talk. Boys, grab a chair."

Mike and Matt hesitated, but Rachel stepped toward Amy. "Please let me help you," she said.

Amy's broad smile made her feel less out of place. "I'd be happy to have you, Rachel." The men all sat around the table, and Amy set four cups—two thick ironstone and two tin—on her narrower worktable and brought a jug from a corner. "If you'd just pour the cider, please."

Rachel went about the task carefully, filling each of the four cups to precisely the same level as she listened to the chief's voice.

"Barkley," he said. "My friend."

Thomas Barkley nodded in silence.

The chief raised his chin and looked at the three white men. "Our people have customs not like yours, but we can live in peace."

"Yes, we can." Tom leaned back to let Amy place his mug before him, and Rachel stood back to watch.

"The day is short, and so I will be short as well. When a woman of our tribe wants to marry, we do not tell her who she must choose."

Rachel saw Matthew look her way, and she quickly lowered her eyes, her pulse racing. Being in his presence again brought on unaccustomed feelings. She wished she knew for sure that he had meant what he said about asking for him and his family. Was it presumptuous of her to invade their household like this? He had yet to speak to her directly, but his gray eyes radiated intense emotions that she could almost believe were relief and gladness.

"That is also our custom," Tom said. "The man and the woman have equal

say in the matter."

Amy went back to her worktable and placed four forks in Rachel's hand. Rachel stared down at them. How long since she had eaten with silverware?

"For the men," Amy whispered.

Rachel nodded and tiptoed toward the table. She tried not to make a sound as she circled the table and slid a fork in beside each man, resting it on the polished pine tabletop. She served the chief first, then Tom, who nodded at her.

"Thank you, ma'am," the man called Brown murmured. She couldn't help throwing him a quick glance, as his voice was different from the others.

She drew back and edged around behind Matthew. Even though the chief began speaking once more, Matthew watched her, and she felt a flush rising in her cheeks.

"My son, Running Elk, wished to marry, and he made his choice."

Rachel reached forward to slip Matt's fork onto the table.

"He chose Stands in Timber."

Her cheeks were on fire now, and she dropped the fork. Matt's hand shot out to clamp it against the table and stop its clatter. Rachel pressed her lips together and lowered her eyes, knowing all the men but Red Wolf were staring at her.

"I'm sorry," she whispered.

"It's fine," Matt said. His face was inches from hers, and she drew back, shaking.

"Rachel, could you help me?" Amy's voice was cheery, and the men turned their attention back to the chief.

Rachel hurried to Amy's side.

"Forgive me," Amy said softly. "I'd no idea the chief would get right to the point today. It usually takes hours. I shouldn't have sent you over there."

"It is nothing," Rachel said. In silence she stood and watched Amy's deft hands as she cut the pie and lifted the generous slices onto plates.

"The woman my son chose did not wish to be his wife," the chief went on. "In our tribe, it is her right to refuse a man."

The men all nodded, and Brown said, "It's the same in our society, Chief." His soft tones again drew Rachel's attention.

"He's from the South," Amy whispered.

"Yes," the chief answered Brown, "but I did not know her heart. Not until my daughter came to me and told me Stands in Timber was sad. You must understand, we are fond of this young woman. She has been a hard worker for the village. I expected someday she would take one of our men, and when my son said he wished to have her, I was pleased."

Rachel darted a glance toward the men and saw that they all gave the chief their rapt attention.

"My son and I do not always agree." Red Wolf raised his mug and sniffed it then took a small sip and set it down. "I hoped he would marry soon and maybe. . . I think you say, 'settle down.' "

Tom nodded with a wry smile. "It generally helps a young man mature when he puts down roots and starts a family."

Amy arranged the plates on a tray. "I'll serve them," she said to Rachel, and without waiting for a response, she quickly rounded the table, placing a dish before each of the men.

"Thank you," Matt and Mike said.

The chief looked at the pie for a moment then looked up at her. "You honor me with special food."

Amy smiled. "I hope you enjoy it."

Tom grinned at her as she held out his plate. He immediately took a bite, and Matt and Mike also began to eat.

The chief watched Tom for a moment then lifted his fork and prodded the piecrust with it. Rachel held her breath as he lifted a bite of steaming apples and pastry to his mouth.

"Hot, but delicious," Tom said. He took another forkful and blew on it.

Red Wolf blew gently on his bite of pie then placed it in his mouth. He sat very still.

They all waited, Amy with an anxious air.

The chief swallowed and stood up, facing her. "You have great skill, Yellow Hair Woman."

"Thank you, sir. My husband's mother left the directions of how she used to make this pie, and I followed her instructions. I'm pleased that you like it."

"It is good for the young wives to learn from the older women." The chief sat down again and lifted a large bite, blew on it, and put it in his mouth. He closed his eyes as he chewed, and Amy walked toward Rachel grinning.

Suddenly Rachel wanted to laugh. She turned away and hid her mouth with her hand. Amy's merry eyes danced as she began to cut two more pieces of pie.

"You must try it."

Rachel accepted the dish Amy held out to her and took a bite. The sweet, spicy apples and flaky pastry flooded her senses with memories of long ago. She savored the flavor, swallowing reluctantly.

"He is right," she whispered. "I've never tasted anything so delicious."

The chief began to speak again, and Amy motioned toward two stools. Rachel sat down with her in the corner and continued to eat her pie in small bites while listening to Red Wolf's tale.

"When you came to my village, I was glad to see you."

"I felt the same," Tom replied.

"I was happy to trade with you, because you have been like a brother to me."

Tom nodded. "Your regard means much to me."

"I traded the paint stallion to you for your herd."

There was a moment of silence then Tom said, "Yes, sir."

"But you did not come home with the paint horse." Chief Red Wolf's voice shook with emotion or fatigue.

"Sir, I—"

Red Wolf held up his hand, and Tom stopped speaking.

"You have long been my friend. My son knew this. He wanted the horse, yes, but it had not been decided that it was his. I wished to show my respect to you by selling you one of the best I had, and I decided to sell you the paint horse."

"I appreciate that."

The chief nodded. "And you returned that honor by giving me a large price."

"Well, sir, I believe in paying full value for something like that."

"Yes. When I saw him return riding the stallion, I was angry."

"I'm sorry that happened."

"Not your fault, Barkley. He told me his story. Ha!" The chief shook his head. "I get the men who were with him one at a time. They cannot lie to me, those boys."

Rachel gasped. The chief was showing his disdain for the warriors who followed Running Elk by calling them boys. She had never heard him speak so before. His son must have hurt him deeply by cheating his friend.

"I knew this about the horse, that you were treated bad." Red Wolf leaned back in his chair. "Then my son tells me he wishes to marry Stands in Timber. So I think he will be a better man. I tell him this is a good decision."

Rachel stopped eating the savory pie and looked down at her hands, holding the green ceramic plate. She hadn't guessed the chief regarded her so highly, and the fact that she had disappointed him hurt.

"When my daughter came to me saying that Stands in Timber was sad because she did not wish to marry my son, I was also sad. I talked to the girl. I asked her what she wanted. She is a woman, she can marry or not, as she pleases. And she told me she wished to go to Fort Bridger."

Rachel's chest ached, and she wondered where all this parlaying would take her. Almost she regretted that she wouldn't be Red Wolf's daughter-in-law.

The chief smiled at Tom. "I asked her why. Why Fort Bridger? She can return to the whites if she wishes, but why Fort Bridger?"

He paused, and Tom said, "Why indeed, sir?"

"Ah. She told me that a man lived there—a man named Barkley. I said, 'Thomas Barkley is my friend.' But she said, 'No, not him. His brother. His brother said that he could help me.'"

Rachel felt her cheeks flame once more. She threw an apologetic glance at Amy.

Amy was smiling at her, and she reached over and pressed Rachel's arm. "I'm glad you had the courage to tell him and to come to us," she whispered.

"So, you see," the chief said, "I wanted to change things. I wanted to restore the friendship between us, and I wanted to make Stands in Timber happy. If she chose to stay with us, I would be glad. But I do not ask her to stay with us and be sad. And I do not ask her to marry a man she fears." His voice sank at the end, and Rachel could barely hear his shamed denunciation of his son.

Her heart swelled with gratitude to the old man. He was willing to go against his son, who was young and strong, to make her happy and to offer her freedom.

"It was the right thing to do," Matt Barkley said, and the chief looked at him.

"Yes, Friend's Brother. It was right to bring her here, to you and to Yellow Hair Woman. You were kind to her, she told me, though none of our people knew. And it was also right to bring the horse to you." He turned to face Tom. "The paint stallion is yours, my friend. You bought him."

"Thank you, Chief. I will gladly exchange him for the horse your son left with me."

Red Wolf nodded and stood. "I must go. The day is short." He looked at Matt as the other men got to their feet. "Please bring me the red horse."

"Yes, sir."

Matt hurried out, and the chief extended his hand to Tom.

"I am sorry my son acted as he did. It was without my knowledge."

"I know that, sir," said Tom.

"Running Elk wanted this stallion for his own warhorse, but now. . ." Red Wolf sighed. "I have sent him away with no horses. I told him not to come back until he is a true man and has learned not to treat his father's friend poorly."

"I regret that this has deepened the rift between you."

The old man shook his head. "It will be well. A few of his friends went with him. Someday he will come back, and we will sit down together. But you will take Stands in Timber and treat her with kindness for my sake?"

"Of course. We'll help her find her family if she has anyone left."

The chief nodded. "Thank you. Next time you come to my village, you will not be mistreated." He turned and stepped toward Rachel, and she jumped to her feet. "I speak to you as a father. We will not forget you. My people will welcome you if you wish to return."

Rachel felt tears well up in her eyes. "Thank you."

"Do not dishonor your tribe."

She nodded, and he turned away.

The men went outside, and Amy took the plate from Rachel's hand and set it down.

"Are you all right?"

Rachel nodded, staring at the closed door. It was done. She was back in the white world, and she was terrified.

Chapter 7

As Matt led the chestnut stallion to the corral fence and tied him securely to a post, Mike came and leaned on the fence.

"Want help?"

"Yeah, can you get Rachel's mare?"

"Think she really told him she wants to marry you instead of his son?"

Matt scowled at him, not wanting to admit the anticipation that idea brought him. "He didn't say that."

Mike laughed and ambled toward the barn.

Matt spread the chief's wool blanket on Sadder's back and lifted his saddle off the fence rail. It was made of two sections of tanned hide sewn together and stuffed with deer hair. Wooden stirrups hung from it on rawhide straps. Matt had seen them before and always marveled at how the Plains Indians could ride so well with these crude saddles or no saddle at all.

When he had transferred it and the hackamore to Sadder, Matt led the chestnut stallion out to the dooryard. Mike came behind him with the second horse.

Tom and Red Wolf stood together before the house.

"You are welcome to stay, Chief," Tom was saying. "The sun is dropping. Sleep here and set out in the morning."

Red Wolf shook his head. "Four men wait for me down the river, beyond Fort Bridger. I must be there today." He looked at the sorrel mare Mike was holding. "Barkley, you keep the mare for the woman to ride."

"For Stands in Timber?" Tom asked.

"Yes. My people did not steal her, but she was taken from her home. She lost everything. I will not let her leave us with nothing."

"I'll tell her the horse is your gift to her. But I know you traded for her when she came to you from the Sioux. If her father were alive, I'm sure he would want to repay you. You've treated her well. Let me give you some mares for your breeding herd."

Chief Red Wolf held up his hand in dismissal, and Tom said no more. The old man mounted the chestnut stallion. Matt held his breath, expecting the horse to erupt in protest, but he only sidestepped and pranced as the chief turned him toward the river. Red Wolf cantered away without looking back. Matt watched his straight back and flying black hair until he was out of sight.

"Now that's a horseman," Mike said softly.

"Too bad we don't have him to help us train these nags." Tom walked over to assess the sorrel.

"This is a good mare, T.R.," said Mike. "Four years old, sound, and hacka-more broke. And I wouldn't be surprised if she's bred."

"She belongs to Miss Haynes," Tom said. "I expect that's the only asset she has, besides us."

Mike shrugged. "I guess it's a start on a dowry."

Matt inhaled slowly and began to smile.

"What are you grinning about?" Tom asked.

"I've been praying so hard these last couple of weeks that God would help Rachel. I didn't know how, but I believed He would. Thought maybe we'd wind up taking a cavalry unit up there to get her. But here God brings her to us with no fuss, no hard feelings, and you get your fancy stud back, too."

"God's more powerful than the army," Mike agreed.

"Yes," Tom said. "He changes hearts."

⁓

Amy brought in a pan of hot water and poured it into the tub on the bedroom floor. "Almost ready." She headed back out to the kitchen.

Rachel fingered the smooth, cool cotton dress Amy had laid out on her bed. The bright red calico with blue and yellow flowers was far too flashy. People already stared at her. If she wore this, she would feel like a raging bonfire.

"It's...beautiful," she said. "But..."

"Too fancy?" Lydia asked with a smile as Amy came in with her final pan of hot water.

Rachel ducked her head, not wanting to insult her hostess.

"It's all right," Amy said. "I've got a plain lavender dress you can wear. I just thought that one would compliment your coloring."

"You'll look lovely in anything." Lydia, whom Rachel had learned was married to Michael Brown, stood and gathered up her sewing project. During Chief Red Wolf's stay, Lydia had kept the children quiet in the bedroom. Rachel could see why she had declined to show herself: She was near childbirth and self-conscious about her swollen figure.

"I'll go keep an eye on Molly and Ben while you wash up."

"Here, Rachel." Amy took a skirt and bodice from a peg behind the door. "I think this will fit you."

"I've got three dresses at my house that I haven't been able to wear in months," Lydia said from the doorway. "I may be taller than you, Rachel, but we could turn up the hems."

"You'll be wanting those dresses again soon," Amy said.

Rachel was having a bit of trouble sorting out the clan. "Doesn't she live here?" she asked when Lydia had left them and closed the door.

"No, she and Mike have their own home, down in the hollow. He comes up here to work with Tom most days, and Lydia comes to keep me company." Amy held the skirt up against Rachel's waist. "Yes, try this on. I've got some navy broadcloth, and we can cut out a skirt for you from that tomorrow, but for supper tonight, I think this will do."

"That's not necessary," Rachel said.

Amy looked up in sudden contrition. "I'm sorry. I didn't mean to imply that you shouldn't wear your own things. I just thought. . . Well, I knew you wanted to bathe, and I thought it would be nice to put on something clean."

Rachel swallowed her timidity and took the skirt, holding it up before her. "It's very nice. Do you think the others will mind?"

"What, that you're wearing my clothes? Of course not." Amy slipped her arm around Rachel's shoulders. "Matthew and I have been hoping and praying for two weeks that somehow God would let you leave Red Wolf's village and return to your people. And here you are! I'm thankful to see this prayer answered."

"So am I." A lump constricted Rachel's throat, but she managed a smile. "Thank you for praying. After you left, I thought much about the things you said. I didn't see how God could want me to cause an uproar in the village, and so I kept quiet."

Amy squeezed her shoulders. "You poor thing. I'm not sure I could have stood it, being all alone like that for so long."

"I asked God to strengthen me for whatever lay ahead. Red Wolf was upset with his son, and there was much talk in the village about how he had cheated your husband. It was whispered that the chief would send his son away for dishonoring his name. Then, when Running Elk announced that he wanted me for his wife, the chief seemed to change his mind. He liked the idea, I think, and he spoke kindly to me. I was so overwhelmed I went to the river, back to the spot where you and I and Matthew Barkley talked."

"I remember it well, by the spruce tree."

Rachel nodded. "I knelt and begged God to release me from the marriage."

"But. . ." Amy's eyebrows drew together in a frown. "This is what I don't understand. You only had to speak up. The chief obviously holds you in his regard. He would have listened."

"You would do that. I. . .did not feel I could. In the few days since Running Elk had returned, he and his father did nothing but quarrel. But when he said he would marry me, the chief was happy. He told his son to make gifts to the family I lived with. I did not want to disappoint him and make him angry with his son again."

Amy nodded. "By going along with it, you were a peacemaker. So what happened?" She glanced toward the steaming tub. "Maybe you'd better undress and get in the tub before the water cools off."

Rachel sat on the edge of the bed and removed one moccasin. "What happened was this: Elk Calf Woman. You know her. She showed you to the river the day you came to the village."

"Yes, she's quite a woman."

"Well, she found me by the spruce tree, weeping." Rachel smiled with a little shrug. "Strange how it happened. If I had kept myself calm, she would not have known, but when I went to that spot to pray, the memory of what you and Matthew said returned to me, and I became very. . .homesick, I suppose. I longed for people like myself. I could see that if I married an Arapaho, I would be forever giving up the chance to return to the white world. I wasn't sure God would have me do that, but neither could I deny that I wanted to come here very much."

"So Elk Calf Woman heard you crying?"

"Yes." Rachel began to peel off her leggings. "She took me to her father. I was very frightened, but the chief spoke softly to me. When I admitted I had met you and Matthew, Elk Calf Woman began to shout at her father."

Amy's eyes widened. "What did she say?"

"She. . ." Rachel felt a flush stain her cheeks. "I am not sure I ought to tell you."

Amy was silent for a moment. "Don't, if you don't want to, but I'm very curious."

"Well, she said that her father ought to let me go to the white man. She said she had hoped to be the wife of his brother, but Comes as a Friend rejected her. But if Matthew Barkley wanted me, then her father ought not to refuse to let me go to the man I. . .loved."

Amy blinked twice and inhaled sharply. "She said that?"

Rachel looked down and nodded. "I should not have told you."

"If it's any comfort, Tom told me years ago that the chief's daughter had hoped he would marry her. But your telling of it sheds a bit more light on her character."

"She is proud and very strong. I liked her in some ways. But she scared me, too." Rachel peered at her from beneath her lowered lashes and found that Amy was smiling.

"I can see that. But tell me, is that why you came here? To be near Matthew?"

"No. It wasn't at all what I intended. I started to tell the chief that his daughter was mistaken, that I hardly knew Matthew, and that he had not even hinted at marriage, but the chief was already giving orders. The next thing I knew, he had banished Running Elk from the village. And the following morning, I was riding toward Fort Bridger with the chief and four other men. I couldn't speak in front of them, and the chief seemed determined to deliver me. Besides that, he was riding the horse your husband bought from him. I understood from things he said that he was returning the horse to Thomas Barkley. I feared at first that he was upset with me, but. . .I no longer believe that."

Amy studied her for a long moment. "God has brought you here, Rachel. That is certain. I hope we hear soon from the authorities in Minnesota. And I hope, if none of your family is found living, that you will consider staying here with Tom and me and the children."

Rachel let the offer settle on her heart. This woman who barely knew her was holding before her a chance to live normally with a white family. It was a tremendous sacrifice on Amy's part, and Rachel longed to accept. But doing so would disrupt the household, she knew. She couldn't ask that much of the Barkleys. "That is very kind. I would not wish to trouble you."

"Don't you worry about that." Amy's brilliant smile warmed Rachel's spirit. "I'll leave you to wash now. If you want me to help you wash your hair, just call me."

Rachel nodded and watched her leave the room. She pulled off her doeskin dress and folded it neatly then released her hair from its leather thongs. She laid them on the bright quilt that covered Amy's bed. Glancing about the simple room once more, she took in the colorful touches that made it seem luxurious and welcoming. Amy Barkley knew how to keep a comfortable home.

Already Rachel was beginning to feel a longing for a home of her own. Not a tepee of buffalo hides, but a home like this, where a family gathered in love.

Approaching the tub, she stooped and felt the water. It was warm, like the water that bubbled from the hot springs in the mountains.

A hot bath! She had begged God for many things in the last two years, but this had not entered her mind. Suddenly, she knew there was nothing she craved more. She picked up the cake of soap Amy had left her and stepped gingerly into the tub.

Although supper was served late that evening, the extended family gathered in thanksgiving around the table. Tom offered the blessing, and the dishes Amy and Lydia had prepared were circulated with lively talk. Mike and Tom spoke of their plans for increasing their horse herd, now that they had the stallion they wanted. Lydia and Amy plied Rachel with questions about her life with the Arapaho.

Matt sat midway down the table, between Ben and Mike, caught between the two conversations, listening and putting in a word now and then.

"So, Matt, are you going to help us with the haying tomorrow?" Tom asked.

"Sure, but pretty soon I'd like to start cutting logs for my own cabin."

Silence blanketed the room for a second then Amy cried, "What, you're tired of living with us?"

Matt shrugged. "No, but you folks are getting a mite snug here, and it's time I had my own place."

"What do you want to do on your land, Matt?" Lydia asked.

"Run some beef, I guess. There's always a market for it."

"Well, you help Mike and me cut hay tomorrow, and we'll help you get some logs out the next day, while the hay dries." Tom stood to carve the roast beef. "Pass your plate, please, Miss Haynes."

Rachel handed her plate to Amy, who sat between her and Tom.

"I hope I'm not crowding you," she said to Amy.

"Nonsense. We've got plenty of room. Matthew's just starting to get over his post-army apathy."

"What's that?" Mike asked.

Tom laughed. "You ought to know. When you mustered out, you rode to the fort almost every day and hung around talking to your old cronies."

"That was only because he was watching for letters from Lydia," Amy said. "Once the first one came, he settled right down to build their house, remember?"

"Oh, that's right." Tom placed a large slice of beef on Rachel's plate. "I had to help put that cabin up before I could get a lick of work out of him around the ranch."

Matt watched Rachel's face. She seemed a bit overwhelmed by the talk and laughter. She refused second helpings politely, and he wondered if she was used to such a bounty of food. She was thin, but not to the point of emaciation. He hoped she could adjust easily to the new diet, along with all the other changes that bombarded her.

When the meal was over, Lydia offered to help with the dishes.

"Nonsense," Amy said, stacking the plates. "Mike's going to take you home for a good rest."

"You're too good to us, you and Tom both." Lydia shook her head. "Here you are feeding us half the time, too."

"You were a big help to me today, especially taking care of the children while Chief Red Wolf was here."

"She was just practicing up." Mike squeezed Lydia's hand.

"Well, you'd better make sure she takes it easy now," Amy said. "Don't let her exhaust herself. Rachel will help me with these dishes, won't you?"

Rachel returned Amy's smile. "Of course."

The Browns soon left for their own cabin, and Tom offered to put Molly and Ben to bed. Matt carried the leftover food to Amy's worktable then escaped out the door. He puttered about the barn, removing a few piles of fresh manure and sweeping the chaff from the packed dirt floor in the middle of the barn.

Fifteen minutes later, Tom joined him and carried his lantern to the back of the large tie-up stall they had allotted to the new stallion.

"He seems calm enough in his new home."

"Well, he was snorting some when I first came in," Matt said. "He's not pulling at the halter, though. Not bad for a horse that's probably never been inside in his whole life."

"I don't dare leave him in the corral." Tom hung the lantern on a nail and grabbed a piece of sacking. He edged into the stall beside the horse and began to rub his already glossy coat. "Yessiree, he's a good one." He ran his hand down the paint's near foreleg and lifted it, examining the hoof. "Turned out to be a wise bargain after all."

Matt smiled. "Yep. It sure would save us a lot of work if we didn't have to lock up all the stock at night, though."

"Things aren't as bad as when Pa first came here," Tom admitted, "but I don't want to risk losing my stock or my tools just yet. When things are a little more settled, maybe I'll be more trusting."

Matt went to the wall where their tack hung on pegs and examined the bridle Rachel had used on the mare she rode.

"Braided mane hair," he noted, fingering the long rein attached to the soft leather noseband. "Beats me how they get so much out of their horses without using a bit."

"I saw some bits in their camp. They trade for some, I guess."

"Or steal them."

Tom moved to the other side of the paint. "Takes a lot of patience, to train a horse without a bit, but I suppose it's better for them."

Matt tugged the rein gently, visualizing what the pressure he exerted would do to the horse's nose and poll. "I dunno, T.R. You grew up using a regular bridle. Better stick with it. But it's interesting. How much hay do you reckon you need for the winter?"

"Hard to say. Usually the wind takes the snow away enough that we can put the stock out to graze part of the winter. But you never know when you'll get more snow than normal here, so I'm aiming to prepare for the worst. It pays off in the long run."

Matt nodded. "I remember that one year our horses about starved. I'll help you as much as I can with the hay, but I do want to get my cabin up before snow-fly."

Tom stood and draped one arm over the stallion's back. "Does this domestic bent of yours have anything to do with Miss Haynes?"

"Well, I. . ." Matt shifted from one foot to the other and ran a hand through his hair.

Tom laughed. "You know we're trying to find her folks, Matthew. If she's got kin back East, she probably won't stay here."

"I know."

"You do, huh?"

"Look, I know what you're thinking."

"What am I thinking?" Tom lifted the paint's back foot and stretched his leg out, resting the hoof on his knee.

"That's it too soon to have feelings for her. And I know that. I just. . .T.R., I like her. It's not just because she's pretty, though I don't deny she's easy to look at. And I'm not just feeling sorry for her. If you'd heard her talk that day about how she trusted God to protect her while she was with the Sioux. . .Tom, she was all alone with those Indians. A lot of people would have blamed God and thought He abandoned them, but hard as it was, she kept her faith. I. . .have to admire her for that."

"Uh-huh."

"I mean, I went through some times myself when I wondered if God hadn't forsaken me. Chickamauga. Now that was a bad time. My buddy was shot down right beside me, and. . ." He broke off, not wanting to remember the terror and hardship of war.

Tom set the horse's hoof down gently and straightened.

"Listen, little brother, I'm not criticizing you."

"You're not?" Matt gulped. For some reason, he always felt inferior to Tom. Tom was always sure of himself. Matt had never known him to act impulsively or to make a big mistake.

Tom came out of the stall and patted the stallion's flank. "Nice horse I bought."

"Yeah. Real nice."

"Look, Matt, part of me wants to lecture you and tell you to take your time getting to know Rachel. But the other part. . ."

"What?"

Tom shrugged. "I was introduced to Amy two weeks before I married her. I don't s'pose I'm the man to tell you to take it slow."

Chapter 8

Rachel went to the porch and looked eagerly toward the river. The men had spent the morning bringing in two wagonloads of hay and storing it in the old barn. Tom had poked his head in the doorway to tell Amy they would go to the river to wash before joining the ladies for lunch.

They were coming up the path, and Rachel's pulse accelerated. In the past week, she had begun to know the Barkleys, and Matt in particular. He'd spent the evenings with her, Tom, and Amy after the children were in bed.

Usually they sat on the porch to catch a breeze and talked quietly in the twilight. Rachel was starting to feel comfortable here, as though she could happily spend the rest of her days as part of the close-knit family.

She'd learned that the Barkley brothers and Mike Brown were hard workers, determined to succeed at ranching and willing to put their backs into it.

But it was the private conversations with Matt that thrilled her. He seemed to understand her turmoil as she hovered between two worlds. She found that he was a good listener and surprised herself by confiding in him her worst fears—that she would find no living family members and have no place in the realm of the whites and that Running Elk would retaliate against his father for his loss of position, respect, and his chosen woman and horses.

As to Running Elk, Matt replied that he couldn't predict what the warrior would do, but he assured her, as Amy had, that she would always have a place here in Bridger Valley.

Matt told her some of his private thoughts as well, and Rachel saw that he was troubled by his ambivalent feelings concerning the ongoing War Between the States. Her admiration for him grew as he described his life for the past three years. He was matter-of-fact about it, but she sensed the deep sorrow etched on his heart by the horrors he had seen.

And they talked about God. She was hesitant at first to discuss spiritual things with him, but all of the Barkleys seemed to think it was normal to talk about their Savior in the middle of any conversation. She soon learned that his faith was deep and firm.

Matt noticed her standing on the porch. He lifted his hat and waved to her. Rachel smiled and waved back then ducked inside.

"They're on their way."

"Good," said Amy. "We're just about set."

Lydia was pouring cool water into the cups at the place settings.

"Sit, Lydia," Amy said.

"Oh, stop it. I'm not completely helpless."

"I don't like that backache you've had the last couple of days. Just let Rachel and me do the work."

Rachel reached for the pitcher, and Lydia surrendered it to her with a sigh. "I have to admit, I'll be glad when this is over."

"You will have your little one soon," Rachel said. "All of this will be forgotten."

"She's right." Amy scooped Molly up from the floor and set her on her stool at the edge of the table. "By this time next week, you and Mike will be rocking that baby and wondering what all the fuss was about."

The door opened and the three men trooped to the table.

"Smells good in here," Tom said.

Mike went to Lydia's side and stooped to kiss her. "How are you feeling?"

"The same as I was when you went out this morning."

"Too bad. I was hoping something had changed."

Lydia swatted at him.

"All in good time." Amy set a platter of fried potatoes on the table.

Rachel took her seat, and Matt slid onto the chair beside her. Somehow the places at the table had been rearranged, and for the past few days he'd sat next to her at every meal.

"Is the hay all under cover?" she asked after the blessing.

"Sure is." Matt stabbed a thick slice of bacon and passed the plate on.

"We'll mow that piece down by Mike's tomorrow," Tom said, "but I expect we'll give Matthew a hand with his house this afternoon."

"I thought I'd take a quick ride to the fort to check with the telegraph office," Matt said with a quick glance at Rachel.

"Well, Mike and I can work on the logs while you're gone," Tom said.

Amy cut a piece of meat into small pieces for Molly. "Don't forget to stop at the trader's, Matt. I'm getting low on sugar."

He nodded then leaned closer to Rachel. "I don't suppose you'd like to ride to the fort with me?"

Rachel almost inhaled the potatoes in her mouth. She coughed and reached for her cup.

"Are you all right?" Amy asked.

"Yes." Realizing her face was beet red and they were all waiting to hear what she would say, Rachel lowered her gaze to her hands. "I'd like that."

"Oh, good," Lydia said. "I asked the trader to try to get me a length of flannel for extra diapers. I didn't want to ask Matt, but would you check to see if he's gotten any in?"

"Of course." Rachel threw her a smile but realized her cheeks were still flaming. She couldn't bring herself to look at Matt, and he didn't speak directly to her again during the meal, but she felt his satisfaction.

The five miles to Fort Bridger had never seemed so short. Matt enjoyed every moment as he and Rachel rode at a jog side by side. He rode his brown-and-white spotted gelding, Wiser, and she took the sorrel mare that was her gift from Red Wolf. Amy had loaned her a divided skirt so that she could ride modestly without drawing attention by wearing her buckskins to the fort. The checked blouse she wore was one she and Lydia had sewn this week, he knew, and the outfit suited her, giving her the look of a charming but hardy frontier maiden.

Matt's long thoughts about the war were banished. There was nothing but Rachel and the blue sky and ripe grass. A light wind ruffled her hair, pulling tendrils from her long braid. Her eyes glittered as she talked to him, and Matt's heart soared.

Too soon they reached the fort, and he steered her toward the trading post.

"Hey, Barkley!" a voice called. He turned and recognized one of his former fellow troopers.

"Hello, Wilson. How's the army treating you?"

"The same, I guess." Wilson looked pointedly at Rachel.

"Oh, uh, this is Miss Haynes. Trooper Wilson, an old buddy of mine."

Rachel nodded but kept her eyes downcast. In the awkward silence, Wilson stared at her, and Matt felt a further explanation was needed.

"Miss Haynes is visiting my brother and his wife."

"Well, I'm pleased to meet you, ma'am." Wilson lifted his hat for a moment then replaced it. "Have you ever been to Fort Bridger?"

"No," Rachel said softly, not looking at him.

"I'd be pleased to show you around."

"No need," Matt said. "I was just escorting Miss Haynes to the trader's."

Wilson nodded in defeat. "Say, did you hear about the Indian raid?"

"What raid?"

"A ranch about ten miles east of here was hit yesterday. Some renegades sneaked in and stole two horses. The rancher heard them leaving, and they winged him with an arrow."

"Everyone all right?"

"Guess so. The wife brought him here in an oxcart to see the doctor. They said the Indians just took the horses and lit out of there. Didn't burn the house or anything."

"Huh." Matt glanced at Rachel. Her face had colored, and she was breathing rapidly. "Well, excuse us. I'd best get Miss Haynes in out of the sun." Matt took her arm and propelled her with swift steps into the trading post.

"Sorry," he whispered as they passed through the doorway into the dim interior.

Rachel stopped and leaned on a rack of tools. "Do you think he knew I'd been with the Arapaho?"

"No, of course not."

She took a deep breath. "I'm sorry. I can't help wondering what people think when they see me."

"Well, I can tell you what Wilson thought. He thought you were the prettiest thing he'd seen in months, and he wondered if he had a chance of prying you away from me for a few minutes."

"What for?" She looked up at him with wide gray-blue eyes.

"Just for socializing." Matt smiled. "Pretty girls are hard to come by out here, you know."

She seemed a bit flustered, and he wondered if he ought to apologize. But when she looked around and saw the array of trade goods, she became immersed in shopping. Soon she was comparing the trader's supply of brushed cottons and flannels, trying to find the softest material for the baby.

They left the trading post half an hour later with a bundle of fabric and ribbons and a sack of sugar. Matt loaded his saddlebags and strapped the sack behind Wiser's saddle.

"I ought to have worn a sunbonnet, hadn't I?" she asked.

Matt followed her gaze and saw a woman and a young girl entering one of the officers' houses. Both wore calico bonnets.

"Only to keep the sun off you. No one will think less of you, if that's what you're thinking."

She didn't look convinced.

"One more stop," he told her with a grin.

"The telegraph man?"

"That's right."

When they entered the cramped office beside the post commander's quarters, the telegraph operator sprang up from his chair.

"Barkley! I was just going to send someone out to your brother's place, but Private Wilson told me you were here."

"You mean you've heard something?"

The operator held out a folded piece of paper. "It came in about twenty minutes ago."

"Thanks."

Matt drew Rachel outside and stopped in the shade of the overhanging eaves to unfold the message. He scanned it and looked at Rachel. She was staring up at him, her eyes large and hopeful.

"Did you have a brother named Caleb?"

She caught her breath. "Yes. Ralph, Ephraim, and Caleb."

Matt looked down at the paper once more and nodded. "Seems Caleb survived. He sent this from St. Paul."

She raised one hand to her lips and swayed.

"Rachel?" He reached to steady her and pulled her into his arms. "It's all right," he whispered, stroking her back. "It's going to be all right."

She drew in a choppy breath and clung to him for a moment. Matt turned slightly to shelter her from the stares of any soldiers passing by. Awe washed over him as he took in the fact that she trusted him completely in this trying time. He knew he would stand there and support her for as long as she would allow it.

After a few seconds, she pulled away from him. "Forgive me."

"It's all right."

"Can we. . .what does it say?"

He held the paper out to her, and she peered at it then shook her head. "You read it, please."

"Well, it's addressed to me, and it says, 'I am Rachel Haynes's brother. Parents James and Laura killed at Yellow Medicine, 1862. Please respond if woman you describe is my sister.'"

She closed her eyes.

"Are you all right?" He clutched her arm, afraid she would faint, but when she raised her lashes, her eyes were clear.

"Yes, thank you. I'm. . .I'm fine. We must send an answer."

"Right away. What do you want to say?"

She stood in thought for a moment, and Matt's heart surged with sympathy. "I guess. . .just. . .I am your sister."

She looked up at him with a silent plea, and a bleak thought hit him full force.

"Do you want to. . .uh. . .tell him you'll. . .go back to Minnesota or anything like that?"

She swallowed hard. "I don't know."

Matt seized her hands, crumpling the telegram between them. "Rachel, please don't go. Not yet. We've just gotten to know each other. I'd hate to see you leave."

Her smile was a bit shaky, and she raised trembling fingers to his cheek. Her hand was warm against his skin, jolting him with anticipation.

"I don't think I want me to leave, either."

A sergeant was approaching along the boardwalk, and Matt restrained his urge to sweep her into his arms again.

After the man had passed them, he nodded and inhaled deeply. "All right, then, let's go send our reply."

⌒

It was nearly suppertime when they reached home. Matt dismounted in the barnyard and held his arms up to Rachel. She hesitated only an instant then swung her leg over the pommel and hopped down. He folded her in his embrace for a moment, and she savored his warmth and the comfort of his strong arms around her.

"You go in," he whispered. "I'll put the horses up."

She drew away from him and turned toward the house, but as she took a step, the door opened and Tom came onto the porch with Molly in his arms.

"Where you been?" he called.

"We heard from Rachel's brother," Matt said.

Tom stared at him then at Rachel. "Your brother?" Ben appeared in the doorway beside him, and Tom came down the steps. "That's wonderful, Rachel. An answer to prayer."

"Yes." She couldn't help smiling. She and Matthew had smiled all the way home, partly because Caleb was alive and partly because of the current that jumped between them. Now she realized she had a large family here in Wyoming to share her news with. "We sent our message to him, and then we waited for a reply. He's coming out here."

"That's. . .good news."

"Do you mind?" she asked.

"No, of course not." Tom swung Molly up onto his shoulders. "Is he planning to take you home with him?"

Rachel glanced at Matt, suddenly embarrassed. "I'm not sure."

"We'll take it as it comes," Matt said, "but I'm thinking. . .*we're* thinking Rachel might rather stay here."

Tom grinned. "Well then, we'll see what the Lord brings."

"Where's Amy?" Rachel asked. "I can't wait to tell her."

"She's over to Lydia's. You might want to go over. Amy can use your help."

"You mean. . .?"

"I expect Lydia's having the baby tonight."

"I'd better get right over there!"

Matt fumbled with the thongs that held the sack of sugar to his saddle. "I'll ride over with you and bring the horses back."

"Bring Mike back, too," Tom said. "He's probably driving Amy and Lydia crazy."

Chapter 9

Matt tossed more wood into the stove. It was a warm night, but no one objected. The coffeepot was steaming, and he couldn't think of anything else he could do to help Mike. The expectant father had not stopped pacing for an hour, across the large kitchen and sometimes out onto the porch, where he would gaze down the path toward his little house in the hollow.

Tom sat at the kitchen table near the lantern, whittling away at the end of a new ax handle. Matt watched him try the handle into the ax head, then take it out and resume his carving.

The brothers looked up as Mike entered the kitchen once more and paced to the worktable, turned, and headed back to the door.

"Relax, Michael," Tom said.

"You'd think they'd let us know something."

"They'll tell you when there's something to tell."

Mike picked up the ax head, looked at it, and then put it down. "At least she's got Amy and Rachel with her. Do you think I should ride to the fort for the surgeon?"

"Oh, come on, Mike," Matt said. "You know Dr. Arnold. He's all right for patching up bullet wounds, but babies?"

"Amy's been through two deliveries of her own and helped three other women," Tom said.

"It wouldn't surprise me if Rachel's learned a thing or two about birthing from the Indians, too," Matt said.

Tom nodded. "That Rachel is quite a gal. She was showing Amy just the other day where to pick some herbs to dry for poultices."

"I'm glad she found out she's got kinfolk," Mike said absently as he walked to the doorway then turned and walked back across the room with measured steps.

Matt took three mugs down from the shelf. "Coffee, Mike?"

"No, thanks."

"Sit down and drink it," Tom said.

Mike sighed and pulled out a chair, sitting down across the table from Tom. "Is that hickory?"

"It's hickory."

"You got wedges?"

"I got wedges." Tom picked up his sandpaper and smoothed the end of the handle once more.

"Takes forever to get a good fit," Mike said.

Tom shrugged. "I might as well do something if you're going to keep me up all night."

"Don't sit up on my account," Mike told him, but Tom only smiled. "She's going to be fine."

"T.R., I'll just die if anything happens to her."

Matt hesitated with the coffeepot in his hand then set it back on the stovetop. "Let's pray again."

"I been praying for hours," Mike said.

"It's good to pray together." Tom set the ax handle aside. "Come on, Matthew, bring a chair over."

The three men sent their heartfelt petitions to God, pleading for Lydia's health and the safe delivery of a strong baby. Matt knew Mike was remembering his first wife, Martha, and their little son, Billy, who had died in a cholera epidemic while Mike was soldiering on the plains. Then there were the babies Lydia had lost already. It was a lot of grief for a young man to bear.

Lord, please don't let Mike have more cause for sorrow, Matt prayed silently. He wondered if Tom had been this upset when Amy bore her children. *Probably.*

Glad I wasn't here. That thought was followed by a wave of guilt, and Matt added to his private prayer, *Thank You, Lord, for giving Tom and Mike the close friendship that's sustained them through so much. If I'm in this situation someday, I can't imagine two fellows who'd be better company.*

When their prayers were ended, Matt rose and went to the cookstove for the coffee. "How long do you think it will take Caleb Haynes to get here from St. Paul?"

"He can take the train part way," Mike said, "then the stage."

"Two or three weeks," Tom guessed. "Maybe longer."

Matt sighed. How long did he have to convince Rachel to make her life here?

"How about that coffee, brother?" Tom asked.

Matt poured three cups. Mike accepted his without protest, and Matt sat down with them again.

"You aim to marry her, don't you?" Tom asked.

His words made Matt misjudge his first swallow of the hot brew, and he gasped, pulling in cool air.

"Didn't mean to startle you," Tom said.

"Well, that's my hope."

"She's a very nice girl," Mike said, "but with her brother coming. . ."

"I know. She might decide to go back and live with him and his family.

There could be other relatives, too, that we don't know about yet."

"Keep praying about it." Tom took a sip of coffee then set his mug out of range of his work on the table.

"You want me to keep the fire up?" Matt asked.

"Let it go out," Mike growled before Tom could speak. "It's way too hot in here."

Tom leaned back in his chair, fishing in his shirt pocket for the steel wedges he'd bought at the trading post. "Let it burn down, and bank the coals, Matthew."

Mike cradled his coffee mug in his hands. "If things don't go right with Lydia, I'll wish I'd got the surgeon."

"You want me to ride to the fort?" Tom asked.

"You wouldn't."

"I would. Just to give you peace of mind."

Mike stared down into his coffee mug. "I'm not saying Amy's not capable."

"I know that."

Mike stood up. "Nah, don't go. I don't think Doc Arnold ever even finished his medical training. I don't guess I want him near Lydia. Like you say, he's better than nothing in an Indian fight."

Matt had let his mind drift, but Mike's words homed in on his train of thought.

"Of course, if I went back in the army. . ."

Tom and Mike stared at him.

"You're thinking of reenlisting?" Tom asked.

Matt felt his cheeks redden. "I don't know. Sometimes I think. . .well, I left before things were settled. I didn't finish the job."

"You did your part," Tom said. "If anyone ought to join up, it's me."

"You've got a family," Mike said. "Besides, you may not have served officially, but you've done a heap of work for the army. The emigrants passing through Wyoming Territory owe you a whole lot for all the scouting and negotiating you've done."

Tom shrugged. "I guess I understand how you feel, Matt. But you were in the cavalry for three years before the war, and then you and your outfit went through three more years of hard fighting."

Matt set his mug down. "A little fighting and a lot of maneuvering and short rations. I'm just glad I had a horse. Those fellows who had to march are the ones who took the worst of it."

"Infantry always has it hard," Mike agreed. "I've got to admit, Matthew, there are days when I think I ought to sign up again myself. I mustered out months before the war was declared. Sometimes I think I ought to be back there, fighting for Tennessee and the Union. I know I served my time—five years total, but still. . ." He took a sip of his coffee.

"Just a second," Tom said. "You two had better not off and join the army again. You'd be leaving me here alone with two families to support. I need you both."

Mike gave him a rueful smile. "Don't worry, T.R., I decided in '60, when I met Lydia, that I was never going back East. I left Martha behind in Tennessee when I came out here, and. . .well, I'd never leave my family behind like that again. But that doesn't mean I don't think about it."

Matt nodded. "I'm staying, too, unless I hear God telling me otherwise. But when I was back there, and I saw Tennessee, I kept thinking about you, Mike. It's a beautiful place. All those trees and hills, but not the wind and dry prairie like there is out here. It's just so different. Trees everywhere. And no Indians, at least none that I saw."

"Yeah, it's good horse country." Mike sighed. "It's completely different here, but. . .I've come to think of this as home."

They heard soft, quick footsteps on the porch, and Mike leaped up.

"Mr. Brown!" Rachel flew through the doorway, panting.

Mike hurried toward her and took the lantern from her hand. "What is it? Is Lydia all right?"

"Yes, she's fine, and she's asking for you."

Mike was out the door, and Rachel pulled in another deep breath.

"Here, sit down," Matt said, guiding her toward Mike's abandoned chair. "I'll get you some coffee."

"Do we dare to ask how things are going?" Tom asked.

Rachel looked at them with wide gray-blue eyes. "Of course. I forgot to tell him, didn't I? It's a boy."

⁓

Two weeks later, Rachel donned her buckskin dress and leggings and headed her mare, Sees the Eagle, toward Matt's half-finished cabin. She hadn't been near it since the first logs were rolled into place for the foundation, and she was eager to see the progress the men had made.

Matt was on the roof nailing boards in place. He wore his broad-brimmed hat and faded uniform pants, but his shirt was neatly hung on the sawbuck beside the cabin, and the August sun beat down on his tanned shoulders.

Rachel hesitated. She didn't want to embarrass him. The Barkley men were modest, but still, Matt knew she'd seen a lot of Sioux and Arapaho men wearing less than he had on. Even so, she decided she'd better make her presence known before she got too close.

Sure enough, as soon as she called to him, Matt turned to see who was coming then slid to the edge of the roof and hopped down. By the time Rachel and Eagle reached him, he was buttoning his cotton shirt.

"Hey! What are you doing out here?" he called with a grin.

"Amy helped me pack a lunch. She says it's a good day for a picnic."

"Sounds good to me."

She dismounted and turned to face him. "Good, because I wasn't sure you'd think so."

"Why wouldn't I?"

She shrugged and looked away. How could she explain the turbulent feelings that ambushed her whenever she was close to him?

"Let me help you." He stepped closer and reached past her to unfasten the saddlebags.

She ducked under Eagle's neck and untied the jug of cold water that hung on the other side. "We got a telegram."

Matt's head jerked up, and he stared at her over the saddle. "From Caleb?"

Rachel nodded. "He'll be here tomorrow."

Matt whistled softly. "Are you excited?"

"Yes."

"You haven't told me much about him."

She tried to call up memories of her brother and the untroubled family life they'd enjoyed before the Dakota War. "He was nineteen when it happened. He was courting a girl. I don't remember her name, but her father was the sutler at the Indian agency."

"What's he like?"

She shrugged. "I don't know. Bossy. Very big-brotherish. You know."

Matt's eyes focused off beyond her, and he nodded. "Yeah, I had two big brothers. I think I understand."

"Two?"

"Yeah. I guess we never told you about Richard. He died about eight years ago."

"Oh. I'm sorry. Any more?"

"Just my sister, Rebecca."

"Amy told me about her. Her husband's in the army, right?"

"Yeah, he's a captain now. He's back East somewhere with Rosencrans."

"Who's that?"

"One of the generals."

"Oh."

"Rebecca's in St. Louis." Matt gestured toward the cabin. "Here, let me tie this horse up, and we can sit in the shade."

While he tended to Eagle, Rachel stepped up onto the threshold of the little house and stood in the doorway. It would be snug—just one large room about the size of Tom and Amy's kitchen, with a loft protruding over half of it. Big enough for a single man. Or a couple starting out.

The sunlight spilled in through the open side of the roof on the back half of the cabin and shone in slashes through the cracks between the boards Matt had nailed to the roof on the front side.

"What do you think?" he asked from behind her.

She turned, startled to find him close to her, holding the saddlebags. He stood on the ground outside, putting them at eye level.

"I like it."

He smiled, and her heart raced. "I'm glad." He touched her sleeve lightly. "First time I've seen you wear that since you came here."

"Does it bother you? I thought it would be better than wearing Amy's riding skirt all the time. She said she'd help me stitch my own split skirt, but. . ." She didn't finish the thought that until Caleb arrived her future was unsettled, and starting new projects seemed foolish.

"It doesn't bother me. I think you look fine in it." He reached out and ran his fingers over the beadwork on the yoke over her collarbone. "Reminds me of the day we met. Did you do all this yourself?"

She shook her head. "An old woman in the tribe gave it to me. When the Sioux brought me to Red Wolf, I was wearing leggings, a blanket, and the remains of the dress I was captured in. Yellow Bird Woman was kind to me. She had made this dress, perhaps for herself or perhaps to trade—I'm not sure. Anyway, she brought it to me and told me to wear it. I asked her later to teach me the fine beadwork, and she did begin to show me. I helped bead a cradle board for my friend West Wind's baby, and I made these moccasins."

He looked down at them. "You did a good job."

"Thank you."

"You'll be needing boots this winter, though. We'll have to see if the cobbler at the fort can make you some."

"Matthew. . ."

His gaze met hers once more, and she caught her breath. In his eyes was the plain truth. He was not thinking in terms of her leaving with Caleb.

"You're beautiful, Rachel. . .in either culture."

He leaned toward her, and she knew he was going to kiss her. It frightened her and at the same time thrilled her. But was this what God would have her do? In His grace, He had preserved her brother's life, as well as her own. He was bringing her brother, one she had thought dead, all the way from Minnesota. Was it fair to decide her life before Caleb even arrived? Because she knew that once Matt Barkley kissed her, she would never leave the Green River Valley.

She stepped back with a little gasp, and Matt stared at her, wide-eyed and uncertain.

"I'm sorry!" she choked.

He stepped up to the cabin floor, leaned against the doorjamb, and eyed her cautiously. "No, I'm sorry. I. . .shouldn't have. . ."

"Matthew! Please. Let me. . .it's just that, with Caleb coming, I don't know what I should do. I believe now that I can live in either world, wherever God takes me. In the Arapaho world, I would have survived, and in the white world, I will be content. But here. . .here in this valley I feel as though I'm between the two, and I'm not sure yet where I belong. Can you understand?"

He looked up at the rafters and the sky beyond. "Maybe. At least, partly. Guess I had some of those thoughts when I was back East, away from everyone I loved." He smiled at her. "But you like the cabin?"

She nodded. "I like it very much. But I thought you were just going to cover it with canvas."

"Well, lumber's hard to come by in these parts, but I had a chance to get up in the hills and get some bolts of fir, so I thought I'd go ahead and lay boards on the roof, and then I'll make shingles as I find time."

"Is that something I could learn to do?" she asked.

Matt's grin melted her reserve. "I imagine you could, if you're still here."

"Matt, I'm sorry!"

"Now, don't keep saying that. I shouldn't have tried to rush things."

She bit her lip and nodded. "All right, then. We'll wait and see what happens when Caleb gets here."

They sat together in the middle of the cabin floor, and she unpacked the biscuits, boiled eggs, apples, and oatmeal cookies from the saddlebags. She handed Matt two tin cups, and he poured water into them.

"How's Lydia doing?" Matt asked after he offered the blessing.

"Great. But Mike's going to move her and the baby up to Tom and Amy's this afternoon."

"What for?"

"Amy told Mike it's too hard for her to go back and forth every day to help Lydia, but Tom said Amy just likes the company and having the baby close."

Matt chuckled. "So she browbeat Mike until he agreed?"

"No, she got her husband to convince Mike. I heard Tom telling him their wives won't be happy until they're together."

"That sounds about right. Amy takes a notion, and T.R. carries it out. I never thought I'd see my brother so besotted over a woman."

Rachel laughed at his description. "You're talking about a man who's been married—what?—six years?"

"Something like that. Oh, I don't mind. Tom's a lot easier to live with now than he used to be."

"Well, he seems pretty levelheaded to me. And it's probably best for a short time. They're putting the Browns in the back bedroom, and I'm going to sleep with Molly for a week or so. Mike said he'll bring Lydia and little Michael up in the wagon later today."

"It'll be fun to have the baby in the house."

"He's already grown a lot."

"I'll bet."

"Of course, it might be harder to sleep if he cries much. I think Mike is worn-out from getting up in the night to change him and bring him to Lydia."

Matt reached for an egg. "I haven't heard him complain."

"I don't think he's a complainer. He's so happy to have a healthy little boy! But he looks tired." Rachel smiled and passed him an apple. "I think that's why he agreed so easily to stay with Tom and Amy for a while."

"Mike will be a terrific father. But how does this affect the arrangements during Caleb's visit?"

She frowned. "They'd decided on it before we knew when he would be here. But Amy says they have plenty of space."

"I can almost hear you thinking you're causing Amy extra trouble."

"Well, I am," she admitted.

"She loves it."

"I try to help her with the laundry and housework."

A bird flew in through the open side of the roof and perched above the doorway, on the stock of Matt's rifle. Rachel tossed a biscuit crumb toward it, and the bird sat watching her without moving.

"Got your gun rack up, I see."

He smiled. "Yeah, I don't want to take any chances, after what we heard about Indians raiding for horses. I keep the Spencer where I can get at it quick."

"Is that the special gun Chief Red Wolf wanted?"

"Yep. I got it before the battle of Chickamauga. When they issued those repeaters to us, everyone could see right away what a difference it would make. I thought to myself, 'The West needs these guns.' When I got out, I took a chunk of my back pay and bought one just like it for T.R."

"That's quite a gift you gave your brother."

"Yeah, he was pretty tickled when I gave it to him."

"Did you win the battle?"

Matt winced. "Not exactly."

"I'm sorry."

"It was a bad one." He tossed a crumb over toward the doorway, and the bird swooped down and picked at it.

"I'm glad you came through that battle and were able to come home," Rachel whispered.

Matt nodded. "Me, too." He smiled suddenly. "That day we met you, when we left the village and Running Elk stopped us. . ."

"You told me about that."

"Yeah, well, I was afraid he'd grab our rifles, but I guess he was concentrating so hard on the stallion that he wasn't thinking about them. His men got the drop on us, though. Scared me, I'll tell you."

Rachel folded back the linen towel that wrapped the biscuits and selected one. "Maybe he just figured that would be pushing his father too far."

Matt laughed. "Of course, he didn't know Red Wolf had already tried to talk T.R. into trading his rifle for that horse."

He looked into her eyes for a moment, and Rachel took a deep breath. There was so much unsaid between them. Was she right to delay saying those things until after Caleb came?

Heavenly Father, she prayed silently, *am I missing out on something fine that You have planned for me?*

Matt looked down at his lunch then met her eyes again. "I was going to wait and bring you down here to see the house after it was finished. But that was before I knew Caleb would be here so soon. I'm glad you came today." He took a big bite of his biscuit.

"So am I. And, Matthew, no matter what happens. . .I mean, even if I feel I should go away with him. . ."

Matt stopped chewing.

She looked away and grimaced. This was much harder than she'd expected. She'd imagined a carefree interlude, but instead it had brought an onslaught of emotions. The little bird fluttered up to the gaping hole in the south wall that would be a window and winged out over the prairie.

"Matt, I don't want to lose touch with you."

He swallowed. "I won't let that happen."

Chapter 10

Matt stood beside Rachel, watching the stagecoach lumber into the yard before the trading post.

"Fort Bridger!" the driver yelled. "One-hour stop."

Rachel bounced up and down on her toes, and Matt smiled. He wanted to reach for her hand but restrained himself from doing it.

She wore the new dark blue dress and bonnet Amy had helped her sew. Her beaded moccasins barely showed beneath the skirt until she bobbed up and down. Then her hemline swayed, showing off her footwear.

"What if he's not on it?" She looked up at Matt as dust filled the air from the rolling wheels of the coach.

He smiled down at her. "He's here. He said he would be, and the stage is on time."

She bounced again, chewing the knuckle of her index finger and staring toward the coach. The guard leaped down and swung the door open, and the passengers began to climb out.

Two women were first. Matt recognized them as wives of officers serving at the fort. They were met enthusiastically by their families as three men disembarked behind them.

Rachel grabbed his arm. "There he is!" She stepped away from Matt, calling, "Caleb! Over here!"

A bearded young man stared at her then grinned, opening his arms to her.

In silence Matt watched him fold Rachel against his chest, murmuring something in her ear. Tears sprang into Matt's eyes. He dashed them away with the back of his hand and sent up a swift prayer of thanks.

Rachel kissed her brother on the cheek then pulled him toward Matt.

"Caleb, this is Matthew Barkley. He's the one who sent the first telegram. I've been staying with his family."

"Mr. Barkley." Caleb's gaze swept over Matt as they shook hands.

His frank stare gave Matt license to do the same, and the two men stood for a couple of seconds, each sizing up the other.

Caleb Haynes stood several inches shorter than Matt. His hair was a bit shaggy, but Matt excused that in light of his long trip. His clothes appeared to be store-bought and a bit citified for Bridger Valley. His eyes interested Matt more than anything. He believed a man's eyes told much about his character. Caleb's were darker than Rachel's, almost a coffee brown, and when Matt gazed into them, he read mistrust and apprehension.

"We'd like to have you as our guest at the ranch as well, Mr. Haynes," Matt said.

Rachel smiled. "Oh yes! You'll come with us, won't you? Matt drove his brother's wagon here so we could take you and your luggage back."

Caleb frowned. "Well, I don't know, Rachel. I was hoping you'd be ready to get on the next coach with me and head back to St. Paul."

Rachel's crestfallen expression triggered Matt's protective nature.

"I'm afraid that's impossible." He kept his voice cordial and smiled as he said it but left no room for doubt. "Miss Haynes left all her things at the ranch. We expected you to visit for a few days."

"You don't have to go back right away, do you?" Rachel asked. "You've come so far. I. . .I'd like you to meet my friends and see what the country is like here."

By Caleb's face, Matt got the idea that he'd seen about all of Wyoming he wanted to see, but he settled the matter by saying, "The next eastbound stage won't leave until tomorrow, anyway."

"Well. . ." Caleb turned and looked at the men unloading the baggage from the back of the coach. "How far is it to your place, Mr. Barkley?"

"Only five miles."

"We'll be there in half an hour," Rachel promised. "The horses move right along."

Matt nodded. "My brother and his wife would be very disappointed if they didn't have the chance to meet you."

Caleb sighed and surveyed the rustic buildings that comprised Fort Bridger and the town growing about it. "Let me get my bag."

Matt grasped Rachel's arm gently while her brother was occupied. "Would you like some time to talk to Caleb privately? I can find a place."

She looked up at him in confusion. "We can talk on the way to the ranch."

"All right. I just thought you and your brother might like a chance to. . .well, you know, to talk things over without me being there."

She hesitated then swallowed hard. "He wants me to go right back with him."

"Yes, I heard." He waited as she sorted out her thoughts. As she studied Caleb, who was claiming his bag from the stagecoach driver, her anxiety was plain on her face, and Matt felt another tug at his heart.

"Look, Rachel, you know we'll all support you, whatever you decide to do. If you and Caleb need some time to talk family talk in private, I'll see that you get it tonight."

"Thank you. There's a lot to discuss, I guess."

He nodded. Caleb was returning, carrying a carpetbag.

"I'll bring the wagon over," Matt said. He had deliberately left it a short distance away from the stagecoach stop in front of the trading post, and he walked along slowly, giving Rachel a few minutes, at least, to get used to her brother.

Rachel eyed her brother cautiously as Matt ambled away from them.

"So...did you have a good trip?"

Caleb barked a short laugh. "Worst roads I've ever seen in my life."

"I'm sorry."

He shrugged. "The sooner I put them behind me, the better."

She inhaled carefully. This wasn't going well. She opted for a different topic. "Do you live alone now, Caleb?"

"No. I guess I didn't tell you. Sarah and I were married in February."

"Sarah," Rachel repeated. Of course, that was her name. "Congratulations. How did her family fare?"

"They killed her pa that day, too. He was at the agency. But the rest of the family was safe at their house. Her mother remarried last fall." Caleb kicked at a loose stone, scowling.

"What do you do in Minnesota now? Are you farming?"

"No. I've been working with a builder in St. Paul this past year, but he wasn't too happy about me taking all this time off."

"I'm sorry."

"Well, don't get upset about it." Caleb set down his carpetbag. "Probably I should have just sent you the stage fare and let you come on your own, but I wasn't sure what shape you were in."

"I'm fine."

He cocked his head to one side. "Are you really?"

"Yes."

"Them Sioux..."

"They didn't hurt me. Not much. We marched for three weeks, and that was hard, especially after what I'd seen them do to Ma and Pa..." She let the thought die, unwilling to examine those memories again just now. "But after we got to where their friends had horses, it was easier. What did they do to you? Did they take you? I thought for sure you were dead."

"They didn't get me."

She blinked as she tried to comprehend that. "They didn't?"

He shook his head. "I hid."

"But they burned the house, and..."

"I got down the stream bank and lay flat in the water. They ran past me and never even saw me."

Rachel exhaled in a puff. "So you didn't see anything?"

Caleb stared down at the dusty ground and shook his head. "After they were gone, I waited a long time, and then I ran to the agency."

"You didn't go to our house?"

"It was burnt."

She tried to imagine herself in the same situation. If she'd known the family had been butchered, she supposed she wouldn't have wanted to see that. But if she thought there was even a feeble chance that any of them lived and needed help... She knew she would have gone to the house to see for herself.

"I met Mr. Johnson on the road. He got some soldiers, and they went out to our place. They came back later and told me everyone was dead. They brought Pa and Ralph back to bury them, but...they said Ma and the rest of you kids were in the house when it burned."

"And all this time..."

"We weren't the only ones hit that day. Look, if I'd 'a known you were alive, I would have tried to find you. But everyone said you were dead."

She nodded. "It's all right. It's not your fault."

He squinted at her in the bright sunlight, and his eyes looked older than his twenty-two years, with deep creases etched in the skin at their corners. "Are you sure you're all right now? I heard they did awful things to some of the captives."

Her memories flooded her mind. The terror she lived in those first few weeks was almost unbearable. Finally it subsided, and she learned to cope. There were difficult times and moments of fear, but she had survived them all.

"God brought me through it," she said softly.

Caleb eyed her for a moment then looked away. "Maybe."

"What do you mean, maybe?"

"You say God brought you through it? Well, why didn't He stop it from happening? That's what I say."

"Caleb, I'm here now. It could have been much, much worse for me. I was frightened. Even those last few weeks before I came here, I was scared. They planned to...to marry me off to an Arapaho warrior."

His eyebrows lowered in a dark frown.

"But I prayed," she continued. "And God brought the Barkleys to the village to give me hope. Not long after that, the chief brought me down here to their ranch and gave me my freedom."

Caleb spat on the ground. "The way I see it is God took a nap the day of the raid. Where was He then?"

She stared at him, speechless.

A horse and wagon pulled up close beside her.

"You ready to go?"

She looked up to see Matt smiling at her.

"Yes."

Rachel climbed onto the wagon seat before Matt could get down to help her. She sat with her shoulders stiff, staring off toward the mountains.

"Sorry I'm putting you out of your room," Caleb told Matt that evening.

"That's not a problem." Matt tucked a few clean clothes into his saddlebags. "My cabin is almost ready for shingles, and if I sleep down there, I'll get it done sooner. I'm glad you can be closer to your sister this way."

"You're building a cabin?"

"That's right. I've been staying here with Tom and Amy since I left the army, but it's time I had my own place." He slung the bags over his shoulder. "Didn't you tell me you work for a builder?"

"You. We built several houses last summer, and a store."

"I ought to have you take a look at my project. You could probably give me some good advice about the shingles. Of course, I have to use what I can get out here."

"Lumber's hard to come by?"

"Yeah. I plan to make my own shingles, but it will take awhile."

"Can you get cedar?"

"There's not much around here. I was planning to use fir. Think that will work?"

"Sure, but they won't last as long." Caleb looked out the window toward Tom's pasture. "My boss is working on a hotel right now. I should be there." His shoulders drooped.

"I'm sorry this trip has disrupted your life," Matt said, "but it's good for Rachel that you came. She needed to see you and learn how things are in your family and all."

"What's left of it." Caleb sighed and turned toward him. "I know she wants me to stay a few days."

"Could you do that? It would mean a lot to her. Give her a chance to get used to all the changes."

Caleb's eyebrows drew together in a pensive frown, and for the first time, Matt saw a slight resemblance to Rachel. When she was worried, she puckered her forehead like that.

"I suppose it's costing you money, since you're losing work," he offered.

"A couple more days won't matter, I guess. I do want her to be comfortable with me. I know she went through a lot."

"They didn't let her see any white people for two years. Every time outsiders came to visit, they hid her." Matt watched his face and was gratified that Caleb's brown eyes showed a hint of compassion.

"If I'd just known she was alive!"

"No sense taking on about it. She's found now."

"I can't thank you enough for that."

Matt shrugged. "It was actually my sister-in-law who discovered her. Amy went off to bathe in the river, and she stumbled onto Rachel. I can't help thinking that Rachel wanted to be found, though."

"Of course she did! Why wouldn't she?"

"Well, it's complicated."

Caleb jerked his chin up. "You're not saying she enjoyed living like a savage?"

"Easy, now. The tribe she was with is pretty civilized. Their chief is a reasonable man."

"But she said they were going to force her to marry a violent man."

"That. . .isn't quite what she said at the supper table. They did expect her to marry Running Elk, but no one was forcing her to go along with it."

"So now you're saying she wanted to marry that heathen?"

Matt inhaled and forced himself to unclench his teeth. "I'm not saying anything. I suggest you relax tomorrow, talk to Rachel some more, maybe stroll around the ranch if it's not too hot, and eat some more of Mrs. Barkley's good cooking."

"I appreciate the good care your family has given her," Caleb said, not quite meeting his gaze.

"It's been nothing short of a joy to have her here. The Lord has blessed us by allowing us to help her."

Caleb clenched his hands into tight fists and shook his head. "That's another thing. My parents were God-fearing people, but they weren't outspoken about it. I don't remember Rachel being fanatical, either, but now it seems all she wants to talk about is God and how He delivered her from those Indians."

"I'd have to agree with her there."

"It wasn't God. It was you people going there. Circumstances."

Matt put his arm against the doorjamb and leaned on it. "God uses both people and circumstances."

"Well, from what she's told me, if the chief's daughter hadn't taken her part, she might still be up in the hills with them and living with a savage man without benefit of clergy. And it sounds as though she wouldn't have objected on her own."

Matt shut the door and stepped toward him. "You can't talk like that. Rachel is here because she wanted to leave the Arapaho, and God brought her the opportunity to do that. It's true, she narrowly escaped a miserable life of being married to a man she didn't love. She didn't want that, but she would have endured it because she thought it was the right thing to do. She had no one else to tell her otherwise."

"But if she was free to go all that time, why did she stay with them?"

"It wasn't like she could just walk away into the wilderness. She stayed with them for a lot of reasons, fear being the most prominent. But even though she was afraid, she hadn't been mistreated, at least not by the people she was with the last year. Not up to that point. But she was feeling some pressure to take a husband."

"How could she even consider it?"

"You can't let her think you blame her or think less of her because of what happened to her. She had no outside contact while she was with them. For two years she was steeped in their ways. It's natural that some of their customs—things we find distasteful—would seem commonplace to her after she's lived with them so long."

Caleb stared at him for a long moment, his posture becoming more rigid as he stood there.

"Barkley, I'm taking Rachel back to St. Paul, and I've only been married a few months. I'm asking my wife to take her into our home as a sister. But if Rachel is going to be all sympathetic to the Indians who massacred our families, that might be too much to ask."

"I'm only saying that she understands them now in ways that we don't."

Caleb's eyes narrowed. "I'll ask you one question. Is my sister apt to be a poor influence on my wife and the innocent children I expect we'll have?"

"What do you mean?" But Matt thought he knew what Caleb meant, and he felt suddenly sick.

"I mean, is my sister still a decent woman? Or has she—"

Matt held up one hand. "Just hold it right there." He resisted a strong impulse to punch Caleb and sent up a silent prayer. *Lord, am I the one to answer that question? If I tell him to ask Rachel, just his asking could harm their relationship irreparably.*

"Your sister is the finest, most courageous woman I know. She's worthy of your love and respect, not suspicion and shame."

Matt opened the door to the steep stairway leading down from his loft room to the kitchen.

"Barkley."

He stopped on the top step and looked back. "Yes?"

Caleb came toward him, his head bowed. "This has been very difficult. It was unexpected, and. . .well, it was hard to arrange the trip and explain it to everyone. My wife, my boss. And then there's the expense. I'm afraid the fatigue of the journey has affected my thinking, as well. I'm sorry."

Matt nodded, although the excuses seemed flimsy. "I realize the events of the last few weeks have been a major inconvenience to you. But that is nothing compared to Rachel's ordeal."

"You're right, I know. But she seems so different."

"All she's asking is a few days to come to terms with things."

Caleb stepped back into the bedroom. "All right. I'll stay a few more days."

Chapter 11

W atch it, Ben!" Matt called. His nephew was climbing on the sawhorse in the middle of Matt's unfinished cabin. Tom had come down to help Matt with the roofing during the cool hour between supper and sunset.

Ben stared up at the underside of the roof. "Where are you?"

"I'm up here," Matt replied.

"Daddy's up here, too, and we can see you, so behave yourself!" Tom leaned out over the board he was nailing in place and let Ben see the top half of his face. "Don't be climbing, or I'll have to leave you home next time."

"I've got to go down for more shingles." Matt scooted over to the edge of the roof and jumped into the grass. When he straightened, he looked into the house. "Hey, Ben, come here. I'll give you something to do for me."

The little boy ambled to the doorway, looked at him, and then stared up overhead.

Matt laughed.

"I'm not up there anymore. Come here, you rascal." He lifted Ben down to the ground.

"See all the little scraps of wood lying around? If you gather them up for me and stick them inside, that will give me some kindling later on. What do you think of that?"

Ben stared at him pensively for a moment then said, "You got no fireplace."

"That's right, I don't. Know why?"

Ben shook his head.

"I'm gonna have a stove instead. No fireplace."

The boy frowned. "We got a stove and a fireplace."

"I know, but this is a small house, and I figure I don't need both. A stove is safer and quicker than building a fireplace. I asked the trader to get me a wood-stove. Can you gather up the wood scraps for me?"

Ben stooped and picked up the end of a roofing board Matt had trimmed. He carried it over to the threshold and stuck it up on the floor of the cabin.

"Good work," said Matt. "You keep it up, and I'll let you ride Wiser tomorrow." He thrust a bundle of shingles into his canvas pack and climbed back up by way of a rude ladder he'd constructed from two saplings with board scraps nailed between for steps.

"Rachel seemed quiet at supper." He opened the pack and passed Tom a handful of shingles.

"She did at that."

"Do you know what that's about?"

"Her brother, most likely. He keeps pushing her to go back to Minnesota."

Matt frowned. "What do you make of him?"

Tom stuck two nails in his mouth, positioned a shingle, then took the nails out one at a time and drove them home.

"He's an odd bird. But then, I calculate he thinks I'm one."

"Yeah, I had the feeling last night that he was... embarrassed by Rachel and her history."

"That right?" Tom put more nails in his mouth.

"Well, he seemed to think his wife might not receive her too kindly if she'd soaked up too many Indian ways."

Tom arched his eyebrows but kept working in silence. Matt sighed and reached for a shingle. "I just wish I knew which way she's leaning."

"You want her to stay?"

"You know I do."

"Better tell her."

"I did."

"Tell her louder."

"Daddy, I can see you now."

Matt whipped his head around and saw Ben at the top of the ladder. "Oh, boy. T.R., your son has come up to help us."

Tom took the nails out of his mouth. "Benjamin, I told you not to climb."

Ben's chin drooped to his chest. "I was lonesome."

Matt was closer to the ladder than Tom. He inched over and scooped the boy into the crook of his arm. "Come here." He carried Ben over near his father and set him down on the sloped roof, where he could brace his feet on a short board nailed down to keep the box of nails from sliding.

Tom shook his hammer gently at Ben. "I'm going to have to leave you home next time."

"No, Daddy!"

"You disobeyed."

Ben's face crumpled, and two tears streaked down his dusty cheeks. "I'm sorry."

"Ha. I'll just bet you are." Tom shook his head. "You'll have to stay home tomorrow. And don't you tell Mommy you climbed up here, or you'll have to stay home two days."

"I won't." Ben's voice quavered, and he looked to Matt for support.

"Here, hold this for me." Matt placed a shingle in Ben's hand. "Now don't move. Just be ready to hand that to me when I need it."

Ben gave him a shaky smile. "Sure, Uncle Matt."

Tom sighed and began to unbuckle his belt.

"You're not going to whip him, are you?" Matt asked.

"No, I'm going to buckle him to something so he can't fall."

"Oh. Good idea." Matt took his suspenders off, too, and Tom fastened them to his belt and tethered Ben to a rafter.

"Now stay put," Tom said. "We're trying to get Uncle Matt's house done."

"Then you can get married," Ben said, watching Matt with solemn blue eyes.

"Married?" Matt laughed and wiggled the boy's booted foot. "Where'd you get the idea I was getting married?"

"From Mommy. She told Aunt Lydia you're making this house for you and Miss Rachel."

Matt didn't know what to say. It didn't seem right to contradict such a wise little fellow. He picked up his hammer and a shingle.

"Are you making it for Miss Rachel?" Ben asked.

Tom checked the makeshift harness once more. "Quit that, now, or Uncle Matt will get cross with you."

"We need to head back, Rachel. I've stayed here so long I probably won't have a job left when I get home." Caleb stood beside her in the Barkleys' kitchen, watching as she filled the coffeepot for tomorrow's breakfast.

Rachel bit her lower lip. It was time to make known the decision she had already made. Caleb had stayed two days, and his restlessness told her more than his words. It wasn't fair to keep him here longer, expecting her to return to Minnesota with him.

She covered the coffeepot and set it over near the cookstove. She could hear Amy's and Lydia's voices murmuring softly in the back bedroom.

"Do you want to leave tomorrow?" she asked.

"Can you be ready?" Caleb leaned on the edge of the table. "I'll ask Tom if he or his brother can drive us to the fort."

"I. . .Caleb, I want to stay here."

"Now, Rachel, look, the longer we put it off—"

"I'm not putting it off. You go tomorrow. You need to get back to Sarah and your work. But I'm staying here."

His baleful stare pierced her, and she felt guilty. "I'm sorry you came here for nothing."

"You belong at home with us."

She shook her head. "No, I don't. I'm starting a new life here, Caleb. I appreciate you coming all the way out here, and I'm glad we've had this time together, but—"

"It's Matt Barkley, isn't it?"

She felt her cheeks flame. "What if it is?"

Caleb squinted at her. "Has he proposed marriage to you?"

"No."

Caleb let out a short laugh. "What if he doesn't? What will you do then?"

She tried to swallow the lump in her throat. For the past two days she had hardly seen Matt, but she was sure he was only staying away to give her time alone with her brother. "I. . .will deal with that when I have to."

Caleb scratched his chin through his beard. "I can't figure these men out. One minute they tell how they've fought Indians, and the next they're telling what good friends they are with the old chief who brought you here. But he kept you hidden for two years, and—"

"I was only in his village one year."

Caleb shrugged. "What difference does it make? He kept you in captivity and enslaved you, but they say that he's a good man."

Amy came from the back bedroom with Molly draped in slumber on her shoulder. She smiled at Rachel on her way through. "When my husband comes home, would you please tell him I'm heading for bed?"

"Certainly."

Amy's bedroom door closed, and Caleb said, "You can't stay here without an honorable proposal of marriage, Rachel."

She frowned. "As opposed to what? A dishonorable proposal?"

"Exactly."

She felt her cheeks flush. "I told you, I'm not leaving."

"And I say you must."

"Why?"

"You have no income, Rachel. If you don't have a husband, you have to stay with us."

"Tom and Amy are happy to have me stay here."

"You can't ask them to put you up indefinitely."

"Why not? I've been making myself useful with the housework and the children."

Caleb scowled at her. "I haven't seen young Barkley hovering around you much. You're dreaming of something that may never materialize. I suggest you pack your things. We'll leave on tomorrow's stagecoach." He turned and marched up the creaking staircase.

∽

It was dark when they walked back to Tom's house. Tom carried Ben on his shoulders, and Matt toted his Spencer rifle and their tools.

"Are you sleeping here tonight, Uncle Matt?" Ben asked.

"No, not tonight."

"You can sleep with me."

"Thanks, Ben, but I just came for a few minutes. I'm sleeping down at the cabin."

Ben was yawning when Tom lifted him over his head and lowered him into his arms.

"Come on, fella. High time you were in bed." Tom carried him up the porch steps.

Mike spoke from his chair on the porch. "I almost came scouting for you two."

"Well, we wanted to use every bit of daylight," Matt said.

"I got all the livestock fed and locked up."

"Thanks, Mike," Tom said. "Are the gals inside?"

"Yes, Lydia's gone to bed. Amy told her she'd better sleep while the baby's asleep, and I thought that was good advice. I think Amy's putting Molly to bed now."

"What about Rachel?" Matt asked.

Mike looked up at him with a half smile. "Seems like she was poking around the kitchen a minute ago."

Matt followed Tom inside and stood his rifle in a corner. At Amy's worktable, Rachel was dipping water from a bucket into an iron kettle. She glanced up and smiled at Matt as he approached her, setting his pulse going double time.

"Good evening."

"Hi," he said. "I was hoping you were still up. Are you too tired to take a little stroll?"

"No, I don't think so. Let me fetch a shawl."

She left him for a moment, and Matt sent up a prayer for wisdom. She'd made it clear she needed time to make up her own mind, but Matt wasn't sure he could wait much longer.

As they walked across the porch to the steps, Mike rose and stretched. "Good night, folks."

" 'Night, Mike," Matt said.

Rachel called, "Good night, Mr. Brown."

Matt took possession of her hand and waited for some sign of acceptance or rejection. In the starlight she gave him a shy smile, and a thrill shot through him. He walked on with her toward the pasture, encouraged enough to reclaim her hand when he'd helped her through the rails.

"I like to get out in the middle of the field and look at all the stars."

"They're beautiful," she whispered.

They walked down the hillside until Matt could see the roofline of Mike and Lydia's little house below. When they were a fair distance from the fence, he stopped and stood for a minute, just looking at the vastness of the sky.

"Rachel, I've asked God to show us what's best for both of us, and. . ." He turned to face her, and she looked up at him. Matt grasped both her hands and took a deep breath. "I know you need time to sort things out with Caleb, but. . . well, I don't want you to forget about me in your sorting."

"I haven't."

"Are you sure?"

She lowered her lashes, but a smile lingered on her lips. "I think about you all the time."

He kept silent for a moment, basking in that knowledge. "I'm glad. Tom was saying how I ought to speak up and make sure you knew I wanted you to stay."

"I. . .know that."

"I hope I'm not being too pushy about it." He drew her hands up to his chest and cradled them there. "Rachel, I love you." It had jumped out without his even thinking of saying it, but it was a part of him now, who he was, and he needed for her to know that.

She didn't speak for an excruciating moment. Matt's pulse hammered, and he swallowed down his rising panic. She couldn't leave now! *Lord, please! I believe You've placed this love for her in my heart. Please give me this one thing.*

"I love you," she whispered.

He pulled her toward him and kissed her beneath the shimmering stars. She rested in his arms, and he held her close for a minute. His mind leaped to the future, planning their life together in an instant.

"With your permission, I'll speak to Caleb in the morning."

"He wants to leave tomorrow."

"Are you ready for him to go?"

She pulled away and looked up at him with soft, trusting eyes. "Yes, I think I am. I'd like to keep in touch with him and Sarah, but my life is here now."

Matt's chest felt tight, as though his lungs would burst. He folded her in his embrace once more, kissing her satin-smooth hair, and allowed his heart thirty seconds to slow down. "We'd better go back."

"Yes." Rachel gently disentangled herself and smiled up at him.

Matt caught her hand and began walking with her up the slope toward the fence.

They ducked through the rails and went on toward the porch. He didn't want the interlude to end, but he wanted to do things right. Besides, he had no doubt several people in the house were listening for Rachel to come back inside.

In Matt's mind, it was settled. He would come back early for breakfast. If Caleb wanted to leave, he'd drive him to the fort, and somewhere in there between Amy's flapjacks and the stage stop, he'd make it official. The thought of what to-morrow evening might bring was only mildly disconcerting. He was sure Rachel would say yes when he made his formal proposal. Still, it wouldn't hurt to get a few

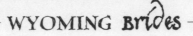
pointers from Tom and Mike as to how to word it.

They mounted the steps, and Matt turned out of habit to look back at the barnyard. A movement in the shadows beyond the barn caught his eye, and he stopped, holding Rachel back. She turned, too, and followed his gaze but did not speak.

Matt held his breath, staring. He almost shrugged it off, but then he saw it again. A stealthy shadow slid from the side of the henhouse and merged with the shadow of the barn's west wall.

"Get inside."

Chapter 12

Rachel gulped. "I saw it."

Matt didn't look her way but continued to stare toward the barn. "My rifle's in the corner. Can you get it?"

He slipped behind the upright that supported the porch roof, and she darted into the house. The kitchen was dark, but she felt along the wall to where she'd seen Matt rest his gun earlier. The cool barrel met her fingers, and she lifted the weapon, pointing it toward the floor and grasping the smooth stock.

She paused in the doorway, but nothing seemed to have changed, so she slid forward and put the rifle in Matt's hands. "How many?" she whispered.

"Not sure. Get Mike and T.R. I doubt they're sleeping yet."

She flitted back inside and hesitated while her eyes adjusted from dimness to near dark. The windows were not shuttered, and she could make out the squares of gray where they were. She made for Tom and Amy's bedroom door and knocked softly.

"Mr. Barkley? Tom?"

"Yes?" came Tom's muffled voice.

"There's something out near the barn. Matt needs you."

After a short pause, the door opened, and she stepped back.

"What is it?" Tom asked.

"Maybe horse thieves. We didn't get a good look, but Matt told me to bring you and Mr. Brown."

"Where's Matthew?"

"On the porch."

"All right. Fetch Mike."

Tom was at the doorway in three strides, his long arm reaching up for the rifle that hung over it. Rachel hurried through the big room to the door of the back bedroom, part of the addition the Barkleys had made to the original ranch house.

"Mr. Brown?" she called. There was no answer, so she tapped softly on the door. "Mr. Brown, we need you."

She heard Lydia's voice murmuring and then a stir. The baby began to whimper. Rachel waited, and a few seconds later the door opened.

"I'm sorry."

Mike rubbed his eyes. "It's all right. What's the matter?"

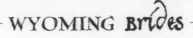

A gunshot split the air. Rachel jumped, and Mike grabbed her shoulders. The baby wailed.

"What's going on?"

"Maybe Indians. Matt and Tom are outside."

Mike ran back into the bedroom and came out carrying his Colt Dragoon six-shooter.

"Help Amy and Lydia with the kids and get the shutters up."

He ran for the door.

"Rachel?" Lydia called from the bedroom.

She stood in the doorway shaking. "I'm here."

"What's happening?"

"Someone's out there around the barn."

"Horse thieves?"

"Maybe."

Another shot sounded. A moment later the three men burst through the front doorway, and Matt slammed the door and barred it.

"Tommy?" Amy stood in her bedroom door.

"Everyone get down!"

Rachel dove toward the window beside the kitchen table and struggled with the heavy shutter. Matt came to her side.

"Let me do that. Keep low, Rachel. They've got muskets."

A bullet shattered a pane in the other window and imbedded itself in the wall beyond the cookstove.

Mike, who had gone to put that shutter up, leaped to one side, flattening himself against the wall. In the momentary silence, he said, "Now that's close, T.R."

"Amy!" Tom shouted. "Get the kids in the back with Lydia. Mike, you got a weapon?"

"Daddy!" Ben ran from his room, straight for his father.

Rachel intercepted him and pulled him under the table with her. "Easy, Ben. It's going to be all right, but we've got to keep quiet."

The stairs creaked, and she heard Caleb's shaky voice.

"Barkley? What's going on?"

"We're under attack, Mr. Haynes. Keep your head down."

Peeking out from between the chairs, Rachel saw Lydia in the back bedroom doorway holding little Michael.

"Bring Molly to me," she called, and Amy carried her still sleeping daughter toward her.

Mike gingerly raised his shutter. Matt ducked low and grabbed the other side to help him lift it. With both windows covered, the room was plunged in inky darkness.

"Think we dare light a lantern?" Matt asked.

"Maybe a candle," Tom said. "We're likely to trip over each other, or worse, if we don't have some light."

"We can't keep these shutters up, T.R.," Mike said. "They'll break into the barn first thing."

"I know it. What do you suggest?" Tom's voice came from near the hearth. A match scratched, and everyone looked toward the flare of light as he put the flame to a candlewick.

"If we open the shutters, they'll keep shooting in here," Matt said.

"Well, we'll get all the women and children in the back, and we'll be careful," Mike told him.

"Maybe you should just let them take what they want," Caleb said.

Tom scowled at him but didn't bother to reply. "All right, we'll open the shutters, but when we do, they'll have targets again."

An arrow broke a pane on the window nearest the table and thudded against the plank shutter. Rachel heard the glass tinkle onto the porch floor.

Matt looked down at her, where she still crouched with Ben under the table. The little boy was clinging to her with both arms around her neck.

"You all right?"

"Yes," Rachel said.

Amy came back from the bedroom, peering about. "Where's Ben?"

"He's right here." Rachel crawled from beneath the table, pushing Ben before her.

"Take him to the back," Tom said. "Amy, can you round up any extra weapons and cartridges?"

"My pistol is upstairs," Matt said.

"I'll get it." Caleb went up the staircase to the loft room.

Peeking out through a crack at the edge of the shutter, Mike called, "They're going for the barn door, T.R. Douse that light, and I'll drop this shutter. If we don't keep up a steady fire, they'll have that lock off."

Rachel hugged Ben to her chest and scrambled for the back room. As soon as she reached the door, Tom blew out the candle, and she was once more in darkness.

"Lydia?"

"Here. Bring Ben in and shut the door so the children can't run out and get in the way."

Behind her, Rachel heard the creak of the shutter being lowered once more, and Tom's low order, "Get down, Haynes!" It was followed by a flurry of gunshots, and Ben threw himself against her, whimpering.

Rachel stroked his head. "Shh, it's all right." Her eyes became accustomed to the darkness, and she noted that the small bedroom window was still open. She fumbled to shut the door then eased Ben down on the bed with Lydia, Molly, and the baby.

"I'd better put that shutter up."

"Can you manage?" Lydia asked.

Rachel squeezed in beside the pine dresser and grasped the edge. Boards nailed horizontally to two pieces of wood formed the shutter, and it hung down on hinges. She heaved it out from the wall, then upward, and stood on tiptoe to turn the wood blocks that would hold it in place.

"There!" She turned toward the bed and felt her way to Lydia's side.

"Too bad we couldn't close the outside shutters, too," Lydia said. "Tom will probably have to replace a lot of glass."

Rachel was grateful for the security the inner shutters afforded them.

Molly stirred and began to whimper, and Michael let out a wail.

The door opened a crack, and Amy whispered, "You've got all the children, right?"

"Yes," Rachel said. "We're all here."

"Mommy!" Ben wriggled toward the edge of the bed, and Lydia grabbed the back of his nightshirt.

"You stay with Aunt Lydia and Miss Rachel. Be a good boy." Amy closed the door again.

"Mommy!"

Rachel pulled Ben to her. "It's all right, Ben. Mommy has to help your father now. Don't fuss."

Ben sniffed. "I don't fuss. I'm a big boy."

"That's good. Just stay right here with me."

"We'd better spread a quilt on the floor and keep low," Lydia said. "Can you fix it?"

Rachel felt for the extra quilt she knew hung over a chair back. During her own days of sleeping in this room, she'd never needed it during the warm nights, but she had admired Amy's handwork. She unfolded it, then plopped Ben in the center.

"Come here, sweetheart." She lifted Molly and sat down with her, and Lydia eased off the bed, sitting down with her back to the wall and putting the baby to her breast.

It was suddenly quiet.

"What do you suppose is happening?" Rachel asked.

"I don't know, but we'd best stay put and keep the children quiet."

"But Amy's out there."

"Amy can handle a gun as well as a man."

"I can shoot."

Lydia frowned. "I doubt they have an extra weapon for you. And besides, I need you."

Rachel's senses urged her to run to the outer room, if only to gain information. Surely there was something active she could do. This was like hiding in the woods when strangers came to the Arapaho village, only worse. Her friends were in lethal danger.

A wild yell came to them from outside, and Molly burrowed her head into Rachel's chest, sobbing.

"There, honey, it's all right."

The deafening report of a rifle fired from inside the building belied her words.

Rachel hauled Ben against her side and clutched the two children. She knew those yells. She had heard variations of them in the Sioux and Arapaho villages, when warriors going out to raid had danced about the fire. Those times she was allowed to flee to her tepee and hide until the reveling was over.

But not the first time she heard them. When the Sioux attacked her family's home two years ago, she could not escape the house. Hostile warriors blocked the doorway and windows, and she had cowered into a corner, awaiting the worst.

"Let's pray," she called over the noise, and Lydia immediately launched into a low, earnest petition to God.

Suddenly a shot followed by a closer yell sent a shudder down Rachel's spine, and Molly screamed. Rachel squeezed the two children even harder.

"That wasn't any Indian!"

Lydia gave a shaky chuckle. "No, that was my wildcat of a husband from Tennessee."

⁓

Matt crouched below the window frame. Mike stood sentinel beside the other window, and Tom knelt by the doorframe. Without being able to see her, Matt knew Amy was huddled near the cookstove, trying to load one of the two muskets they had. He could hear Caleb Haynes's ragged breathing from where he sat on the floor, aiming Tom's pistol toward the door. Matt hoped he wouldn't panic and shoot wild.

He edged up to where he could see outside—just enough to let him watch the only entrance to the barn. If the Indians shot the lock off, the dozen horses inside might be lost.

"How many do you make?" Mike whispered.

"At least four."

"Six," Tom said from the doorway.

"Think we can get the sash up?" Matt asked. "I'd hate to have to replace every single pane." He and Mike, both grasped the crosspiece on the lower window sash, shoved it up, and then waited in silence. All was still.

Matt tried to keep his focus, not letting his thoughts roam to their usual destination these days—Rachel. His plans to discuss their future with Caleb were insignificant now. He needed to be vigilant, to ensure that any of them had a future.

Lord, help us to get out of this scrape. If You want us to lose the horses, I reckon we can stand it. But let us come through without anyone being hurt, if that can be part of Your plan.

A shape suddenly materialized, and Matt saw that one of the attackers had taken cover behind Tom's buckboard in the yard. He started to draw a bead, but the Indian was pulling back his bowstring. Matt ducked, and an arrow thunked against the window frame outside.

Rachel eased closer to Lydia. The baby seemed to be sleeping in his mother's arms, despite the tension and occasional blasts of gunshots.

"What will we do if. . ." Rachel glanced toward the shuttered window.

Lydia gulped. "I don't know. I feel helpless."

"Me, too."

"If it weren't for the children, I'd have a weapon in my hands. Mike and I stood off a band of Sioux once."

"Really?"

Lydia nodded. "I was never so scared in my life. Mike was wounded. But I was healthy then. I was able to help him."

"You're right about the children. We have to keep them safe. And you can't be out there loading rifles. You just had a baby."

A flurry of gunshots caused them all to cringe, and Michael shrieked. Lydia cuddled him close. "Sh, sh, sh."

Rachel set Molly down and crawled to the dresser.

"What are you doing?" Lydia asked.

"Looking for something we can use to defend ourselves." Rachel stood up, feeling the items on top of the dresser. A hairbrush, a small tin, and a wooden box. "Did Mike have a knife in here?"

"He's probably got it with him, but check the second drawer." Lydia reached out to grab Ben. "Hold it, little fellow. Stay here with us."

"I want to help Daddy."

"Not this time. He's doing fine." A crack from a rifle beyond the bedroom door punctuated Lydia's sentence, and Ben scrambled back to her side.

It grew still once more.

"Maybe they're quitting," Rachel said.

"Mike told me once the Sioux like to attack four times."

Rachel pursed her lips. "I guess they do that sometimes. It depends on a lot of things. But anyway, I don't think those are Sioux."

"What do you think they are?" Lydia asked.

"Renegades. Maybe. . ." Rachel pulled the second drawer open, careful to make no noise. "You heard about the raids lately?"

"Yes."

"I wondered if it was Running Elk and his friends."

Lydia gasped. "Wouldn't that be something if he came here to steal horses and found that paint stallion he wanted so badly?"

"I think..." Rachel felt the contents of the drawer, patting the folded clothes. Her hand closed on a leather sheath and the cool handle of the knife it held. "He didn't pick this ranch by accident. He knows the stallion is here."

The moon had risen, and Matt could see Tom's face, set like granite in the pale light. His gaze never wavered from the barn door across the yard.

Matt eased over to the side of the window hole again and peered out. He couldn't tell if the man behind the wagon had moved or not.

"It's quiet," Amy said. "Think they're gone?"

"No. They won't leave without the horses," Tom said so low that Matt could barely hear him.

"There can't be too many of them," Mike said, "or they'd make a charge."

"Maybe they're trying to bust in around the back of the barn," Matt suggested.

Mike shook his head. "We'd hear something."

"I could go out the back of the house and circle around," Matt said.

"No," came Tom's voice. "Too dangerous. I'd rather lose all my horses than lose you."

Matt sighed, longing to try it but relieved that he didn't have to.

"Are you praying?" Tom asked.

"Sure am," Mike drawled.

"Haven't quit for a second," Matt said.

Caleb's dry laugh came from behind them. "It's not praying that will get us out of this fix, gentlemen. It's ingenuity and superior fire power."

The others said nothing. Amy crawled toward Tom with one of the muzzle-loaders. "Here, this one's ready. Where's the other?"

"Mike's got it."

"You need a reload on the musket, Mike?"

He slid the long gun toward her across the floor then returned to his stance beside the window, his pistol pointed into the quiet night.

"I figure they're not going to reload many times. They're already using their bows more than their guns. If we could pin them down, we could run them right out of ammunition and chase them off."

"You may be right," Tom said, "but they're slippery. Just when I think I know where one's hiding, he fades away to another spot."

"Why don't you pray more?" Caleb said with a laugh.

"God knows what we need," Matt said.

"Maybe so, but I'll tell you one thing. If we live through this nightmare, my sister is getting on the stagecoach with me tomorrow."

Matt turned toward him. "You can't guarantee her safety in Minnesota."

"Well, it's a lot less dangerous there now than it is here, and that's a fact." Caleb shifted his position.

A volley of arrows flew in through Mike's window, and they all ducked then sprang to their firing positions.

Tom and Mike both squeezed off a round.

When the reports faded, Tom said, "They're trying to keep us busy so they can rush the barn door. Look lively over there, Matthew. If you see anything move near the barn, shoot it."

"I'm going to need more cartridges."

"You got more?" Tom asked.

"Up in my room. There's powder and a pouch of bullets for the Colts, too."

"I'll get them," Amy said.

Before she could move, Caleb rose. "Let me go, Mrs. Barkley. I think I saw the box of cartridges on the chest up there."

Matt heard him cross the room but kept his attention on the eerie scene outside. Shadows rose up near the hay shed and the barn, and movement flickered near the wagon. He threw a quick shot toward the wagon then hit the floor again.

Several arrows whizzed over his head and shattered against the fireplace. One found a less resistant mark.

"Oof!" Caleb hit the floor, and then he screamed.

Chapter 13

M r. Haynes!" Amy crawled toward Caleb.

"Stay back, Amy. Let me get him."

Matt crept forward, grabbed Caleb's shoes, and pulled him toward the wall.

"Get him in our bedroom," Tom said. "Amy, shut the door and you can light the lamp in there."

Matt dragged Caleb toward the doorway, and Amy went ahead of him. As he pulled Caleb toward the bed, the light flared and steadied. Amy replaced the lantern chimney and shut the door.

"Got him in the leg," Matt said.

"I'll help you lift him." Amy picked up Caleb's feet as Matt got his arm under Caleb's shoulders and hefted him onto the bed.

Caleb moaned.

"Gonna get your quilt all bloody," Matt said.

Amy brought a folded towel and shoved it beneath Caleb's leg. The arrow shaft stuck straight up from his thigh, with blood oozing through his pants leg around it.

Caleb opened his eyes and stared at it. His breath came in shallow gasps, and his eyes darted from Matt's face to Amy's and back to the arrow.

"Take it out!"

"Are you sure?" Matt asked.

"Wait," Amy said. "I'll get something for a bandage. She opened her wardrobe and rummaged, coming back with a pillowcase.

"Ready?" Matt asked.

Caleb nodded, and Matt took the arrow in both hands. Caleb gritted his teeth, and Matt pulled with all his strength. Caleb screamed as the shaft came out then lay panting.

Matt held the arrow before him, staring at the point and the fletching design. A bead of sweat dripped off his forehead onto the floor.

"There, Mr. Haynes," Amy said, "I'll bandage this and get you some water."

"I'm going to die, aren't I?" Caleb gasped.

"Not in my house. It's a flesh wound. When things calm down, I'll tend you properly."

"The point stayed with it," Matt told him. "That's good. It's not stuck in your leg."

He opened the door to the kitchen. Mike and Tom were at the two windows. Matt crouched and hurried to his brother.

"T.R., look at this."

Tom glanced toward the arrow then back out the window. "Arapaho. I know. I saw the ones that came in earlier. Is he gonna make it?"

"Oh yeah, but he's already whining."

"Get Rachel out here," Tom said.

Matt hesitated then laid the arrow on the floor and headed for the back bedroom.

"I see one!" Mike whipped his rifle up and fired.

"Get down, Mike!" Tom yelled, and Mike ducked behind the casement.

Matt opened the door to the back bedroom. "Rachel?"

"Over here." Even in the melee, the sound of her voice thrilled him.

"We need you out front. Stay low."

"What happened?" she asked, following him in the kitchen.

"Your brother's hurt but not bad. Amy's tending him."

They reached Tom's side, and Rachel sat down below the window.

"Do you want me to reload?"

"We're set for now," Tom said. "But please look at these arrows."

She took the two shafts he extended and examined them in the moonlight. "Arapaho?" Matt asked.

She nodded. "Not just Arapaho. That's Running Elk's arrow." She touched the distinctive wavy lines of paint that ran along one of them, representing elk horns.

"His father sent him away," Matt said.

"Yes, and several of his friends went with him."

Tom scratched his chin. "There've been raids in this area where horses were taken. I figured it was him. He wants the stallion."

"Maybe we should let him have it," Mike said.

"Maybe."

Matt touched his brother's arm. "Tom, you can't just let him get the best of you like that."

Tom shook his head. "This is bigger than the horse, Matt. Caleb's already injured. Do you want to wait until someone else gets hurt?"

"Matthew, get to your post," Mike barked, swinging his rifle up once more.

Matt sprang to the side of the window.

"They're going for the barn door again," Tom said.

A wave of bullets and arrows flew between the barn and the house, and Rachel lay on the floor, covering her head.

"Got one!" Matt cried.

"But they've got the barn door open," Mike said. "They must have shot the lock off."

"None of them made it inside, did they?" Matt asked.

"Don't think so."

"You two reload," Tom said, setting his Spencer aside and picking up his Colt pistol. He stared out the window.

Rachel sat up.

"You'd best get out back again," Tom said.

"Can I help Amy?"

"If you could take care of your brother, she could come reload my rifle for me."

Rachel crawled to the door of Amy's bedroom. She entered and shut the door quickly so the light wouldn't spill out into the kitchen longer than necessary.

"Caleb," she whispered. "Are you all right?"

"I'm going to die, Rachel."

"He'll be fine." Amy was tying a strip of linen around the makeshift bandage she'd made. "The bone's not broken. It'll be sore for quite a while, but he'll heal."

Beads of sweat stood on Caleb's forehead as he squinted up at Rachel. "You tell Sarah I died defending you and your friends."

"Now, Caleb, Amy's good at nursing, and she says you'll be fine."

He swore, and Rachel turned away.

"There's water in the pitcher," Amy said.

Rachel went to the washstand, soaked a cloth, and then returned to the bed to bathe Caleb's brow.

He frowned up at her. "So much for your prayers."

"You think prayer is useless?" Amy asked.

"It's not God who will save us. If we get out of this, it will be because your men shoot well, not because you pray hard."

Rachel flinched. "Caleb, please. We all believe in God's providential care. You don't have to agree, but at least be respectful of the men who are defending your life."

"Oh, that's right." He shook his head then snarled at her, jabbing his finger toward her in anger. "We should have gotten on that stagecoach the day after I came. This is your fault."

In the stillness, a deep voice called from outside, "Barkley!"

Rachel stiffened.

After a pause, she heard Tom Barkley shout, "What do you want?"

"It's a diversion," Mike yelled. "They're going for the barn." He let off several rounds and pulled back behind the casement. Matt eased into position and fired three times. The third time he pulled the trigger, there was only a click. He grabbed his Colt and raised the pistol, then ducked back as he saw two warriors ready to loose arrows. They thunked into the thick planks that framed the window.

Mike again leaned toward the window and squeezed off two shots. Matt followed up with two more.

In the lull that followed, both men hurried to fill the chambers of their guns.

"I'm pretty sure I took one down," Mike said. "There can't be many left."

"Barkley!"

They all froze and stared at each other.

Rachel came to the bedroom doorway, and Matt whispered, "Get down!" She crouched by the wall and waited. Amy came and knelt beside her.

Tom edged the front door open a crack and yelled, "Quit the tricks, Running Elk. What do you want?"

"I want Stands in Timber."

Rachel's wide eyes were the only feature Matt could see clearly as he stared toward her. Her dark dress blended in with the shadowy wall behind her, and her hair was part of the ebony frame, but her eyes shimmered in her pale face. She was afraid, and he longed to chase that fear away. The thought of Running Elk carrying her off to a life of oppression, forcing her to do his bidding, brought on a slow, burning rage.

Tom shouted, "Do you want to talk in peace?"

"Send out the girl."

"Your father told her she was free to go."

"You know my father and I do not agree in all things." The derisive voice sent a shudder down Matt's spine. *Lord, I won't let him have her. You know that.*

Tom hesitated only a moment. "I'm not giving her up, Running Elk."

"Then you and your family will burn."

Amy caught her breath. "Tommy, they'll set fire to the house!"

Rachel stood. Her legs wobbled, but she walked toward Tom.

"Get down, Rachel." His voice was etched in granite, but she kept walking.

"It's not worth it. We're talking about ten lives. Your precious children. Your friends. Your wife."

"We can hold them off."

"Can we?" she asked.

Tom peered out the crack then looked over at his best friend.

"Mike?"

"I'm pretty sure there's only four of them left, T.R. They might get close enough to fire the house from behind, though. We can't see them there. Maybe it's time for one of us to go out the back."

"No."

"Well, then, I'll go upstairs. Isn't there a window on the back up there?"

"Yes."

Mike tucked his revolver into his belt and picked up his musket and bullet pouch. "I'll bet you anything that while Running Elk's keeping you talking, one of his men is sneaking around back."

Rachel strode to the door and yanked it open.

"Rachel, don't!" Tom leaped toward her, but she took a step forward, forcing herself not to think what Matthew's reaction would be.

I have to do this. God, protect me!

A bullet splintered the wood beside her head, and Rachel flinched then stood tall in the doorway. "Here I am."

Running Elk shouted a command, and all was still.

As she stepped across the porch, she made out the shape of the warrior on his horse, coming toward her from beside the barn. At the bottom of the steps, she stopped. He sat straight and commanding on the back of a big gelding that looked white in the moonlight.

The lurid paint smears on his face reinforced the memory of her capture and the massacre of her family. She would not stay hidden in the ranch house and be the cause of another mass slaying. Not Amy and her children. Not Lydia and the baby. Not the valiant Barkley brothers and their stalwart friend, Mike. Not her brother Caleb, who was spared in that other raid.

"You get a horse and saddle," Running Elk said in his own tongue. "Be quick."

She walked slowly toward the barn, and he turned his horse to move along beside her. She knew Mike and the Barkleys had their guns trained on him but would not fire with her so close to him.

She had almost reached the barn door when another man emerged from within, leading a snorting horse. He took it up close on the other side of Running Elk's mount, and the chief's son swung from the gray he'd been riding to the back of the proud paint stallion.

"You're not taking that horse," Rachel cried as the second warrior mounted the gray gelding.

Running Elk frowned at her.

"Get your mare. We go."

The impatient stallion pawed the ground and snorted, tossing his black mane. She clenched her jaw against the onslaught of fury that overcame her.

"Give the horse back."

Running Elk laughed.

She stepped toward him. "I'll go with you, but only if you leave that horse here."

"You are not making the terms of this truce." His dark eyes raked over her, and she shivered. "You look better in the dress of the people," he said.

Rachel didn't waver, though her instinct was to look down at her cotton dress.

"If you take that stallion from Thomas Barkley, you will not take me."

He grunted, and she stared at him, determined not to blink. She couldn't tell if he was amused or enraged.

"You have no say in this." He turned the stallion sideways. Rachel knew she was still between Running Elk and the window where Matt was watching. She wondered if Tom or Mike would find the opportunity for a clean shot from one of their positions. She doubted Tom would chance hitting her or the paint, but she wasn't so sure about Mike Brown. At that moment, she was so angry she didn't care what happened. She only knew that she would not give herself up and leave Tom once more robbed of the stallion.

Lord, give me wisdom, she prayed, staring into Running Elk's glittering eyes. She knew the others inside were praying, too, all except her brother. *Show Caleb You can preserve us, Lord. Show him and Running Elk that You are all-powerful.*

"Come," Running Elk said again. "If you do not, we will burn the house."

Rachel couldn't move. Had her bones melted, leaving her feeling so weak and unable to move?

"You hear me?" he shouted. "Look!"

She turned as he pointed and saw another warrior at the side of the Barkleys' house holding a lighted torch. He had prepared a pile of dried grass and pine boughs beneath the window of the room where Lydia and the children huddled. A saddled brown horse was waiting for him, tied to the corral fence at the side of the house.

With sick apprehension, Rachel turned toward the barn to get her mare, Sees the Eagle.

A gunshot roared from above, and she saw a quick movement from the upstairs window. The warrior astride the gray gelding fell from his horse's back without a sound.

Strong arms encircled her waist. Rachel gasped as an unseen assailant lifted her, but he held her so tightly she couldn't breathe until he released her into Running Elk's arms. The chief's son pulled her onto the saddle with him, and the man who had lifted her leaped onto the horse of the fallen warrior.

The Arapaho beside the house threw his torch onto the pile of tinder and sprang toward his mount.

Chapter 14

Matthew and Tom rushed out onto the porch as the three horses galloped away. Matt raised his rifle and sighted, but held off, not willing to risk hitting Rachel. He lowered his gun and tore for the barn.

"Hey!" Mike called from the upper window, and they whirled around.

At once Matt saw black smoke billowing up from the side of the house.

"Fire!" He ran toward the blaze.

Tom leaped onto the porch and yelled through the open window, "Everyone out. We've got a fire!"

He leaped off the end of the porch and ran to Matt's aid. A moment later, Mike burst from the house carrying a wool blanket. Amy followed with two dripping flour sacks.

The flames had not yet caught the log walls, and Matt kicked the burning pile apart then stomped embers. Mike, Tom, and Amy soon extinguished the rest of the blaze, and they all stood panting.

"Thank You, Lord." Tom turned to embrace Amy.

"Come on," Matt said. "We've got to get Rachel back."

Mike shook his head. "You'll never catch them."

"Running Elk and Rachel are riding double. That horse won't last forever."

Matt ran into the barn and lit the lantern with shaking hands. The horses snuffled and shifted in their stalls. He didn't stop to count, but he thought the only animal they'd taken was the paint.

As he threw his saddle over Wiser's back, Mike strode in. "Tom's going to stay here with the women and children."

Matt nodded. He couldn't ask them to leave their families defenseless to help him.

"And I'm riding for the fort."

Matt stared at Mike as he grabbed a bridle from the wall and headed for Amy's big gelding, Kip.

"You mean. . ."

"I mean it's foolish of us to take off after them alone. I made that mistake when Lydia was captured. You can go with me, or you can track those Arapaho and try to keep up with them. I'll come along as quick as I can get some reinforcements."

Matt nodded, thinking about the options as he fastened Wiser's cinch strap. "I'll follow them."

"Right. Leave me some sign."

Matt led Wiser out, and Tom met him in the dooryard with Matt's pistol and what was left of the box of cartridges for the repeating rifle.

"Take these."

"You got plenty?"

"My magazine is full. I'd go with you if things were different."

Matt nodded. "I know. You need to be here."

Tom rested his hand on Matt's knee for a moment. "Take care, little brother. We'll be praying for you. Oh, and by the way, Caleb asked us to pray for Rachel."

"Huh. That's something."

Amy ran from the porch carrying a tapestry workbag.

"Matthew! Take this. It's quilt scraps. You can leave a trail for Mike."

"Thanks."

Matt hooked the handles of the small bag over his saddle horn, turned Wiser toward the hills, and urged him into a canter. He doubted they had ten minutes on him, but those ten minutes might make the difference on whether or not he would ever see Rachel again.

⌒

"Let me go." Rachel squirmed against Running Elk's hold, to no avail.

He chuckled mirthlessly, close to her ear. "You told me you would not go with me unless I left the horse with Barkley. But now you come."

"Against my wishes."

"So." He urged the horse on along the rocky trail. "If I leave the horse now for Barkley, you will come with me?"

She hated the way his hands snaked around her waist and held her against him.

"You set their house on fire," she spat out.

"I should have done it sooner. We could have taken all their horses and not lost three valiant men."

"Valiant! You are nothing but cowards. Attacking innocent people, trying to burn up women and babies to make their men do what you want."

He grunted. "You went to the brother of Comes as a Friend. My sister told me you would be his woman."

Rachel clamped her jaws together and said nothing.

His arm tightened about her waist. "You are with me now. I hope your man is in the burning house."

Rachel seized his hands and tried to pull them away from her waist.

"Let go of me!"

He held her tighter and laughed.

⌒

The moon shone from a cloudless sky, and Matt was able to see the hoofprints clearly. One horse was unshod, but the paint and the third mount, the big gray, had iron shoes. He kept Wiser at a gallop while the trail was plain and knew Mike would be able to follow the signs as easily.

The marauders had chosen a path that followed the river for a few miles, across relatively flat terrain, and passed close to a homestead. The point where they splashed into the Blacks Fork was easy to spot. Matt rode Wiser straight across and picked up their trail again on the north bank. Running Elk and his friends were headed across the valley, toward the foothills. They weren't wasting any time.

Matt crossed a rocky rise and flagged the way with one of Amy's scraps when he found the hoofprints again. He would soon be in rugged territory, and he wanted to close the gap quickly, before he hit the mountains.

Was Running Elk headed toward his homeland? Maybe he planned to go back and have things out with his father. Or perhaps he thought the tribe would accept him if he came back with horses and his chosen bride. More likely he would hide out in the hills and do some more raiding to build up his resources before he faced Red Wolf again.

Another stream flowed into the river. To Matt's surprise, Running Elk had swerved to follow its course toward the buttes that loomed above the valley. Matt rode along as quickly as he dared, occasionally dropping more scraps of calico.

After half an hour, he stopped to study the ground. The horses had waded into the water here. But where did they come out? He rode Wiser to the other side. The Blacks Fork was summer shallow, but this stream, coming down cold from the summits, was up to the gelding's belly. Matt stopped him when they reached the far bank. As he'd suspected, the horses he was pursuing had not left the stream here.

He walked Wiser upstream in the water, watching both shores for a sign of their passing. Matt recalled that a few prospectors had come up this way to hunt gold when he was a boy. A light breeze blew in his face, and he shivered. A few minutes later he found a place where horses had slipped and scrabbled for their footing on the far side. Wiser was glad to leave the rivulet, and they followed the rising trail, cantering while he could see the telltale hoofprints.

After fifteen minutes, Matt stopped. He was no longer certain he was going the right way. Somewhere ahead, another stream rushed down from the mountains.

Rachel! Where are you? He tilted his head back and gazed up at the star-strewn sky. "Lord, I need your guidance. I can't lose her now! Please show me the way."

Wiser raised his head and whinnied.

Matt jerked to attention as he heard the faint answer from far ahead.

⌒

The paint stallion had fallen behind the other two horses. The moon's light showed Rachel the others as they waded along in another stream.

She leaned forward, over the paint's withers and neck as he toiled in the water. Falling off into the cold water might not be so bad. She had looked for an opportunity since they set out, imagining she could choose the time and place to tumble from her captor's grasp, but Running Elk held her in place with arms like the branches of an oak tree.

The paint's sides heaved beneath her legs. He wasn't used to this strenuous labor, with the weight of two people on his back and the water resisting every step.

Ahead of them, the gray horse, white as milk in the moonlight, turned to the far bank and climbed out of the stream with a groan. The brown horse followed, clawing at the low bank before he found his footing and leaped from the streambed.

Running Elk pushed the stallion along behind them. When he reached the bank, the horse stopped and lowered his head to drink.

With a harsh grunt, Running Elk squeezed the paint's sides and dug his heels in behind the stallion's ribcage. The horse coughed and stood still. The warrior gathered the long single rein of the hackamore Rachel had used on Sees the Eagle. It was the bridle chosen by the man who stole the paint from Tom Barkley's barn and brought him out to Running Elk. Now the chief's son used the end of the hair rein to whip the stallion's flanks, and the paint shivered and heaved his front feet up onto the bank. Rachel felt a moment of panic, wondering if he had the strength to leap up the bank from a standing position. She felt his muscles tense as he pushed to leave the rocky streambed, but the stallion's hind hooves slipped, and they fell back and sideways, crashing down in the icy water. Her right foot touched bottom, but the horse lurched over off his side before his weight crushed her leg against the rocks.

She started to push away from the struggling horse. Her mind raced. Could she shove herself downstream and come out on the far bank? Was it possible that this was her moment to escape? She couldn't outrun them, but perhaps she could lose herself in the dark ravine and hide until morning. The gurgling of the water would mask the sounds of her flight.

Suddenly, she realized that Running Elk had loosened his hold on her. He was no longer seated behind her but was thrashing in the cold, waist-deep water. Instead of pushing away from the paint, Rachel seized handfuls of his mane and clung to the horse as he fumbled to get his feet under him.

The stallion rose, and the water streamed from his body and Rachel's clothes. She was above the surface of the stream now, and to her surprise, she saw that the other two warriors had gone on and were high on the trail above. Apparently they hadn't noticed the paint's effort at the stream bank.

Running Elk spoke a harsh command, and she glanced toward his voice. He was two yards from the horse and wading slowly toward her.

Rachel leaned forward, seized the wet, dangling rein, and pulled the stallion's head around. She eased back behind his withers and kicked. The paint moved with slow steps through the swirling water, away from Running Elk. As they approached the bank they had come down earlier, she lay down and wrapped her arms around his neck, still holding the rein and linking her fingers beneath his throat.

"Lord, give him strength," she cried.

The stallion jumped up out of the water and into a canter, running down the ravine the way they had come.

Chapter 15

Matt touched the stock of his rifle in its scabbard and gouged his heels into Wiser's sides. He was close. He would not wait for Mike while Running Elk carried Rachel beyond his grasp. Wiser snorted and leaped forward.

"Come on, fella. We've got to catch that paint!"

That horse! Matt wished for an instant that his brother had never seen the black-and-white stallion. Tom hadn't even had him long enough to name him, and he'd been stolen a second time. That horse was nothing but trouble.

Wiser surged forward toward the sound they had heard, and Matt let him canter for a short ways then held him back.

"Easy, now," he murmured, stroking Wiser's neck. The gelding heaved a breath out, and Matt listened. He could distinguish staccato hoofbeats growing louder each moment.

"Steady, boy." He sidled Wiser to the edge of the trail, where he hoped they would blend in with the shadows of a sprawling rock formation. Wiser's white patches would stand out, but if the approaching rider was surprised, Matt would still have time to react. He pulled his rifle out and held it at the ready.

Rachel pushed the stallion on at a breakneck pace. She knew she was risking both their necks, but fear drove her. She had no doubt that Little Turtle and Three Killer would be close behind her. It wouldn't take them long to realize what had happened and dash to overtake her.

The paint stumbled, and she lurched forward with a gasp. When he straightened, she let him go on at a trot.

"I'm sorry," she whispered. "I don't want you to get hurt."

They burst out into an open stretch, and she stared ahead, trying to make out a landmark.

There should be another stream soon. Lord, please help me find it!

The paint let out a whinny, and she slapped his withers. "Hush! Do you want to tell them where we are?"

The horse stretched forward eagerly, and she let him run with his head low, allowing him to choose his own path, so long as he didn't turn back toward the high ground.

They cantered toward a large rock, and she thought she recognized it. They would reach that other stream soon, and they needed to wade in and follow it downstream.

As they tore past the big rock, the paint shied so violently she almost went off over the side. As she pulled on his mane to right herself, she saw what had caused him to leap aside. Another horse stood in the shadow of the boulder, and its rider had a rifle trained on her.

She gave an involuntary squawk then concentrated on maintaining her seat.

"Rachel!"

The shout came from behind her, and relief flooded her churning soul.

"Whoa!" She didn't dare let go of the stallion's mane to give a good pull on the rein, but he dropped his pace to a trot, then a walk, and looped around to face the back trail.

Rachel sat low on his back, panting and peering toward the oncoming horse and rider. No question, it was Matt Barkley on his paint gelding.

He galloped toward her and pulled Wiser up short beside the stallion.

"What happened?"

"We stumbled in a stream, and I got away."

"Are you all right?"

"Yes, but they'll be coming." She pushed her wet hair back out of her eyes and realized she was shivering with cold.

"You're soaking wet."

"Don't worry about that. We need to hurry."

"All right. Stick with me."

Matt took the lead and turned toward the ranch, pushing Wiser into a canter. The stallion needed no urging to fall in behind him. He seemed to have regained some energy.

They reached the next stream, and Wiser plunged in. The stallion hesitated, and Rachel wondered if he was wary after his recent experience. She squeezed her legs around him, and he stepped down off the low bank, then stopped and pawed at the shallow water.

"You coming?" Matt called.

"I think he's thirsty."

She let the horse lower his head, and he drank in long, noisy gulps.

Matt brought Wiser closer to her.

"Sorry," she said. "Running Elk wouldn't let him drink before."

Matt looked back behind her, toward the rising ground of the foothills dotted with a few small trees.

"I hear someone coming."

"Little Turtle and Three Killer."

"Come on. We're good targets here in the stream." He took Wiser straight across against the current, and Rachel pulled the paint's head up and followed.

There was no time to wade along the way they had before. She knew the Indians had done that to avoid leaving a trail, but now speed was the only concern.

The stallion struggled as he exited the stream; the bank was higher on this side, but he gained the level of the valley floor. Soon they were flying along the edge of the rushing rivulet, back toward the Blacks Fork and the Barkley ranch.

From behind them, a terrifying shriek ripped through the night, and the paint leaped forward, almost slamming into Wiser's tail. The gelding kicked at him, and the stallion responded by running up alongside and snapping at Matt's leg.

Matt slapped the stallion's muzzle. "Cut that out!"

Rachel steadied her mount and made him keep his distance, with a couple of feet separating him from Wiser. When he was cantering smoothly, she looked back.

"That's Running Elk. He's riding the gray horse Three Killer had before."

"You see him?"

"Yes. He's over the stream."

Matt pulled his pistol and turned to look back.

Matt held his breath and squeezed the trigger. The horse behind him faltered, but he was sure he'd missed. He fired once more and turned forward.

"That won't stop him, but it might make him a little more cautious. Ride, Rachel! Keep ahead of me if you can."

"The horse is tired."

"I know. Just keep going."

From far ahead, he heard the report of a rifle.

"Oh no." Rachel stared at him. "How could they—"

"It's Mike," Matt said. "He went for help. Ride toward them."

"What if they shoot at us?"

"They won't. He probably heard my shots and fired once to let us know they're there."

They tore along the stream bank faster than was prudent, but Running Elk was maintaining his distance behind them.

Matt stared ahead, looking for the bulk of oncoming horses, and at last he saw a dark, moving mass. *Good old Mike! He's brought the whole garrison out!*

He grabbed Rachel's rein from her hand. "Hold on!"

He clucked to Wiser and steered him for the middle of the line of troopers, taking Rachel and the paint along with him. As soon as they were close enough that he knew his words could be distinguished, he shouted, "Mike, they're right behind us."

Wiser and the stallion charged through the line of horsemen. The troopers' mounts sidestepped to give them clearance then closed behind them.

They galloped a few more yards, and Matt eased up on Wiser. "Okay, fella.

Whoa, now. We made it."

Both horses halted and stood with their sides heaving. Matt jumped down from the saddle and hurried to Rachel. He held his arms up to her, and she wriggled off the paint's back and into his embrace.

He held her tight against his chest and kissed her damp hair. "You're freezing cold!" He rubbed his hands briskly over her soggy sleeves and the back of her dress.

"I'll be all right." Her shivering told him otherwise.

"Come on." He walked with her, keeping one arm around her waist and leading the docile stallion with the other. He realized his initial estimate was an exaggeration. Only a dozen troopers had come to their aid, and they were off in a flurry of hoofbeats. One tall horse hung back and walked toward them in the moonlight.

"Mike!" Matt swung his arm over Rachel's head and reached for Mike's hand. "God bless you! Don't know as we could have outrun him if you hadn't been here."

Mike swung to the ground. "It shocked me to my boots when I saw you had Rachel."

Matt grinned. "She's something, isn't she? She rescued herself. All I had to do was guide her on home. But she's wet to the skin and freezing."

"It's ten more miles home. We'd best build a fire." Mike began to rummage in his saddlebag.

"Don't tell me you've got matches," Matt said in amazement.

"I still keep a tinderbox in here."

"That's an old soldier for you."

"Yeah, well, I'll let the young soldier mosey over to that brush yonder and get me some twigs."

"What am I going to do with this horse? I don't think he knows the ranch is home yet."

"Let me take care of him." Mike reached for the rein, and Matt gladly turned the stallion over to him and headed for the low bushes.

"What happened to the other two Indians?" Mike asked a few minutes later when Matt returned with a meager handful of sticks. He had arranged his tinder and was ready to strike a spark.

"Don't know," Matt said. He looked toward Rachel, who huddled on the ground, shivering.

"They were ahead of us when I got away," she said. "Running Elk must have grabbed Three Killer's horse. I don't know about Little Turtle, if he came with Running Elk or if the two of them stayed behind."

"Well, those troopers will find out. And you'll have a story to trade with Lydia." Mike struck the flint to steel and blew cautiously on his glowing pile of cattail fluff and pine twigs. When it flared, he sat up and fed the blaze with Matt's twigs.

"Keep it going. I'll hunt around for something more substantial." He ambled off, kicking at clumps of grass, looking for a mound of dried dung.

Matt looked over at the three horses. Wiser and Kip stood with their reins hanging down, but the paint was hobbled.

"Where'd the hobbles come from?"

"Mike's saddlebags," Rachel said.

Matt sat down beside her. "He must carry a whole general store around with him. Are you sure you're all right?"

"Yes, I'll be fine."

Matt slid his arm around her and pulled her close. "God is good."

"Yes, He is very good."

Matt tipped her chin up and gazed into her eyes. "I love you, Rachel."

She smiled, and he bent to kiss her.

"You're warm," she whispered, snuggling in against his shoulder. Matt held her, staring into the fledgling campfire and feeling content until a rough nudge on the back of his head sent his hat tumbling. He fumbled for it and whirled to look up at his assailant.

Rachel laughed. "Wiser wants some attention, too."

Matt sighed and scratched Wiser beneath his forelock. "You dumb horse."

Chapter 16

In the gray before dawn, Matt, Rachel, and Mike rode into the barnyard. Tom came from the barn carrying a pitchfork in one hand and his rifle in the other, and Lydia and Amy rushed out of the house to meet them.

"Praise God!" Amy cried, enfolding Rachel in her arms. "Come inside and have a hot breakfast and tell us all about it."

Tom leaned the pitchfork against the barn wall and reached for the paint's rein, and Rachel surrendered it to him. "I hope he's going to be all right, Tom. Running Elk pushed him pretty hard, and then I asked him to work even harder. He seemed to be limping a bit toward the end."

"I'll check him over, but don't you fret about him. We're just glad you're safe." He took Wiser's reins. "Get her inside, Matthew. I'll tend to these nags."

Mike was still kissing Lydia, holding her in an ardent embrace and letting Kip's reins dangle from his fist.

"Hey, Mike, let go of the reins," Matt called with a laugh.

Lydia pushed Mike away, ending their kiss and flushing to her hairline.

"Just glad to be home," Mike said with a chuckle. "Amy, I've got to say, this horse of yours may be twelve years old, but he's still got the heart of a lion and the endurance of a locomotive. Smoothest horse I ever rode, too."

"Thanks, Mike. That's why I told you to take Kip." Amy turned toward the steps. "Let Tom take care of him, and come get some coffee."

"No, I'm going to rub him down myself. This is one heroic horse."

"The stallion didn't do so badly, either," Matt said. "He carried double weight for about fifteen miles then raced on back with Rachel. T.R., I think he's going to give you some great colts."

He kept his arm around Rachel's waist as they followed Amy and Lydia into the kitchen.

"Did you get any sleep?" he asked Amy.

"Not much. The children slept, but I was a bit on edge, I'll admit. And Tom sat up all night watching for you and wishing he'd gone along with you."

"He knew his place was here with you and the children."

She smiled as she brought the steaming coffeepot to the table. "Yes, he knows, but I still think he was a little itchy, knowing he was missing something out there." She poured out two mugs of coffee.

Lydia called, "I'm putting the biscuits in the oven, Amy. Shall I start cracking eggs?"

"Yes. Rachel, you're shivering," Amy said. "Are you sure you're all right?"

"She got a little dunking, and her clothes are still damp," Matt said.

"Well, you just get right into the bedroom and put on something warm." Amy set the coffeepot back on the stove. "I'll bring you my brown wool dress. Or do you want a hot bath?"

"No, I'll be fine," Rachel said, "but I would like to change my clothes. How is Caleb?"

"He's asleep. He moaned and groaned for a couple of hours, but I dosed him well with chamomile, and he finally dropped off."

Amy went with Rachel into the small bedroom she shared with Molly.

"I really think you need a hot bath. Let me put some more water on to heat, and after breakfast you can have a nice, long soak."

Rachel reached out on impulse and hugged her. "Thank you. I can't count the ways you've helped me. I can never pay you and Tom back."

Amy squeezed her. "You don't need to try. A month ago you never would have let me touch you like this. Just having you here and seeing you shake off the fear and sorrow you carried then has been more than enough reward. And watching you with Matthew...well, that's an extra blessing. I hope I'm not wrong in thinking we'll be sisters soon."

Rachel clung to her a moment longer and wrinkled her nose as she felt the sting of tears in her eyes. "You are a gift from God. And I don't think your hopes are misplaced."

Sergeant Hoffman sat at the table with Mike, Tom, and Matt. Amy set the table while Lydia put a second pot of coffee on to brew. Then the two women brought platters of biscuits, eggs, and fried ham to the table.

"We lost the other two in the hills," Hoffman said regretfully, staring into his mug. "That's excellent coffee, Mrs. Barkley."

Amy smiled. "Thank you, Sergeant. There'll be more coming in a minute."

"But they've got Running Elk in custody," Matt said.

"Oh, they've got him all right," Hoffman assured him. "Took him to the fort. The lieutenant wanted you to know he won't be around to bother you anymore. And I expect those other two will hide out for a while then hightail it back to their village."

Rachel came with soft steps from her bedroom, wearing a dark dress and her soft moccasins. Her hair was brushed and freshly braided, and her eyes held a look of peace, though the skin below them was darkened, showing her fatigue. She returned Matt's smile across the room, then lowered her gaze and joined Lydia near the stove.

"Come sit down, Rachel," Amy called.

She glanced toward the table. "Oh no, I can wait."

"We're all going to sit down together. Come on. You, too, Lydia."

Lydia smiled and handed Rachel a dish of butter. "Could you carry that, please? I'll bring the applesauce."

Matt stood and held a chair for her, and Rachel set the dish down then took her seat beside him, hardly looking at him but sporting a vivid blush.

After the blessing, the men dominated the conversation. Hoffman speculated that the horse Running Elk was riding when captured could be returned to its rightful owner soon. Matt half listened but for the most part kept his attention on Rachel. When he'd finished a plate full of food, he reached surreptitiously for her hand under the edge of the table. She darted a glance toward him, then looked away, smiling, and squeezed his hand.

"I'll make a plate for Caleb if you'd like to take it in, Rachel," Amy said. "I'm sure he'll be awake soon."

"Oh, let me fix it." Rachel released Matt's hand and rose.

He watched her flit about the kitchen, loading a plate for her brother.

Thank You for bringing her back safe, Lord! And thank You for. . . for letting her love me.

Anticipation swelled in his heart. She scooped eggs onto the plate, holding her mouth just so, her hands working with delicate precision. Matt inhaled slowly and made himself quit staring at her.

Mike was smiling at him across the table. "Another biscuit, Matthew?"

"Thanks."

Mike winked. "All things work together. . ."

Matt nodded as he reached for the butter. "They sure do."

"I want the surgeon to look at it." Caleb lay against a mound of pillows in Tom and Amy's bed, with his breakfast plate balanced on the quilt that covered his legs.

"All right," Rachel said. "I'll ask Matt if he minds going to the fort and asking the doctor to come look you over."

"Maybe I should have him take me there in the wagon. Then if the doctor says it would be all right, I could get on the stagecoach." Caleb stirred and flinched. "It's so painful, though, I don't see how I could sit on one of those coaches all day."

"No, you'd better stay here and rest for a few days, at least." Rachel poured a glass of water for him and set it on the bedside table.

"It must be infected. It hurts so much!"

Rachel suppressed a smile. "Caleb, you were shot twelve hours ago. I think the pain is natural for the type of wound you received. It's a bit early to be talking about infection."

"Well, I still want to see a doctor."

"All right." She refrained from repeating the disparaging comments she had heard the Barkleys make about Fort Bridger's current surgeon. "He might be able to give you something stronger for the pain."

"Didn't I smell coffee?"

"Yes, Lydia made a fresh pot while the sergeant was still here. I'm sure there's some left."

Rachel went to the kitchen and found Amy fixing a plate for Ben, who sat yawning at the table. The room was full a few minutes before, but now Ben and his mother were alone.

"Well, look who's up!"

"Hi, Miss Rachel." Ben's blue eyes were wide with admiration. "I'm real happy that Uncle Matt saved you."

She smiled and tousled his hair. "So am I."

She poured Caleb's coffee, took it to him, and then returned to the kitchen. Amy took the boy's plate to the table and set it before him. "There you go, Ben. If you eat every bite of that, you can run out to the barn and help Daddy."

"Where is everybody?" Rachel asked.

"Molly's still sleeping, and Lydia went to feed the baby. The men are out in the barn tending to the stallion."

"Is he all right?" Rachel swallowed hard, remembering the horse's fall in the stream and the way she'd pushed him afterward.

"Oh, Tom thinks he strained a tendon, but it's not permanent." Amy poured boiling water from her teakettle over a pile of dried leaves in a yellow earthenware bowl.

The front door opened, and Matt came in. His eyes lit when he saw Rachel, and she smiled at him.

"Is the poultice ready?" he asked.

"Almost. I need to wrap it." Amy took a linen towel and began to spoon the saturated leaves onto it.

"Caleb wants to see the surgeon." Rachel looked to Matt for assurance, feeling somewhat embarrassed. She didn't want Amy to think she doubted her nursing skills.

"I can ride to the fort and ask him to come," Matt said.

"Good idea." Amy's deft fingers tucked in the ends of the towel. "He's probably got more disinfectants and painkillers than I have, and it will give Caleb confidence that he's going to live."

Rachel couldn't help smiling. "Yes, and perhaps he can impress the need to rest upon my brother. He suggested he might take the stagecoach today."

Amy stared at her. "Absolutely not. How would he brace himself on those rough roads?"

"I expect he'll listen to the surgeon."

Amy nodded. "I'll take this out to Tom."

"You don't have to. I'll do it," Matt said.

"Well, my son wants to go help with the horse doctoring. Looks like he's about finished his breakfast, so I'll just take him on out there." Amy smiled at the two of them and hustled Ben outside.

As the door swung to, Rachel sensed Matt watching her. Her stomach fluttered when she felt his tender touch on her sleeve.

"Looks like we're alone."

"Yes." She stared at the black buttons on the front of his shirt. Matt slipped his hands along her arms and stepped toward her. Slowly she let her gaze travel up to his face. His jaw was shadowed with a day's growth of whiskers. His mouth was set with determination, and his eyes. . . A surge of love and longing swept over Rachel, and she cast aside her self-imposed restraints and catapulted into his embrace.

Matt gathered her close with a deep sigh and stooped to kiss her temple, where the hair was pulled back into her braid.

"I can't tell you how awful it was to see you hauled off by Running Elk," he whispered.

She stroked his back, enjoying the sense of belonging brought on by his gentle caresses. "That's over, Matt."

"Yes. I don't ever want to be apart from you again."

She tipped her face up and kissed his scratchy chin. "I love you."

His lips found hers, in a long, sweet kiss, and then he held her close, with her head cradled over his heart. "Rachel, will you. . . I haven't had a chance to talk to your brother yet, but. . . Well, I don't want to go even as far as the fort without knowing. Will you marry me?"

"Yes. No matter what Caleb says, yes. I belong here now, with you."

Chapter 17

The August sun beat down on the wedding party a week later as they rode from the Barkley ranch toward Fort Bridger. Amy drove the wagon, with Rachel beside her on the seat. The bride was attired in a new dress of palest blue organza and shoes of soft, black leather. The horses were smartly groomed, with ribbons twined in their manes and tails.

In the wagon bed rode Lydia and the children, along with Caleb Haynes, who sat with his left leg stuck out stiff before him on a cushion of folded blankets. His carpetbag, packed and ready for his journey back East, and a handmade wooden crutch lay beside him. The wedding had been timed so that he could enjoy the cake and celebrating for an hour or two before boarding the coach.

Matt waved to Rachel and rode ahead with Tom to make sure the arrangements were in place while Mike rode his bay mare along beside the wagon.

A festive mood enveloped Fort Bridger. At first glance, Matt could tell the troopers had policed the parade ground, chapel, and mess hall in preparation for the wedding. Everything looked a little neater than usual, and colorful streamers fluttered from the chapel door. He was honored that they'd gone to the extra trouble on the occasion of a former soldier being married at the fort. No doubt the commanding officer had ordered extra fatigue details to spruce up the area.

Captain Whittier, the fort's chaplain, met Tom and Matt outside the chapel as they tied Wiser and Milton to the hitching rail.

"Fine day for the ceremony," Whittier said.

"Couldn't be better," Matt agreed with a grin.

Whittier's brow puckered. "Well, perhaps it could be a little cooler, but the Almighty knows best."

The brothers followed him inside.

"You fellows can sit here on the front pew while we wait for things to start," the chaplain said. "When the guests are seated, I'll have you come stand over here, in front of the pulpit." He explained a few other details, and Matt nodded, trying to keep his mind on what Whittier was saying.

Troopers began filing in through the double doors, and the chaplain left them to greet the guests. All of the officers' families would attend, of course. The wives seized on any pretext to dress up and enjoy a social gathering. Most of the enlisted men would come, too, since nearly all of them knew the Barkley brothers, and there were rumors of cake and punch for everyone afterward outside the mess hall.

Matt's heart began to pound as the buzz in the pews behind them grew. The sergeant who directed the post band took his seat at the pump organ and began to play wheezy chords that might belong to a hymn Matt learned as a child.

Matt rubbed his jaw and shifted. His new jacket didn't feel quite right, and it was getting warm in the chapel. He could feel beads of sweat dotting his forehead and coursing down his back.

"I might suffocate before this is over." He tugged at his collar and wondered if he could loosen his tie just a bit.

Tom grinned at him. "It'll be worth every agonizing minute. Trust me."

"Oh, I'm not worried about the 'til death do us part.' It's the here and now that's killing me."

"You got a fine woman."

Matt smiled and stretched his long legs out before him, slumping a little lower against the back of the pew. "I know it. I'm figuring marriage will be one long adventure with Rachel."

Tom arched his eyebrows. "Well, if she's anything like Amy, it will be more like one adventure after another. Just give yourself time to breathe in between."

Caleb leaned on his crutch and scowled as Rachel fumbled with his jacket, trying to pin a stem of blue cornflowers to his lapel.

"Are you sure this is what you want?" he asked.

Rachel pressed her lips together and straightened his collar. "You know it is."

He sighed. "I guess I do. And I'm not saying Matt's not a good man. I just…well, I was hoping you'd come back and be part of the family again. Sarah was, too."

She smiled. "Sarah will do just fine without me, and so will you."

"I expect that's true. You'll write?"

"Of course. And you must answer."

Caleb nodded and glanced toward where Amy was waiting near the chapel door. The soldiers, except for a few standing duty, had surged into the austere building, and Lydia went in holding young Ben by the hand, while Mike carried their baby and Molly, one in each arm. The wail of an organ soared out over the valley.

"Almost time," Amy called from the steps.

Caleb looked down at Rachel, still frowning. "Look, I'm sorry if I caused you any distress. I'm really glad you came out of the Indian village, and…well, I'm happy for you and Matthew."

"Thank you." She smiled up at him, treasuring the peace in her heart. "This is the right thing for me to do, Caleb. I'm sure God wants me to marry Matthew."

He nodded. "He told me he feels that way, too, so I guess you can't go wrong."

The music changed, and Amy gestured frantically. Rachel steadied Caleb as he hobbled up the steps with his crutch. He leaned it against the outside wall and crooked his elbow, and she tucked her hand through his arm.

"You both look wonderful." Amy kissed Rachel's cheek and stepped into the doorway.

The sergeant started into Wagner's familiar "Bridal Chorus," and the chaplain hurried over to Matt and Tom.

"All right, boys, come stand over here now."

Matt rose, gulped in air, and then took his spot with Tom beside him. Whittier nodded at him soberly, and Matt felt sudden panic.

"You got the ring, T.R.?" he whispered.

"I got the ring."

"What about the money? I gave you the money for the chaplain."

"Shut up and look at your bride."

Matt followed his gaze toward the aisle and saw Amy approaching with slow, confident steps. She was lovely, as always, in her best Sunday dress, but beyond her, pausing in the doorway with the light behind, was a vision even more beautiful: Rachel, with a wreath of prairie flowers in her hair, holding her brother's arm. As Matt held his breath, she began the processional down the aisle toward him. Caleb had set aside his crutch and managed to keep pace with only a slight limp, though his teeth were clenched in a fierce grimace.

Matt saw only Rachel after that first glance. She floated toward him, love shining in her face. The dress made her eyes appear more blue than gray, and the wildflowers she held accented them. Her face colored to a delicate pink as she advanced, and Matt pulled in an achy, sweet breath of contentment.

Rachel and Caleb stopped before the chaplain, and all the guests settled into their seats with a rustle of anticipation.

Matt managed to maintain a dignified demeanor until Whittier asked, "Who gives this woman in marriage?"

Caleb looked Matt in the eye and nodded. "I do."

Matt's joy was echoed in Rachel's smile as he reached for her hand and pulled it gently into the crook of his arm. They stood facing the chaplain together, and he felt the warmth of her hand and the glow of her love as they began their new life together.

A Letter to Our Readers

Dear Readers:

In order that we might better contribute to your reading enjoyment, we would appreciate your taking a few minutes to respond to the following questions. When completed, please return to the following: Fiction Editor, Barbour Publishing, Inc., P.O. Box 719, Uhrichsville, OH 44683.

1. Did you enjoy reading *Wyoming Brides* by Susan Page Davis?
   ❏ Very much—I would like to see more books like this.
   ❏ Moderately—I would have enjoyed it more if _____
   _____
   _____

2. What influenced your decision to purchase this book?
   (Check those that apply.)
   ❏ Cover   ❏ Back cover copy   ❏ Title   ❏ Price
   ❏ Friends   ❏ Publicity   ❏ Other

3. Which story was your favorite?
   ❏ *Protecting Amy*   ❏ *Wyoming Hoofbeats*
   ❏ *The Oregon Escort*

4. Please check your age range:
   ❏ Under 18   ❏ 18–24   ❏ 25–34
   ❏ 35–45   ❏ 46–55   ❏ Over 55

5. How many hours per week do you read? _____

Name _____

Occupation _____

Address _____

City_____ State_____ Zip_____

E-mail_____